P9-CFF-429

THE WOLF'S BOY

EASTON PUBLIC LIBRARY
PO BOX 2
EASTON CT 06612
WITHDRAWN

SUSAN WILLIAMS BECKHORN

DISNEY • HYPERION
LOS ANGELES NEW YORK

Copyright © 2016 by Susan Williams Beckhorn

All rights reserved. Published by Disney-Hyperion, an imprint of Disney Book Group. No part of this book may be reproduced or transmitted in any form or by any means, electronic or mechanical, including photocopying, recording, or by any information storage and retrieval system, without written permission from the publisher. For information address Disney-Hyperion Books, 125 West End Avenue, New York, New York 10023.

Printed in the United States of America

First Edition, June 2016
1 3 5 7 9 10 8 6 4 2
FAC-019817-16074

Library of Congress Cataloging-in-Publication Data
Names: Beckhorn, Susan Williams, 1953–
Title: The wolf's boy / by Susan Williams Beckhorn.
Description: First edition. | Los Angeles ; New York : Disney Hyperion, [2016] | Summary: "Marked as tabat—the unlucky one—Kai and his wolf, Uff, must brave the long winter together and learn what it takes to survive on their own"—Provided by publisher.
Identifiers: LCCN 2015016834 | ISBN 9781484725535
Subjects: | CYAC: Prehistoric peoples—Fiction. | Wolves—Fiction. | Survival—Fiction.
Classification: LCC PZ7.1.B4348 Wo 2016 | DDC [Fic]—dc23
LC record available at http://lccn.loc.gov/2015016834

Designed by Maria Elias and Rachna Chari

Reinforced binding

Visit www.DisneyBooks.com

37777124909896

THIS LABEL APPLIES TO TEXT STOCK

To the wolf cousins of my life:

Spike

Jessica

Oakley

Cedar

George

Genny

Spike II

Chloe

George II

and

Curry

PROLOGUE

The man stopped to sniff the air. Cave bear, but not close. The valley was filled with the sounds of birdsong and rushing water. He shifted the baby in his arms and continued on to the denning grounds of the yellow wolf pack. The child was strong, but one of the tiny kicking legs was curled like a withered leaf.

The man's eyes were dead with sorrow. Still, he could not go against the law of the People. He laid his son beside a hollow under a great pine stump and turned away.

Yellow Mother had just two pups that year. She heard the child's cry and found the baby among the litter of bones at the mouth of her den. She nosed him carefully. He turned his cheek to her touch. The wolf opened her jaws, lifted the child, and gently carried him into her den. She laid him beside the others. There, the human pup found comfort.

The wolf licked the baby's twisted leg, giving it much attention. Time does not matter to a wolf. She licked and straightened the curled leg over and over. The pups grew. The sun and the moon shone into the entrance of the den many times.

The People knew death well, both swift and slow. *White teeth tearing flesh.* The human mother felt as if her own heart were torn open. She was grateful to think that her child did not suffer long. Still, her arms were empty, and she ached for him. Could the spirit of a misty-eyed little boy live now in one of the wolves?

One night as she stared into the darkness of the reindeer-skin hut, she heard a new note threaded into the singing of the wolves. It called to her, like the beckoning sound of her father's little bone *osa*, or the voice of a lost child. . . .

As one dream-walking, she too went out to the denning grounds of the yellow wolf pack. She carried a gift—a slab of deer meat. A full moon floated up out of the hills while she sang her own song to the wolves. She poured a mother's longing for a lost babe into the night. Then she was silent.

Suddenly, Yellow Mother sang back from the warmth of her den, a low, crooning song. The woman did not know what to think. And then she heard the muffled squalling of a pup—not a wolf pup; a human pup.

The woman crept to the entrance of the den and peered inside. In a ray of moonlight, the wolf's eyes glittered back at her. The woman's eyes widened when she saw the tiny round head of dark hair between the bundles of puppy fur.

The two mothers stared at each other. The wolf resumed her licking of the curled leg. The woman watched for a long time. Then she began to talk to Yellow Mother. She told how her child had been taken from her and that he had been hers first. She talked most of the night. In the early dawn, Yellow Mother licked the pup one last time. Quietly, the woman took her son back.

Then, holding him fiercely to her breast, she walked back to the *immet* of the People.

ONE

CHAPTER 1

I could not get free. The string of spit dripped closer. My brother was good at this game. I struggled, but he held my wrists above my head.

Sen and the others had found me alone in the grassland where the herds of bison, horses, and woolly rhinos came to feed. I was gathering dried dung for the fire—women's work. The boys were on their way back home from the willow copse. Each carried a *keerta* with a flint point. Each had several ptarmigan swinging at his waist. Each walked tail up, stiff-legged—like young wolves, full of the success of their hunt.

My knee landed a blow to my brother's middle. He grunted.

"Do it, Sen," Xar urged. "Spit on him!" His voice cracked with excitement.

"Wolfboy, try to run now!" shouted Uli, craning his head over Fin's shoulder.

"Run? He can only hop like a toad!" Xar called back, snorting at his own joke.

Sen let his spit drip again. I tried to twist away. It stretched out a finger's length . . . *slppp!* He sucked it back up at the last instant.

Again.

And again.

The boys howled. They danced, holding their *keertas* over their heads. Soon, each of them would kill a deadly beast, as Sen had, to become a blood-hunter—but what would I be? I tried to swallow my fear.

"You would have been smarter to tend the fire beside your *ama*," taunted Xar. He grinned, sucking loudly at the gap where he was missing a front tooth. I hated Xar's broken grin, hated the whistling sound he made, hated his bristled scalp and pale eyes. "A lame pup makes good bait!" he hissed, staggering and lurching to show how I walked with my stick.

Xar was the closest to my age, the loudest to mock me.

Fin and Uli instantly set on him, raking his back with fingers held in pretend claws and snarling. A pair of slobbering hyenas. They fell against each other, weeping with laughter.

Xar was right. A single person, with no *keerta*, even one with two good legs, might be stalked by a cave lion—or worse. It wasn't the hungry season. Still, I could have met an Ice Man. It was bad to be alone, especially for me. I was *tabat*, cursed. It was forbidden for me to hunt or even to handle a weapon. I had nothing but my work blade to protect me.

But I was twelve winters old, almost a man. Anger burned in my stomach.

I often slipped away alone.

Sen's eyes narrowed. I fought with all my strength, but could not wrench free. Suddenly, his shoulders shook with laughing. Wetness splashed across my face. Into my mouth. I spat back. Hated my brother. I would have pounded my fists into his teeth, the way Xar's father did to him that time, if I could have. But I saw a flash of something in Sen's eyes—regret?

"Sorry, Kai," he whispered. He started to wipe my face with a hand, but the other boys jeered. He glared at them. Then he leapt to his feet and shouted at me, "You should never have been born! The yellow pack should have eaten you and cracked your bones!"

A spatter of laughter came from the river path. Had I not had enough? I didn't need the pack of girls mocking me, too.

Mir was the tallest of them. Her laughter bubbled out through perfect teeth. Her hair gleamed like sunlight on water. Her eyes were bright stars. It was no secret that those eyes looked only at Sen.

I sat up, tucking my twisted foot out of sight.

"Your little brother looks like a wolf, Sen!" said Mir. "His eyes make me shiver. Careful, or he will bite your leg! You don't want to be a cripple, too!" Several of the other girls laughed with her. But two of them did not.

"Leave Kai alone!" said Cali. She gripped her *keerta*. My brother took a step backward. Cali could throw a weapon well. Her eyes and hair were the color of dark wood. She wasn't beautiful, but she was good to see. Still, I knew that when my brother looked at the girls of our *immet*, the only one he really saw was Mir.

Sen's cheeks flushed. "I was teaching Kai a lesson," he muttered.

"There's a dead marmot near the gravel hills, Sen. Why don't you vultures tear at that instead?" It was Cali's little sister, Vida, who spoke. Her eyes, as brown as Cali's, snapped hot sparks of anger. Everyone stared at her in surprise. She was only eleven winters old and usually shy as a brush hen.

Vida and Cali were Rhar's daughters. Rhar was the headman.

Ignoring them, Sen gave Mir a slow smile. Then he ran off with the other boys. I watched their long legs moving so easily. The shafts of their *keertas* glinted in the sun. The girls followed. Cali strode ahead, straight and silent. I saw Vida scowl and jut her chin at another girl. Then she glanced back at me, a question in her eyes. I shrugged to say it was nothing. Her face brightened a little. She turned and followed her sister.

I was still breathing hard. The crushed grass smelled of spring. I reached for my stick and yanked myself to my feet. I could still hear the boys yelling as they ran—as if they had just won a fight with the Ice People. It was a great honor to spit on one's enemy. I was not much of an enemy, though.

Part of me hated Sen, but part of me didn't blame him. He had not asked for a crippled brother. Secretly, he used to make play *keertas* for me. We had mock hunts and battles with Ice Men when no one watched. If I fell behind on the trail, he waited.

But things had changed. Now, at fifteen winters, my brother could read a trail nearly as well as our father. He could hurl his *keerta* so that it thrummed when the stone tooth struck the heart of its prey. He could run like a young horse, far over the open land, without tiring. He was the first of his friends to become a blood-hunter by killing an animal that could as well have killed him—a black aurochs bull with great white spots, like storm clouds, on his hide and huge horns.

Since then, I had become invisible—or something shameful to Sen.

I slammed the scattered dung back into my basket and dumped it beside a rock. Cripple or not, I was nearly old enough to be a hunter. There was nothing wrong with my eyes, my arms, my hands. I could climb high into a tree. I could swim and dive in the icy water of our river.

Scrubbing hard at my eyes with the back of my fist, I stumbled to the torrent running down from the snowbanks. A hunter does not weep. I crouched on my good leg, plunged my face into the icy water, rinsed my mouth, splashed my cheeks. Then I shook the wet hair from my eyes. Not curling yellow hair, as my father and Sen and little Suli had, or even brown like my mother, but straight black—like the tips of wolf fur. *Wolfboy.*

Did I really look like a wolf? Mir was not the first to

say so. Even my mother sometimes brushed the hair from my eyes with her hand and asked, "What are you seeing, Kai? Who gave you those eyes? They glow like amber in the firelight." I had glimpsed them myself, staring back from the surface of still water. An odd brown—almost golden—with green sparks. Strange eyes. *Wolf eyes.*

I could have gone home. Ama might have needed me. Our Bu was not always an easy baby—and my little sister, Suli, could be more trouble than help. But I still seethed inside. The things I felt half choked and half blinded me.

There was a place I liked to go.

I made my way now to the *immet* of the yellow wolf pack and crawled into an abandoned den under a great pine stump.

CHAPTER 2

It was quiet at Torn Ear's den. I became still, waited. The wolves knew my scent. They would not be troubled. I let my thinking go where it would. A memory flickered. I was perhaps four or five.

Ama helped me over the rough places, calling to the wolves as we came. The wolves sang back. Yellow Mother met us on the trail. We called her pack the *imnos*—friends—because they liked to live near the People. They were small wolves, in many shades of yellow. They were curious, sniffing at a broken basket or playing with a worn-out fur. The gray pack were the *lupta*—wild ones. They kept to themselves.

Yellow Mother's amber eyes did not look for the gift of bones that day. They went to me.

"Thank you again for our Kai," Ama whispered.

Very slowly, the wolf placed one paw in front of the other. I was not afraid. Her whiskers quivered. Her nose almost touched mine. Then she licked me.

Other times, Ama and I would be digging roots or picking white ear mushrooms. Where there had been no wolf a moment before, Yellow Mother would suddenly appear. She might sniff my foot or let me rub her ears. I saw her many times, and each season's pups as well. But then one spring when the pack returned to their denning grounds, Yellow Mother did not come.

I missed her.

Torn Ear was Yellow Mother's daughter. She was strong, playful, and beautiful as smoke. Of all the pups of all the litters that I had known, she was my favorite.

I had named Torn Ear's big mate Shine. His fur was like autumn grasses. The two of them were the leaders. Mostly, they taught the others to obey with a downward thrust of muzzle on muzzle. Sometimes there was a snarl or a lifted lip showing an ivory fang. The wolves had their quarrels. I had seen fights that ended in belly-up yelping. Sometimes blood spattered the ground and a beaten wolf limped away from the pack with his tail tucked between his legs.

Once, I watched as a strange wolf tried to join the *imnos*. There was something about him that was wrong, but nothing I could see. It was over in moments. A fury of slashing teeth. Blood in the snow. A stiffening carcass. Tufts of fur blowing away on the wind.

But for the most part, they were kind. They greeted each other joyfully, tumbling and wrestling. They hunted together as men did. There were low members of the pack, like the young male I called *Lan*, uncle. He guarded the pups while the others hunted. But he had a rightful place. He was not despised.

~

Now, hidden in the old hollow under the pine stump, I watched as three pups spilled from Torn Ear's den. They tumbled and yipped. A fourth, smaller one crawled to the entrance, eyes barely open. It did not come farther. Lan stepped out of the brush. He had been there all this time! He lay down and was swallowed by a tangle of baby wolves. They tugged his tail, hung from his ruff, all the time snarling.

I watched until dusk when Shine returned alone. Something was wrong. The big wolf limped. His belly did not bulge as it did when the hunt had been good. One at a time, the others of the pack slunk back to their own dens. Dried blood darkened Shine's flanks.

Where was Torn Ear?

The three larger pups jumped on their father. They licked at his lower jaw until he emptied his belly for them. It was a small pile of meat—perhaps a hare. The three ate. The fourth pup hung back in the mouth of the den. It was not ready for such food. It wanted milk.

But Torn Ear did not come.

CHAPTER 3

The night beasts would be waking and hungry. Slowly, I turned for home. The outside of my twisted foot was as calloused as the bottom of my good one. Still, it ached when I walked. Often I stubbed it on roots or stones. It was an ugly thing. I could hide it when I sat, but I would feel stares as I walked through the *immet* of the People. *Wolfboy*. Tabat. *Why did his mother bring him back?*

My mind raced ahead of my feet. How long could the smallest pup live without milk? What had happened to Torn Ear?

As I approached the *immet*, the smell of roasting meat made my mouth water. Smoke hung over the cluster of *takkas* crouched in the shelter of the cliffs. I could hear children laughing and screeching. A woman's voice scolded. A baby squalled. It came to me suddenly that the *immet* of the People was like the denning ground of the *imnos*. There was a headman and his mate. The hunters went out and brought food back. It was much the same.

In front of our *takka*, my brother and father squatted beside the fire. Sen smoothed his new *keerta.* Apa heated pitch to help hold the point in place. This would be the first *keerta* with Sen's new sign on it, a curving aurochs horn for the bull he had killed.

Keertas were sacred and powerful. They meant life. My brother's hands worked patiently, shaving tiny curls of wood one after another into a neat pile on the ground. My own hands clenched as Sen ran his fingers along the surface searching for rough places. A *keerta* that could kill game or save a man's life was full of magic. Luck hovered over a hunter and his tools. And no one—especially one as unlucky, as *tabat*, as a cripple like me—could touch a hunter's things.

I eyed my brother's new *keerta* with a bitter taste in my mouth.

Sen. It wasn't easy getting used to his new name. But I tried hard to remember, because when I forgot he reminded me with a fist jabbed into my shoulder. I had a few of my own names for him that I did not say aloud.

Sen means *steady one.* The name we had called my brother for as long as I could remember was *Bol*, tree. But now he was a blood-hunter of the People. He had shed his boy's name as a snake slides out of its skin.

The night of Sen's kill, Vida's father had roared out the story of how my brother had stood his ground when the bull charged. "He judged the distance. He did not throw wildly or too soon, but waited for a foreleg to stretch, baring the ribs over the heart. Then he threw! And only then he sprang aside—so that he felt the hot breath of the beast as it thundered past!"

Rhar spread his arms wide. "The bull shook his horns. He thrashed while the lifeblood foamed from his nose!"

I could see it all as if I had been there. It was no soft-eyed ibex or saiga Sen had killed, but an aurochs bull—perhaps the most dangerous beast to hunt except for the great mammut. *My brother, a blood-hunter.*

Then Rhar marked Sen's forehead with the blood of the bull. Apa was stiff with pride. Ama wiped tears from her eyes. My throat hurt so that it was hard to breathe. I knew that I too could hurl a *keerta* straight into the heart of death, if someone would just let me try. Still, I smiled for my brother. I was glad for him. He could not help it if he was favored by the spirit of *Tal* any more than I could help being cursed.

Mir glowed that night like a star in the sky. It was almost as if Sen's honor belonged to her. For the rest of the evening, she hung on his arm the way flower petals cling in the long grasses. The elders, full of feasting and good humor, saw them and smiled.

I looked over at Vida where she stood with some other girls, and we made crossed eyes at each other. She did an imitation of Mir, tossing her hair back.

That night, Moc-Atu, our shaman, came to our *takka* for the final ceremony. He mixed burnt bone, ground bloodstone, and icestone with fat to make his colors. I crouched in the shadows, watching each thing he did.

"Go away, *tabat* one!" my brother hissed at me. "This is a thing only for a blood-hunter."

But Moc-Atu shook his head. "The wolfboy stays. It hurts nothing to watch." My brother was silent then. One did not speak against Moc-Atu. Then the shaman made the great aurochs bull on the hide wall. He made running legs and white spots and a mist of red spurting from its nostrils. It seemed alive in the flickering light of the stone lamp. I watched. My eyes never left his hands. Others crowded in behind us to see.

Then, at a word from the shaman, Sen pressed his hand against the wall of the *takka* and Moc-Atu blew a mouthful of red color over it so that when my brother took his hand away, the ghost of it was still there. *The hand that killed the bull.*

~

"You tempt the big cats, coming in so late," Apa growled as I approached. His eyes were the color of blue ice. I looked at him and shrugged as if I did not care. He stared at me a moment, then shook his head and went back to his work. Sen did not look up, but Suli ran to me, hugging my legs, making me stumble. "Get off me, Bramble," I said, smiling.

Ama shifted Bu, who was fussing himself to sleep on her shoulder. She nodded toward the hearth. I ate the last of the soup and gnawed some deer ribs they had saved for me. Darkness fell, and with it, the air grew cold. The tops of the willows began to stir. It would rain before morning. We moved inside for the night.

Nearby, a wolf howled. I turned my head, listening. It was Shine. There was something in his voice like cold fingers at the back of my neck. I went to the opening of our *takka* and looked out. After a time, Shine's voice was joined by others from the pack.

I did not hear Torn Ear.

Shine howled again. *Where are you?* The sound filled the grassland where the horse herds stamped and drowsed. It swelled over the patches of forest where the bands of aurochs lay. It rose over the cliffs of the river gorge, even above the rushing of the river.

I sat down again. Suli scuttled over to me clutching the pinecones she had been playing with. She settled herself bottom-first into my lap.

"Tell it, Kai. What are they saying?"

I could not tell her that Shine was calling for his mate.

I took a breath. "That deep voice, like Moc-Atu, is Shine telling the *lupta* that the *imnos* are very strong this year. The high voice—the one like wind whistling over snow—that is one of the younger females. I call her Mist because her fur is almost white. She sings that there are pups in the den and the grays must stay away. And all the yipping is the yearling wolves saying they are big and part of the pack now."

Suli nodded. In the firelight her eyes were those of a small owl.

"How can you know that, Kai?" my father asked roughly.

"Kai is talking about his real family," Sen sneered. "They're calling him to come live with them again."

"Hush, Sen." Ama stirred the fire and added a chunk of dried dung. The flames danced high. On the walls of our *takka,* the painted beasts seemed to leap and rear. The hand shadows marking my father's blood kills and the new one that belonged to Sen waved eerily.

I opened my mouth to speak, but Sen cut in. "Maybe I will get myself a good new wolf pelt tomorrow." He knotted the sinew holding his point in place and trimmed the ends close. Then he twirled the *keerta* slowly in his hands. The flint was killing-sharp. Sen lifted this new *keerta* and sighted along the shaft—at me. It shone, deadly and beautiful, in the flickering light.

"Sen, that is enough!" Apa snapped. I glanced back at my brother. He was a black silhouette now, face turned, shoulders a stony ridge, as he hunched over his work. The *keerta* was finished. Now he was carving his sacred sign in it. He was stiff with resentment. But he held his tongue. He would not go against our father.

"More, Kai?" Suli begged. She loved to hear about the yellow wolf pack.

In a low voice, I continued. "Shine is the big father. He is the headman. His teeth are white as ice, and long as Apa's gutting blade. He can run faster than any of his family. But he is gentle with his pups. He lets them climb over him and chew his ears and tail. He slides out his great tongue to pant, half-closes his eyes, and seems to smile. I think he is very proud of his children."

Suli had two big pinecones that she pretended were Shine and Torn Ear. Three little ones were the pups. "What about Torn Ear?" she demanded.

"Torn Ear is brave and strong," I whispered. My voice cracked. I swallowed, hoping Suli wouldn't notice. "Once she fought a band of hyenas to protect her litter, and one bit her so that half her ear is gone now. But she is still beautiful."

Suli touched one of the big pinecones gently. Her hands were very sure for a four-year-old. Already she could hold a bone needle and sew a bit if the holes were punched for her. She murmured, "Poor Torn Ear." Then she nestled the three little pinecones close to the side of her mother wolf.

I slid my eyes sideways to see if Sen was hearing all this, but he was lost in his work. Apa's eyes were closed. I didn't know if he was listening or not. Bu slept soundly at last, in his basket of furs, and Ama was busy at the hearth. I let my thoughts slip back to the times I had watched Torn Ear with last season's pups outside her den.

Yellow Mother taught Torn Ear to trust me. She let me come very near. But once I crept too close, and hardly knowing what I did, my hand moved toward the pups. Torn Ear stiffened. There was a low rumble in her throat. I scuttled back a respectful distance.

Now, for Suli, I made pup sounds, "Unhh unhh unhh," and pushed the tiny pinecones at their mother. Ama turned, and I saw the worry in her eyes, so when Suli said, "Do it again, Kai," I shook my head.

"You should go to sleep now," I told her. "I will take you out to make your water."

"Thank you, Kai," Ama said. I picked up my stick and got to my feet. Outside, the stars danced to the singing of the wolves. I wanted to throw back my head and answer them, but I did not dare.

Back inside, Suli was not sleepy. She tugged at my stick. "Draw horses, Kai."

Even then, I could draw many animals. I did not know what magic in my hand made lines that became a thundering horse or a snorting rhino. Sen used to watch, but now he scuffed his feet across my pictures. When Ama saw my drawings, her eyes shone. Sometimes she turned her head, squinting, and pointed to where a tail was too long or an eye not right. Even Apa thought they were good. I could tell by how he studied them. But he worried. "Do not let others see, Kai. It may be unlucky for one who is *tabat* to make pictures."

But Moc-Atu had said it did no harm for me to watch him draw.

Once when I was small, I tried to make a person with my

lines, but my father put out a hand to stop me. "*Nah*, Kai." His voice was suddenly tight. "It is forbidden. We draw only the beasts that feed us. To draw a man is *tabat*."

Now Suli tugged again at my stick. "Make it be a snake, Kai!"

I shook my head.

Stubborn, she tucked the handle of it under her arm and hobbled a few steps.

I smiled, but in my heart, I did not smile. The stick I used for walking could never be far from me. Everything Apa made was beautiful, and my stick was as well. He had searched long for a hornbeam sapling that bent at the root. That part went under my armpit. A branch had to grow sideways as well, on the same side. That, cut short, was for my hand. The distance between root and branch must be just right. He measured the space between my armpit and hand carefully with a thong, marking it with knots.

Hornbeam is very strong. He cured it by the fire and whittled it smooth. Night after night, he rubbed it with sand until it was as soft as one of Bu's cheeks. Then he worked tallow into the wood so that the grain showed. It was like a mysterious world that you could touch the surface of but not enter. Lastly, he wrapped the head of it with layers of fur to cushion my armpit.

Apa had made many such sticks for me over the years. I had grown this past winter. Before much longer, I would need a new one. This stick that my father made for me was a thing I both loved and hated. Without it, I could not walk.

Suli lost her balance, and Ama put out a hand to catch her. "Suli, that is enough," she said. My little sister sat down by the fire, stroked the smooth wood of my stick, and hunted all over it. Then she looked up at me and asked, "Where is your sign, Kai? I can't find your wolf."

"Kai means pup, not wolf," I told her. "That is all I am."

Apa had not carved a sign into the stick for me as he did when he made things for the others. Each of them had a sign. Apa's was the head of a bison. Ama's was a singing blackbird. Sen had his aurochs's horn now. Even Suli had a tiny owl carved on the bottom of the little *das* she ate and drank from. Every one of the People had a sign.

Except for me. I was not a real person with a real name.

"Bed, Suli," said Apa firmly, but there was a smile in his voice.

Far into the night I lay staring in the dark. Stars glittered between racing clouds in the smoke hole overhead. After a time, rain began to spit against the side of our *takka*. Where was Torn Ear? The embers of the fire glowed faintly. What would happen to the smallest wolf pup? The bigger ones could eat the food Shine brought for them, but the little one still cried for milk. I knew that if Torn Ear did not come back, it would die.

CHAPTER 4

At daybreak, Bu cried. I sat up. Was the little pup also waking now in Torn Ear's den? Was it, too, whimpering with hunger? How long could it live without food?

Ama took my baby brother outside to feed him. The rain had stopped. If Torn Ear had made it home, she should be warm and dry now. But then I remembered the mournful tone of Shine's voice.

My father and Sen still slept. Suli was curled in the warm spot Ama had left. I knew that my mother liked this quiet time. I heard a red-paint bird whistle *see see see su*. Ama whistled back to him.

I dressed and went out. Ama turned to me. "The sunbirds are back," she whispered. "I can hear them in the willows." I nodded. *Tal* was strong on a spring morning like this. Everything was full of life. Then I said in a low voice, "I am going to see if Torn Ear returned in the night."

Ama put a hand on my arm. "It's not full light yet. I don't like you to go alone."

"I am not so slow as Apa and Sen think. I'll be careful."

It wasn't possible, but I was sure I could hear the pup calling to me.

"If the mother wolf is dead, the little pup won't live. There's nothing you can do," Ama said, gazing into my face.

"I have to know."

My mother sighed, touched my forehead in the gesture of parting, and whispered, "*Tal* keep you." She let me go, but not without another deer rib left from last night's meal. I stripped the bone hungrily as I went, even though the fat was hardened to tallow.

It was warm enough to be barefoot; still, I was glad for my *anooka*. Mist made a ghost lake in the valley. It clung like ibex wool to the trees on the hillsides. Bellowing and snarls echoed from upriver. A cave lion had ended the night's hunt well.

Before I reached the denning ground, I heard another sound—a long, low howl.

Shine.

I paused to listen—not a song, a moan. Cupping my hands around my mouth, I sent my own call back. Shine did not answer.

I hobbled faster, cursing my lame leg, stumbling and bumping, picking my way over the rocky knoll. A branch slapped my face. *Please let her be there, please.* I tripped, scraped my knee, but did not feel it. Finally I came into view of Torn Ear's den. I stopped, leaning on my stick. *There.*

Torn Ear lay near the entrance, as she sometimes did. But not resting, nose on forepaws, one ear batting a fly, enjoying the sun. No. She was on her side, legs stiff. Her fur was rain-soaked and matted. I closed my eyes.

Dead.

She had dragged herself home sometime in the night. There was a trickle of blood at the corner of her jaw. I knew what that meant. It was an injury to her insides. Wolf or human, we sometimes give much for our meat.

I fell to my knees beside Torn Ear and buried my face in her fur. Under the cold, clinging strands of outer fur, the soft under-fur was dry. It smelled of golden wolfness, sweet and sharp. I had seen many dead animals, but not often a wolf. She had let me come close, but seldom to touch her. A thought came—*Torn Ear was my sister.*

My face twisted. How far had Torn Ear crawled on her belly, across rocks, over rough ground, trying to reach her pups? I scanned the hillside. Shine had already left to hunt again. The pups must be fed. I spied Lan for a moment before the uncle wolf melted into the underbrush. Then I turned to the den.

The opening was partly screened by a trailing vine. Warily, I crouched, pulled the tangle back, and looked inside. "Little wolves," I called softly. Muffled yips. I listened, thought I could hear a weaker cry among the others. "You have to come out. I can't help if you won't come out."

But I could not coax them to me. Again, I looked over my shoulder. If Lan was watching, he gave no sign. Placing my hands on either side of the den opening, I peered into the tunnel. This was a much deeper den than most. Walls of sandy earth. Rocks jutting. A tangled net of roots. I made a whimpering sound in my throat, and once more the pups answered. *So narrow.* Sen could never have squeezed his shoulders through. But my shoulders were not big.

My hand slipped, knocking loose dirt and pebbles. Fear gripped my belly. What if I got stuck or the tunnel caved in on me? How did the wolves know it was safe? But they must know. The walls of the tunnel were worn smooth. They went in and out of here often. Again, I called to the pups, and they whimpered back. Then my vision went dark. I was in a dream. Or was it memory? *Shadows. Puppy cries. Warmth.*

The fear loosened its hold. I breathed. I could do this.

I set down my stick and slithered in on my belly. The brightness of day was gone. Slowly, my eyes made out roots arching overhead. A slab of stone formed a sort of roof. Using my elbows, I pulled myself forward. I called to the pups. They answered me.

The tunnel took a downward twist. I found handholds, dragged myself along, forcing my way into Earth Mother's heart. My own heart pounded in my ears. Was I really doing this? Once my shoulder jammed against a root. I thought I could go no farther, but I clawed away enough dirt to slither forward again. Some of it rained on my head. Got into my eyes. Inside my clothing. I blinked hard. Rubbed it away.

Small scraps of light glimmered from the tunnel opening behind me. Now I could make out a wider space ahead. The wolves had chosen well. The tunnel was dry. It smelled of earth and the muskiness of wolf fur.

Dark bundles crowded together in the shadows. I heard them snuffling. Then suddenly, all went black and a trickle of earth fell on the sole of my good foot. I froze. Something had come into the tunnel behind me. *Lan.* I was trapped. He would tear at my legs. I knew what wolf teeth could do. Once I had watched Shine open a reindeer's belly with a single pass of his fangs, even as it lay, eyes wide, bleeding out from its throat.

I tried to draw my legs away. Then something moist and cold touched my foot. Lan's nose. I felt the wolf's breath as he carefully smelled each of my feet, first the good one, then the twisted one. He licked it once.

I will not harm them, I cried silently to the uncle wolf. *I have only come for the small one who cannot eat meat yet.*

Almost as if Lan heard and understood, the nose went away. There was a slight scraping sound. Slivers of light again. I waited until my heart slowed once more.

Then I reached into the warmth of the nest. There was a puppy snarl of terror. A fuzzy shape moved away from my hand. I tried to grasp a leg, but needle teeth sank into my fingers. I let go, fumbled for another pup, and was bitten again. I paused, leaving my hand in the nest. Waited. The air was thick, like being under heavy furs. I forced myself to breathe slow and deep. Tried not to think of being trapped under the ground.

Then something touched my palm. A small nose sniffed

my fingers. Licked them. Which pup was it? There was no way of knowing for sure in the darkness, but my heart said this was the one. Very gently I closed my fingers on the loose skin at the scruff of its neck. I pulled it toward me, away from the others, who kept snarling fiercely.

I shuffled backward out of the tunnel, clutching the pup to me with one hand. I squeezed past the place where my shoulder jammed. Worked myself upward past the rock. All the time I murmured to the small handful of fur, holding it close to my face, smelling its sweet breath. "Hush, I will not hurt you," I whispered.

At last I was out again, squinting in the light. I crouched, holding the tiny wolf under my chin, and breathed. Then I lowered my arms to look at it. The pup wriggled onto its back. It blinked its eyes, nuzzling desperately for milk. A little female.

I glanced up—to find both Lan and Shine less than a leap away. Legs locked, fur bristling along their spines, they blocked my path. They stared at me through eyes closed nearly to slits.

Shine licked his lips showing his great tearing teeth. *I am dead*, I thought. I dropped my eyes. *I am only taking the one you cannot feed*, I begged him silently. One breath. Two. Ten. My heart thumping so hard I was sure they could hear it. *Yellow Mother gave me my life. Let me try to give your pup hers.*

From the corner of my eyes I saw the two wolves drop out of their challenge stances. The ridge of fur along their shoulders went down. Shine tucked his hindquarters and sat. He sniffed the body of his dead mate. Licked her torn ear. Whimpered once like a pup himself. My heart twisted. *I am so sorry, my friend.* Then he turned his eyes back to me. I glimpsed the sadness in them before I looked away. Lan glanced at Shine once and then lowered his eyes.

They had agreed. With my eyes still on the ground, I nodded. Then holding the pup to my chest with one hand, I picked up my stick and backed slowly away, one step at a time. I could feel them watching.

"Thank you," I whispered.

CHAPTER 5

When I reached the *takka*, my mother was sorting and brushing dirt from a basket of mushrooms. They were the kind that look like wrinkled skin. We call them *mora*, old-man mushrooms. She had a basket of greens, too. Her woman's hunting had been good. My mouth watered. With my free hand, I grabbed a handful of the greens to eat raw.

Ama clucked her tongue, but she did not slap my hand away. Bu was asleep in his sling on her back, his little head bobbing as she moved. My father and brother were up in the highlands, hunting.

Suli crouched by the fire. Her face split into a grin when she saw me. I rubbed a smudge of soot from her cheek with my thumb. "Careful, you're losing your *ah-bu*." With one hand, I helped Suli stuff it safely back into the little sling on her back. It was made from scraps of leather and wool and was very ugly, but Suli loved it fiercely.

"Not *ah-bu—ah-bah*! She's a *girl*, Kai. Bu is a *bu*."

"I forgot."

"Kai," my mother said, her eyes questioning.

I did not answer. Instead, I opened the front of my *anooka* and showed her the wolf pup nestled against my chest. It turned to the light and whimpered with hunger. Ama's eyes widened. Suli's mouth opened. "Torn Ear is dead," I told them. "The other pups are bigger and can eat meat, but this one needs milk."

My mother stared at me. "What are you going to do with it, Kai?"

"I don't know. She is hungry. I owe my life to the *imnos*. There must be some way to feed her."

My mother didn't answer. The pup cried and nuzzled weakly against my chest. At last, Ama said, "There is a way that sometimes works when there is no milk."

She took the leg bone of the deer from our night meal, smacked it open with a rock, and scraped the marrow into a small *das*. Then she ground a bit of the bone into paste and mixed it with the marrow and some broth to make a rich gruel.

"Give it to me," she said.

I put the pup into her hands, and she touched the tiny muzzle with her fingers. The little black nose snuffled. Suli crept close and reached out to stroke its fur. The pup licked her fingers. Suli giggled.

Then my mother showed me how to dip a finger into the gruel and let the pup lick. At first the pup turned away, but suddenly, she attacked ravenously. Ama laughed. "You cannot eat without some manners," she scolded softly. She handed her back to me. The pup lapped gruel from my fingers until it was gone.

I ran my hand over the little belly. It bulged now like a filled waterskin. Suddenly the pup grunted and a stream of wetness dampened my front. "*Ayee*, you little leaking *bah*," I whispered. I held the pup over the ground until she was empty. Then I held her close again, and stroked her head. She nudged my hand when I stopped. She liked my touch.

She sighed, nestled, and was suddenly asleep.

Ama laughed softly. "It's good to see you smile, Kai." She stroked the baby fluff. "Soon she will be able to eat soft meat. You must feed and care for her. Bu and Suli are enough for me. But Kai, a wolf is not the same as a baby crow, and your little thief-bird was trouble enough before he flew away last fall. Apa may say no."

My eyes flew up to meet hers. He could not say no. After all this, my father could not say no. I would not *let* him say no.

But my father was my father. And I was only Kai, the son that would never be a hunter. The nameless one. What could I do to make him let me keep the little wolf? And Sen—what would he do? He had been gentle with my baby crow, had hunted eggs and caught mice to help feed it. But that was last year.

I spent the rest of the day in a blackness of fear. The pup was lonely at first, whimpering, seeking her brothers. I made a nest for her from an old ibex fur that was used for wiping feet, near the opening, where we kept our winter *sabas*. She seemed to know my pair. She rested her chin on the one my mother had made to fit my twisted foot and slept soundly for a time.

A few days before, Apa and Sen had used the game net to capture a saiga antelope. The creature had torn a hole as it thrashed and kicked. I was not allowed to knap flint into *keerta* points, but I was allowed my work blade. I made good twine and nets. My knots were strong. Very strong, as I had found out the time I bent to pick up a spilled basket of hazelnuts and suddenly the net came down over my head and shoulders, throwing me to my knees. I fought like an animal, nuts flying everywhere, with Sen's laughter like stinging bees in my ears.

"Let me go!" I shouted. I struck and kicked at him until he finally loosened the net.

"I didn't mean anything, Kai," he said. "You were just so easy to catch."

My twisted foot was bruised where I had kicked one of the hearth stones. I rubbed it. Tried to keep my face empty. Suddenly he was the old Sen again. "Sometimes I hate *Tal* for twisting your foot," he whispered, handing me my stick. Our eyes met.

"Maybe *Tal* had a reason," I said, with a shrug.

"But you were a baby. You did nothing wrong."

"*Tal* gives two arms, legs, eyes, ears. If one is hurt,

the other grows stronger. Maybe Tal is trying to make me stronger."

He eyed me strangely. Then he looked down. "You would have been a good hunter," he said softly.

As I knotted and twisted the fibers of the net back together, I worried. What if Apa would not let me keep the little wolf? What if Sen hurt her? Over and over I scolded Suli, "Leave her alone, she's just a baby. She needs to sleep. Play with your *ah-bah* and your pinecone wolves."

After a while, the pup woke and cried at being alone. She needed to make water, and her belly was empty once more. I carried her outside. Suli laughed as the tiny thing squatted.

"At least she's doing it outside," I told her.

I made more gruel as my mother had shown me. "Hurry, Kai, she's hungry!" Suli said. She was right, the pup yapped and cried while I worked. Then Suli made me let her feed the pup. A lot was spilled, but only because the little wolf was so greedy. It was good to see her eat. Now, instead of falling asleep, she wriggled around in my lap, sniffing carefully. It was as if she was learning who I was with her nose. She was stronger already.

Bu watched, big-eyed. He laughed, reached out, and grabbed a fistful of fur before I could stop him. *"Nah!"* I cried, thinking the pup would bite, but she only turned and nuzzled my baby brother's fat hand.

Now the pup was wakeful. She didn't like being alone. Suli held her close, cradling her in her arms. "You have a wolf *bah* to go with your *ah-bah* now," I told her. My sister nodded, grinning. The pup nosed one of the tangled yellow braids that hung down Suli's shoulders. She found the rawhide tie, and began to tug and chew. Suli giggled. Then the pup found her string of beads. They were only made of wood, but Suli was very proud of them. "*Nah!*" she scolded.

I took the pup back to my own lap. The *imnos* had always lived near the People. Sometimes they followed us on hunts. But no family of the People had ever taken one into their *takka*. Never. Was it wrong? The little wolf licked me. *Shine, Torn Ear, see this. Your pup is alive. I will feed her. I will raise her for you.* But how?

It was nearing dusk. All around the *immet*, fires were being built up for the evening. There was little to fear from the Ice Men now. They were seldom seen during the warm months. Still, the fires would be kept burning all night to ward off hungry beasts—and thieving wolves. Sometimes a yellow wolf was bold enough to steal unwatched meat.

~

I thought about the Ice Men. Once, when I was small, I had seen one. It was early spring. The women were trying to catch fish. Vida and I had built a small trap of stones to catch minnows in the shallows. They flashed in a silver cloud, the way swirling snow blows over frozen ground, as we chased them into our trap.

I remembered stopping. Sniffing. Listening. There was a

prickling at the back of my neck. I lifted my head, turned, and stared across the stream. Nothing. Just rocks and low bushes. Beyond that, open land in patches of green and yellow. A herd of horses grazing. Far-off blue humps that were hills.

Nothing moved.

But then my sight changed. It came into a different way of seeing. Eyes—deep-set and shining—watched me from the shadows. There was thinking in those eyes. And hunger. I took a step closer, with the river water running cold past my shins. Then I made out the rough clothing and the shape of the man crouching in the brush. His features were jagged, but he was a kind of a man. Stocky, hairy, and ragged, but I was sure of it—a man.

He smiled, showing strong white teeth. Nodded at me and made a gesture of eating, then for me to come to him. I had a strip of dried meat in my carrying pouch. Maybe he smelled it—wanted it. I took another step toward him, but then stopped.

"Look, Vida," I whispered. "There is a creature . . . like a man. It . . . he's watching us from across the stream. In the willow thicket. There!" I pointed. "I think . . . he wants us to come across to him."

Vida looked up from where she was kneeling in the shallows. She leapt to her feet shrieking, "Run, Kai! It's an Ice Man—they eat children!" Suddenly I was stumbling after her, and all the women and children were running. I hobbled as fast as I could over the gravel. My brother was ahead with the bigger boys. I saw him turn to search for me, heard him shout to my mother. Ama looked around, eyes wild, snatched me up, and fled after the others. But I could not help staring over her shoulder as she ran.

There were three of them. They stumbled away from us, crashing through the tall reeds along the river. I saw terror in the dark eyes that stared back at us.

When we reached the safety of the *immet*, a party of hunters went out but found nothing. Ice Men were not fast runners, but they had gotten too good a start. Ama held me tight, patting my back. "Hush, Kai, you must not cry. See, Bol does not cry." I looked at my brother. He was crouched by the hearth, shoulders hunched, clutching his elbows. His face was the color of bone. His lip trembled, but he was not crying, would not cry, for he would be a man someday, and a hunter does not cry.

"What were they? Who?" I stammered.

Ama took a shaky breath. "They are animal-men, Kai. They live in the north where the ice stays forever in the mountains. They are few and shy, but fierce, and very strong. An Ice Man can break a person's back with just his arms. They cannot speak as we do or even sew clothing and *sabas*. They do not make long *keertas*. Their weapons are short and heavy. They cannot throw them as we do." She shook her head, biting her lip.

"Do they eat children?" I asked, trying hard not to cry again.

She wouldn't look at me. "In the deep of winter, when food is scarce, sometimes they come at night." Her voice fell to a whisper. "They steal children, Kai. I cannot tell you why. Last winter we were lucky and they didn't come—just that lion the one time. You are too young to remember the winter before, when so many had the coughing fever. My friend Imi was killed by an Ice Man and her little boy taken. They stole all the meat in their storage pit.

"Imi's man, Baq, and your father and some of the other hunters set out after them. There was a battle by the crossing at the little river where the big boulders are. The Ice Men sheltered behind the rocks. Our *keertas* were not much good there. Baq was killed, and another of our men. The Ice Men got away with the boy. I don't know why they come now. Winter is over. There is food." Angrily she brushed away her own tears.

"But, did they . . . eat . . . the boy?" The words hurt to say. Still, I had to know.

"I don't know." Then Ama saw the terror on my face. "Don't be afraid, Kai. No one can throw a *keerta* like your *apa*. He will not let anything harm us."

For a long time after that, the face of the Ice Man at the river haunted my dreaming, beckoning me to come and be eaten.

~

But this evening, such terrors were far away. There was only the worry of my father and Sen coming home from their hunting to find my wolf pup. The spring air was sweet. We sat by the outside fire pit, and Suli danced around with the pup at her ankles. Suddenly, she yelped and hobbled to me on one foot, sobbing.

Ama shook her head, saying, "Suli, I told you not to run over Apa's work place." I made Suli sit and hold out her foot to me. I studied the bottom of it until I found what she had stepped on. "You go from sunshine to rain very quickly, Bramble," I told her.

I looked up, pretending to see something over her shoulder. "Is that a woolly rhino grazing across the river?" Suli twisted around to look. In that moment, I pulled out the splinter of flint and tossed it back to Apa's work place.

The hills became smoky shapes and the watch star came out over the cliffs. Ama turned her head at each sound, a burst of laughter from another *takka*, a stick of wood snapping, the thump of grind stones. There were worry lines between her brows. My father and Sen were late.

I took my grandfather's *osa* from its secret place. It was made from the hollow wing bone of a great vulture, my most precious thing. In his last days, when he had little breath to play, Apa-Da had been trying to teach me. "Hold it so, Kai. Put your fingers here and here. Breathe like this—*feeeeeu*—and let it out slowly."

My squeaks and sputters made Sen laugh.

In all my remembering, so many nights had been filled with the sound of my grandfather's *osa*. It whispered stories that carried me to sleep.

His music was magic. It was his heart song.

The morning after my grandfather walked away from us forever into the winter night, I found his *osa* lying beside my bed. For many days I could not look at it. Then suddenly I knew what Apa-Da had asked of me. I must be the one to play the *osa* now.

I tried, but I was a very bad *osa* player. My breath ran out. I had trouble covering the holes. I made squawking sounds. Sen liked my playing because it gave him a chance to mock me. "*Ayee!* My ears! Careful, Kai, you sound like a dying rabbit. See, the vultures are circling already!"

I hid the *osa* in a hollow under a stone, where my brother wouldn't find it. Now I did not play it if he was near. But when I was sure that he was not around, I worked at trying to make good sounds. For Apa-Da. Somehow he might be listening. He would not laugh. I was getting better at finding the notes, but I thought I could never make the little hollow bone sing as my grandfather had done. I did not have a heart song.

I tried a high, dancing tune now. Some of the notes were sour. But Suli sat quietly, listening, with the wolf pup curled in her lap.

Then I played the song I remembered best: the one, a little sad, that made me think of moonlight on the frozen river in winter. Again I missed some notes. The baby wolf stared hard at me. Suddenly, she lifted her sharp little muzzle and sang with the *osa*.

When I finished, I looked at my mother. "I cannot play like Apa-Da," I said.

"Not yet, Kai," my mother agreed, "but still, I like to hear it."

~

At last, I spotted Sen and Apa. Each carried the quarters of an ibex. Apa carried the skin and head as well. It was a male. The long horns curved down over his shoulders like two new moons. Hurriedly, I took the wolf pup back from Suli and ducked inside to put my *osa* away. Then I crouched near the opening, waiting.

When she saw them, Ama laughed softly, the lines of worry gone. There was a clattering sound made by the rows of teeth on my father's *anooka* as he set his burden down. Sen did the same, throwing his shoulders back so that the teeth of the aurochs bull, sewn to his *anooka,* clicked together loudly. He was taller now than Apa, though still skinny. He brushed a hand over the front of his head where the yellow hair was cut short. The rest was pulled into a tail at the back of his neck, the way hunters wore theirs.

"Sen killed one as well," Apa told Ama proudly. "He gave it to Mir's family." My parents' eyes met. They smiled.

Suli reached for the beautiful horns. Apa chuckled, touching her cheek with a calloused hand. "Patience, my Suli," he said. My father stepped inside the *takka.* "We will have a good new waterskin from the hide. . . ." He broke off, his nostrils working over the blood scent of the freshly killed ibex. Then he turned to me where I crouched.

"I smell wolf."

CHAPTER 6

There was no use trying to hide what could not be hidden.

"The one I call Torn Ear was killed," I whispered. "The other pups can eat meat, but this one is too little. She would have died."

My father stared. Sen came inside to see. His lip curled. "Kai has brought home his little brother!" he said. "A pup with a pup." His voice was like sour fruit.

I glared at him.

"Hush," said Apa. For a few breaths, he was silent, thoughtful. Finally he squatted beside me and held out his hands. Trembling, I put the pup into them. I looked up at him, silently pleading. Those hands could break the neck of a small animal in one swift motion.

He held the pup, stroking her fur and running the tiny tail though his fingers. He could not help a trace of a smile. "How did you find it, Kai?" I told him about crawling into

Torn Ear's den. His face went very still. "You did that?" he asked in a low voice. "You were not afraid?"

"She would have died."

"That took courage," Apa said. Something glinted in his eyes. Pride? For me? But then his expression changed. "I do not know what you have done bringing one of the wolves into our *takka*," he said. "There is enough talk among the People about you, Kai. Better to take it back to its den. The People have lived the way we live forever. As have the wolves. If *Tal* had meant for wolves to live with humans, it would have been so from the beginning."

I tried to say that the *imnos* were our friends. That they had always followed the People wherever we went. But it came out in a croak like a scared animal.

Ama spoke. She had come in behind us with Bu in her arms. "There is no law to be broken by keeping a wolf."

My father laughed. "That's because no one has ever done it. Have you ever watched a pack take down a deer? Do you want those teeth near Suli and Bu?"

"The wolves saved Kai as a baby. Yellow Mother never forgot him. She never hurt him," Ama said. "It seems right to save one of theirs."

Sen snorted. My parents' eyes met again. They spoke to each other without words.

Apa was quiet. The silence between them grew. My stomach clenched like a fist. Ama settled Bu in his basket and turned to build up the inside fire. The light played on my father's face. A little sad. Thoughtful.

At last he sighed. "Keep it for a while, Kai, but if there is trouble, you must give it back to the *imnos*."

"Her," I said softly. My father's eyes flickered to mine, and the corner of his mouth twitched. Then he handed the pup back to me. She nested in my arms, warm against my chest. She seemed already to know she was safe there.

"It will steal our meat. How can a wolf live with people?" asked Sen.

"I will teach her to find her own meat," I said wildly. "She will become one of us." What had made me say that? I had no idea how to hunt.

Sen laughed. "When it grows big and eats your share, you will be glad for me to put my *keerta* into its heart. Wolf fur is very warm."

Something hard as a stone rose in my chest. "She can keep me warm alive," I said to my brother.

Apa and Sen went down to the river to wash. Apa came back soon, but Sen was gone a long time. When he returned, he combed out his wet hair and struggled to knot the long part at the back of his head. "Here, let me do it," said Ama, smiling. Sen's cheeks flushed, but I was amazed to see him give her the comb.

"She is a lucky girl," Ama whispered, almost to herself, as she finished. Sen did not reply, but strode off in the direction of Mir's *takka*.

Not long after that, I saw the two of them sitting together on the great flat rock behind the *immet*. They were gazing out over the open land. Sen's arm was around Mir's shoulders.

The evening meal was good. Along with the fresh meat, there were weeping roots roasted whole in their skins and the greens with their sharp spring taste. There were also the mushrooms, sizzled in fat rubbed on the cooking stone.

I offered the pup a tender bit of meat. She licked at it, but turned her head, so I made more marrow gruel for her. Once she was full, I could not get her to stay in her corner. Over and over, she dropped to sleep as I stroked her soft fur. But when I turned away, the little wolf woke, crying pitifully.

Apa grumbled.

My brother cursed. "Maybe you should take your yipping pup and find your own den, Wolfboy," he hissed at me.

I carried the pup back to my bed. The little wolf nestled against me. She stretched out a foot, bumping my nose. I ran a finger over her muzzle. It was shorter than most. Her little skull seemed rounder, too. "Will you be one of the People?" I whispered to her. "Or should I be one of the *imnos* with you?"

CHAPTER 7

The wolf pup stirred where she was tucked into the front of my *anooka*. She poked her head out and sniffed the air. I sniffed, too. Storm. I scanned the sky. To the west the clouds were muddy and billowing, like smoke from rotten wood. Down along the river, the willow leaves shivered. "There will be lightning soon," I called to the others. "We should go back."

"What's the matter, Wolfboy? Are you afraid?" asked Xar. We were on the cliff trail, cutting juniper for torches. At least, I was cutting torches. Sen and his friends had spotted some ibex grazing on the tufts of grass growing among the rocks higher up and left to track them—with no success. Now they were back, hurrying. I had nearly all I could carry. I started binding the pile together. My hands were sticky with sap.

"Women's work," Sen muttered.

"I smell sky fire. See how fast the clouds run," I said. "The pup smells it, too."

"More likely you and that beast are calling the storm, *tabat* one," said Xar, chopping at a root.

"Go back if you're scared," said Sen.

"I'm not afraid, it's just that it's stupid to be on the cliffs in a thunderstorm." I hefted my load, got my balance with my stick, and started down the trail.

"I don't hear any thunder. *Tal* is still holding back. We have plenty of time," Uli called after me. He stripped branches and tossed another stem with its pitch-filled root onto his pile. He didn't joke now. He hurried.

I had just reached the shelter of some trees when the air went blinding white, with a crash overhead like a rockfall. Hot needles stabbed through my *sabas*. The pup yelped. A great wind swept around us with rain like a waterfall. More sky fire flashed. A juniper burst into splinters and flame. I scrambled under a stone ledge. The others yelled in fear as they raced past me. Their faces were blue in the flashes of light.

Bolts of sky fire struck all around us, crash after crash. I could not think. On the slope nearby, a dead tree was hit. Far below, the storm tore through the *immet*. Another stab of sky fire and the *takka* of Xar's family blew apart, flames devouring it.

At last the storm passed, but I was a long time picking my way down the slippery trail. Soaked and shivering, I stared at the soggy mess of the *immet*. Xar and his father struggled to reset the remaining blackened poles of their *takka* while his mother sobbed over the smoldering ruins. As I made my way past them, they turned to stare. Xar's father spat on the ground. Three sets of cold eyes followed me.

The *takka* of my family still stood, but part of the covering had been ripped away. The frame showed like bones. My father and brother were already at work repairing it. Ama and Suli were laying bed furs out to dry. Rivers of rainwater choked the fire pit and ran along our footpaths. It was over, but I could not forget the look in the eyes of Xar and his family.

CHAPTER 8

Bu is going hunting and he kills a big cave bear!
Bu is going hunting and he kills a big lion!
Bu is going hunting and he kills a big leopard!

Holding my small brother under the arms and letting his feet thump the ground, I sang to him. I did not envy those stout little legs that kicked so hard. I was glad for them. Each time I said an animal's name, I bumped his forehead with my own and Bu squealed.

It was the day after the storm. I was keeping him happy so my mother could work. The sun shone and things were drying out. Bu opened his mouth wide, showing four white teeth in his gums. I play-growled and he bent forward, trying to bite me. "*Ayee!*" I said. "You are savage, little brother!"

"I'm a wolf pup, too!" Suli cried, throwing herself in my lap. The pup woke, and in another moment I was in a tangle of arms, legs, paws, and nipping baby wolf teeth. Suddenly Suli yelped and ran sobbing to Ama.

"Kai, don't let the wolf hurt your sister!" my mother cried. My father looked up from the blade he was shaping.

"It's just play," I said, but my gut clenched. The pup yipped, trying to root under my chin, wanting to wrestle again. *Wet nose, licking tongue, pricking teeth!* "You are growing a mouth full of flint blades!" I scolded, pushing her away.

She sat down. Now her mouth was a tiny round yowl of emptiness.

"I think she's hungry again," my mother said. "I can take Bu. Suli, you are not hurt. Go feed her, Kai."

After the pup ate, I found a scrap of hide. The pup bit onto it, yanking hard. I tugged back. She slid on her bottom, but did not let go. Suli begged to try this pulling game. The pup growled, and my little sister laughed, forgetting her tears.

Later, the others watched while Suli and I played the tugging game with the pup. Once Suli pulled and the scrap of hide flew from her hand. The pup yipped. Where was it? She put her nose to the ground, snuffling. She circled away, then back again. When she came close, her tail began to wave. She searched with her nose until she found it.

"Hold her while I hide it," I told Suli. I hid the scrap under a mushroom basket, inside a cooking container, behind a waterskin. Each time, the little wolf sniffed and found it.

I glanced back to find Ama smiling and Apa grinning broadly. My father ran a hand over the pup's fur. She shook the scrap, wanting to play again. But when my eyes caught my brother's, Sen quickly looked down and pretended not to be watching.

Now Suli held the piece of hide over her head. The little wolf crouched, opened her mouth, and yapped, "Uff!" Then she said it again, "Uff, uff, uff!" until Suli tossed it to her. The pup pounced and carried it off with her tail in the air.

"If she's to be one of us for a time," Ama said, "I think she must have a name."

"We can't call her *Kai*," said Sen. "We already have a good-for-nothing pup. This one will grow into a ferocious hunter!"

"The *imnos* don't attack people!" I said. Still, I knew what my father would do if she hurt any of us.

"What name will we call you?" I asked her.

The pup did not hesitate. She yapped again.

"Uff!" repeated Suli.

Ama laughed. "I think she has told you her name, Kai."

"Uff," I said softly.

CHAPTER 9

The pup who had named herself Uff watched whatever I did—as if I were her *Tal*. The thought made my chest hollow. I could hear Apa-Da's voice in my head, as if he were still beside me, reciting the words told by the fires of all time. I knew them like breathing.

Tal is in the seeds that become great trees and in the mountain peaks that bite the sky. Tal spits fire, roars, and flings rain. Each new sun is Tal. Tal is in the earth and among the stars. Tal is fire that eats wood to give the heat of summer in winter, blackens the land, yet is the green that lives again.

I might be her *Tal*, but Uff was not afraid of me as the People are afraid of our *Tal*. Fearlessly she nipped at my legs or chewed on my stick. "*Ayee!* You are a clinging bramble, like Suli," I told her. Uff nipped my fingers and tried hard to chew my nose off. But if I yelped, her ears went down and she stopped.

My little wolf spoke, but not in words. She talked with her ears and tail and also in yips and *uffs*—demanding, humble, or happy.

One day my brother and his friends went duck hunting. It was not easy to creep close enough to hit the birds. When spooked, they would fly, quacking, down the river, leaving only a feather floating on the water. But Sen brought down two. Ama stuffed each with herbs and weeping roots, wrapped them first in leaves, then clay, buried them in a pit of coals, and let them roast all day.

By evening the smell of roasting duck made it hard to think of anything else. Everyone's mouth watered as Ama finally dug them out of the coals and broke away the covering.

"That was good hunting, Sen," said Apa, wiping his chin with the back of his hand. Sen grinned with his mouth full. I pressed my lips together. I wanted to say that the meat was stringy and flavorless. But it was not. It fell from the bones in tender chunks.

"Apa-Da loved a roast duck," said Ama. "I once saw him eat a whole one himself when there was plenty."

"And then he would belch," said my father, chuckling. "Such a belch! I think everyone in the *immet* could hear it."

"I think the birds were frightened off their roosts," said Sen.

"And the horses on the grassland thought a lion was after them!" I added. We all laughed, remembering.

Suddenly, Uff lunged for my duck leg. I saw my father's eyes flash our way. I chewed a mouthful until it was soft.

Then I fed it to Uff with my fingers. She was crazy for this new food. She trembled all over, ears pricked, tail quivering. In her hurry to gulp it down, she tried to eat my fingers, too. "Ow!" I pulled my hand away. There were two small drops of blood on my knuckle.

Suli immediately spat out her own mouthful of meat for the pup. Soon my sister had to be told to eat some of her food herself. Now Apa frowned. "I think you must take her back to the pack before long, Kai. A grown wolf eats much. The time will come when we cannot spare any meat. You remember last winter?"

I stared at him. The words cut my heart. How could I send Uff away?

"But she doesn't know how to hunt," I stammered.

"How do you plan to teach her?" my father asked. I opened my mouth. Closed it again. I had no answer. My brother shook his head as if I was a crazy person. I wanted to hit him. Hard. But I knew my father was right. Each of the People did a share of work to keep us all alive. Even Suli helped scrape hides and pick berries. I did my part, though it was not the part I would have chosen. What could Uff do for the *immet*?

Yes, I remembered last winter. I wished I could forget it. I held Uff close now, staring at the fire, as the bitter memory filled my head.

The cold time had been endless. All of our storage pits were empty. We boiled lichens, old bones, scraps of rawhide, hoping for signs of thawing weather. But the winter went on. My belly felt sucked against my spine. My dreams were all of roasted meat, fresh greens, duck eggs. When she climbed into my lap for comfort, the bones of Suli's little bottom were sharp. She and Bu whimpered day and night.

When food is scarce, the old people will sometimes offer themselves to *Tal* so that a younger belly may have their share. Apa-Da's eyes had grown so weak that I had to help him find his walking stick and his drinking *das*. He joked and called me old man too, because we both used sticks to walk. My throat hurt and my eyes stung now with the remembering.

As long as he was able, my grandfather did what small tasks he could. But at last he could not grasp his tools. Ama and I fed him as if he were a small child. Apa and Sen had to help him rise to his feet to walk. Once I saw Sen brush tears away. Our Apa-Da had always been there, telling stories, playing his *osa*, working flint and leather.

One night, while we slept, Apa-Da dragged himself to his feet. He left his warm bed furs behind and walked out into the night naked, and alone. The next morning, my father followed the tracks. He came back with his eyes streaming. He took Ama in his arms and said in a rough voice, "Your *apa* has walked to the world beyond."

Apa-Da's share of food kept Ama's milk flowing for Bu. It

kept Suli alive until the early spring when the reindeer herd came up from the south once more.

At last we heard the cry, "The deer are coming!" At first, I saw just a brown smudge at the edge of the world. Then heads came out of the dust as they approached the river crossing. They were not beautiful and fat as they would be in the fall. Their coats were faded and worn bald in places. They had no antlers. But they were beautiful to us. I held Suli up to see. "Soon you will taste meat again," I told her.

"Let me join the hunters!" I begged my father, "It's not so hard to kill a deer as it comes up out of the river."

His face went rigid.

"At least let me carry your extra *keerta*!"

"*Nah* and *nah*, Kai," he said in a choked voice. "Do not even think of it! We can't afford *tabat* to blacken this hunt."

I watched as Apa and Sen gathered their weapons.

I watched when the hunters took deer as they came out of the river. That was all I could do—watch. Then I went back to my work with the women, hands blistered from slicing meat to dry in the smoke of the willow twig fires.

The reindeer herd splashed across the river for two days. We worked hard. Skins pegged out on the ground and racks of drying meat made it difficult to walk through the *immet*. Soon the herd would disappear into the north. We would not follow. Ice Men were there.

And suddenly the reindeer were gone.

Now, as Uff gnawed on a duck bone, my heart twisted. I could not lose her, too. If only my grandfather could have waited for the reindeer herd. But one way or another, a hunter, even an old one, gives life to his family. One day, even Bu would keep a family of his own alive. The People must live. Each of us knew this thing. We did not need to speak of it. Now we had meat. But the time would come when we would not.

CHAPTER 10

"You cannot play with the wolf pup all the time," Ama said, but she smiled as she handed me a waterskin to fill. I reached for my stick. Uff's eyes caught the movement. She was up, ready to go.

"Alright," I said to her. "You're big enough to see the world for a little while."

The path to the river was stony. The pup balked at the steep places. She cried until I helped her. Still, she would follow. After a few steps, she grew bolder. She scampered from rock to rock. Then suddenly, she was going too fast. Her feet tangled. She tumbled over herself, yipping. But in a moment, she found her feet again. She opened her mouth in a little wolf grin and galloped after me once more.

We reached the sandy place beside the river. Uff lunged for my waterskin. She latched her teeth into it, hanging on with all her strength. "*Nah*, Uff!" I tugged it away before she could make holes in it. She was excited now. She ran at my ankles. I had seen wolf pups playing with sticks. "Play with this, Little Bah," I told her, breaking off a branch and giving it to her. She seized it in her teeth and pattered along behind me.

The girls liked to come to the pool in the river where waterskins were filled. Usually they ignored me. But when they saw Uff, they hushed and stared.

"There's the wolfboy with his pup!" I heard Mir say in a loud whisper. I was glad Sen was not there to hear her.

Jyn looked up from twining a feather into Mir's hair. Her eyes widened. "Kai really *is* a wolf! He talks to it! He'll tell the pack to hunt us!"

"That's foolishness," said Cali. "Wolves hunt deer and mice, not humans, and it's just a baby."

"I saw Suli playing with it," said Vida wistfully.

"It will grow big and hungry with horrible teeth. I wouldn't like a grown wolf following me," said Mir.

Uff felt the wet sand under her feet. She stopped short, lifted a paw, and looked at me anxiously. "Water," I told her. "This is where we get water. Here." I scooped some from the stream and offered it to her. She nosed it, then lapped from my cupped hands. The girls stared, silent.

Now Uff saw the moving stream. She did not understand it. Sunlight touched the surface, yet it was clear as air. She tried to bite a pebble on the bottom and got a nose full. She sat down hard. Sneezed. The girls laughed, and she spooked at the sound. I stumbled after her and caught her up. "It's just the river," I whispered, holding her close. "And the girls. They are alike, always babbling and laughing."

"Can I touch her?" It was Vida. She had left the others and come to my side.

"You can hold her," I said, putting Uff into her arms. My little wolf wriggled, licking Vida's face. Vida stroked Uff's fur and looked up at me, her eyes shining. "Once I found a baby rabbit," she told me. "Its fur was just this soft. But my mother wouldn't let me keep it." Uff licked her face again. "She likes me!"

"Of course she does," I said. I felt my face suddenly redden. "She has a name," I added. "I call her Uff."

Vida nodded. "I will be your friend, too, Uff," she said to my wolf.

"Vida!" The voice was shrill with fear. I looked up. Vida's mother was striding toward us. "Don't touch the wolf. It's *tabat*, like Kai." She grabbed Vida's elbow and pulled her back toward the other girls. I heard her hissing, "I have told you to stay away from that one!"

"He's just a boy. He's not some poison thing," said Vida crossly, shaking her mother's hand away. But she went.

~

As I struggled back up the path carrying the full waterskin, I suddenly knew what I would ask my father. He was there, outside the *takka*, with Bu and Suli. I did not see Sen or my mother anywhere near. I stopped to watch. Apa had made a play *keerta* for Bu. The tip was padded with soft leather instead of a stone point. Bu waved it in the air, growling fiercely.

Something stabbed my heart.

Suli also had feelings. "I will hunt, too!" she said, her face stormy.

"*Eya*, my Suli," said Apa, taking her onto his lap, "but girls don't have the strength and speed of boys. You will learn to throw a *keerta* to defend yourself and hunt rabbits and such. But mostly you will learn women things. Women have little time for hunting."

Suli's lip trembled. "I don't want to be a woman!" she said. "I want to be a blood-hunter, like Sen!"

Apa grinned. "I hope you do not become a blood-hunter. You would have to kill something fierce and big that might hurt you."

"Apa," I said. My voice cracked.

He looked up at me. Raised an eyebrow.

I set down the waterskin. Straightened my shoulders. Shuffled my feet. Tried again. "Apa," I said. "If Uff could hunt her own meat, she wouldn't need ours. But I can't teach her if I don't know how to hunt myself." His shaggy eyebrows drew together. The blue eyes held mine. I took a breath. "I do not ask to use a *keerta*. The twine I make is strong. You have used it with no bad thing happening. Let me set snares. I know how it's done. Apa-Da used to let me go with him when he set his. Sometimes..."

I searched my father's face carefully to judge whether or not I should say this. "Sometimes he let me be the one to find the game trail, or place the loop, or cut the twigs and bend a willow and set the notches. No *tabat* thing happened. Apa-Da's snares caught many small animals. If I could catch such game, I could feed Uff—and maybe somehow she would learn to hunt them herself."

Hearing her name, Uff came and sat beside us with her head to the side, listening. My father's eyes shifted to her, then they dropped. He seemed to be seeing nothing for a very long time. At last he said, "Alright, Kai. But you must do this alone."

CHAPTER 11

And so I set my snares.

At first I didn't go far from the *takka* with Uff. Often I had to wait for her. She would come trundling along the path after me. Her tongue hung out. Her eyes were bright. When she tired, I tucked her into my pack-basket and carried her. But soon her legs lengthened. She no longer tripped over her big paws. Wherever I went, she followed.

A hunger that had been inside me was filled. With Uff at my heels, I was no longer alone.

For many days, my snares caught nothing. Over and over, I whispered the hunter's prayer for luck: *Nnnnn-gata, nnnnn-gata*.... But still they would be empty—always empty. I didn't stop trying, but I couldn't neglect my work. There was the endless task of gathering fuel. There was not much wood near the *immet*. Old bones could be burned, but dried dung was best for a quick, hot fire.

One morning, I shouldered my pack-basket, called to Uff, and set off. I didn't go close to the great hearth, with its circle of flat ground worn bare by many feet. The women came there to sew, work hides, and talk, while the children played and the old people told stories.

As a little boy, I had spent much time at the great hearth, helping my mother with her work. But my heart had burned to be with the other boys. There had always been stares and whispering. Now a wolf pup followed me. Who had ever seen such a thing? If Rhar blew his aurochs horn, I would have no choice but to go hear what was to be said. But otherwise, I kept away.

There was a place that was used for throwing *keerta*. The boys spent much time there. I stopped at a distance to watch them. I couldn't help myself. I held my breath with each toss, willing the *keerta* to fly straight and hard to its mark. No one saw me at first. Sen and his friends took turns. They used a reindeer hide stuffed with moss for testing their skill. Someone had set a skull where the head should have been, and drawn a mark on the hide to show the killing place. A ghost deer. Every time it was hit, the skull with its broken antlers fell over and they shouted. The hide was tattered from the many *keertas* that had pierced it.

I copied their stance: opposite foot forward, arm held back and high—the sudden forward motion and snap of the wrist. *Eya!* Even leaning on my stick, I was sure I could do it.

Then Xar spotted me. I started to turn away. His eyes were hard. Cold. I did not want to look into them. Xar kept the front of his hair hacked so close to his skull that the skin showed through, white as bone. It was as if looking fiercer would make him so. It was said that Xar's father had once run away in a fight with a boar. Another hunter had died because of that. We all knew that the bruises on his son's face and the missing tooth were not accidents.

"The pup brought one of his wolf friends," Xar said over his shoulder to the others. Then he grinned at me, his tongue sucking loudly at the gap in his teeth.

"It follows him like a child!" said Uli. He was so short and thickly built that the others often called him Ice Man, which made him very angry.

"Wolf-*ama*!" called Fin. I didn't mind Fin so much. There was no meanness in him; he just liked to tease. But the others were not so kind.

"You'll need to kill a lot of game to feed your wolf *bah*!" Uli added with a sneer.

"It won't be a baby next winter," muttered Sen.

"He's not allowed to hunt—a *keerta* would split in two if he touched it!" said Ptyr, laughing.

"Cripple!" hissed Uli.

"*Tabat* one! Get away from our throwing place." Xar's voice was like ice.

Sen's cheeks reddened. He spat on the ground. "Kai is growing the hide for my new winter robe," he told them.

My mother was wrong. Their words were not just words. They were aimed like *keertas* at a mark. I could not make my heart as tough as hide. The words cut me. And they did not grow tired of mocking me.

"A man fights those who hurt him," my father had said. I had promised him that I would not touch a *keerta*, but my hand itched to hold one now. Still, I knew I could not fight a bunch of older boys.

"A bad foot isn't everything. You must find what there is in you that *is* strong." It was Apa-Da speaking in my head now.

Suddenly there was a hiss, a soft thud behind me, and gleeful shouts. Uff yipped and scooted sideways. I turned to see Xar's *keerta* still quivering, its point buried in the ground barely a hand-span from where Uff had been a moment before. I grabbed her up with my free arm and hobbled quickly away.

"You didn't have to do that!" I heard my brother say to Xar. I did not hear more.

Once Uff and I were at a safe distance, I knelt beside her to catch my breath. She had gotten over her fright. She gazed at me the way Shine's followers looked at him—not so much at me as *into* me. I gazed back. Her eyes had lost their blue color. They glowed deep amber now. "He's a stinking pile of hyena dung," I told her. "Someday I'll fight him. You do not think I am *tabat*. You don't hate me for my bad foot." I put my forehead against hers. "You are my friend," I whispered.

She licked my cheek and gently bit my nose. I stroked her shoulders where a few long, glossy hairs with black tips were growing through the puppy fluff.

"Come," I said to my wolf. "Let's go set more snares."

CHAPTER 12

ff, *NAH!*" I tried to yank my mother's *saba* away, but Uff tugged back, tail waving, play growling. The moon had grown full again, and she had grown strong. "It's not a game—give it to me!" My voice frightened her. She dropped it. There was a gaping hole gnawed through the toe.

"Kai, you can't let her do that!" My mother snatched the *saba* from my hands. "Look what she's done!"

"I'll mend it," I said. "Please don't tell Apa."

Ama opened her mouth to say more. She looked down at Uff, pressed up against my legs, shivering. She closed her mouth again.

"Please," I begged. "See. She knows it was wrong. She just wants to use her teeth now that she has them. Like Bu." My mother smiled. I fetched the sewing things.

That day, Uff stared at me as I gnawed on a bone from the shoulder of a deer. "So, Little Bah, you want bigger game?" Uff's eyes did not leave the bone. "Well, then. I've had enough." She lunged for it, dragged it from the fire circle, and tore at it with her front teeth, grinding sideways with her back teeth. She chewed for a long time. At last, she fell asleep, one paw stretched over her prize.

Others were watching. I met my father's eyes. "Kai," he said, "it's a long time until the deer come back to us. The wolf is growing bigger. Are you catching anything in your snares?"

I looked down. Shook my head. I still had caught nothing.

"You must be doing something amiss, some careless thing." My father's voice was gentler. "Think. Become the rabbit or the ptarmigan. The small creatures are not stupid. They see us and hear us move. The marmot can feel the earth tremble when the horses run. He smells the smoke of our fires. He tastes meat eaters on the wind."

I expected Sen to say something cutting, but he only raised an eyebrow at me as if to make sure I was listening. I stared at him, mouth open. Did my brother want me to be able to kill game for Uff? For myself, too?

See, hear, feel, smell, taste. A hunter used all these things. He stalked game not just with his eyes but with ears, nose, and even his open mouth, tasting the air with his tongue.

Of course.

I snatched up my stick and pack-basket. Then, calling to my wolf, I hurried off.

The day was gray with mist and the ground was damp. Softly. *Eya*, that was how I must walk. Stalking.

Uff had little trouble with this. She was still young, with the big paws of a pup, but her feet knew how to be soft on the earth.

I came to my first snare. Sprung by last night's wind and rain, or a wary animal, but empty. Uff's nose worked carefully, studying it. *Smell*... I inhaled, mouth open. Damp moss. Sweet bramble blossoms. Then I sniffed the sleeve of my *anooka*. Wood smoke. Meat. Sweat. I smelled the palms of my hands. *Eya*, they had an odor, too. *I have left my smell.*

I swung back on the trail to where a boar had rooted under a hazel bush searching for old nuts. The ground was torn open by its sharp hooves. I scooped handfuls of dirt, rubbed it over my hands, arms, feet, legs. Then, quietly, carefully, I went back to my snare and, handling it as little as possible, set it again. "*Nnnnn-gata*," I whispered.

The next morning, as I was setting out to check my snares, Uff suddenly raced out of the *takka* with Suli's *ah-bah* in her mouth. My sister stumbled after her, screaming. I followed as fast as I could. Uff circled, dodging bushes and boulders. This was a good game!

"*Nah*, Uff, give it back!" I scolded, trying not to laugh. At last she let me come close enough to catch it by one arm. I tugged, but she shook her head, tugging back. The leather tore. Suli cried.

When I finally pried the *ah-bah* from Uff's teeth, she yelped. Blood in her mouth. I crouched to look. One of her little fangs hung by a shred of flesh. I opened her jaws. In the back of her mouth, big teeth were growing. I caught my breath. Teeth are sacred. They are life and they are death.

"You are growing up," I whispered. In a quick motion that she hardly felt, I jerked the loose tooth free.

Suli had caught up to us. She sobbed over her *ah-bah*. "I will sew her arm back on," I told her. "But look, Uff is growing new teeth." I tucked Uff's baby tooth into the pouch around my neck where I kept my sacred things, hoping Apa had not noticed. He was sitting by the fire eating his morning meal.

But Suli ran to him. "Uff is growing new teeth," she announced.

"Suli, hush!" I hissed.

"Great big ones! As big as cave lion teeth!" Suli added, holding fingers curled like fangs up to her mouth.

My father's brows came together. He stared at my wolf and shook his head.

"Come," I said to Uff. I needed to check my snares.

The first one was sprung. Empty. The second was still set. I trudged on. Uff looked up at me anxiously. I knew she was hungry. "Maybe we'll find something for you left from some creature's kill," I told her, but that was not likely. What the big beasts did not finish, the hyenas and vultures picked clean.

As we came near the next snare, Uff brushed past my legs, ears and tail up. She stopped. Growled. "What?" I whispered. I pulled a branch aside and there, dangling by its hind legs, was a rabbit! Dead.

I closed my eyes. *Thank you.*

~

Now I caught small game almost every day. But Uff was growing fast. Her belly was always empty. My father and brother did not have luck with every hunt. Sometimes I shared the small meat I caught with my family. I felt pride watching them eat. Twice, as I tended my snares, I came very close to red deer coming to the river to drink, and once closer than I liked to a big spotted cat lying out on a log. If only I, too, could use a *keerta*... I gritted my teeth. If only.

One afternoon, I was startled by Ama's cry of anger. Scattered rushes everywhere. Uff feasting on strips of dried meat. The basket she had ripped open on its side. Bu wailing.

"*Ayee, ayee, ayee!*" my mother cried, trying to snatch up the remaining pieces. My father grabbed Uff, yelping, by the scruff of her neck and dragged her outside. He picked up the broken basket and found that it was empty. He smacked it on the ground. Kicked it away.

How could one small wolf eat so much?

"Kai, I told you she would steal from us!" my father shouted. Sen sat on his heels and smirked. Then Uff tried to crawl back inside on her belly to burrow under my bed fur. I dragged her out again.

"Bad, that was bad!" I told her. I turned to my father, my stomach wrung into hard knots. "She doesn't know it was wrong. To her, food is to eat. Wolves eat when there's food and hunt more when it's gone. She can learn. Please give her one more chance! Please."

"How do you know a wolf can learn?" Then my father sighed heavily. Shook his head. "I don't know why I give in. Until winter, Kai. She can stay until winter—but only if you don't let this happen again." He walked away to cool his anger.

"I will make a new basket," I called after him.

"We could tie the other baskets, and anything else she might get into, out of her reach on the poles of the *takka*," said my mother. I looked at her gratefully.

"Where Apa and I will bump our heads," grumbled Sen. But he helped us to do it, which was good because he was so tall. "It looks like we live in an upside-down place, with all our food stored over our heads," he muttered when we were done. "People will think we are strange."

"I don't care what they think," I said.

That night I did not take my eyes from my little wolf. When she wriggled close to Bu and Suli, hoping to steal their meat, I scolded her, pushed her away. "*Nah*, you must wait," I whispered.

Uff put her head to the side. Whined. *I am hungry.*

"I know it's hard. You'll have what's left when we're finished. *Nah!* Stay there!"

Uff struggled. The hunger water dripped from her mouth.

Until winter. I heard the words over and over again in my head. I couldn't send Uff back to her pack. She would be a lone wolf to them. They might kill her. If she couldn't hunt for herself, she'd starve. As she lay resting her muzzle on my knee, watching me work, I didn't think she would willingly go. This was her place, beside me.

The moon would grow full twice more before cold weather came again. There was still time.

CHAPTER 13

Coming home with Uff at my heels one day, I saw Sen and many of his friends gathered around the outside fire pit. They were talking eagerly, laughing. Uli and his sister, little brown-haired Hani, who lived in the *takka* nearest to ours, were there. As usual, Uli was full of loud talk and jokes. Mir and Jyn, who always shadowed her, sat at one side of the fire. Mir was wearing her good *anooka*, stitched and decorated with tiny river shells, as if it were the reindeer feast and not an ordinary day.

Even Cali and Vida had come. Spitted over the coals, the entire haunch of a small horse was roasting. Cali was tending it, singing softly to herself. Vida and Hani were playing the pebble game. "*Ayee*, Hani, you are a shaman-girl!" Vida exclaimed as Hani lifted a *das* to show her which one she had hidden the pebble under. Uff trotted over to Vida waving her tail.

I straightened my shoulders. The day had been very good. Uff's belly was stuffed with marmot, and at my waist hung two rabbits.

"Look, Kai," Sen called to me. "We chased it away from the herd, running in turns, and cornered it against the foot of the cliff. Rhar said we could roast this part for ourselves. He said the older hunters could not have done it, that it takes young legs to outrun a horse!"

I joined them warily. Xar made a play of being me, hobbling around the fire pit, leaning on his *keerta* as if it was my stick. Then Fin pranced after him on all fours, being Uff following me—funny, because Fin was so big and clumsy. Mir and Jyn squealed, hands over their mouths, eyes bright as sunbirds.

Somehow I did not mind their teasing so much today. Even if I could not chase game or hunt, as the others did, even if I could not have a *keerta*, I had Uff.

"Remember that time we stole the seed cakes from Ptyr's grandmother?" asked Uli.

"You didn't!" said Jyn, eyes wide.

"Oh, yes, we did," he answered. "She may be bony as an old cow aurochs, but she can move fast! She grabbed her stick and chased us away, shrieking. She caught Fin too, and hit him over the shoulders as hard as she could, but he was laughing so hard, he didn't feel it."

Uli could tell a good story.

Then Mir leaned close to Sen, letting her hair fall across his arm. "Your lame brother is becoming a great hunter!" she said. "Perhaps your mother can sew a new sleeping fur with those two big rabbit hides he has brought home!"

Sen frowned. "Leave him be, Mir."

"Will your wolf let me touch her?" Fin asked. I searched his face. Nodded.

"She likes it when I rub her ears, like this," I told him. He crouched beside me and cautiously held out his fingers. Uff sniffed them. She moved the tip of her tail a little and sat quietly. Fin ran his hands over her glossy fur. He was very careful. I could see him swallow nervously. When my wolf did not growl or try to bite, he laughed a soft laugh.

Xar moved toward Uff. One side of his mouth was turned up in a smile that was not a smile. His eyes were expressionless. He reached for her. I stepped in front of my wolf, opening my mouth to say *"Nah,"* but Uff's amber eyes narrowed. She lifted her lips, bared her big new teeth, and said *nah* herself with a sound in her throat that I had never heard her make before.

Xar jerked his hand back. "Why do you want that ugly beast?" he asked. "She's dangerous."

I could hardly breathe for my anger. "Come," I said to my wolf, and ducked into the *takka* to hang the rabbits out of her reach. She followed me reluctantly, neck fur bristling.

When we came out again, they were all sitting around the fire pit, each sipping a *das* of steaming broth. Sen got up and filled one for me. "Don't listen to what he says," he told me in a low voice. My eyes flickered to his. I smiled, and took the *das* from him.

I turned to find a place to sit, and as I did, Xar slid one of his feet in front of me. I stumbled. Uff yelped, dodged, and tangled me even more. I fell forward, broth slopping out of my *das*—and all down the front of Mir's *anooka*. It must have burned her. At least she screamed as if it had. Everyone else was laughing.

Except my brother. He leapt at me, shouting, "*Tabat* one!" He yanked me to my feet. Pounded my face and gut. I sprawled back to the ground. His foot caught Uff in the ribs. She yelped and cowered against me.

Everyone was silent. I reached for my stick. Got to my feet. Tasted blood from my lip. My left eye was already swelling. Sen's face was white, with red splotches over his cheekbones.

"You are not my brother," I said, and spat on the ground.

With Uff at my heels, I turned and made my way down the path to the river.

CHAPTER 14

The next morning, I went early to check my snares. There would be no hiding the bruises on my face in the daylight.

Uff followed. Whining and *uff*ing, she burrowed her muzzle into the tunnels of mice and the hollows where rabbits had hidden. She sniffed the flattened grass where the red deer had lain.

It was hard to shake the black feeling I had against my brother. It had kept me awake for a very long time, wishing that I could run away with my wolf. If only we could live by ourselves. But we would both need to learn to hunt before we could do such a thing.

There must be a place in this world for us.

Maybe I wasn't looking. One moment he was not there. And then he was. The shaman, Moc-Atu, appeared out of the shadows as if by some magic. I stared at him with my mouth open like a fish. Even Uff was wary. She came to me, tail tucked, and pressed herself against my leg.

It was whispered around the fires that Moc-Atu had lived nearly five tens of winters, but no one really knew how old he was. He lived by himself at the outskirts of the *immet.* His skin was like leather that had been folded over and over and left for many seasons in the wind and sun. His *anooka* was thin and shiny with wear, with patches over patches at the elbows. His hair and beard were twisted into braids the color of old snow.

"Wolfboy."

Was it a question or just a thing to say?

"Boywolf."

I tried to speak, but no sound came from my mouth. The shaman tilted his head and laughed, wheezing slightly. The braids of his hair whispered with the tiny shells tied to the end of each. A big spiral shell hung around his neck. It was like none of the little mussel and snail shells found in our river.

"Is there something wrong with your tongue as well as your foot?"

I shook my head. My mouth was dry as cracked earth. "N-no. It's just that I didn't see you at first."

His stick was clenched in a hand like a dried-up bird claw. It was hazel wood, with an owl's head carved on the top. I had seen with my own eyes the tiny living owl that sometimes flew to his shoulder when Moc-Atu stood on a rise at twilight chanting prayers to *Tal.*

He raised his stick and pointed it at me. "You must look more carefully, boy-with-no-name who is called Kai. Our headman has spoken to me. There is talk among the People about your wolf."

My eyes flew to his then, even knowing the horrible thing that would happen when I looked directly at him. "What do they say about her?" I whispered. It was not just that the eyes peering out from under the wrinkled forehead and shaggy brows were two different colors, or even that the blue eye stared up at the sky while the dark eye seemed to pierce my spirit.

He did not answer for a moment. Then, the blue eye did its terrible dance. It rolled wildly. Right. Left. Up. Down. I felt light-headed. I clutched the handle of my own stick so that I would not fall. The old man threw back his head and laughed again—the thin, wheezing cackle. His braids echoed the sound.

At last, when he had caught his breath, he leaned toward me. The blue eye settled beside the brown one. "Rhar fears you and your wolf."

"Me? How could . . . ?"

"He fears *tabat*. The People say that you were born with *tabat* and should not have lived. Now they say that you bring more evil with the wolf. They fear misfortune."

Moc-Atu took a step closer. He was frightful to look at, yet he did not smell fearful. He smelled of herbs and juniper smoke.

I noticed now that his staff had more than the owl's head

carved into it. Something like icy fingers seemed to brush down my spine. *The head of the owl sat on the shoulders and body of a man.*

Owlman.

Manowl.

I took a deep breath. "Uff is good!" I said. "I think *Tal* led me to her. *Tal* wants her to walk beside me. She will not hurt the People."

"She will not hurt a person who does not hurt you," said Moc-Atu. He reached out one of his claws and stroked Uff's head. She had relaxed now and faintly waved her tail. It was the first time an adult person besides my mother or father had touched her. The shaman's blue eye wandered, then suddenly stopped moving and focused directly on me again, seeing side by side with its brown mate. "You are strange like me. You are *other.*"

I could not think of anything to answer. It was true. I was strange. Having a wolf follow me wherever I went was strange. Did people fear us as they feared Moc-Atu? Were we both *other*?

"Listen to your wolf. She has much to teach you. It is your power. When you have learned, the pictures you draw and the music of your *osa* will come alive with that power."

Moc-Atu turned and walked quickly away. I stood, stunned, staring after him. *How could he know about my pictures and my music?* He went along the gravel path, away into the dancing shadows and light of the willows, faster than I could walk. And then he was gone. He had walked so fast for one as old and bent that I thought perhaps Moc-Atu's staff was just for show.

That night I dreamed of wolves—black shadows that came pouring into our *takka* as we slept—as many as the salmon swarming up the river. They ripped open our baskets and devoured our food. Then I saw that a wolf had found my grandfather's *osa* and was playing it. The People gathered to listen.

Suddenly it was me playing and Uff singing beside me. My breath was strong, the notes sweet and clear. People came in a huge gathering, faces without counting, shining in the firelight. Then the People began to howl. And suddenly, they were not people. They were wolves. All those voices together, singing with my *osa*.

I woke then to the sound of the yellow pack's moon song. Uff was awake also. I could just make out her shape in the dark, sitting up, head turned to the side, ears pricked. She was quivering all over. Pulling her head to my shoulder, I whispered, "That is the *imnos*. You were born to them, but you are part of my pack now."

CHAPTER 15

Summer was the full time. The days passed quickly as my wolf pup grew. But winter would come again. There was much I loved about winter—the world gone white, nights of songs, stories, games. But the cold time could be cruel. I looked often at the empty spot by the fire that had been my grandfather's place. We were all very careful not to sit there in case his spirit wished to visit.

Often now, my brother went to see Mir in the evening. Then I would take out Apa-Da's *osa* and play it as best I could. Sometimes when I managed to make a few notes sing, I could feel my grandfather beside me.

We gathered and stored as much food as we could against the time when game would be scarce and the plant world sleeping under the snows. But Uff did not understand. How could she know what lay ahead? The world she knew had always been warm and fat and easy.

Summer faded. Now came the salmon, running in their

own great herd up the river. The stone weirs had tumbled apart since last season. There was much splashing and heaving, many shows of strength, lifting and hurling rocks back into place. Rhar hefted a boulder nearly as big as his chest. Fin dropped a smaller rock on his foot, making his toenail turn black.

I could not kill the fish, but I could help drive them into the traps. It was wet work, with much shouting. Crows and ravens fought over the piles of leavings. It was also smelly work, rank with willow smoke and fish stink. The boys were fierce in their killing of the salmon. They yelled in triumph and notched the shafts of their fish *keertas* with each one they took. Sen's had many notches.

After a while, my knees were bruised and bleeding from falling on the wet rocks. I stopped to watch the fish *keertas* flashing like a storm of sky fire. My fists clenched. If I could not run easily through the shallows, driving the fish, I could swim. I would drive them in my own way. I slipped into the deep pool downstream and plunged after the dark shadows of the salmon. It was a green, cold, rushing world under the water, but I liked it. Here, I was not crippled. My arms and one good leg drove me forward. I was a bird flying. I came up for a breath, shook the wet hair from my eyes, dove again, breathed and dove, until I was tired.

When at last I came out, I found Uff curled on top of my clothing, shivering hard. Her eyes were white with fear. She did not understand what had happened to me. I crouched beside her. My teeth chattered. The hot sun on my shoulders was good. "Don't be afraid," I told her. "I may not be a good walker, but I'm a very good swimmer. See? I've come back to you."

The moment she knew it was really me, Uff leapt on my chest, yipping. She was crazy with relief. She nipped my nose and slapped my cheeks with her tongue. Then she raced away and back to me in a wide circle. At last, she rolled onto her back, showing me her belly.

The next time I came out of the river to warm myself, Uff was not there. I looked up and down the gravel bank. There was no half-grown wolf anywhere to be seen. Suddenly I heard women's voices scolding, shrieking, "*Ayee! Ayee!*" A crash, the sound of splintering wood. A commotion by the fish racks. I yanked my *kanees* back on and made my way quickly up the path in time to see a long rack, laden with rows of drying fish, lurch and topple to the ground. Women struggled to retrieve fish from the smoking fires. Ama chased my wolf, swinging a willow branch over her head.

I saw Uff sprinting away with an entire split salmon in her mouth!

"*Nah*, Uff!" I yelled.

But she didn't listen. I followed, stumbling, panting. She streaked away to a safe distance. Then she swallowed her prize before I could come close. How could I tell her that the curing fish were not for her? There, on a rock in the sun, Suli and Hani sat feasting on their own stolen fish. They picked the sweet flesh from the bones, the rich oil dripping down their chins. Nobody minded. But a wolf pup was not a child.

"That was bad!" I scolded, when at last I caught Uff. I grabbed her by the ruff of fur around her neck and shook her. "The fish is for winter. It is for people, not for wolves. You had a rabbit from my snares this morning—isn't that enough? Apa will make me send you away if you steal our food!" Uff crouched and tucked her tail. She stared up at me anxiously, but even so, she could not help licking the taste from her lips.

I saw now that Xar had come up from the river behind us and seen the whole thing. He was dragging a heavy load of salmon, spitted through the gills on a forked stick. One of the big, gleaming fish still thrashed and shuddered. He had not bothered to kill it.

Holding his fish *keerta* up to his ear now, Xar listened as if it were speaking to him. His eyes grew wide. Then he nodded and grinned at me, but it was not the smile of a friend. "My *keerta* whispers that she is tired of fish," he said. "She would like to taste the heart of a thieving wolf."

Sucking softly on the empty space in his gums, he sighted along the shaft of his *keerta* at Uff. I could not keep my eyes from going to the bone point. I put an arm protectively around my wolf, shielding her with my body. "If you hurt Uff, I will..."

"If I hurt her, you will what?" Xar did not need to remind me that I had nothing but my hands and my work blade to fight with.

"Kai, you cannot let the wolf steal from us!" It was my father, breathing hard, angry. He had come running to see what had happened. But his anger was not all for me and my wolf. He turned to Xar and grabbed the stick of spitted fish from him. Swiftly, he snapped the neck of the salmon that was not dead. "What kind of hunter does not kill his prey but hauls it back to the *immet* still flopping?" He spat the words out as if they tasted bad in his mouth. "A hunter kills quickly. He honors the life taken."

Xar turned to leave, but not without a grin at me and a shake of his *keerta*.

I did not meet my father's eyes. I made Uff follow me to a place downstream, away from the fishing. There had to be some way to get her to hunt her own fish. "Look," I said to her, trying to make her see the dark shapes of the salmon finning their way over the pebbled shallows. "There is meat for us all in the river." She squirmed in my arms, trying to turn back toward the fish racks. She had grown so big I could barely hold her.

Then I remembered something I had watched Torn Ear do for last year's pups.

I scanned the surface of the water until I spotted a killed salmon that someone had missed. It floated toward us. "Uff, see this!" I set her down, waded in, and grabbed the fish. "See!" I said again. I held it out to her. Then I plunged it back into the water and shook it so that it splashed and seemed alive again.

Now Uff saw.

Her tail stiffened. Her ears came forward. I let the fish drift toward her. At the last moment I snatched it back and shook it again. Uff crouched in the shallows. Water dripped from her belly. Her eyes were locked on the salmon. Once more, I made the fish seem to swim. Uff trembled all over. I let it go. With a great splash, she pounced and came up with the salmon in her jaws. She shook it so that if it were not already dead, it surely would have been. She carried it to shore, tail high. I stumbled after her. "You did it!" I cried.

Uff shook herself now, getting me even wetter. Then she snatched up her fish again and trotted off with it, tail waving in the air. "*Eya*, it's yours," I called after her. I couldn't believe it. She had done it. I sat down, suddenly tired, and watched her eat.

Now that she knew how to catch the fish, Uff joined in the drive. She stalked the shadows in the river. Over and over, she plunged her muzzle under the water to snap at them. Now and then, she caught one.

Some of the men stopped to watch. They laughed and pointed. "Look," I called to my father as Uff waded to the shore, dragging a thrashing salmon between her front legs. It was so big she stumbled over it. She killed it, carried it up the bank, and lay down to eat it.

Apa nodded. "That's good, Kai."

~

It had been a good day, but that night there was more happiness. Sen did not eat the evening meal with us. Instead, he ate with Mir's family. He came back late. Ama put down her sewing quickly. Apa raised his eyebrows. My brother's smile was very big. There was something in his eyes, his face. He seemed to be shining with joy that could not be held inside.

"I have spoken with Mir, and with her parents. We will be joined at the reindeer moon." He picked Suli up and spun her around so that she squealed with delight.

I bent my head over the rabbit skin I was working. My father was pleased. "You will need many reindeer skins if you are to build your own *takka*."

Ama stood up, took him by the shoulders, and gazed into my brother's eyes. "My small boy has grown into a strong and well-looking man," she said. "Mir is very beautiful." Then she added softly, "I hope she will be a good mate for you."

CHAPTER 16

Uff's nose found the scent of many small creatures now—mice, voles, rabbits, and such. They all scurried or leapt away before she could catch them. Whenever I caught a rabbit or a marmot in one of my snares, I wriggled it for Uff, trying to make it seem alive. She shook the animal as if it were her scrap of hide.

One morning, she snuffled her nose into a nest full of half-grown mice. The tiny beasts exploded everywhere, running between Uff's paws and under her belly. One darted up over her face and between her ears. It leapt into the long grass and disappeared. Uff looked confused. But suddenly, one more mouse ran from the broken nest. My wolf pup pounced, snapped her jaws, and swallowed. I could hardly believe it.

All by herself, Uff had caught a mouse. I had not taught her how. Somehow she knew.

It was another small step.

~

At last *Tal* stopped calling the salmon to come up the river to us. Many of the fish seemed to grow old. They died. Bears and other animals ate these, but we did not. The rest swam back down the river to wherever they had come from.

The few remaining berries shriveled. The bushes turned red as blood. All along the river, willow leaves turned the color of old sunshine.

I gathered moss for the winter lamp wicks and Bu's night wrapping. It was not a hunter's work, but it was one less task for Ama. When my pack was nearly full, I straightened up. I looked at the autumn world.

My wolf stood motionless beside me, sniffing the air. Her head came nearly to my waist now. She turned to look at me—serious, gentle, and wise all at the same time. The puppy clumsiness was gone. Her legs had grown long and slim. Her paws did not seem too big anymore. "If Apa makes me take you back to your pack, I will always know you," I whispered.

Uff bowed, asking me to play. She snatched the clump of moss I was holding. Then she raced in a wide circle, teasing me to chase her. My pup was back.

~

All day now, wherever we went, Uff hunted mice—behind the *takkas*, along the river, in the long grass of the open land. Her belly was a pit that could not be filled.

Snares do not kill every time. One day I found a big marmot caught only by a foreleg. Uff usually took great interest in helping me check my snares, but she had stopped to sniff and dig at its burrow. The marmot thrashed and growled when I came close. There was terror in its eyes. I had never killed anything so big. “I’m sorry,” I said. I looked for a rock. A streak of yellow fur hurled past me. With several hard shakes, Uff snapped the marmot’s neck.

“It is very nearly big game,” I told her. “You will have a piece for yourself.”

Apa and Sen had not been so lucky on their hunt. The marmot was welcome. The night was cold, and we cooked inside. The scent of the sizzling fat, as it roasted slowly, made our mouths water.

Waiting, watching the fire, I followed the shifting flames. The coals broke apart and made pictures in their shapes: a mammut with a tiny blue eye raising its great humped head and shoulders out of a bog, a rocky hillside with sparks that were ibex grazing, a waterfall tumbling out of a cliff. I could never grow tired of watching fire.

“Tell me about Moc-Atu,” I said to my father.

He raised his head from his work and stared at the fire a moment. “Moc-Atu was old when I was a boy,” he said. Sen and Ama and Suli looked up, listening. “He was like you, Kai—touched by the dark one—*tabat*. Even his mother could not look into his eyes without dropping her own. They say he can start a flame from cold ashes with those eyes. Like you, he was not meant to live.

But his father was a shaman. He would not let him be killed.

"His name was just Moc then, the crazy one. He was violent. He fought anyone who spoke to him. They say he tried to jump from a cliff and fly, that he tried to live underwater like a fish, that he walked through a fire pit and was not burned. One day he disappeared on a journey to the south. He was gone for three years. On the day we painted his father's face with bloodstone to return his body to the spirit world, the one called Moc came back with his own face painted to be our new shaman. He did not tell anyone what had happened to him or how he knew to come back. He only said that his name was now Moc-Atu—the crazy one who is changed. He never hurt anyone again, but he has healed many."

When the meat was cooked, my father said, "Since you helped kill it, Uff, you may eat, too." He tossed her a juicy morsel. Uff caught it in midair. Apa laughed and tossed her another. Hope swelled in my heart.

But the next night there was trouble.

My mother was working a basket by the light of a stone lamp. Sen was visiting Mir. I took out my *osa* and played a few notes. Uff's ears twitched as she lay sleeping by my side.

Suddenly Uff leapt to her feet, knocking over the lamp. In another moment, there was fire. The flames traveled fast, lighting bundles of herbs and running up toward the roof.

My father grabbed a waterskin, slashed it open with his

work blade, and splashed it on the flames. I threw dirt and ashes over the burning fat from the lamp. Snatching up the little ones, Ama ran outside. Uff spooked into the dark. People came running, but the fire was already out.

Burnt fur, smoke, a wet, smoldering mess. One whole piece of the *takka* wall was ruined—the one with Sen's handprint and the picture of the aurochs he had killed.

"Kai," my father said, "at daybreak, take her." His voice was hard, but his eyes were filled with pain. My pain.

My brother had come with the others. His chest heaved in anger. "See, it's true. Kai is *tabat* and his wolf also is *tabat*!"

But in the morning, my father found the marks of a big cat, nearly a hand-span wide, not ten paces from the outside fire pit. Only Uff had known. Apa was silent a long time. Then he looked at me. "Alright, Kai. She can stay," he said, "until winter."

Ama and I replaced the ruined section of the *takka* and Moc-Atu came to make a new painting. He took packets of ground stone from his pouch and put them into my hands. "You have seen how it's done. Make the colors."

I stared at him. I could not refuse.

Then, after he had traced the shape of Sen's bull, he said, "My eyes are tired. Finish it."

My mouth opened. I tried to say, "*Nah!* I cannot!" but nothing came out. Slowly, with trembling fingers, I picked up a *das* of color and began. First, the white of the eye and nostrils, the spots, then the black—but not solid black. I rubbed white into the belly, so that it seemed to swell with life, made darker lines where the legs joined the body, made shadows showing muscle and ribs, made the blood.

When I was finished, I looked at Moc-Atu. His eyes settled together on my work. He smiled. "So," he said, stroking Uff's head.

CHAPTER 17

There was a scuffle in the long grass and a sharp bark. "What is it, Uff?" Suddenly a big rabbit burst from its hold almost under my feet. She chased it in a great circle. In its terror, it ran nearly into my legs. I stood like a stupid person. The rabbit had escaped. Uff looked at me as if to say, *Why did you not do your part?*

"My part?" I asked aloud. "I can't hunt. I can only set snares. It's *tabat* for me to touch a weapon."

I had seen boys throwing sticks to kill small animals. It was not easy, but it could be done. *Was a stick a weapon?* It was not much of a weapon. "Well, then," I said to Uff, "we will find another rabbit." I took a dead branch and smacked it across a rock until I had a stout, short piece to throw.

I followed Uff back across the open grassland. Soon she tore off after a second rabbit. This time I was ready. She brought it in a circle back to me. I flung the stick hard in a sideways motion, catching it as it ran, stunning it. I fell on it before it could recover, and snapped its neck. Then I looked up into the expectant eyes of Uff. "*Eya*, it's half yours!"

I cut the rabbit apart with my blade. "It's your kill and mine, too. We are small-game hunters now." I whispered these last words. Uff ate. I looked at my half. I had snared many small animals, but I had never killed one this way. My heart thudded hard. This *was* hunting.

"Here." I held out my share. "Fill your belly."

Uff was strong and sleek. Winter would come, but my wolf pup was becoming a hunter. She could survive.

Still, she had not given up chewing.

That afternoon, I came into the *takka* looking for her. She was curled up on my bed, chewing a stick. She held it between her paws. Her eyes were half-closed, her head tilted to one side, as she ground her teeth into the wood. A scattering of splinters lay on my sleeping fur.

My heart seemed to stop inside my chest.

It was not just any stick. It was long and white and smooth. Sen's new hunting *keerta*.

"*Nah!*" I yelled, grabbing it from her. "Bad! You're bad!" Uff dodged out of my way, tail between her legs. She had never heard my voice like this. Suddenly I realized that Sen's *keerta* was raised in my hand as if I were going to strike her. She was afraid of me. My stomach heaved. I lowered my arm.

What had she done? The end of the *keerta* was a mess of splintered wood. I stood staring at it. There was a deep tooth mark right through Sen's sacred sign. I could feel drops of sweat on my forehead. Nothing could be unluckier. *Please make this not have happened*. But there it was. I could not undo it.

Or could I?

The damage was only to the end of the *keerta*. The rest of it was unharmed. What if I were to carve off the chewed part and shave it smooth again? Do it quickly, before Sen and my father returned... With shaking hands, I gathered tools from Apa's work place—this too was forbidden. But I had watched my father and brother making weapons all my life. I knew what to do.

My first thought was to go to my hiding place in the old wolf den, but there was no time for that. I ducked into the *takka*, leaving the *kep* pushed aside to let in light so I could work. Uff followed me. She was uncertain, ears down, tail half-tucked. She knew she was bad, but she didn't understand why. My heart felt sad for my wolf. Still, I could not speak to her.

Carefully, I put the *keerta* between my knees and began shaving away the damaged wood with Apa's curved scraper. My hands were shaking so that I dropped it, nearly hitting a hearthstone. *Tal, do not let me break my father's best scraper, too!* I took a deep breath to make myself still. Then, a small bit at a time, I shaved off the shredded wood. Was it possible that my brother would not know? It would be just slightly shorter now. Would he see? Would it feel true in his hand? If Uff had chewed much longer, I could not have repaired it.

Eya, that was better. I worked until all the tooth marks

except the deep one were gone. I ran my fingers over the smooth wood, touched the perfectly shaped point. *So sleek. Beautiful. Deadly.* A blood-hunter's *keerta.*

Again and again, a thought pushed its way into my mind. *What would it feel like to use this keerta—to send it whistling through the air, clean and hard—to hunt like a man?* I shoved the thought away.

I looked at the deep mark through the twisting aurochs horn. *How could I possibly fix that? Could I fill it in somehow? With pitch? Yellow clay?*

I hurried to the riverbank for the clay. On my way back, I pried a bubble of oozing pitch from a spruce tree and warmed it in my mouth. I worked a bit of clay into the pitch. Then, very carefully, with the tip of my blade, I pressed the mixture into the tooth mark. With dry sand, I rubbed the freshly carved wood until it was as smooth as the rest of the *keerta.* I peered at my work. Maybe, just maybe, Sen would not see.

I checked again to see if anyone was coming. No one yet. I took down a pouch that Ama kept hanging from one of the support poles. It held the last of the reindeer fat. There would be no more until the fall hunt. I opened it, dug out a bit with my fingers, and quickly rubbed it into the wood. *Eya.* It looked very nearly, *very* nearly, as good as new. I was turning to set the *keerta* near Sen's sleeping place, when the thought wriggled again. *What would it be like to throw a keerta—just once?*

Before I knew what I was doing, I had stepped back outside. I dropped my stick and placed my feet in a wide stance.

Then I raised my brother's *keerta*. There was nothing wrong with my arms. Surely I could throw a *keerta*. I sighted on a patch of soft moss many steps away. Then I snapped my arm forward, and let the weapon fly.

"Kai!"

CHAPTER 18

My father's voice was a harsh bark. I turned quickly. Apa stood behind me. His eyes blazed. My brother was beside him, face white, eyes wide—not so much with anger as with fear. My father put a hand on his arm to hold him back.

"Give it to me," Sen said between clenched teeth. With my eyes on the ground, I hobbled to the *keerta*, aware as never before of each lurching step. I tugged it from the ground. The point was unharmed. Carefully, I wiped the earth from the flint, made sure the binding was clean. The silence pressed on my ears as if I were underwater. I closed my eyes for a breath. Then I carried the *keerta* back to my brother. Without looking at it, he wrenched it from me.

"You knew you were never to touch a weapon!" There was pain in Apa's voice, but also ice. The muscles of his jaw were tight, the hand that gripped his own *keerta* clenched and unclenched.

I stared at the ground. Something was in me—my own anger working. All this. All my life. *Why?* Suddenly it burst from me. I met my father's eyes and let my words fly. I wanted to hurt him. I wanted to hurt Sen. "My arms are strong! My eyes are good! I only want to be a hunter and do my part. I don't even have a name or a sign like a real person. You treat me as dirt! As less than dirt!"

I thought my father would strike me then, but he did not. I saw a great sadness in his eyes. He stepped toward me and tried to put an arm around my shoulders. "You are lucky that you live," he said.

"I am not lucky, I am *tabat*! There is no worse luck! You left me for the wolves to kill. You should have had the courage to do it yourself! I hate you both!" I spat the words out. Sen did not answer. He grabbed a handful of sweet herb. Furiously, he scrubbed the shaft of his *keerta* all over with it, as if he were trying to disguise the human scent on the parts of a snare.

"We will take it to Moc-Atu," my father whispered to him.

Neither of them spoke more to me. When Ama returned with the little ones and learned what had happened, she began to weep. She looked at me with sad, reproachful eyes. Only Suli, Bu, and Uff seemed not to know what had happened.

That night, I sat hunched on my bed. They only knew that I had handled Sen's *keerta*. They had no idea what my wolf had done to it. Uff crept to my side. I pulled her close, rubbing her shoulders until she was easy again, but my thoughts spun. It was bad enough that I had thrown my brother's *keerta*.

What if they saw Uff's tooth mark? Would they drive her away? Would they kill her? I cupped her face in my hands.

"I won't let them hurt you. If they make me send you away, I will go with you," I whispered to her. But I did not know where it was that we would go.

I was grateful for the comfort of my wolf curled beside me. I listened to the sounds of my family breathing. With all of us inside, our *takka* was not a very big place. But on this night, I felt far from the others. I longed to be able to sleep as Uff did now, and to forget.

Sometime deep in the night, we were awakened by shrieks coming from the direction of Uli's *takka*. Uff sprang to her feet, neck fur bristling, snarling. Apa was up just as quickly, *keerta* in hand. He kicked at the outside fire to waken it and lit a torch. Sen and I threw on dried dung to make it blaze high. In the red light I saw that one side of their *takka* had been ripped away, slashed by great claws. A huge leopard was dragging someone in its teeth. Uli and his father were fighting it. "There may be another—guard them!" Apa shouted to Sen, and ran to help. They hacked at the cat until it dropped its burden, screaming its rage, and disappeared into the night.

Sen gripped his *keerta*, panting, searching the dark all around. "What is it?" Ama called. She crouched, clutching the little ones. Their eyes were those of creatures caught alive in snares. Shouts now, and wailing.

It was Hani, her voice a raw keening that made my skin crawl. Someone was hurt or dead. I fought back panic.

Sometimes the big cats hunted in pairs. *Suli. Bu.* My eyes flew to the walls of the *takka,* expecting claws to slash through any moment. They were only thin reindeer hide. *I will not let*… I fumbled for my work blade. Slid it from its sheath.

Rhar's horn sounded, two short blasts followed by a pause. All the hunters must come now. Sen, too. He hesitated. Then my brother looked at my half-grown wolf standing at the entrance of our *takka.* She was braced on stiff legs, her great white teeth bared. The growl that rumbled from her throat was not that of a pup. A strange look of appreciation came over Sen's face. Ama put Bu into my arms. She took up one of my father's *keertas* and went to stand guard at the opening beside Uff.

Suli attached herself to my leg. She was too frightened now to make a sound, but I could feel her shuddering. "Hush, little Bramble, we won't let anything happen to you," I whispered, stroking her head.

"It's alright," Ama whispered. "Rhar would not signal all the men to come if it were not safe to do so. The cat must have been killed or wounded."

But there could be a second one. I had never felt so worthless. Surely I was at least as strong as my mother, cripple or not. "Let me take a *keerta,*" I said through clenched teeth.

She shook her head. She would not look at me. "It is *tabat.*"

I gripped my work blade harder. Well, then. If that was all I was allowed to fight with, so be it. I looked again at my wolf. "Suli, Bu," I said, "see Uff's teeth? She will protect you."

With my mother and the little ones, my wolf and I waited in the darkness.

The hunters were gone until just after daylight. When they returned, four men carried the dead leopard between them. It had been wounded. They had followed the trail of blood, by torchlight, up into the highlands and cornered it against a cliff. They had lashed its feet to a pole. The head hung limp, staring eyes clouded over now, with the tongue clenched between its huge teeth. Dragging heavily along the ground, the tail made a snake mark in the dust. People gathered silently, eyes wide, whispering, pointing.

"That's the cat we saw cross the river last spring."

"It's so big!"

"Almost as big as a cave lion."

"Did it have a mate?"

"No. It traveled alone."

That was some relief.

I swallowed. I held Suli up so she could look. "See, it is dead. There's nothing to be afraid of now." Uff approached the leopard on stiff legs, hackles raised, growling. She sniffed it carefully until she was sure that it would not move.

Uli and Hani's mother had been killed, her neck snapped like a hare, when the cat burst through the wall of their *takka*. She had tried to shield their Bu, who still lived, but he had not escaped the terrible claws. Moc-Atu was working over him now, but everyone knew it was hopeless. Before midday, there were two corpses to bury.

Moc-Atu mixed the bloodstone and painted the faces of the dead. Ama held Hani as if she were her own child. Uli stood bravely beside his father, but I could see he was biting his lip. The women placed a few late flowers in the grave, and the men covered the bodies. There was nothing more to do.

I wondered if I had somehow caused this to happen, when I touched my brother's *keerta*. But these things always happened. Who could stop a big cat from clawing its way into the *takkas* of the People while they slept?

Fires burned. People kept watch, but still, the great beasts sometimes had their way.

CHAPTER 19

On a white morning of frost, the cry came at last. Fin ran down the cliff path, leaping from rock to rock, calling out, "The reindeer come!" Men scattered for their *keertas*. The women began setting up the drying racks. Children were sent for armloads of willow twigs for the smoke fires.

We stood on the knoll above the river crossing to wait. I shivered in the cold morning, watching my older brother uneasily. Sen seemed nervous as he checked his hunting things. His laughter and jesting were louder than usual. *Had he noticed anything odd about his* keerta*?* He and Apa had brought the weapon to the shaman and it had been purified with bitter-leaf smoke and much chanting.

Now Moc-Atu danced a prayer to the deer spirit. We gathered to watch. Wearing a headdress of a skull with antlers still attached, he whirled in a circle, his strange eye rolling wildly, his braids flying. The rattles he wore clicked at his ankles and wrists. He chanted the ancient words in his ancient voice:

Mind of the herd, come to us!

Body of the herd, come to us!

Spirit of the herd, come to us!

Nnnnn-gata!

In the distance, I saw three of the *lupta* trot to the top of a rise, noses to the wind. Closer at hand, I spotted a big, golden wolf with a handful of followers. Shine and the *imnos.*

Suddenly Uff leapt to her feet. Black specks appeared in the sky. Ravens! Now, on the far side of the river, came the cloud of dust, closer and closer until I could see the forest of antlers, hear the clicking of their ankle joints, smell the mossy scent of them. They plunged into the river and began swimming.

Moc-Atu sang his song, high and thin, over and over. Men shook their *keertas*. Women held their work blades to the sky. They had become a hunting pack, like the wolves. Suddenly Moc-Atu stopped. The headman, Rhar, raised his fist. There was a great cheer.

It was time.

Uff circled, hackles up, panting. My stomach lurched. "*Nah*, Uff! *You* cannot!" I grabbed her by her neck fur. She fought to get away.

I couldn't hold her much longer. With one hand, I unfastened my *jahs* from my waist and tied an end around her neck with a knot that would not choke her. She threw herself sideways, shook her head.

"Give her this, Kai!"

It was Vida, carrying the foreleg of a deer. "They're starting to bring in the first ones," she panted.

Uff leapt for the deer leg. She did not see me tying the other end of the *jahs* to a small tree, but settled down to eat. Vida ran a hand over her fur. Uff waved her tail.

I crouched, jabbing the end of my stick into the dust. Vida knelt beside me. Suddenly I felt her hand over mine, holding it still. "Why are you so angry, Kai?" she asked.

"They will never let me take part in the hunt," I said.

"Kai, you do have a part—use your eyes!" she answered. "Your mother showed me the aurochs that you painted. Look at the living deer—how beautiful they are. See those two that have crossed safely and are browsing—how the bull reindeer licks the nose of the cow. You could draw that, Kai! You could do that for the *immet*."

I stared at her.

She cast her eyes down, cheeks flushed. "I should go now. If my mother sees, she'll be angry." Vida got to her feet and sped away.

Before nightfall, the blood of the deer stained river and bank, and still the herd kept coming. I watched as other hunters besides those of the People began to gather at the crossing. The air grew black with circling ravens and vultures. We worked until dark.

The big cats, wolves, hyenas, foxes, even stoats and weasels would move in now. And still the herd kept coming.

Apa and Sen returned to the fire long enough to eat much

of the sizzling haunch Ama had ready. "I have killed nine deer," Apa told us, "but Sen has killed ten—*ten*!" My brother grinned. "It was just luck," he said. "*Nnnnn-gata!* I have a lucky *keerta*."

My mouth went dry at his words.

~

Now the dangerous part began. The herd could be gone by morning. There were still killed deer to bring in. It might seem like plenty, but winter was long. Nothing could be wasted.

Carrying torches, Apa and Sen headed back to the crossing with the other hunters. The moon gave little light. Under the stars, our hunters and their flickering torches looked very small. I watched as they built fires. In the red glow, they stood guard over and fought for the remainder of our winter meat.

Ama put Suli and Bu to bed. Then she came back outside to sit with me. "I cannot sleep," she said. Her voice was low and tense. I flexed my shoulders, trying to ease my aching muscles. Together, we listened to the shouts of the hunters and the surly snarling of hungry beasts. It would be a long night. Beside me, Uff slept uneasily. Now and then, her ears moved, listening to the sounds. The men shouted and banged sticks together. Moc-Atu thudded on his drum. Out in the open land, hyenas shrieked their anger. Foxes yapped on the hillsides.

Suddenly there was a roar followed by a scream made by

no animal. Shouting. Uff leapt to her feet. In the wavering light of our fire, my mother and I stared at each other.

Then Ama cried out, "Someone is coming!" Together, we peered into the dark, in the direction of the river crossing. Two men stumbled up the pathway to the *immet* carrying a third. As they came closer, I could see that it was Apa and a man named Reo. The one they carried was my brother.

CHAPTER 20

They brought him inside and laid him on his bed. His face was blood and torn flesh. My mother knelt beside him, moaning as if she felt the wound herself. I crouched in the shadows, with Uff. Ama pressed moss against Sen's forehead to try to hold back the bleeding.

My father was beside her. "It was a cave lion." His voice choked. "Sen's *keerta* split . . . the beast took him down. The *keerta* should not have broken—it was a good *keerta*. . . ." He stopped speaking and stared at me. Then he turned back to my mother. Several other hunters now stood by the opening. A chill wind had come up. I could feel it sweeping in around them.

My father spoke again in a rasping whisper. "The *keerta* was cursed! Kai . . . the *tabat* one . . . he disobeyed. He was never to touch a weapon. . . ."

I could not speak. My father's words cut like flint. Ama pressed her face into Apa's shoulder.

One of the men placed the broken *keerta* carefully beside Sen. "We'll ask Moc-Atu to come," he said very low. They went back into the windy night. Some of them would return to the river crossing. My gaze fell on the aurochs-horn mark near the end of the *keerta*. The pitch and clay repair had fallen out. Uff's deep tooth mark was clearly visible.

It is true. I have done this. I have killed my brother.

I was about to say this to my father when he got to his feet. He took up Sen's shattered weapon, staring at me with hollow eyes, as if he were seeing me from a great distance. "I was a fool to think it could be cleansed." His voice broke. He flung the *keerta* into the fire. I watched the shaft burn to gray ash. The beautiful blade split in two. My father did not look my way again.

Numbly, I carried water and helped my mother bathe the wounds. The bleeding would not stop. The lion's claws had ripped the flesh from Sen's scalp, down across both eyes, to his left ear. Both eyelids were torn—one nearly off. We found deep tooth marks in his shoulder. I had to put my ear to his mouth to hear his breath.

Moc-Atu came with rattles and incense. I shook all over as if I were freezing. I wanted to go away from my family in the night and never return. But Moc-Atu put a stone lamp into my hands. He did not look at me, but said in his rasping voice, "I need light for my work. See and know."

I bit my lip. I saw well enough. I knew what I had done.

Ama sat, clutching Bu and Suli. I wiped away the blood

so that Moc-Atu could see to work. My wolf curled herself up on my sleeping fur and lay there unmoving, but her eyes never left me.

The shaman threaded my mother's finest needle with a length of hair from a horse's tail. I tried to keep my hand steady holding the lamp for him. I could not take my eyes away as he made careful stitches, one after another, slowly closing the wounds. There were beads of sweat on his forehead.

Apa's face was a mask. "I will track the lion and bring its heart for Sen to eat so that he will take its strength and live." The ragged sound of his voice made me shiver.

Moc-Atu nodded. "I have seen that save a hunter. *Nnnnn-gata*. It is a good magic."

My father lit a torch. Then he went out alone into the wind and dark.

At last Moc-Atu finished. The light from the stone lamp flickered over my brother's face. It shone on the shaman's cheekbones and brow, making his eyes caves of shadow, and the lines in his face so deep that he seemed as old as the earth itself. I looked at my brother. Blood oozed through the stitches. The shaman wrapped Sen's head in fresh moss and strips of clean, soft hide.

Then he crouched beside him. I fed the fire, as if doing so would keep Sen alive. The dancing light shone weirdly on the shaman's face, making the shadows behind him blacker. Moc-Atu's voice began as a hoarse whisper. I had heard the words sung for others: for the little *bah* before Suli who left us, burning with fever, then suddenly gone cold and still on a frozen winter night. For the grandmother I could barely remember—except for the cough that was finally silent. For my mother on an endless day after Suli's birth.

Tal, do not leave us!

Spirit, do not leave us!

Far into the night, Moc-Atu chanted. He sang without stopping, until his voice was little more than a croak. I thought the old man might fall over with exhaustion, but he did not. The spell of the chanting seemed to hold me upright, too. I had no thought of sleep. My eyes seldom left my brother.

Sen lay very still. He looked thin and strangely shrunken.

Uff was pressed against my leg. My hand stroked her fur. My eyes watched my brother. *It was me. I did this.*

Toward dawn, Apa returned, his face lined with dirt and sweat. He could barely stand. In his hands was the heart of the cave lion, still warm—red with its blood. With her sharpest blade, Ama quickly cut it into small pieces, anger and fear in each slashing cut. Then she boiled the meat into a strong broth.

When at last Sen woke, his hands fumbled at the wrapping around his head. "It's only a scratch," Ama whispered. "Soon you will heal. Drink this. It's made from the heart of your enemy. It will make you strong again."

Below the bandage, Sen's face was so swollen that I did not know him. He spoke a few words then. "I struck . . . but I was afraid. . . . It was not a good thrust. The cat . . . fell on my *keerta*. My eyes . . ." But Ama hushed and crooned to him, made him drink the heart broth, until he fell asleep again.

Moc-Atu did not leave his side for three nights. I was sent for whatever he needed that could still be found growing: chaga fungus, *keerta* leaf, bristle-stem, moon root, sleep root, black seeds, sticky vine. These had to be fresh and perfect. He sorted through what I brought, grumbling and muttering to himself. The tiny shells in his braids whispered together. His blue eye rolled. He tossed anything shriveled or brown aside and sent me to find more. What was good, he made me grind and brew. Other things he had in his medicine pouch: dried roots, strange powders. He kept a poultice of these herbs on the wounds. Now wetness seeped through the moss and hide. The shaman sniffed carefully for the smell of death. Nodded.

Again and again, he said to me, "See and know." I saw the oozing, torn flesh of my brother's face. I saw the fever burning in his body. I knew what I had done. Still, I stayed by Sen's side. I could not leave. I watched Moc-Atu feed him sips of willow-bark broth and heart broth. I listened as he chanted until he had no voice left.

Deep into the third night, Sen began to thrash. A sound came from deep in his throat. Suddenly he screamed. He sat up, tried to stand, clutched at his head, fell back, gasping. Then he was very still.

I couldn't breathe. Moc-Atu leaned forward and put his

ear to Sen's chest, a hand to his cheek. Then he turned to me. In terror, my eyes met his. Both the blue and the brown held mine steadily. Slowly, he smiled. "The fever has left," he whispered.

CHAPTER 21

Sen would live, but he was thin and weak. I could not leave his side, and Uff never left mine. When my mother changed the wrapping over the wound, she averted her eyes. The healing wound was ugly. Many people came with gifts and kind words. The hunters came to show him honor. They stood about uneasily in the cramped space of our *takka*.

"You made a good scratching tree for the lion," Reo tried to jest. The others chuckled, but there was no heart in it.

Apa unrolled the pelt of the lion. It was huge. Beautiful. He had strung the fangs and claws of the cat. Firelight glittered on them as he put this carefully around Sen's neck, saying, "The beast was dying from the wound of your *keerta* when I found it. It is no shame for a hunter to be scarred. These claws will help you track the lion's brothers to mark one of them as this one marked you."

Fin came alone. He had no jests. He squatted by Sen's

side and said nothing. If he had spoken, he would have cried. Finally, he got up and turned to go. "Get better, friend," was all he could manage.

Vida and Cali came. Uff greeted Vida. I saw that Cali wore her ordinary clothing, but her hair was combed back and she had bone rings in her ears. She gave Sen a *das* filled with choice bits of deer loin, roasted with herbs. "My mother made this . . ." she started to say, until Vida interrupted, saying, "*Nah*, Cali, you . . ." But Cali shook her head to tell her to hush.

They told stories of her brother. "Bim lost his tooth, but he swallowed it, so he could not show it to anyone. He roared until my father gave him a deer tooth to hush him," said Cali.

"Kai, you must eat, too," Vida said, turning to me. "It's very good."

I shook my head. I hoped that she could not see the storm of blackness inside me.

Day after day, never even once did Mir come to see my brother.

Rhar visited alone. The headman was like the sun when it rises. He glittered with the teeth of his many kills. He did not look at me, but his eyes rested on Uff for many heartbeats. I felt more than heard the low rumble in her throat. She eyed him, head low. "Hush," I whispered to her.

The headman pulled a long blade of white flint from his pouch. "Here is a new *keerta* point for your next hunt," he said roughly. Sen could only feel with his fingers the deadly edge and perfect shape. He whispered his thanks.

Rhar turned to my father and motioned to speak with him. They went outside. Uff got up and stalked to the opening. I watched the two men move off to where their talk would not be heard. The headman looked my way once and made a gesture with his hands. Apa stood very still, staring at the ground. Then Rhar pointed to my wolf. I saw my father shake his head. Rhar growled a warning and strode away.

~

Later I stood beside Uff and gazed at the cold world. The first snow was falling. Winter.

When grandfather knew that his place by the fire was worth more empty, he had walked out into the winter night and never returned. I had been marked at birth by the Dark One. I could see it clearly now. I had nearly killed my own brother. Rhar could not know what Uff had done. But I was *tabat*. I was the wolfboy with the twisted foot and I had handled my brother's *keerta*.

I knew now what I must do. I put my hand on Uff's head. I did not know how much longer she would be safe with the People. But still, I could not leave my brother. "We will go as soon as I know if Sen can still see," I whispered.

Days passed.

For long spells my brother sat near the entrance to our *takka*, brooding under the darkness of his bandages. His hands hung limp between his drawn-up knees. He spoke little. Suli tried to put her *ah-bah* into his arms, saying, "Here, Sen, you can have her," but he pushed her away.

"It was a good present," I told her, stroking her tangled hair. "Sen is too sad now, even for gifts." Uff licked her cheek. "See, Uff knows."

Secretly I gathered what I would need. I was ashamed. I did not have the courage of Apa-Da. He had walked without pack or blade, without even clothing, into the cold to end his life.

I did not want to live, but I did not have the courage to die.

I made myself a new fire kit. Fire was first. Then, with a guilty heart, I took three good cores from Apa's store of flint, and a suitable tine of deer antler for shaping edges. If my work blade broke, I would need a new one. Flint was life, too. I gathered my snares and tied them into a tight bundle. I made new needles for my sewing kit. I found a bark *das* that could serve for both cooking and eating. I took my *osa* too, but my bearskin sleeping cover was too heavy to carry. I would have to leave it behind.

I packed travel cakes made for winter hunts. I had worked as hard as anyone pounding dried berries, nuts, and meat together to make them. Still, something inside me hurt. Sen might never hunt again, or at least not this winter. I was taking food from my family.

Last of all, I ground a chunk of bloodstone and tucked the powder into my pouch of sacred things along with Uff's baby tooth, the stone shell I had found by the river, and the little rainbow stone my mother had given me long ago. Bloodstone paint was used for the death ritual. If Uff were to die, I could help her find the spirit world by painting her face with it. If I were to die . . . well . . . if I knew that I would die . . . I could use it for myself.

There was little need to be secret. When Ama was not busy with the work of the reindeer and Bu and Suli, she was cleaning and wrapping Sen's wounds. There were lines in her face that I had not seen before. She scarcely saw me. To my father, I thought I was already gone.

Once I heard him say to my mother in a harsh tone, "It is my fault." For the smallest moment, his eyes slid to me. Then they fled back to my mother's. She shook her head. The muscles around her mouth tightened. She looked away.

So.

She should not have taken me back from the wolves. He should not have let her do it. That is what my parents thought. They were frightened. Of me.

Another time, when we were alone, I said to my brother, "I'm sorry."

He said nothing for a long time. One hand went to the wrapping over his eyes. In a halting voice, he said, "Kai, I think . . . it was not your fault. Remember the times I let you play with my *keerta* . . . when we were small? No *tabat* thing happened then. A hunter can be hurt in many ways. I was afraid . . . I think this time I was not steady. My aim was not sure."

I reached for Uff where she lay beside me. I stroked her head. She rested her chin on my knee. Then I said very low, "Maybe my friendship with a wolf angers *Tal*."

My brother put out his hand. For the first time, he felt the softness of Uff's fur. Stroked her head. Rubbed her ears. She licked his fingers. "I have wanted to touch her and to be her friend . . . as you are. I was . . . Kai, I had envy . . . envy for *you*!" There was amazement in his voice. I swallowed hard. Sen continued, "Maybe *Tal* gave her to you because of your foot," he said. "Maybe you needed a friend. I haven't been a friend to you for a long time."

I looked at him. He could not see the tears in my eyes.

Then he said, "I remember when you said that *Tal* gives us two arms, legs, eyes, and ears, in case one is broken or hurt. That the other grows stronger. That maybe *Tal* is trying to make you stronger. But what if both my eyes are gone? I would no longer be a blood-hunter. I would not have Mir. I do not think I'm strong enough to live like that."

"You have to be strong enough," I said. "In the wolf pack, each wolf has a place."

I wanted to believe my brother—that it wasn't my fault—but I was filled with terror of the danger I might be to my family. Rhar wanted me and my wolf gone. Would he kill Uff when I wasn't looking? I beat my fist against my useless leg. Why did it have to be like this?

I knew what I must do.

On the day of the reindeer moon, the day that Sen and Mir were to have been joined, Ama took the binding from

Sen's wound. We watched in silence. He blinked in the light. His right eyelid was thick with the new raw, red scar, but with the help of Ama's gentle fingers, it opened. Three raised lines from the lion's claws raked his forehead and down the side of his face.

Apa sat back on his heels, watching. His eyes showed no feeling, but over and over, his fingers worked the small bundle of magic things he wore around his neck.

Sen's eyes watered. He squinted, turning away from the sun. He put his hands in front of his face and moved his fingers. At last, in a voice so low that we could barely make out his words, he whispered, "The right one blurs, but I can see." He did not smile. Then he was weeping. My father looked away so as not to see my brother's tears. He drew a great breath and put a hand on his shoulder. "You will hunt again," he said.

But Sen turned from him. "I am ugly now," he whispered. "I am marked as Kai is. Mir will not have me."

My chest ached. *I did this.*

The full moon shone brightly that evening, but there would be no joining ceremony, no wedding feast. Others celebrated the reindeer harvest. My family did not. I sat silent, one arm around Uff. I tried not to hear the drums and laughter coming from the great hearth. No one spoke to me.

It was time for me to go.

CHAPTER 22

It was later that night, when I was alone with Uff and Sen in our *takka*, that the other boys came. Suli had begged, and Ama and Apa had finally taken the little ones to watch the hunters dance the Reindeer Dance. We were by ourselves. Not saying much, but not angry either. As we sat by the fire, I carved a small wolf from a piece of deer antler. For Suli. She would miss Uff. We would leave that night, after my family slept.

Sen's friends were disappointed that there had been no marriage celebration. We heard loud voices, laughter. Then Fin stumbled through the opening of the *takka*. Several others followed him. Uff leapt to her feet with a growl. She liked Fin, Uli, and Ptyr well enough. But she had not forgotten Xar. I held her back by the scruff. "*Nah,*" I said to her. I sidled toward the opening. Maybe I could escape.

The boys smelled of drink. Uli still had a half-full skin

of it. His hair was shorn for his mother's death, and his eyes were still dark with grief. Fin took the skin from him and offered it to Sen, saying, "I saw your parents leave. It should have been a wild feast—your feast, Sen!" He wiped his mouth with the back of his hand. "Help us drink this! My father made a lot of it for this night. He won't miss it. He has already drunk so much of it himself that he sleeps like a winter bear!"

"It will open your eyes to all the other girls," said Uli. "Jyn doesn't care how a boy looks. She likes us all."

I edged past my mother's cooking things. Sen took the skin willingly and drank. He coughed. Made a face. Then he drank again.

I was nearly outside, pulling Uff along with me, when Xar saw us. He lurched in front of me. "Where do you think you're going, *tabat* one?" His words were slurred from the drink.

"It wasn't Kai's fault," muttered Sen.

Xar raised his eyebrows. "That's not what the headman says! It's not what my father and I say." He spoke to Sen, but his eyes never left mine. He swayed on his feet, and the firelight made his shadow loom over us—a huge, flapping thing. "Rhar says your *keerta* broke because your brother thought he would try being a hunter."

He pointed at Uff. "He says the wolf is *tabat*, too."

"Come," I said to Uff, and tried again to leave.

Xar slammed a foot in front of my stick. Smiling. Ugly.

"The moon is full, a good night to hunt wolves! I will count to ten while you run, Kai." Snorting over the word *run*. "Then the hunt begins!" He started to draw his long blade.

Fin grabbed his arm. "Leave Kai alone!" But Xar threw him off. Held up the blade, gleaming in the firelight. "Perhaps I will skin your beast while she still lives!" A step closer. "Start running, Wolfboy.... One... two..."

Uff roared, broke away from me, and sprang for Xar's throat. He put his arm up. She sank her teeth into it, shaking her head, furious—beautiful. Xar screamed. Fin and Uli helped me drag Uff away from him—the fire knocked apart, singed fur and leather, fighting all the while. I had to pry her jaws open. All of us panting.

Fin laughed, shakily. "You deserved that, Xar!"

Xar stumbled away, cursing. His arm was red with blood.

Moments later, Vida and Cali came running.

"Xar told my father that Uff attacked him!" Vida panted, fear in her eyes.

"She was only trying to protect me," I said.

"Xar pulled his blade on Kai," said Uli.

"He was acting crazy," agreed Ptyr.

"Rhar says he will kill Uff at daybreak," said Cali.

"What will you do, Kai?" Vida was near tears. She knelt and put her arms around Uff.

I heard Cali say very low to my brother, "We heard that your eyes have healed. I am glad."

He nodded, put a hand up to the scars, but he did not look at her.

"Come, Vida, we cannot stay."

As they left, Vida turned and held out her hand to me in the friendship sign. I reached my hand to hers and clasped it. "Thank you," I managed to whisper.

Then I watched the two sisters, running back together in the moonlight. I wished I had said more to Vida. I wished I had said good-bye.

TWO

CHAPTER 23

The night was cold. Owls called their terror cries to their prey. A snow cat screamed. The *imnos* sang to the moon. Uff raised her head, ears pricked. Her body quivered.

At last my family was all breathing deep and steadily. I rose silently and pulled on my clothing. Quietly I shrugged into my pack-basket and took up my stick. I could just make out the forms of the others in their sleeping furs.

I will not ever see you again.

I bent and tucked the little carved wolf into Suli's hand. Touched her forehead. *Tal keep you, little Bramble.* She murmured something in her sleep. Her fingers closed around it, but she didn't wake. Then I slipped outside.

Uff bounded after me. We would have to move fast. Outside, the world was blue and huge. The tree branches were black bones. Only the river broke the stillness. I made my way down the steep path to the river trail, Uff close at my heels.

One time only, I turned to look at the *immet* of the People. The dark shapes of the *takkas* huddled at the base of the cliffs. A few fires flickered.

I will never return to this place.

Always, the hunters went out to the east, the south, the west. Never to the north. The story was told of the grandfathers' grandfathers who, in desperation, had once traveled north during a hungry winter. A band of Ice Men took them by surprise in a ravine, killing most of the hunting party. The fearsome men-who-were-not-men wore only shaggy furs. Their *keertas* were short and crude. They did not throw them, could not throw them as we did. But their strength was crushing.

With so few of our hunters left, many of the People died that winter. North was the direction of fear. But I could not stay in the hunting grounds of my people. They would track us and kill Uff. I could not move fast enough to escape our hunters. She would not leave me. There was no other choice. The world was very big. There had to be a place for us.

It was not easy going. The snow wasn't deep, but there were patches of ice. After a time, a light wind began to blow. My path led up and out of the river valley, following a smaller stream. It was the one the People called the Forbidden River.

Uff ranged ahead of me now, tail high. She seemed to feel no sense of dread, but bounded through the fine dry snow. Her nose worked the cold air. The thought came to me, *What will become of Uff if I die?*

The night grew old. The moon was still a white disk near the edge of the world when the sky began to pale into morning. Wind stung my eyes, but I was glad. Our tracks would be swept away. Uff was safe—at least from Rhar's *keerta*. My empty belly groaned. Apa-Da would not have eaten, but then Apa-Da would have let the cold kill him by now.

At sunrise, I stopped without planning to. My hands reached into my pack-basket without my will. I ate a travel cake, sharing with my wolf. The strength of it spread through me. My thoughts were a confused tangle.

My food won't last long. I must hunt. Some beast may be hunting me. How can I hunt or defend myself? I have no weapon. My foot aches. But I have to keep going. I have to find game soon. But it is tabat *for me to hunt. I am a curse to my people, my family. I should die. But Uff deserves to live. She did not mean to do anything wrong. I should find the* imnos *and give her back to them. But they might kill her. I have to live—Uff needs me. . . .*

I sank my face into my open palms. Uff came then and leaned into me as I crouched in the snow.

I slipped an arm around her shoulder. A new thought came. I did have something like a sign. A living sign—and it was Uff. I alone of the People had such a thing. I had a wolf who was my friend. And she alone of her kind had me. I belonged to her as much as she belonged to me. Perhaps I was not so much the *wolfboy* as *the wolf's boy*.

Moc-Atu had said that she was my power.

My power.

After what seemed a very long time, I raised my head. A fish eagle appeared high in the pale morning sky above us. Strange. It was very late in the season to be seeing one. It hovered over a deep, open place in the river. Balanced. Perfect. I thought I must look like a clumsy lump to it, sitting beside my wolf with my bad leg stretched out to ease the ache. I watched the big black-and-white bird. Its eyes were fixed on something in the river. Then it plunged. For a heartbeat it disappeared into the icy water. It was no longer in this world at all. Then it burst out of the river, a fish clutched in its talons.

It was a thrashing pike. The bird flew with its burden to an outcrop at the bend of the river. It stumbled when it landed, fought with its wings for balance. Suddenly I saw that the great fish eagle had only one foot. It held the fish with just the one set of talons. It had to stand upon the stump of the other while it fed.

"The Dark One has touched you, yet you hunt and live," I whispered aloud. It had to. The bird had no foot at all. Yet it was still proud and strong.

It came to me that I had no people now to whom I could bring misfortune. I was not in their hunting grounds. Why should I not make a weapon? The fish eagle hunted and lived. Why should I not do the same? The bird lifted its head to glare over the distance at me with fierce eyes. Then it bent to feed again, shredding the pike with its hooked beak.

CHAPTER 24

I moved faster, continuing along the Forbidden River. Through the afternoon, I searched for a campsite. Tail high, Uff plunged her muzzle into drifts, snuffling for mice. She turned to look back at me with a clump of snow on her nose. The sense of blackness had lifted from my heart. *Uff will live! I do not have to die!*

I saw many tracks in the snow: ptarmigan under a birch tree, the straight line of a fox, the sweep of an owl's wing where it had plunged after a mouse—whose tracks ended in that place.

But nothing that looked human.

I would need fuel, a fire to keep night beasts away, shelter from the wind. Not enough snow here to burrow into. I would have to build a brush *takka*. There were plenty of willows along the stream that I could cut. Already the light was fading.

The way narrowed. There was just enough room to walk along the graveled edge where a spring flood had cut under the overhanging bank. Dead trees had fallen, crisscrossed—a tangle of branches and roots.

I almost did not see the cat.

She was young and hungry—careless. Still, she was big enough. There was a skittering of pebbles and ice. I turned to see her launch herself from the rocks above. I raised my stick and dodged sideways so that she carried me down with her weight alone. No tooth hold. Snarling, she writhed, trying to grasp me with claws and teeth while I beat at her with my stick.

Uff flung herself at the cat. Dodged, slashed, snarled like a grown wolf. Eyes wild. Teeth snapping. *A cat will lose heart. Do not give in to a cat*—my grandfather's voice in my head. The cat seeking a hold on Uff's throat. Claws scrambling. Gravel flying. Fury I had never known before. "*NAH!*" I screamed. I swung my stick over and over at the creature's head. Suddenly, she turned and leapt away down the riverbank. Flowed over the rocks like a great tawny, speckled ghost.

I lay back panting. The surrounding hills seemed to echo silence after the sound of the battle. Did that really happen? Uff came to me, licking my face, whimpering. I sat up. She was bleeding from a foreleg and a cut across her muzzle. My *anooka* was shredded with long slashes down one shoulder, but the double layers of reindeer hide had saved me from a mauling. Blood ran from my nose. I couldn't remember bumping it, but I must have. That was all. The sturdy hornbeam stick that Apa had made for me was not broken.

It was some time before I could breathe easily again. I held a fistful of snow against my nose while I checked Uff's injuries. "You helped to save me," I whispered to her. "This will heal. You'll have a scar, I think, to tell of your courage." A lick and a quick nip to my sore nose. She had not lost her humor.

Before dark, I found a campsite at the base of a boulder. I cut willow saplings and bent them into a small shelter. It took much time to weave the branches so that I could stuff leaves and moss between them for warmth. I gathered fuel. Kindled a fire. Darkness was coming.

Now. My fist tightened on the handle of my stick. I studied the cluster of trees around me. Most were bent by the wind. But in the distance, there were a few straight ones. *Keerta* wood.

Slowly, with my work blade, I cut through the wood. Hands shaking. *I am doing this.* I watched it fall with a thump and puff of snow. Then, crouching by my fire, I did the thing that I had watched many times before, but had never done myself.

I made a *keerta*.

After trimming off the top of the sapling, I peeled the bark and scraped and smoothed it. I cured it in the hot ashes, turning it when it began to smoke. I shook the weariness from my head and kept working. I would have a weapon when the sun rose.

I heaped dry wood on the fire. Then I reached into the bottom of my pack and brought out one of Apa's flint cores. I looked closely at the grain, trying to feel the way that it would break open when struck. Apa would know where to tap to work the best pieces from it.

Apa.

Angrily, I brushed away a tear. *I will not cry. I will do this.*

With a round stone, I tapped the flint as I had watched my father and brother do so many times, searching for the place where it would split. All the while, I listened carefully for any sign of dark spirits. But if they objected, they held their tongues. In my heart now, I knew that what I was doing was right. The People, the headman, my parents, were good. They had meant to do what was right.

But they had been wrong.

A person should do what he was able to do. A one-legged bird could hunt and live. A cripple with no name could make weapons and use them. *Tal* had shown me. *I will do this!*

At last, I saw a tiny crack forming. I struck now with the heavy end of my antler tool. The rough shell of the flint broke away in a curved flake—glossy, gray stone inside. The next flake was bigger, but split off badly. *Ayee!* A wasted piece. I made a lot of mistakes, but at last, I managed to coax several long flakes from the core piece. There was not much of it left.

I took up the best of the big flakes, handling it carefully.

Wrapping it in a scrap of hide to protect my fingers, I pressed the tip of the antler tool against the edge. A flake snapped away. Another. Bit by bit, I worked the smooth, sharp flint into a shape like a pointed leaf. I turned it over in my hand. Not like my father's—but not so very bad.

I worked faster. Exhausted. I cut the notch in the shaft. Fit the point to it. Bound it tightly in place with wet sinew.

There.

I turned the *keerta* in my hands, sighted down the length of the shaft, tested the strength of my lashing. It was sturdy, lethal—and beautiful in the fearful way of weapons.

"See!" I said, showing it to Uff. "We will hunt and we will live!"

One thing more. I would carve my sign. My hand moved, then stopped. Not my wolf. She was too much like a person. The carved wolf for Suli was different—a plaything. One could not make a sign that was the image of a person. It would be wrong.

Then I knew what to do. With the tip of my work blade, in the thawed earth beside the fire, I made lines until I was satisfied. Two wings. Each with the inward curve between shoulder and elbow of a fish eagle. A single set of talons, open, ready to grasp prey. Strong. I studied it. Nodded. Then I picked up my *keerta* and carved it into the shaft. *Tal* speaking through my hands. *My sign.*

I pulled Uff close, felt the warmth of the fire on my face, gazed at my *keerta*. I was very tired, but at last, it was done.

When I crawled to sleep, I was stiff with cold. Uff squirmed around in a circle to settle herself, as she always did before going to sleep. I pulled her close so that her head rested beneath my chin, grateful for her warmth. Then I checked to be sure my *keerta* was within reach. I had a weapon to protect myself. No, I had two weapons.

I had my *keerta* and I had my wolf.

CHAPTER 25

I *am still alive,* I thought. No other beast—no Ice Man—had sniffed us out and attacked in the night. I crawled from my warm nest, Uff scrambling out behind me. She stretched and shook the leaves from her fur, tasted the air. *It's a good world! Let's get going!* she said with all of herself. I ruffled her shoulder fur and shared a travel cake with her.

As I chewed my portion, I thought of Vida.

She had never mocked or teased me as the others did. Last fall I had made a tiny basket of fine, perfect rushes for her. It was just a plaything, the size of a bird nest. I filled it with crow berries and left it in the crook of a pine root near the great hearth, where we once played. I had known she would find the gift there and might guess where it came from.

My thoughts returned. Now I must learn to throw my *keerta.* Hardly believing it was real, I reached for it and closed my fingers around the shaft.

There was a rotten stump in an open place a short distance away. A white-and-brown fungus like a brush hen's tail grew on it about three hand-spans from the ground. Not good to eat, but a very good target.

I started at a distance that a boy half my age would stand. *Little boy! Ayee*, I was mocking myself! At least there was no one else here to mock me. I could miss the entire stump as many times as there were days in winter—which after that first morning I was pretty sure I had done—and no one would laugh. I tried to remember just how I must place my feet. It was not easy. I raised the *keerta*, pulled my arm back . . . *Steady* . . . With the other arm, I balanced my weight and reached for my target. It was as if the reaching arm told the other where to throw. *Now!* The *keerta* flew a distance and then skidded sideways through the frozen leaves and thin snow cover.

I held my breath, waiting many heartbeats without moving. *Tal* did not strike me dead. Nothing happened. I went to my *keerta* and picked it up. Hobbled back to my throwing line. Threw again. *Clumsy—Suli could throw better than that!*

"Arggh," I said in exasperation after limping across the clearing many times to fetch my weapon. "I couldn't hit a mammut if it was fast asleep, lying on its side, next to you, Uff!"

Uff opened her mouth wide and spilled out her tongue in a wolf grin.

"You are laughing!"

She waved her tail.

Over and over, I flung the *keerta*. Over and over I missed. My cheeks burned with anger. I wanted to break the *keerta*, burn it as my father had done with Sen's. Miserable thing that would not fly where it should!

Still I kept on throwing.

Again.

Again.

Then—*thunk!*

I stared in amazement. My *keerta* quivered, its point firmly embedded in the stump, barely a hand-span from the fungus. "Hah!" I shouted, so that my wolf leapt up with a surprised *Uff!*

Then I backed up a few paces and threw again. I knew that in one day, I could never learn the skill of throwing a *keerta* like a hunter of the People, but I did not stop. Many more times, the *keerta* skidded, bounced, and flew wrong. But finally, I was able to hit the stump over and over again. With each throw, I pried the point gently from the soft wood and tested the binding of sinew. Tonight I would make another point in case this one broke. This one must do for today.

By the time it grew too dark to see, my arm shook so much I could barely raise the *keerta* to my shoulder. But three times, with a shout of triumph, I had hit the target.

The next morning my muscles were stiff. I rubbed away as much of the pain as I could. I set a few snares, then went back to the stump. Now I stood a proper distance away. *You have grown up, little Kai!* At first it seemed I was back to the beginning.

What had I heard my father tell Sen so often when he was discouraged? *Throw until you can do it without thinking. A hunter becomes his* keerta.

After a while, the *keerta* began to sing. It flew more truly with each throw. By the end of the day the fungus was gone and the stump looked as if a woodpecker had torn away the mossy outside, opening the white heart.

The third morning, when I stretched my shoulders and throwing arm, the muscles felt different. I gripped my upper arm. Still sore, but harder. My forearm was stronger, too. My shoulder had fire in it, as if it were made for this.

I must hunt now.

We continued onward. I had no idea where I was going. I just wanted to keep moving. I was in the land of the Ice Men, but now I had a *keerta* and I could throw it. I shifted it in my hand, still getting used to its heft. But how would I travel with it? A whole person could have jogged over the thin snow, balancing his *keerta* in one hand. How would I manage both stick and *keerta*? I could not give up either. I tried a few steps. Struggled for balance. Then quickly, I knew. Instead of carrying the *keerta* in line with the ground, I used it as a second stick to lean on. I could move faster this way. *I could have used a* keerta *a long time ago,* I thought grimly.

I could not travel fast, from sunup to sundown as the hunters of my people did. But I would go as far as I could.

Maybe the Ice Men would not bother a single human person. I had nothing to steal. I would keep going. The stream wound through open land now. Birds chittered in the clumps of willow shrub. A raven called overhead, playing in the wind, following me. If I brought down game, it would sound the kill cry to call the sky pack. "I'm doing my best!" I whispered to the great black bird.

My wolf trotted effortlessly, tail up, as if she was saying, *This day is good, Kai!* Suddenly, she plunged her face into the snow-covered bracken and spooked out a big hare. There was a fast chase, snow flying. I clenched my *keerta*, watching helplessly. Too far to throw it. She was not swift enough to catch the hare. It would get away from her. Then I saw.

I whistled sharply. The chase went on. I whistled again and suddenly Uff knew as well. *Bring it to the* keerta*!*

With a burst of speed, she turned the hare. It sprinted back to me. I was ready. My *keerta* caught it cleanly so that it kicked its last before I could reach it. I grabbed it up by the ears, holding it over my head. Uff leapt about, snapping at it.

"You and I are a pack," I told Uff, ruffling her fur. "Together, we will eat." I did not say *live*, but I was thinking that. Really, it was the same thing.

CHAPTER 26

For many days, Uff and I traveled along the Forbidden River, moving up toward the mountains. They were jagged white teeth in the distance. *Wolf teeth. The teeth of the world.* If the land was forbidden, the spirits seemed to be looking the other way. I saw no sign of Ice Men. I also saw less game. At night I set snares, but caught little. The travel cakes were gone. I began to be hungry.

All along our route now were huge boulders and rocky outcroppings. The river ran faster as the land rose higher. I built brush *takkas* to sleep in. Each night by the fire, I rubbed my twisted foot. My right *saba* was worn nearly through. I combed the woolly under-fur from Uff's coat with my fingers and stuffed it into the *saba* to keep my foot dry. My body ached for meat.

I had to find deer soon.

The mountains were all around now, huge and brooding.

Sacred Tal. I caught glimpses of them through the snow-laden firs. They came together to form a narrow pass. Here a great blue sheet of ice loomed like a sleeping bear. I would not go up there. That was where the grandfathers had said the Ice Men lived.

It began to snow, covering the ground as deep as my knees, and still falling. Uff snuffled, sneezed, and raced in circles, but I began to struggle. She filled her belly with mice, but I was empty. A hunter would make snow-walkers. It would be a puzzle to figure out how to strap one to my twisted foot. Still, I knew I must try.

I found a clump of willows and hacked off some branches. There was barely room to sit up inside my shelter, but at least I was warm. Uff squeezed in beside me. Using my snares and the remainder of my sinew, I made a pair of snow-walkers. Tomorrow I would hunt again.

I woke to a strange blue darkness. Was it still night? What had happened to the day? I pulled the branches away from the opening. We were buried in snow. "Dig, Uff!" I cried. Together we tunneled into the blinding sun. It was well up in the sky. I caught my breath. *Ah!* With its thick fur of snow, the world was . . . *other.*

I had to tie the snow-walker on my bad foot so that it cut painfully. There was no other way to make it stay on. Apa would have figured out something better. I tried a few awkward steps. I did not sink into the drifts. Uff spooked, dashed away, then sidled back to me.

"You can run over the snow," I told her, "but for the deer,

things will be different." I was right. Before the sun was very much higher, Uff stopped. Her nose quivered. I caught up with her, panting. With no food, I was weak. Stalking now, creeping, Uff led me to a clearing. I scarcely dared to breathe.

Uff turned to me, questioning. Gripping my *keerta*, I crawled after her on top of the snow.

I am a wolf now. A wolf of the People.

We worked our way closer. Uff knew to approach from downwind. I had not taught her this. At last, I saw movement through the trees. Looming antlers. A small herd of reindeer trapped here by the deep snow. They were feeding on lichen growing on the spruce branches. Uff trembled. Looked at me. I grasped the loose skin at her neck, holding her back. *Wait.*

A big female moved slowly toward us, ears twisting nervously as she fed. I had to get closer. I could not miss. She took a step. I wriggled forward. The deer's head came around. Ears questioning. She stamped once. The other deer turned. I froze.

After a time, the reindeer went back to feeding.

I eased myself closer. Everything in me cried *Now!* I was shaking all over. I could not do this. *You have to do this.* The deer was no more than ten paces away, partly hidden by branches. Very slowly, I drew my arm up. Steady.

Tal, please give me this.

I flung my *keerta*. There was a soft thump as it hit her squarely between the ribs. She reared, bleated, tried to run. But Uff was away from me now. My wolf threw herself at

the deer's throat and brought her down. The deer crumpled to her knees, blood running from her mouth.

It was over.

I turned my face to the sky. *Thank you!* It was not a blood kill, but it was a hunter's kill—swift, clean, and much meat. Together, my wolf and I had done this.

By the time darkness fell, the snow had stopped. Long into the night, I sat savoring tender chunks of roasted meat with my wolf beside me. I cut the two longest teeth from the deer and carefully bored holes in them. Then I stitched one to each shoulder of my *anooka*. At last, I took out my blade and cut the long hair away from my face. I burned it in the fire for *Tal*.

CHAPTER 27

We moved on. Winter deepened, but we were not hungry. I had dried much of the deer meat and cached the rest in a snowbank covered with branches. I could go back to it if I needed to.

There was more game here. Uff understood now what my *keerta* could do. We hunted well together. I thought perhaps I had come far enough. I would find a sheltered place, get more deerskins, build a proper *takka*, live in it until spring. It was the first time since I had left that I'd thought about the time when the world would grow warm again. *Ha!* There was very much more winter to get through before then. Still, *spring*. I grinned. Maybe we would live to see it after all.

I kept looking over my shoulder. I was very far north now. I sniffed the air carefully, trying to pick up any scent. Several times I stopped to look around. Was something or someone

watching us? Uff, too, was uneasy. She paced behind me, hackles half-raised, tail stiff.

One day there was a break in the cold. The air had warmed, so I unlaced the front of my *anooka*. Ahead was an opening in the trees. As I stepped into it, a thundering roar came. I looked up. A wall of snow, trees, and branches snapping, churning, rumbling toward us.

Uff scrambled desperately away.

The river of snow took me. It carried me, fighting and clawing, spinning, up, down, gone. Choking me.

Suddenly it stopped.

There was no sound. I couldn't move. Pain in my right arm. I tried to breathe, but couldn't. I was suffocating. I opened my eyes to half-light.

I was buried.

I would die now.

My mind drifted. I was moving through walls of stone toward a fire somewhere deep in the earth. I saw pictures. Red spots, and then zigzag lines. A great black-and-white aurochs bull. A bear. A black bird. An owl. A running horse. *Why a horse?* My brain could not think of an answer.

Scratching.

Digging.

Whining. Scrabbling.

Just when I felt myself going away forever, claws raked my face. A hot tongue washed my nose. There was sweet air.

"Uff!" I said aloud. But my voice was a whisper. She

clawed at the snow. I tried again to move. My left arm found its way free. I helped her dig. It took a long time. My right arm could not help. If I moved it, a sound like a wounded hare came from my mouth.

"Dig," I begged Uff, through gritted teeth. But she did not need to be told. She was wild-crazy to have me out of the snow. When they were finally free, my legs were as dead as frozen meat. I beat on them with my good hand. At last blood flowed in them once more. Somehow my pack-basket was there in the snow beside me, mostly in one piece.

I looked at my arm. My throwing arm. I saw the way it was bent between elbow and wrist. *Finished*. An arm broken like that would heal crippled and useless. There would be no more hunting, no more reindeer. I laughed bitterly.

The leg and now my arm. I had thought *Tal* was on my side. *So stupid*. *Tal* had not smiled on me. No. *Tal* was playing with me. *Tal* had let me think I could live—only to batter the life from me slowly, as a cave lion toys with a wounded bird. It seemed absurd now. I had fought my way out of the smothering snow just to die a slow death of pain and hunger. I staggered in a circle, clutching my arm, face turned to the empty sky, weeping, furious. *What more can you do to me?* I drew my work blade. *Do I have to finish it myself?*

All things try to live. Apa-Da's voice was inside my head. Without intending it, my hand opened. I dropped the blade into the snow, fumbled after it. Could not find it again. Uff licked my face. I tried to push her away, "You should have let me die!" I screamed at her. But she would not stop tugging at the sleeve of my good arm, trying to get me to leave this fearful place of churning, smothering snow.

There was the head of my stick. I tugged it free and got to my feet. I managed to thrust the bare hand of my broken arm inside my *anooka* so that it would not freeze. Well. Maybe I could get back to my last camp. Perhaps there were coals left for fire. With one arm, I could not make a new one. I had meat for a few days. Then the night beasts would eat me. I fumbled for the pouch at my neck where I had put the bloodstone powder. At least I could die with my face to the south and my family. Apa, Ama, Sen, Suli, Bu.

Vida . . .

I wavered.

Blackness.

CHAPTER 28

A smell woke me. It was too much work to open my eyes. I tried to think what it might be. My head felt as if it were packed with woolly fur. There was a familiar scent of roasting deer meat, but there was this other, puzzling odor. Animal, but not any creature I knew.

There was another puzzle. I wasn't cold. *Was this death?* But I could feel the warmth of a fire. Pain in my right arm. I moved the other and found Uff pressed up against my side. My wolf. My good wolf. My friend. I was not dead.

I tried to open my eyes, touched my eyelids cautiously. They were swollen nearly shut. Suddenly I felt the panic again of being swallowed and smothered by the wall of snow, and a fear sound came from my mouth.

Another sound answered me: "Ummmmm."

Someone was there. Still I could not find my way out of

the wool inside my head. Gentle fingers touched my face. Warm, wet, fragrant moss bathed my eyes.

Uff moved her head to rest her chin on my chest. She made the little welcoming sound in her throat that she made for a friend. Again, I lifted my hand to my eyes. Now I was able to open them.

A person was turned from me, bent over the fire. I squinted. I saw walls. *Walls of stone.* I reached out my good hand and touched one. We were not in a *takka* of the People. My heart raced. We were inside walls of stone. A cave. I had heard of such a thing. I had seen caves where a man could lie down and take shelter for a night. Cats and bears used them. But this one was larger than any cave I had ever known. And there was fire. Then I saw a *kep* of hide fixed over the cave opening so that the smoke could make its way out at the top.

A stone takka.

My eyes traveled again to the person by the fire. His back was massive, more so because he was wrapped in bearskin. *Why would a person wear a sleeping robe?* The man's hair hung in shaggy clumps. And the hair...was as red as the coals of the fire.

He turned. My breath went out of my lungs in a rush.

He was an Ice Man.

A man, but not a man of the People. Brows like mossy shelves over eyes that glowed with fire on each side of a broad nose. They were strange eyes, all dark—like some beast, yet filled with knowing. And humor, I was sure of it.

Did he think I was funny? The big nose with its wide nostrils worked. The Ice Man was smelling me, too.

Under the cape of thick black fur, laced together at the shoulders, I glimpsed a powerful chest, with hair nearly as thick as the bearskin. His stocky limbs bulged with muscle. He wore more scars on his body than I had ever seen on a man of the People.

Why hadn't he killed me? Why hadn't he killed Uff?

He was roasting deer meat. Had he dug up the cache I had made? Had he been following us? Watching?

The Ice Man held out a chunk of it to me on the end of his blade, making a deep sound in his throat. His meaning was plain. *Eat.* I hesitated. But Uff did not. She was no fool. Meat was meat. In one swift motion, she rose and gulped the offered food. If I didn't want it, she surely did.

The Ice Man bent over and made a sound that I knew. He laughed. It was deep and hoarse, but it was laughter. Then he crouched before Uff, touched his forehead to the ground, and chanted a song that made the air quiver.

He thinks she is magic because she doesn't run with a wolf pack, but follows me.

I didn't refuse a second piece. While I was gnawing it, holding it with my good hand, the Ice Man peered at my injured arm. I saw now that the sleeve of my *anooka* had been cut open, the broken arm held between sticks and sinew over a padding of dry moss. It was swollen and bruised, but straight.

The Ice Man had made my broken arm straight. I did not think even Moc-Atu himself could have done such a thing. *Could it heal? Would it not be a useless thing like my foot?*

The Ice Man showed me his own arm. I could see a knot in the muscle. He made gestures so that I knew it had once been broken. He laughed and flexed the muscle to show me that it was strong now. Very strong. He showed me a slightly crooked finger. He pointed to his cheekbone. His leg. *His leg!* My mouth opened. All broken. But he was not a cripple.

I knew that Ice Men could not speak as the People do. Still, I thought I should try to say something. "Thank you," I said. "Good." I pointed to my arm. The Ice Man looked puzzled. Then I touched my chest and said "Kai." I put my hand on Uff's head and said "Uff."

His face broke into a grin, showing two broken teeth on one side. The Ice Man pointed to himself and uttered a deep sound that was half singing and seemed to me to go on forever. It sounded something like "*Oooni-alu-kas-pah-vard-ahhh...*" But there was much more to it than that. All the time his great calloused hands were swimming through the air telling a story that went along with the sound he was making.

I could not repeat all that, so I said the first part hesitantly: "Oooni?"

There was a sound like a wheezing bear might make. The Ice Man was laughing again.

"Well," I whispered to Uff, "maybe he will not eat us."

Oooni wrinkled his forehead. He gestured toward my wolf and uttered something that sounded like "Ahhhuff," working his hands at the same time, making a moving shadow on the wall in the firelight.

For the tiniest moment, I thought I saw the image of a wolf running through deep snow, its tail held high. I shook my head. "How did you do that?"

He looked intently at me. "Khhhaiii," he said, while his hands made shadow pictures of a hunter killing a deer. *Khhhaiii*... The sound of my name-that-was-not-a-name seemed to ring in the air and fade into nothingness.

I started to shake my head to say, *No, that's not me. I'm only a crippled pup that will never grow into a hunter.* But Oooni must have watched me kill the reindeer. He knew me only as a hunter.

I met his eyes and nodded. "*Eya.*"

I saw that Oooni had carefully gathered my things: stick, *keerta*, pack-basket, even the wreckage of my snow-walkers. They were in a row along the far wall of the cave. I watched now as Oooni inspected each item carefully. He was especially interested in my *keerta*, studying the length of the shaft and the way the point was bound into the split end of the sapling.

I asked with gestures to look at Oooni's *keerta*. It was short, made of heavier wood. The point was well formed, but too thick to be set into the wood the way the People did it.

Then Oooni gave me a bitter-tasting drink that made the

pain in my arm fade and my head swim. Sleep overtook me again.

In the morning, I pointed to my twisted foot and made Oooni understand that I wanted my stick. I pulled myself to my feet. There was pain, but I was able to walk outside. I found that Oooni had made a great heap of firewood. The tool he used, with its big stone head, was almost too heavy for me to lift. He did not need snow-walkers to travel in deep snow. I saw that instead of boots, Oooni wore hide wrappings bound with leather straps. He had brought the remainder of the deer, but he ate much of it himself. I was sure that between the three of us, every scrap of it would be devoured in a day or two.

There was a thing I needed to know. It kept gnawing at me. *Are there others?* The stone *takka* was big enough so that other people could have slept there. Where were they? There was a tool-making area at one side of the fire pit with many fragments of flint lying about. More Ice Men must have been here at some time.

Somehow, I made Oooni understand the question: "Where are your people?" He stared at me. I could not make out the expression in the eyes under those fiery brows. Then he gestured for me to follow him down the hillside to a level place. Here, he bent and scooped the snow away with his hands. I saw a heap of rocks. Oooni sang and gestured a name. He crouched and swept off a smaller heap of rocks. And another. And another—this one very small. Each time he sang a name—his hands told more. Tears ran down his leathery cheeks.

Even though I didn't know what the rumbling words and gestures meant, I understood enough. These were his people. "They're dead?" I asked using signs as well as words. "All of them? All of your people, dead?"

Oooni rose and pointed to the mountains. There were more Ice Men.

CHAPTER 29

The moon grew big, waned, and began to grow once more. From time to time, Oooni went out and hunted. Uff wanted to go with him, but I would not let her. The ache and the swelling in my arm faded. Outside, the winter howled like a hungry thing, but the cave held the heat of the fire so that I could go without my *anooka* and still be warm.

I cut pieces from the reindeer hide to make a new *umee* to replace the one lost in the snow. Oooni had scraped it while I slept for so long. At least Ice Men knew how to work hides. Now Oooni watched as I opened my sewing kit and threaded a bone needle with a long strand of sinew. He did not take his eyes from my hands as I punched tiny holes with my awl and carefully stitched the hide. Sewing with my left hand was very awkward, but Oooni seemed to think it was a sort of magic.

He studied the reindeer teeth that decorated the shoulders of my *anooka*. He could not stop himself from touching them. His eyes glowed as he turned them to see the holes I had drilled and how I had sewn them to the leather.

"You should see my father's *anooka,* and the headman, Rhar's. They're covered with teeth—cave lion, bear, aurochs, wolverine . . ." I tried to tell him, making signs and sounds for each animal, but he only partly understood.

Then I offered him the needle to try stitching for himself. He stared at me. I took one of his big, hard hands, with its broken nails and many calluses. I tried to get him to hold the needle, but he could not pinch such a tiny thing. Oooni's hands, so weathered, made me think of the pads of Uff's feet. I had seen him put a hand under his bearskin. He had no other way of keeping them warm. I pointed to my *umees*. "Where are yours?" He laughed, opening and closing his great paws, and shook his head.

Yet he had made his *keerta*. And he could kill with it. But not from a distance. He must be a deadly stalker to get close enough to kill with just a thrust. I remembered the feeling that I had been followed. Had he been close enough to kill me or my wolf and neither of us had known it? And what if he didn't hit the killing place of a beast? What if the animal struggled or fought back?

I understood the scars and broken bones.

Night after night, staring into the Ice Man's fire, sharing meat together, trying to share our thoughts, I wondered: What was the difference between us, really? The sounds and gestures Oooni made were strange, but I was sure now that it was a way of talking. I could not understand it very well. I tried to copy him, but we both ended up laughing. A few things were the same. Smiles. Frowns. Head shakes. Nods. Hand gestures. Raspy laughter when I tried to tell how I had gone into Yellow Mother's den for Uff. Wide eyes when he understood what I had done. Tears for his dead people. The sharing of food.

Why was Oooni caring for me? I could see no reason except kindness. It was against everything I had ever known about Ice Men.

Uff did not wonder. Each time Oooni went out and came back again, she bowed and waved her tail. She leapt up, trying to lick his face. He was her friend. She would have followed him if I had not held her back. I was terrified of losing her. "Stay here with me," I whispered to her. "We don't know him. Maybe he eats wolf."

~

The days were slow while my arm healed. I was tired of smoke, of darkness, of sitting still. I longed to be outside. "Wait, Oooni," I said one day as he was about to leave.

He drew his eyebrows together, frowning, and shook his head. He muttered something. Motioned for me to stay.

Uff was on her feet now, pacing back and forth by the hearth, whining to go. "I know I cannot throw my *keerta* yet," I said, "but my arm doesn't hurt so much now. Just let me walk behind you. Maybe Uff will scare up a ptarmigan." I pointed to a heap of feathers in the corner, pointed to Uff, flapped my arms.

Oooni's face broke into a grin.

My snow-walkers were beyond repair, but I could make my way in his trail. I picked up my stick. "Just let me walk with you—a short walk," I pleaded.

He paused. At last, he agreed. He bent, took up a handful of the ptarmigan feathers, and held them out to Uff. *What was he doing?* My wolf sniffed the feathers carefully. Oooni put a finger to his nose and then to his eyes. Looked at me. *What?* Then he put a finger to Uff's nose and to her eyes. *She sees with her nose.* Yes! Of course. I knew that, but it took Oooni to make it into a thought for me.

Then the Ice Man tucked a strange thing into the rough *jahs* he used to hold the bear fur closed around his waist. It was made from several fist-size rocks tied together with long strips of leather. He took up his *keerta* and went out, letting me follow.

The sun glittered. I breathed the cold air. Uff snapped at the snow, tossed a stick in the air. I watched Oooni stalking through the drifts ahead of me. Silent. Powerful. As alive to the world as a wolf. From a distance, I had watched my father and brother stalking game, but Oooni's way was different. Somehow he became the trees, the bushes, the dried grasses. . . . He moved like a shadow. I felt very awkward, making my way behind him.

We came through a grove of pines. Suddenly Oooni's hand shot out behind him, shaking the branch over my head, sending a shower of snow down my neck.

"What?" I sputtered, shaking it out of my hair. Then I saw that he was peering back at me, eyes dancing, actually holding a big hand over his mouth to keep from laughing. It was a very old trick. Sen and Uli had played it on me many times. Oooni looked so funny that I couldn't be angry.

I grabbed a fistful of snow and flung it at him, smacking his hairy chin. He bellowed with laughter. Then we threw snow at each other until we both collapsed. Uff loved it. She raced back and forth between the two of us, snapping at the flying snow, twisting, spinning in the air, all the while yipping like a pup.

So much for silent hunting. At last we got to our feet, brushed ourselves off, and continued on our way.

We came to some willows. Ptarmigan sometimes hide under the drifts. Suddenly Uff froze, nose working the air, quivering all over. For a moment, Oooni's eyes met mine. I nodded. He did not raise his *keerta*. Instead, he took the strange weapon of rocks and straps from his *jahs*. He nodded back at me.

"Now, Uff!" I whispered. She surged forward. In a thunder of wings, a group of ptarmigan burst from the snow. Oooni flung his weapon. It snaked through the air, taking down not one, but three birds. *Three!* Uff snapped up a fourth one herself.

There was a deafening grunt-snort. Something black exploded from under a hazel bush. A red-eyed boar, tusks slashing, charged us. A young one, but dangerous enough. Oooni shoved me away. Uff lunged, snapping at its snout, just giving Oooni time to snatch up his *keerta* again. I had never seen anything like the power behind the thrust he made. A hideous squealing. And then stillness.

"You killed it, Oooni!" I said, panting.

"Eyahhh." He was touching the boar very gently at the sacred place between the eyes, murmuring something. He knew. *A hunter honors the life taken.*

At least I could carry some of the kill home. We were making our way back when we heard a distant drumming far across the open land. It was a herd of some sort, coming toward us. Oooni made a sign that meant horses. I stared at him. I saw only a dark mass and a cloud of snow. How could he tell they were not bison? Did those strange, dark eyes see farther than mine? At last I made out the arched necks and streaming tails. Now we could see wolves following, seven of them, beside and behind, keeping pace. The horses were mostly unafraid, but some of the yearlings were nervous. They whinnied, broke away, joined back again.

At the tail of the herd, a horse stumbled. It was an aged mare, gaunt with the slow hunger that comes when teeth are gone. Suddenly there was a flurry of fur—a wolf dragging at the throat, three at the flanks. I grabbed for Uff and held her back. It was soon over. The pack fed while the herd moved on.

Oooni shifted the burden on his shoulders and turned to me. His eyes were bright. He nodded, and said a word I had learned: "*Ummmb.*" Good.

"Good?" I asked.

He nodded again. Gestured to the lead mare. Made gestures showing how fast she was, how strong. Pointed to the stallion, also strong, beautiful, trotting now, with his nose to the wind, legs lifting in a high-stepping dance over the snowy ground. Oooni pointed to the wolves. He spoke again, and even though I did not understand all his words, suddenly I knew. *The wolf pack made the horse herd swift and strong.* They were not two separate things. They were part of each other. They were *Tal,* which is all things. Life. Death. *Tal.*

"*Eya,*" I said.

In Oooni's cave that night, I ground charcoal and mixed it with fat from the boar to make a glossy black. He watched, eyes glinting, as I drew the horse herd on the wall. The wise lead mare. Her stiff black mane. The stallion, nostrils wide, tasting the wind. I paused then, wondering how to show them galloping.

Oooni reached out a hand. Dipped a finger in my paint. He squinted his eyes. Then in a flurry of motion, he traced legs, not two, not four, many legs, dancing legs, galloping horse legs, moving, pounding. Moving.

I sat back with my mouth open. Yes. That was how to do it.

CHAPTER 30

One night, soon after, Oooni motioned for me to show him my arm. With his blade, he carefully sliced through the straps. The splint fell away. I touched the chafed skin where the sticks had rubbed. I opened and closed my hand. The shrunken muscles of my forearm flexed. The place where the bones had broken was still swollen and sore, but the arm was straight. Weak, yet it worked. I looked at Oooni. The Ice Man nodded. He flexed his own arm to show me that the arm would soon be strong again, like his.

The next morning, Oooni took his *keerta* and was gone until very late. At last my wolf made her *uff*ing sound. I went outside, and there was Oooni coming back through the snow, carrying the entire hindquarters of an aurochs cow across his shoulders!

"*Tal*, that is huge!" I helped him bring it inside. Uff leapt at the fresh meat. "*Nah*, Uff, get down! You must wait!"

But Oooni took up his *hahk* and with one motion, severed a lower leg and gave it to her.

His face broke into a misshapen grin. One of his eyes was purple and swollen nearly closed, but he rumbled with satisfaction as he set down his burden. He made cutting motions. I nodded. I would start butchering it—roasting some. Then he left again. Before dark, he returned with the skin and the front quarters. It was a huge amount of meat for two of us, even with Oooni's great hunger. We both laughed over the heap of it while Uff begged for—and got—more scraps.

While the meat was roasting, I removed the cutting teeth from the jaw of the aurochs cow. I drilled a hole in each of them. Oooni watched me intently. I could not see how to sew the teeth to his bearskin cape. At last, I strung them on a length of sinew and put this around Oooni's neck. He studied my gift, turning the teeth over in his thick fingers.

But then he took the string off. He gestured at one of the teeth and then at me. I did not understand. He tried to put the string of teeth around my neck. I shook my head. "*Nah*, you killed the cow. These are yours," I insisted. Oooni shook his head. He would not be satisfied until I strung one of the teeth on a new length of sinew and put it around my own neck. Then he allowed me to place the string with the others around his neck once more.

Over and over he touched his necklace. He turned the teeth in his big fingers, feeling how they hung securely on the sinew. Then he held his hands out, palms up, first to me and then to my wolf. "*Mehu*," he said.

It took me a moment to understand. Then, hesitantly, I nodded. "*Meh . . . u*," I said, and held my hands out to him and to Uff. "Yes. *Mehu. Imnos.*"

Friends. We three were friends.

"*Immmnosss . . .*" agreed Oooni, and we grinned at each other.

I wished we could talk well enough to share stories, as my people would have done. I imagined my family living in a place like this, made of stone. It would be so warm, such good protection from storms and beasts. It would be so easy to defend ourselves here.

I stopped myself. They would never know. I was not going back. I was not ever going to see my family again.

When we could eat no more, Oooni began to sing a rolling song from deep within his chest. It filled the cave. In the flickering light of the fire, he did his best to tell the story of his hunt to me. First he was the aurochs cow, digging for dried grass under the snow. She twitched her ears, snorted, flicked her tail. Then he was himself, the hunter, seeing the cow. His eyes grew big. He sniffed her scent. He rubbed his belly and licked his lips. Then he showed the long, stalking hunt, on hands and knees, working his way close. Uff whined. She understood. Finally, *Hah!* The fatal thrust when he was so close he could almost reach out and touch the beast. How she had flung her head back, smacking her skull into his cheekbone and blackening his eye.

We laughed together. It was good to laugh.

Reaching for my pack-basket, I drew out my *osa*. Perhaps

Oooni would not care that I played it badly. I unrolled it from its rabbit skin. My hand and wrist were very stiff. But I was able to hold the *osa* and cover the holes. Curious, Oooni watched. I lifted it to my lips and played a few notes. They were not good ones. Still Oooni's eyes widened. I tried the moon song, which is easy. Oooni's mouth opened in amazement. I grinned back at him. He gestured for me to play more. Uff rested her chin on my knee.

I tried another song. The sound filled the cave and thrummed in my ears. Now my notes were truer. I had never made the *osa*'s voice sound so rich and sweet. The stone walls seemed to sing back to me. Uff pricked her ears and made a sound in her throat. Oooni's eyes were huge with wonder.

I played another song, the one about the reindeer herd traveling. Then I played the song of the spring reindeer feast. It would not be long now until the great herds were on the move again. Oooni smiled broadly, his big hands dancing in the air with the voice of the *osa*.

I began the song of ice melting and the greening of the world. Oooni started to hum deep in the back of his throat, and the cave suddenly came alive. The sound vibrated against my skin. Uff turned her head to the side, looking at each of us. Then she rose on her haunches, lifted her muzzle, and joined us with her own song.

Oooni sang words in his deep voice. The hairs at the back of my neck prickled. The sound was old, as if it came from the beginning of time. It was the song of the Ice Men.

I do not know how long the three of us made music

together that night. All I knew was I was happy. We were friends. My chest swelled with the goodness of it. It filled the cave, making the fire burn more brightly. The sound swirled out into the starry sky with our smoke.

In the morning, I woke to the sound of icicles dripping. I heard the far off whinnying of the herd of horses. But the cave was silent.

Oooni was gone.

CHAPTER 31

He had taken a great chunk of the aurochs meat, so I knew he must be traveling. He would not be back. He had stayed with me until my arm was healed, had brought me meat to last until the arm was strong enough for me to hunt for myself again. Then he had left.

I was not surprised. I didn't understand why Oooni had taken care of me. But in my heart, I had known that the day would come when the Ice Man would leave.

Something hurt inside my chest. My . . . friend . . . had left me. Oooni had never thought anything of my lame foot. Just like Uff, he had accepted me the way I was. I stroked Uff's head. "At least I still have you. It's just the two of us again."

She looked at me as if to say, Eya, *there is me and there is you*. My arm was weak, but it was healing. And much of the winter had passed. I had a safe place to stay until the weather warmed, and I was strong again. But I didn't want to stay longer than I had to in Oooni's cave. The ghosts under the rock piles made me shiver.

There were things I could do. I needed a new stick for walking, and I could make a new pair of *sabas* with the aurochs hide. In the woods nearby, I found a grove of hornbeam trees and among them a likely sapling. I found chaga fungus on one and hacked off a piece to replenish my tinder supply. It was good medicine too, if I got sick.

Spit and dung! It took a long time to hack through the tough little tree, and longer to trim, peel, and smooth it. I worked on it for several nights. This stick would be nearly two hand-spans longer than the old one, a little more than I needed, but perhaps I would grow that much. I could always cut it shorter if I did not. When it was finished, stout and beautiful as such a thing could be, I carved the sign of the fish eagle into the top of it.

My sign.

I could not think what to do with the old one. My father's hands had made it. I could not burn it or throw it away. There was a narrow ledge, about shoulder height, near the back of the cave. I placed it there.

Outside, day after day, the wind howled, piling snow around the entrance to the cave. Often we heard wolves singing to one another as they hunted. Uff would raise her head to listen. "It's another pack, Little Bah, not ours. We are a small pack—the two of us—but we have a good den." Oooni had left us firewood. We were warm. Uff spent most of her days curled up beside me, but each time I went out, she leapt up, eager to run through the snow. Her tail hung low with her disappointment when I didn't go far from the cave. "We'll hunt together again soon, my friend. Soon," I told her.

My arm throbbed. I had to stop and rest it many times as I worked. But it was healing. I flexed it, turned my hand this way and that, tried lifting things with it. Each day it was a little stronger, the ache a little less. "Thank you, Oooni," I whispered into the smoky shadows. I touched the aurochs tooth around my neck.

The *sabas* took longer. Aurochs hide is very tough, which is why it is so good for the purpose. It took much effort to make it pliable. As I scraped the hide, I remembered doing such work when I was small. I could hear Sen and the other boys laughing as they practiced throwing *keertas*. The ache of wanting to be with them made me chop and stab with the scraper.

"Go easy, or you will slice right through, Kai! Do not mind it. All work is good, and needed," Ama had said. But that did not make my anger any less. "Cold can kill a hunter as surely as a cave lion," Ama had added, as she patiently stitched seams that kept out the bitterest wind. She did not need to add that the loss of a hunter could kill a family, but she did repeat the old words: *The life of the People is stitched together with gut and sinew.*

One morning, we woke to sun and wind from the south. I was nearly finished with the hide. Soon I could begin cutting and stitching. After a time, I had no choice but to stop. The muscles in my arm were shaking. I had to rest. Sitting back against the rock wall, I said, "Little Bah, I'd let you do your part and chew this hide to soften it for me, but you would do too good a job. There'd be nothing left!" She turned her head to the side, listening. I was grateful to have her to talk to. "At least you can have the tail!" I hacked it from the hide and tossed it to her. She jumped up and snapped it out of the air, shook it as if it were alive. Then she bowed, looking at me from the corner of her eyes, asking me to chase her.

"Alright, alright," I said.

So we went out. The day was warm. Slip-sliding in the melting snow, I hobbled after her. She pretended to go one way, then whipped around me on the other side, bounding in crazy circles, tossing the aurochs's tail in the air and catching it again. Never letting me get close enough to snatch her prize. She had grown even more, was filling out. Her coat shone. For a moment, I remembered her, a handful of fur, shivering and hungry, when I brought her out of Torn Ear's den. My wolf—so big now!

Then, over the snow, from somewhere away to the west, came a howl—the call of the pack leader. *Ahooooooo! Oooooo!* It was echoed by several others. I turned my head. They were not far off. Uff dropped her plaything and froze, trembling all over. Her ears worked the air. She listened. Suddenly, she lifted her muzzle and called back to them.

Her song was a question at first. Then it changed to a call of longing. I was gripped with terror. "Uff!" I cried. I made my way to her and seized her by her scruff. My thoughts stumbled over each other like my clumsy feet. *You cannot leave me. You and I are a pack!*

But Uff was not a pup anymore. There was no loose skin to grasp, only thick, glossy fur. She jerked and plunged, trying to pull away from me. I felt her strength. *"NAH!"* I said, wrapping my arms around her shoulders. I had never been so fierce with her.

A cold wind had sprung up. *Winter is not over.* On the far stream bank, a single wolf appeared—a big male. Huge. His fur was the color of sun on sand, with a cape of charcoal over his ears and shoulders. He turned to look at us. I saw his breath, white in the air. I saw the wind riffle the hairs of his bushy tail. His yellow eyes did not look at me. He was staring at Uff. But wolves do not mate in the first year or even the second. Uff was too young. I gripped her harder. "You cannot have her!" I whispered desperately to the male wolf. Uff trembled all over. She whined, trying to twist from my grasp.

Six other wolves trotted into sight, sleek, well-fed for this time of year. There was a brief romp. The younger ones shouldered one another, snapping like puppies. A smaller male, grayer in coloring and a bit scruffy, bounded toward the leader. A name for the big yellow male came into my mind without my willing it—*Sand.* He turned the younger wolf aside with a quick downward thrust of his muzzle.

Where was his mate? A pack leader almost always had a

mate. Uff was locked to his gaze now. Sand called softly to her. She whimpered and fought again to get away from me.

Once more, Sand called, clear and wild. Uff's tail waved. She struggled, cried, begged me with a quick lick to my face. Then suddenly, she wrenched free. She ran from me.

I could not believe it. For an instant, I stood silent, watching her dash down the rocky, snow-covered slope. A brief greeting. Then the pack—with Uff in their midst—disappeared over the rise.

"Uff! Uff!"

I screamed her name until my throat would make no more sound.

CHAPTER 32

I slumped to my knees. I did not try to hold back. It was as if I was still feeling the twisting of the broken bones in my arm. *Not Uff. Please, not Uff.* The pack would tear her to pieces. I remembered the strange wolf I had seen killed by the *imnos* so long ago.

She did not know how to be a wolf. I had made her something else. She was my friend. She belonged at my side.

I do not know how long I crouched in the snow. I was stiff with cold when finally I stumbled to my feet again. Wolves could run effortlessly all day. I could only limp. There was no use trying to follow.

Alone.

Oooni was gone. And now . . . Uff. I should have known. Even if she was too young, it was the mating time of the wolves. I should have seen it coming. I could have tied her up—kept her in the cave somehow. Sobbing so hard I could not get breath. Slamming my fists over and over into the snow.

I might as well be dead, too. Leaning heavily on my stick, I made my way back to Oooni's cave. My thoughts had gone blank. Like one half-dreaming, I built up the fire and warmed myself. I could not eat. At last, I curled into a knot and slept.

The next morning, it hit me all over again, like the thundering wall of snow. Uff was gone. *Have you not taken enough from me, Tal—making me grow up a nameless cripple, casting me out from my people? Why must you play with me—let me think I could be a hunter, have a life, have a friend? She was all I had!*

She is only a wolf.

I know. She is not a human person. She is not my sister, or my mother, or my child. It is not like losing one of my family.

But she is *my family now—if she even lives anymore.*

I stared at the thin flames of my morning fire. I thought of how Uff had followed me for so long, like a second shadow. Rested my forehead on my arms. Let the tears burn and flow.

It had never mattered to her if the sun shone or not, if we fed or hungered together, if I was happy or sad—she would not leave me. Uff had stayed at my side from the day I carried her home. We were part of each other. How could she leave? She was a wolf, but not like the others. What did you call a wolf like that?

At last, I ate some cold meat broth left from the day

before. It had gelled in the night. I did not bother to warm it, but ate it as it was. There were chunks of meat in the bottom of the *das*. Out of habit, I stabbed one out with my blade and looked to the place where Uff usually lay. Closed my eyes as the pain sliced through my heart again.

Gone.

Dead, probably.

Would I find her body? Would I ever know what happened to her? I dropped the piece of meat back into the *das* and flung my work blade against the wall.

Many times in the following days, I looked for Uff to greet me, to see her get up from her place by the fire, expected to feel her nose touch my hand. Sometimes I thought I heard her padding softly along behind me as I went out for wood or water. I missed the sounds she made in her throat while she waited for me to roast meat. In my sleep, I reached out in the dark to stroke her head, and woke feeling the coldness of the place where she used to curl beside me, knowing again that she was gone.

"*Tal*, you have taken so much from me," I whispered over and over, "not Uff, too."

More snow in the night. No break in the weather. I did not care if my arm was still weak. There was no reason to stay. But I was trapped in Oooni's cave until I could travel and hunt again. I went back to making my new *sabas*. It was something to do. Blisters rose on my fingers and broke open. I did not mind the pain. I almost welcomed it.

I remembered making the little antler wolf for Suli. I put down my work and leaned my head against the wall. Had I done wrong to make the carving of Uff? Was it *tabat*? Was that why *Tal* had taken her from me? But it was only a plaything. *Ayee.* Suli had loved my wolf, too. My wolf. But not my wolf anymore. Uff belonged to herself—and probably to the spirit world now.

But Uff had dug me free when the snow was killing me. She had helped me fight off the cat. She had learned to hunt with me. She had given me my life many times. Many times. Had I taken hers by not teaching her how to be a wolf? I closed my eyes, feeling the hurt of losing her again and again. Without her, my heart was dead.

I lost track of the days. The wind howled endlessly. Sometimes I ate. When it was dark, I slept. The sun moved in the sky. Slowly the world grew warmer. I lived in loneliness.

But at last, my thoughts began to waken. I needed meat again—but could I hunt without my wolf? Could I? Uff and I had always hunted as a team. *She is your power.* Did that mean I was powerless without her?

I stared at my hands, flexed my arms, looked at my *keerta*. Opening my pouch of sacred things, I took out her sharp little puppy tooth and held it in my palm.

No.

I was not powerless. I was not the same person I had been before I found Uff. I would hunt and I would live—because of her. "You will always be my power," I whispered. "I will not dishonor you by giving up."

At last trickles of melting ice ran down outside the opening of the cave. The nights were filled with a new sound—geese, heading north once more, calling like wolves when they sing on the trail. The mornings were noisy with the voices of returning birds. My arm was stronger. I hunted again, but differently—creeping, waiting, creeping again—as Oooni did. It was difficult without Uff to help track and then turn the prey to me, but I killed and I ate. Soon fish would run in the river. Maybe I could find the reindeer herd when it traveled north again. In the cliffs I saw other caves, all too far up or too small, or not right in some way. But perhaps I could find one suitable for shelter. Soon I would head out again and search. Sometimes I heard wolves in the night. I listened for Uff, but could not tell her voice.

One more day...

CHAPTER 33

As I was crossing a great meadow to the west of Oooni's cave, there came a bellow, like no creature I had ever heard. Then I saw them—mammuts, browsing in the distance! The great bull called again, telling the others to follow. I found the direction of the wind and moved closer. *Tal!* Each beast, with its shaggy coat the color of bloodstone, was as tall as the willow trees they tore at and fed on—a mountain of meat! Useless to a hunter alone like me, impossible for one person to hunt, but such a richness for an *immet* of People, if by luck and courage they could kill one.

There were eight of them. Now I was close enough to hear their great teeth grinding. The old bull swept a half-melted snowbank aside with his tusks to get at the bushes underneath. The tusks were yellowed with age, curved as wind-bent trees, and as long as he was tall. The tip of one had been broken in some past battle. The females muttered and stamped as they fed, so that I felt the ground shuddering under my feet. They curled their snake-noses around bunches of grass and twigs, and fed themselves that way. Two small ones, last year's babies, tussled in a thawing mudhole.

It would be foolish to go closer. I took a deep breath. What I was seeing was magic, yet real. It was a thing few people had ever seen. Almost by itself, my hand went out before me, and in the air, my fingers traced the curve of tusk and grasping snake-nose, the great humps of brow and shoulders, the small, wise eye, the sweep of fur almost the color of Oooni's hair. Which colors would I mix? What words would I use to make another person feel the wonder? If only Uff were here with me to see this. If only I could sit by the fire to make pictures and tell it to someone. It was a thing that would never leave me. It would stay in my mind forever.

I glanced back at a steep-sided ravine that opened onto the meadow. Suddenly I saw a thing. If Uff were here, if there were other hunting-partner wolves, other hunters of the People—together, they could turn a mammut and drive it away from the herd. They could chase it into a narrow place like the ravine. Men with *keertas*, waiting on the cliffs could . . . My heart burned with the thought. *Wolves like Uff could make it possible to hunt the great mammut!*

Other wolves.

Perhaps sometime I could find another pup. Try again. Perhaps. Slowly I made my way back to Oooni's cave to gather my things.

CHAPTER 34

I would find my own cave and make my own life. I knew now that I could do this. Even without Uff, I could do it. I had new *sabas*, a new work blade, and a new stick for walking. Everything I needed was stowed in my pack-basket. Squatting at the edge of the stream, I filled my waterskin for the journey. Warm air moved up from the river valley. Patches of blue sky. Sun glittering on melting ice. What new thing would this day show me? Where would the night find me? I shrugged into my pack-basket and flexed my shoulders. It was a good day to travel.

Then I looked up and saw a wolf—a wolf I did not know and yet *did* know—streaking toward me. She squealed like two trees rubbing together in the wind. She knocked me to the ground with her great paws, slapping my face with her wet tongue. She rolled onto her back and showed me her belly. *Oh, Uff!* Then she leapt up, raced in a circle, and knocked me flat again. Together we danced and chased each other until we were breathless. Together we laughed and yipped our joy.

At last, panting, Uff sat down and gazed up at me. I crouched beside her, took her head between my hands, and put my forehead against hers. "I suppose you are hungry—is that what made you decide to come home, you miserable wolf?" I whispered to her. "If you had waited another day, I would have been gone from here."

Home. We were not home. We would never go back to the *immet* of the People. We had left one home to try to find another. But somehow, with my wolf beside me, anywhere in the world was home.

She was thinner. There was a half-healed slash on her cheek, patches of hair missing along her flanks that were not just from shedding her winter fur. But the lead wolf had not allowed the others to kill her. She was too young for him to have chosen her for his mate, but somehow he had favored her. "I think you have an admirer, pretty girl," I whispered to her. There was a new thing in her eyes. There was a story of her life that I did not know and she could never tell me.

But she was Uff, and she had come back to me.

"There is a thing I have yet to do," I told her. "Come, we will find our new home together—and then someday..." Did I dare to think such a thing? "I, yes, even I—the *tabat* one—will hunt and kill some great beast." My voice hushed to a whisper. "Even if there is no one else to tell of it, I will become a blood-hunter!"

With a last silent thank-you to Oooni, I picked up my new stick and my *keerta*. "We will go now," I said to Uff.

CHAPTER 35

She bounded in front of me as we headed still farther up along the Forbidden River. It was full of tumbled rocks, broken trees, and churning meltwater. The going was uphill, but not difficult. A hunter of the People would have trotted swiftly over the open ground, as a wolf trots for long spaces of time. I laughed wryly to myself. "Perhaps I am slow, but at least when we find game now, I will not miss," I said to Uff. She turned to look at me over her shoulder, then raced on ahead.

By sundown, I had missed five times: a fox, an old, crippled saiga, and three ptarmigan. But, in a flurry of feathers, I took down the fourth bird. We camped in a hollow above the rushing river. Uff looked at me with a question in her eyes after she had bolted her portion.

"What, you want more? We would have had the saiga if you'd pulled your head out of that marmot hole! Tomorrow we'll find something better," I told her.

The land changed. The going became steeper, harder. I searched the cliffs, looking for caves. I wouldn't need to fear attack from beasts in such a place. And if there were other Ice Men, unfriendly ones, perhaps I could defend myself. But Oooni had been a friend to me. Maybe I could find a way to be a friend to his people if there were any here.

On either side of me were gray walls with slopes of gravel and boulders at their feet. There were still a few patches of ice and hollow places filled with snow, but the new wind coming from the south had scoured most of it away. The sun was bright. There was the fresh scent of open earth. The world was coming alive again.

Uff ranged ahead. She thrust her face into every hole she found. Once she met with some small, fierce creature that sank its teeth into her muzzle. She yelped and let go of it.

Every now and then, she circled back to check on me. She touched my leg briefly with her nose. Then she moved off again. Over and over, I looked at my wolf and grinned. *I can't believe you have come back*. I wondered if her brothers had grown as big as she was now. Then I thought of myself. I was taller, stronger. I carried a *keerta*. I knew how to use it. "I think we have both changed," I whispered to her.

I came around a bend in the river. Stopped. Stared. Out of the cliffs on each side, gray stone thrust itself into an arch—a huge arch as high as the cliffs it grew out of. It spanned the river, which flowed under it, leaving a shelf of tumbled rock just wide enough to walk along. *Oh, Tal! An opening into another world!* The water under the arch swirled deep blue-green, the color of Suli's eyes.

My breath was gone out of me. I was dizzy. I could feel the breath of the river. *What would a new world smell like?* The living stream. A pebble beach. Gravel banks. Trees. A meadow curving back toward more cliffs. All smelling of the newness of spring—new, but familiar. The world on the other side of the arch looked the same as this one.

Was it the same?

I stood, silent, listening with my whole body. Uff was quiet, too. She came to my side and sat still, also listening. Nothing. Just this beautiful, powerful place. It pulled me forward. With Uff close at my heels, a step at a time, I passed beneath the arch. Swallows circled high overhead. They led us through, playing in the currents of the wind. I turned my head up as I walked. The stone arch soared above us. Green vines trailed down from it. More birds dove in and out of nests in hollows in the rock. The water rushed endlessly through the great opening.

We scrambled over boulders and pushed through a willow thicket. Then we were on the other side.

I glanced back the way we had come. Looked forward again, scanning every direction for danger in this new place. But nothing happened. All seemed the same: the river, the cliffs, the sky. Then Uff rushed after something in the bushes, and I saw a reddish-brown shape disappearing up the slope. Just a red deer come down for a drink.

Uff returned to me, panting, excited. "Sorry, Little Bah, next time I'll be ready." I shifted my *keerta* in my hand.

The sun moved higher in the sky. We kept walking. I had to turn my head up to see the tops of the cliffs on the far side of the river. Clusters of ferns grew out of crevices. The rock face was pocked with hollows. Some were big enough to shelter in if I could have climbed up to them.

On our side of the river, the land opened into a level valley, facing south. In summer it would be lush with grass. There were trees and more cliffs farther back from the river. Then, in a fissure in the cliff side, I saw what looked like a path leading upward. Twisted juniper bushes grew out of the rock.

I worked my way up through the trees. The path followed a rock ledge. It must have been used by ibex coming and going to the river, or people.... My heart raced. "Stay with me, Uff," I called softly. I don't know what made me follow the path, but I couldn't turn back. Something pulled me upward.

Uff scrambled ahead, her paws sending showers of gravel down the rock face below us. I made my slow way along the ledge behind her. We came to a place where the trail turned back on itself. I turned and drew in my breath. From here, the stone arch looked like a great mammut crossing the river! The sun shone on the valley below. It was sheltered from wind. A small herd of horses grazed on the fresh new grass. It was a sweet, rich place. So powerful.

Suddenly I thought, *Vida would like this.*

When at last I turned back to the path, nothing. No sleek wolf, no happy, waving tail. I looked behind me, ahead. Uff was nowhere to be seen.

Where was she? There were no trees here to hide her, nothing but rock and stunted juniper. I scanned the path once more. "Uff!" I called. Still nothing. I searched the slope above. Just cliffs, soaring up to the bright blue of the sky and far above, a kite spiraling. How had she disappeared like that?

"Uff!" Turning, I called again, louder this time. Nothing. This was impossible. There was nowhere to hide. "Uff!" Fear in my voice. Had something taken her? Were we in some magic place where a wolf could disappear in a blink of time?

"Uff!" My voice echoed from the gray cliffs. A hunter did not reveal himself so recklessly, but I didn't care. I couldn't lose her again. Once more I filled my lungs and called her name. "Uff!" My voice was almost a scream.

And she appeared. Out of the rock. No, out of a place, a hole, between two rocks. Her paws were muddy.

She came to me, waving her tail, happy. Then she turned as if to say, *Come see what I have found!* I realized there must be a hollow place in the rocks. Uff turned and looked at me over her shoulder. I stumbled after her.

At the back of an overhang, there was an opening. Not so big, but plenty big enough for a wolf—or a person . . . or some other creature. There was no sign of people, no footprints on the path, no mark of humans. With a hand on each side of the rock opening, I peered inside. It was very dark. Black. Silent. A current of dank air wafted out. It was like an ancient breath on my cheeks. Uff slipped past my legs.

"Wait!" I called to her. "*Nah*, you can't go in there! Something might be . . ." I didn't know what. But something. I grabbed a fistful of her fur. "Wait," I said again. She whined, nose working. She had caught a scent. She wanted to go back inside. I felt it, too. A pulling on my whole body, my spirit. The opening in the rock seemed to draw me into itself.

Perhaps this was a better cave than Oooni's small one. I called softly into the opening at first, then louder, an owl's call. "Hoo hoo hoooo!" My voice echoed back to me. There was space inside the cliff. A big space.

"I have to find a torch," I told Uff. Breathing hard, I scrambled back down the path to the place where the juniper bushes were growing. I searched among them, and at last found a length of dead wood with a good knot of root and yanked it free. I fumbled in my pack and opened my fire pouch. The ember of chaga fungus I carried glowed when I blew on it. I fed it dried stuff until I had a small blaze going. Then I added twigs until it was strong enough to catch the root. It crackled and smoked its sweet juniper scent. There was much pitch in the root that would blaze for a long time.

It was not easy to manage the torch with my *keerta* and my stick. But I could leave none of them behind. I felt for my work blade. Then I climbed back up, Uff close on my heels.

Panting now, I paused at the opening—a gaping black mouth. Then, holding the torch before me in one hand and dragging both my *keerta* and my stick in the other, I crawled inside. My wolf scrambled in eagerly after me.

CHAPTER 36

At first there was just a narrow shaft. The torchlight played along it, shadows flickering. Damp rock. Traces of small animals sheltering here. A few hazelnut shells. I remembered wriggling into the wolf's den long ago. Then the opening widened. Blackness. Space. I drew the air of the cave into my lungs. Cool, moist. I stood carefully and lifted the torch high above my head. Its wavering light spilled over rough walls that soared away into blackness. It was huge, this hole under the earth! It was a *world* inside the cliff.

The floor of the cave was smooth. I could stand, no, I could walk here! I tucked my stick under my arm. Then I grasped both my *keerta* and the torch in my right hand.

There was that faint odor. It seemed to be all around me. Uff whined softly. "I think you are a foolish wolf to follow me in here," I whispered to her. But she, too, was spellbound.

I made my way forward. Mud oozed between my toes. Uff went ahead of me now, the fur along her spine bristling. To my right, I saw a side passage. I must not lose my way. But there would be our tracks in the mud to follow back.

Uff's shadow was a great creature with long legs. Mine was also four-legged, a hulking thing. They danced weirdly beside us as we moved along.

I thought of Moc-Atu showing each animal's foolishness of the season in the dance of spring madness. I heard my own breathing. In. Out. In. Out.

I turned.

Teeth!

They loomed out of the dark: rows of great, white teeth, many times taller than myself, hanging down and rising up from the cave floor. My feet wouldn't move. There was a roaring in my ears, yet silence really. I had to tell myself to breathe, keep breathing. Silence. But no—a drip. A faint, slow, endless drip.

Drip.

Drip.

Drip.

And the strange smell. I could not run. It would eat me. Whatever it was, wherever it was, this fearsome thing would eat me. And I could not turn away from it.

The cave drew me deeper into itself. Uff pressed close to my legs. We were inside the teeth now. Uff sniffed a great, dripping fang. It didn't frighten her. I reached out a finger. It was cold and wet. Slick. My torchlight flickered on the surface. Uncountable tiny stars sparkled in the whiteness when the light moved. Shadows leapt across the walls. The teeth were not ivory. They were stone.

Uff was curious, excited. We moved on. The passage opened into a cavern with pale, gleaming walls. We were inside the beast. I held my torch this way, that way, this way again, lighting up the darkness. *Beautiful*. First the arch and now the cave. *Oh, Tal, such power!*

And then I saw a mammut.

Not a living mammut. It was the image, the spirit of a mammut—painted on the wall. The ground-shaking beast, just as I had seen them in the great meadow. Hulking shoulders, powerful snake-nose lifted high, deadly tusks curving.

And there—a hand—a human hand outlined in blood! And then many handprints together. These were the marks of shamans and hunters, like the marks that Sen and Apa had made on the wall of our *takka*. This was not real blood, it was paint blown through a hollow bone.

Someone has been here. A bead of sweat trickled down my spine. I glanced behind me, inhaled deeply again. I could smell something else now. Charcoal. Here and there on the floor of the cave were the remains of old fires. But people could not live here. The smoke from a cooking fire would drive them out. These must have been small fires for light.

Hesitantly, I reached out and touched a red line. It was covered by a film of stone. Had the ones before me been turned to stone? I looked again over my shoulder. Looming walls. A soaring roof of shining stone.

I felt the old ones somewhere in the shadows, beyond my torchlight.

I turned in a slow circle. There, on the far wall! More animals! Trickles of sweat fell between my shoulder blades. Uff's nose touched my leg. "They're not real," I whispered to her, trying to calm myself. But they were—so real. A wall of cave lions, stalking. A big female spitting at her mate. The lions seemed alive. In the flickering light, they moved in the sinewy way of cats.

Tears ran down my face. I sank to my knees before the paintings. These were such pictures as I had seen when I was trapped under the snow. Alive but not alive. Real but not real. Lines with magic in them.

Uff was sniffing the floor and whining. I looked down.

Bones. Leg bones. A shoulder blade. A scattering of large and small bones. But not human. I crouched lower to study them. Some were glazed with the same ice stone. It did not melt when I touched it with my fingers. But it had frozen the bones to the floor of the cave. And tracks. Great wide pads—the tracks of the hind feet looking almost human. Deep furrows left by five terrible claws. Claw marks on some of the paintings. Cave bear. But the tracks were not fresh. They too had been turned to stone.

I glanced around quickly. Tens and tens and tens of bones. Many strange pits in the floor. Had bears scraped out these hollows for winter beds? A huge skull. Bear. Many skulls. Bears came here. And died here.

My torch sputtered. Ash had collected on the end. I tapped it against the stone wall. The ash fell away, and it flared bright again.

Go! But I could not.

"It's alright," I whispered to Uff. My voice was strange in my ears. I felt her nose touch my leg again. The fur along her spine was raised. We went on.

The walls narrowed, changing to reds and oranges like the colors that swirl sometimes in the northern sky. The passage narrowed, turned back on itself. The gut of the stone creature. My breathing seemed to echo from the walls. Still I could not go back. There, on a hanging tooth of stone, the image of an owl. Owls hunted the night. They could see in darkness. I thought of Moc-Atu, with his man-owl stick and his strange eyes. Could the old shaman see where I was now?

Suddenly the cavern opened again to a wall of snorting horses. Beside the horses, two rhinos fought while others paced in a row. Once I had watched rhinos fight like this far out on the grassland. I had seen a cloud of dust, the flash of their eyes, and heard the snort and thud as they came together.

The passage narrowed even more. And then there was a gaping pit at my feet. I almost stepped into it.

My way was blocked by a gullet of blackness. With the tip of my stick, I felt for the opposite rim. I could just reach it. Sen might have jumped across. How deep? I held out my torch, but could not see the bottom. On the far side, I made out a ledge. That was all. I could go no farther.

Then there was a low growl. My heart crashed against my ribs—just Uff rumbling deep in her throat. I moved the torch slowly. Shadows lurched on the stone walls and rock over our heads. She was sniffing something at my feet. More tracks. I bent to see. Cave bear again, but different. These did not shine in the light. I touched one. It was not coated in stone ice. The floor of the cave was soft clay here, the track pressed into it.

Fresh tracks from a bear that was hot and alive. My mouth went dry. I was afraid to move. But surely it was too late in the season for a bear to be here in the cave?

I tried to still my breathing, to listen. . . . I opened my mouth, sniffed, trying to scent anything, tried even with my skin to feel movement in the air. Nothing.

I began backtracking. It was not hard to follow my own trail: the clear print of my right foot, the muddled shape left by the bad one, the pockmarks of stick and *keerta* shaft, the occasional smudge of my torch on the wall. Uff's tracks wandered some, but they were there, too. Through the gut, the great painted belly with the horses and lions. Ahead was the narrow shaft where we had entered. I could see a slant of sunlight now, smell fresh air.

We had just passed back through the great stone teeth when the cave exploded into roaring—all around, echoing, battering us with sound.

Rocks and gravel grinding, spewing, hitting my skin.

Claws scrambling. A huge body plunging toward us in the dark. Uff roared too, in fury and terror. Frantically, I swept the torch before me, behind, left, right.

There! The glitter of eyes, flash of teeth, gaping mouth making that sound—the bear stood on its hind legs, twice the height of a man. The sliver of daylight behind it winked out. It blocked the cave entrance.

I turned and stumbled back into the mouth of the stone beast, the bear roaring after me. The pit lay ahead. I wavered. Trapped.

I had two choices: death or death.

The pit.

The bear.

My mind wandered sideways. There had to be something.

The pit was not wide, but I could not leap across it. There had to be another way. My *keerta*? Lay it across? No—not strong enough. My stick? Would it reach?

Behind me, the bear reared to its full height again. Uff snaked at it—furious, crazed. "*NAH!*" I screamed at her. She would not listen. But she gave me time. Again and again, she lunged at the bear, writhing away as it slapped at her with its great paws. The roaring filled my ears, my body. My teeth clenched. Light and shadow leaping, plunging. A crevice in the wall. I jammed the butt of my torch into it. The fire might keep the bear back a few heartbeats longer.

If there was any way to save Uff, I would need my *keerta*. Carefully, I tossed it over onto the ledge. It slid back toward the pit, then came to rest against a rock. I crouched and reached for the opposite rim with the tip of my stick. *Tal, make it reach!* It slipped and banged down against stone in the darkness below. I tried again. And again, finally hitting a notch between two rocks.

I lowered my body into the blackness. I hung for a moment, felt pain where my arm had been broken. I gritted my teeth. Breathed. *Not far, just one hand over the other, and one more . . .* I pulled myself across to the opposite ledge.

Grabbing my *keerta*, I stood. There was barely room on the ledge to brace my feet and draw my arm back. Uff was between me and the bear. There was no way to save her. But then, she moved sideways. I saw where the *keerta* would hit the bear's heart.

I threw.

The bear staggered, raged. My *keerta* had pierced its chest.

It slammed a paw into my wolf's side and flung her away, back into the dark. Then the beast fell forward. Crashed against the torch, sending the knot of juniper end over end into the pit. The light flared down. A pause. Faint splash and hiss. Then blackness.

Silence.

Blackness and silence.

It was as if my eyes and ears were gone. Something whimpered. Not my wolf—it was me. I took a shaky breath.

"Uff!"

Nothing.

She couldn't be alive. She could not be battered like that and live.

I was frozen.

But all things try to live.

I knelt, feeling for the edge. There. The tip of my stick jammed between the two rocks. If it came loose, I might as well leap into the pit after it. My hands were slippery with sweat. I dried them on the front of my *anooka*. Very carefully, I grasped the stick and lowered myself off the ledge.

My muscles shook. Pain stabbed my arm. One hand. The next. Hanging in blackness. Suddenly, my weak hand slipped. I clung for a moment by the other. A vision came into my mind of the beasts on the walls of the cave. Their life. Their power.

I made the weak hand grasp the stick again. Pain seared my bones. I reached out once more and grabbed with the strong hand. I scrabbled with my good foot, found a jutting rock, and dragged myself out.

I did not move for a very long time, huddled on the cave floor, shaking.

Then I heard something coming toward me in the dark. I fumbled for my blade. Pulled it from its sheath. The scrambling of claws on stone.

Something cold and wet against my hand. I flinched back, ready to strike blindly. Then I heard her whimper. "Oh, Uff!"

Cradling her against my chest, I buried my face in her

thick fur. I felt her all over. She was bleeding from her shoulder, but she was alive.

I crawled a safer distance from the pit and pulled myself upright. I heard Uff sniffing, moved a few steps, and nearly fell over the great bulk of the bear. Already the body under the dense fur was cooling and stiffening. I had killed it. I felt my *keerta* sticking out from the bear's chest and wrenched it free.

In the blackness, I found Uff again. She trembled. How badly was she hurt? We needed to get out. Now.

"You can see with your nose," I said, taking hold of her tail. My voice cracked like an old man's. I took a deep breath. "You must lead us out now."

CHAPTER 37

The light was blinding.

I pulled myself out through the opening behind Uff and stood up. I raised my *keerta* to the sky. "*Tal*, see me!" I cried. My voice echoed from the cliffs. "I am a blood-hunter of the People. I am a man!" Tears streamed down my face. I was not ashamed. I let them flow.

Crouching now, I tended Uff's wound as best I could. She had lain down as soon as she came out of the cave. She whimpered as I gently pulled aside the thick fur, matted with blood, to see where the bear had struck her. I sucked in my breath. I could see white bone under the torn muscle and seeping blood.

I had to stop the bleeding. Removing my *anooka*, I peeled off my *desu* and bound it over my wolf's shoulder.

I shrugged my pack on again. Then I hoisted her across my shoulders and, with *keerta* and stick in my left hand, gripping her legs with my right, I got to my feet. She cried out once, but did not—could not—struggle. She let me carry her like killed game. But she was not dead.

It was too long a walk back to Oooni's cave. She could bleed to death before I got her there. *Tal* had brought me this far. "*Tal*," I shouted now. "Show me!"

There had to be a sheltered place nearby. I stumbled down the path under the cliff face, back to the river, and turned upstream once more. *Hurry*. I passed a place where the land sloped down from the high country. I could see a path worn by hooves. A skull with antlers gnawed away by the small things that chew antler. A reindeer crossing.

I could build a brush *takka* beside the river, but the wind was whistling down from the cliffs. The night would be cold, and there could be other bears. On each side of me now, the cliffs rose again. *Tal, please! If you have ever been with me at all, hear me now! She will die if I don't find a place soon!*

I saw several hollows high up in the sheer walls, but I could not get to them. Not carrying a wolf on my shoulders. The strip of sand at my feet grew narrower. I would have to go back.

But then—I came around a pile of boulders and saw ahead a wide ledge overlooking the river. The sun shone onto it. It was higher than a man's head far back under the cliff. Below the great shelf of rock was a rough slope.

There was a path.

I was panting hard when at last I reached the wide ledge. I laid Uff gently on her side. Stroked her ears. Her eyes were open, staring at nothing. *Don't go away from me—please, no*. Warily I sniffed the air, searching for beasts, any sign of people. A scattering of flint chips. Several fire pits. But gazing carefully into the shadows, I saw no sign of anything living there now.

Water. I scrambled back down to the river, filled my cooking *das*, and let Uff drink. Her tongue pulled at the water desperately. Then she laid her head back down. Closed her eyes.

You cannot die. Please. No.

I used the rest of the water to wash the blood from Uff's wound. The bleeding had slowed. I threaded a needle with the finest length of sinew I could find. Then, taking the skin between my fingers, I sewed it closed, one stitch at a time, as I had seen Moc-Atu do for my brother. She seemed not to feel it. *See and know.* I caught my breath. Was that what the shaman had meant? Not to see and know my wrongdoing, but simply to learn his healing magic?

I ran my fingers over Uff's long muzzle. She was panting. "Little Bah, please live," I whispered to her. Then I gathered wood for a fire. I made broth and tried to make her drink, but her jaws were clenched. *Do not die.*

There had to be something else I could do. What?

The heart of her enemy. But that was still in the beast—in the cave. *The heart of her enemy.* The words came again, hissing like a cold wind on my neck. *I cannot*, I thought wildly. *Tal, do not make me. I cannot go back in there!*

But the voice sighed. *You will have to. It is strong magic. You need strong magic now. There is no other way if you want to save her.* I wrapped my head in my arms. I could not think anymore.

The sun would set soon. I gazed around. This place, this huge open cave in the cliff, was big enough for an entire *immet* of people to live. People had lived here once before. Oooni's people? Why had they left? There was water and wood. One could have a fire without choking on the smoke. Not far away was the crossing where the reindeer passed. The great ledge would be shelter from wind, storm, and beasts.

Tal had heard me, had brought me to this place when I needed it most. *Thank you.* I stroked Uff's head gently. She moaned. "You saved me, Little Bah," I said softly. "I will not let you die."

I knew now what I had to do. Alone this time, I must go back into the cave. I must bring Uff the flesh of her enemy's heart. *It is strong magic.* In the dark of that cold, windy night, my father had done this for Sen. My brother had lived. I must do the same for my wolf.

What if there was another bear? A mate? My gut quivered. But something had happened to me inside the cave. I was still myself, Kai—yet I was someone new.

I hobbled down to the river, stripped off my clothing, and plunged into the icy water. I let it wash away the blood and sweat of the battle with the bear, the salt of the tears from my face. I came out again and dried myself with my *anooka.* In the last rays of the sun, I saw my reflection in a pool of water.

There were the same glinting eyes, the same dark

hair—cut short in the front now, the same nose, mouth, cheekbones, but all somehow leaner. Harder. Then I saw something strange—a flicker of my brother's face in my own. How could that be? We were not alike—but there it was.

Sen. Suddenly I yearned to see him, to tell him each thing that had happened to Uff and me. I wanted to laugh with him. I wanted to show my brother how Uff could track game, chase an animal back to me, help me kill it. I wanted to show him the *keerta* I had made, that I could hunt with it. To play my *osa* for him. He would not mock me now, but would hear the strength and trueness of the notes. The hate and the misery were gone.

And my father—suddenly I knew that he missed me, cared for me as much as for the others. I wanted to ask him to teach me how to make better *keerta* points. Had Suli talked him into making a *keerta* for her? How big was Bu now? And Ama. Was she grieving? It would be so good to see the joy in her eyes when she knew that I lived.

Vida...

I knew then that I would go back to the *immet*. I would show my family and my people who I was—that I was not *tabat*. I saw all this, in that moment, in my face in the river. I was the same, but so very different.

And in the morning, I would bring Uff the heart of her enemy.

Through the night, I lay beside my wolf. I kept one hand on her chest, feeling the faint thudding of her heart and the rise and fall of her breath. I fingered the sacred pouch at my throat, wondering if I would need the powdered bloodstone to help her to the spirit world when morning came. The night grew cold. At last, I slept. I dreamed of lions and leopards, hyenas, rhinos, bears, horses—all the painted beasts of the cave. In my dreaming they were alive. But they were not fearful. They trumpeted and snarled. They sang of the lush green and the red blood of their feasting, the hot stink of their spoor. Life. Death. *Tal.*

At daybreak, I saw that a late snow had fallen.

Uff was alive. She licked my hand but could not raise her head. I dribbled water into the side of her mouth as if she were a pup again. Then I built up the fire so that it would blaze for some time. "There is a thing I must do," I told her. "You're safe here by the fire."

With four new torches stuffed into my pack, I went back to the great cave. My heart hammered like stone on wood as I lit the first. "*Tal*, keep me," I whispered aloud. Then I crawled back inside the black hole.

I missed Uff's eyes and nose. With every step, I was ready to run or use my *keerta*. But all was silent. When I could barely make out the light from the cave opening, I found a crevice in the floor, jammed the butt of my first torch into it, and lit another. Lighting new torches as I went, I made my way to where the bear lay.

I found the creature, cold and stiff. The hide was too precious a thing to leave. Wedging my last torch into a gap, I took out my work blade. I used my stick to lever the huge bulk of the animal as I worked. It took all my strength to strip and slash away the skin. When, at last, it was done, I rolled it into a bundle and tied it with twine.

With blade and hammerstone, I took two of the incisor teeth. I put them into my carrying pouch. Then I hacked the giant head from the body. This was the hardest. I placed it reverently on a great flat rock. It had been a fearsome enemy. Taking a bit of dried sweet herb from my sacred pouch, I burned it for the bear's honor. "You have made me a blood-hunter of the People," I whispered. "I thank you for that."

While the smoke curled into the shadows overhead, I brought out my *osa* and played for the spirit of the bear. The notes were true and sure. The cave hummed—as Oooni had hummed. I closed my eyes, feeling it. Feeling my grandfather beside me. At last, my heart song.

Then I opened them again. Searched the cave wall. Suddenly I saw an eye and the shape of a bear's brow in the stone. A strange magic happened where the rock curved inward. The shadow became the bulge of the bear's shoulders. Did the spirit of the bear want to come out of the rock? Was this how *Tal* had made the beasts? Could they pass through stone from that place of creation? I thought again of the pictures I had seen when I was dying under the snow.

I must make my own image here of the bear. For Uff.

But I was no shaman.

Or was I? *Wolfboy. Wolf's Boy. Wolfman. Manwolf.*

There was a hollowed stone nearby. It held traces of color. Someone had used it before. Quickly I took some of the charcoal from the old fire pits, crushed it, and mixed it with the water and grease I had brought. I looked carefully at the bear's head in the flickering torchlight, closed my eyes, and let the spirit of it come into my mind. Fierce. Bellowing. Strong. I asked the spirit of the old shamans who had been here before me to come into my heart. I had scratched a few pictures in the dirt for Suli. I had finished the aurochs bull for Moc-Atu, and drawn the horses for Oooni, but I had never done anything like this before. The old painters must work through me.

"For Uff," I whispered fiercely. Then, with one long line, I made the shape of the bear on the cave wall. The brow, the hulking shoulders—so. I added the eye. The small ears—here and here...

When the outline was finished, I rubbed my paint onto the rock to make the shaggy fur. The torchlight danced. The image of the bear breathed with life. I shivered.

Now I shook the bloodstone powder from my pouch and mixed it with water. I had no other hollow bone, so, covering up the finger holes, I used my *osa.* I drew in a mouthful of paint. Then I placed my right hand on the wall of the cave, beside the bear, and sprayed the mixture around it.

When I took my hand from the wall, it left a white shadow. *The hand that killed the bear.* I must get back to Uff, but for just a moment, I studied what I had done. My heart swelled.

My bear was a fitting companion to the other beasts who lived on the walls of this cave.

This is what *Tal* had given me to do. This, and the healing work of a shaman. I had found the strength that was in me through the friendship of a yellow wolf. She was my power. All of this Moc-Atu had seen.

Rhar was not here, so I would do it myself. Quickly I sang the prayer to *Tal*, the prayer of life and death. The walls of the cave echoed my voice. *You are the killer of the bear that would have killed you and your wolf-friend*. . . . Then, dipping my fingers in the bear's blood, I lifted them to my brow and made the mark of a blood-hunter. "You, who have been named Kai, are now a blood-hunter of the People. Henceforth, you are no longer Kai."

But Kai is part of who made me what I am now. I am stronger for having been so weak. Kai is in me.

"I am Kai-Atu, the wolf pup who is changed."

The last thing. I hacked through the great rib cage of the dead bear, cut out the heart, and put it into my carrying-pouch. It was a pity there was no one else here to share the bounty of meat. I slashed off enough for a few days. Shaking with the effort, I lifted the huge hide onto my shoulders. I looked back the way I had come, where my torches still sputtered. They were suns of light in the blackness. They showed the way out. Then, grunting with each step, I went back to the great ledge in the cliff.

Uff did not move when I returned. She was very weak, but I saw her throat move as I dribbled the heart broth between her lips. That night was even colder, with more snow falling. The world has a way of taking forward and backward steps into springtime. But we did not feel it. I pulled the skin of the bear, with its long, dense fur, around both of us. Before I closed my eyes, I hung a piece of sinew around Uff's neck strung with half of the bear's claws and one of the two teeth I had taken. The rest I kept for myself to hang beside Oooni's aurochs tooth.

"Little Bah, I think you are different from other wolves as I am different from other people," I whispered to her. She did not move or open her eyes, but her chest still rose and fell. My throat closed. I could not say more.

~

In the morning, the sun filled the great cave on the ledge. I threw back the bearskin. Uff raised her head and gazed at me. She thumped her tail. Life burned in her amber eyes.

AUTHOR'S NOTE

I think it is important to say here that Uff is *not* a wolf, she is an early dog. Because Kai has never known them as any other creature, he calls her a wolf, but he knows she is something different and new. Even though they are genetically close, a dog is not a wolf. A dog has a place at man's side, but a wolf is meant to hunt and roam freely over vast territories. Take joy in the wolf cousin by your side!

WORDS OF KAI'S PEOPLE

ah-bah: female baby doll

ama: mother

anooka: double-layered reindeer-skin parka similar to those worn by the Inuit

apa: father

apa-da: grandfather

ayee: exclamation of distress

bah: female child too young to be counted on to outlive infancy and therefore not yet given a name

bol: tree, the name Kai's brother is given in childhood

bu: male child too young to be counted on to outlive infancy and therefore not yet given a name

das: eating, drinking, or cooking vessel, carved from wood or fashioned from bark

desu: rabbit-skin vest or undershirt

eya: yes

hahk: stone axe

immet: village of the people

imnos: friends; the yellow wolf pack that has come to live near the People has a similar social structure to humans, and is beginning to make the evolutionary leap into becoming dogs

jahs: belt

kai: pup

kai-atu: pup who is changed

kanees: reindeer-skin pants or leggings

keerta: spear

kep: door or covering of stiff hide

lupta: gray wolf pack, which remains wild

moc-atu: crazy one who is changed

mora: old-man mushroom

nah: no

nnnnn-gata: luck; the hunter's prayer

osa: bone flute made from the hollow wing bone of a large bird

saba: winter boot

sen: steady one, the name Kai's brother has earned after killing the aurochs bull

suli: little owl

tabat: cursed, unlucky

takka: reindeer-skin hut

Tal: God, creator, spirit of life

umee: mitten

WORDS OF OOONI'S PEOPLE

mehu: friend

oooni-alu-kas-pah-vard-ahhh: fire-haired traveler with big hands, heart, and voice

ummmb: good

ACKNOWLEDGMENTS

Thanks are deserved by many: First and foremost, my dear husband, Fred, who brings me coffee each morning and makes sure I have time for my writing; our daughters, Fern and Spring, who listen patiently to their mother's ramblings and who make wise suggestions; the divine Patti Gauch, her Heart of the Novel Workshop, and the Heartbeaters group; Rich and Sandra Wallace and their Writing for Boys Workshop, both given through the Highlights Foundation; Kent Brown, for making those good things happen for so many writers; the Rochester (New York) Area Children's Writers and Illustrators group; my Scribblers and Wellsboro, Pennsylvania, critique groups; three insightful young readers: Bennett Sprague, Carson Grover, and Michael Hixon; and Heath Ward, who helped with IT support so I could work on line edits while aboard ship in the Caribbean. Thanks to Brian Fagan for advice on Ice Age mammals and his imaginative description of a Cro Magnon/Neanderthal encounter in his book *Cro Magnon,* which inspired Kai's first encounter with the Ice Men. Thanks to the late Jean Craighead George for endless inspiration and for kindly pointing me toward the Wolf Conservation Center when I asked where I could meet and observe wolves in New York State.

A very special thank-you goes to Mark Derr, author of *How the Dog Became the Dog*, who generously answered my questions at length. When I asked where my story should take place, he said it could have happened many places at different times in history: Europe, the Middle East, China . . . But when he mentioned that it could have happened in France, where the fossilized footprints of a boy and a canine, walking side by side, were discovered in 1994 in Chauvet Cave, chills ran up my spine. I knew I had found both my setting and story. My thanks go also to the discoverers of Chauvet Cave and the French government, who made sure it was never opened to the public and prevented the ensuing damage to the priceless art that would have caused. It was enough for me to climb to the entrance and absorb Kai's world as it is today.

Thank you to my agent, Brianne Johnson, for her belief and bubbling enthusiasm.

Thank you to my editor, Tracey Keevan, for drawing more from me than I knew was possible, with such a light touch, and for knowing exactly what a story needs.

Easton Public Library
WITHDRAWN
AUG 03 2016

Another AIT computer tool is FLUENT, which allows a user to conduct computer searches of documents in a number of foreign languages—including Chinese, Korean, Portuguese, Russian, Serbo-Croatian, and Ukrainian. An analyst can enter English words into the search field and receive relevant foreign-language documents in response. The system then translates the document into English and gives the analyst the option of sending it on to a human translator for more precision.[22]

In-Q-Tel is a nonprofit venture-capital firm that the CIA created in late 1999 and gave $28.5 million in agency funds. It is a legacy of Ruth David, who has recalled that the agency was accustomed to working with large defense contractors but not with the newer, smaller firms involved in information technology innovation. In 2000, In-Q-Tel heard from about 500 vendors who proposed projects that they believed would benefit the agency. Twelve development projects were actually funded.[23]

One In-Q-Tel–assisted project involved a commercial search engine named NetOwl, developed by SRA International in Fairfax, Virginia. NetOwl uses natural-language processing in place of keywords to locate information, and can deduce that a word is a name, an organization, or a place. In-Q-Tel funding has permitted SRA to increase the power of NetOwl—allowing it to identify events and relationships and create structured data from unstructured text. According to SRA's vice-president, Hatte Blejer, it could search the Internet to provide an answer to a question such as "Which high-tech companies were established in northern Virginia last year?"[24]

In-Q-Tel funding was also instrumental in allowing companies to develop the Presidential Intelligence Briefing System (PIDS), which is used to produce the President's Daily Brief (PDB) that only sixteen senior government officials are permitted to read. Previously, CIA analysts had to shuffle hundreds of intelligence cables every day to produce the PDB. The PIDS brings the cables into a Lotus Notes database, performs a variety of search and analysis functions, and then places the brief on a notebook computer. According to Lou Clark, a program manager at In-Q-Tel, PIDS delivers briefs that are more timely because information can easily be added up to the last minute.[25]

A third In-Q-Tel investment may make it easier for the CIA to cover its tracks when collecting information off the Internet. The investment is intended to enhance a piece of software called Triangle Boy, which is produced by SafeWeb of Oakland, California. The commercial version of Triangle Boy allows users who want to examine a website without being detected to go to SafeWeb's website, which acts an intermediary. Anyone monitoring the user's activity would see the traffic between the user and SafeWeb, but not between SafeWeb and the user's ultimate destination. What interested the CIA was the ability of Triangle Boy to permit users to go to any number of innocuous addresses before going on to the actual site of interest. "We want to operate anywhere on the Internet in a way that no one knows the CIA is looking at them," according to a senior CIA official.[26]

SafeWeb also has suggested that the CIA could use the same technology to allow its officers and assets in the field to communicate securely with Langley. Such an application may be part of the CIA's plan, as described by George Tenet, "to take modern Web-based technology and apply it to our business relentlessly."[27]

As another part of the reorganization, most of the responsibilities of the Clandestine Information Technology Office, the joint DS&T-operations directorate office, have been reassigned to the newly created Directorate of Operations Information Operations Center—a center that at one point was going to be assigned to the DS&T. The technical operations element of the CITO was transferred to the DS&T Office of Technical Collection.[28]

The plan to revitalize R&D has resulted in two organizational changes. A chief scientist "will encourage collaboration among the top scientists, engineers, and technologists from across the Intelligence Community, private industry, and academia."[29]

In addition, the Office of Research and Development has been resurrected under a new name—the Office of Advanced Technologies and Programs (ATP). ATP is responsible for overseeing the transfer of new technologies from the drawing board and putting them into operational use. It is to "focus R&D on the CIA's most difficult problems and core mission."[30]

GLORY DAYS

Over the almost forty years of its existence the Directorate of Science and Technology has made an enormous contribution to U.S. intelligence capabilities and national security.

Its development of collection systems, as well as its assorted collection and analysis activities, proved vital to the assessment of Soviet strategic capabilities and intentions during the Cold War. With key assistance from its contractors, the directorate developed and deployed the HEXAGON (KH-9), RHYOLITE, and KENNAN (KH-11) systems and their successors. Each of those systems represented a quantum leap in U.S. intelligence capabilities.

The directorate also guided the development of the A-12/OXCART program. Although that program had a short life, without it there would have been no Air Force SR-71 aircraft, which operated for over two decades and provided valuable intelligence to U.S. national security officials. The agency's efforts in the collection of telemetry intelligence, both from space and ground platforms, were vital to understanding Soviet missile capabilities during some of the darkest days of the Cold War.

Certainly there were missteps—attempting to turn cats into microphones and recruiting psychics are two notable examples. Undoubtedly there were others. But such cases are insignificant compared with the overall accomplishments of the directorate.

The winding down of the Cold War and the emergence of a new world environment have not eliminated the value of the DS&T's contributions. Although the successors to RHYOLITE and the KH-11 are today formally assets of the NRO, they are unmistakably products of the Directorate of Science and Technology. Included are the three advanced KH-11 satellites in orbit, each with greater resolution, area coverage capability, and nighttime capability than those of the first generation. The upgraded version of the MAGNUM/ORION SIGINT satellite, which Bob Kohler fought so hard for and which was temporarily canceled, eventually made it back into the budget and was first launched into its geosynchronous orbit in 1995. Those SIGINT satellites also possess some of the relay capabilities intended to be part of the KODIAK system.

In addition, a number of scientific advances that emerged from the directorate, including its research and development office, not only have augmented U.S. intelligence capabilities but also have aided the work of those outside the national security establishment, including the medical community. Lithium batteries for pacemakers and automatic change recognition applied to the detection of breast cancer are two prominent examples.

It is important to note, both for the sake of history and in charting the directorate's future, that such successes were not simply the result of the directorate carrying out its assigned duties, with the full support of the rest of the agency and intelligence community. Nor were they the result of a cautious, incremental approach.

One element of success was the outside pressure by far-sighted scientists such as James Killian and Edwin Land to develop the agency's scientific capabilities. They were the prime movers in establishing first the Directorate of Research and then the Directorate of Science and Technology.

Another element was the willingness of managers to fight for roles and programs that they believed vital to national security, or to oppose programs they considered useless—even if that meant bureaucratic bloodshed. Had Bud Wheelon not passionately battled Brockway McMillan and the NRO, there would have been no HEXAGON or RHYOLITE. Carl Duckett's lobbying to oppose the Secretary of Defense's choice of FROG was one factor in ensuring that the first KH-11 was launched in 1976 and not 1986.

The DS&T's achievements also required a collection of individuals with advanced technical skills and a sense of adventure—some willing to search for new technical solutions to problems and possibly fail, others willing to man primitive outposts in the Iranian mountains in order to uncover Soviet missile secrets. Leslie Dirks and Lloyd Lauderdale helped bring into being programs that Wheelon and Duckett conceived and fought for.

Another element of success was having an organization that sought to fill important gaps in U.S. collection and analysis capabilities. The DS&T did not try to duplicate what the National Security Agency was doing with regard to COMINT collection, but it did come up with novel ways to provide information that NSA or its military subsidiaries were not collecting—either because of their priorities or their technical approaches to collection problems. As a result, it was the CIA that developed the first telemetry intercept satellite and that deployed personnel to Iran to monitor telemetry from the TACKSMAN sites. Much of the CIA's success resulted from identifying important gaps or shortcomings in other organizations' programs and seeking to fill them.

The directorate's connection to intelligence production—strongest when the agency's nuclear and missile intelligence analysts were part of the directorate, but still strong after their transfer to the intelligence directorate—also helped produce success. The link between satellite developers and analysts that existed at CIA but not at the Air Force Office of Special Projects helped guide the developers' work and motivate them to develop new capabilities that would solve old intelligence problems.

Of course, one factor underlying much of these gains was the presence of a major and very apparent enemy. Despite all the problems that the Soviet political and economic systems imposed on the nation, the USSR was still a formidable military threat—capable of deploying thousands of ICBM warheads and a massive army that could have, at the very least, destroyed Western Europe and the United States as modern civilizations. That threat helped attract many of the best and brightest to service in the CIA.

In addition, during much of the Cold War, CIA science and technology operated at the cutting edge, substantially in advance of what was being done in either the private sector or other parts of the government. For many who liked tough challenges, the CIA was an exciting place to be.

ROAD TO RECOVERY?

How the DS&T will meet the challenges of the future is a chapter of its history yet to be written. It will never be the bureaucratic empire that it was in 1972. Nor should it be. Clearly it is a vastly different world from 1972. The demise of the Soviet Union, the concern about transnational threats including terrorism and the proliferation of weapons of mass destruction to rogue states (with their sophisticated secret police and denial and deception programs), the shift of the development of cutting-edge technologies to the private sector, the deployment of high-resolution commercial imagery satellites, and the shift in the volume and means of international communication mean that priorities and targets have shifted. The volume of information has also increased dramatically, making it harder to find useful information among the flood of data. New collection and processing capabilities have been developed, but much work still needs to be done to enhance collection, processing, and analytical capabilities.

It is clear that the directorate should continue to devote significant attention to how to employ information technology to ease the burden on intelligence analysts. In an April 1999 speech to a technology conference in Raleigh-Durham, North Carolina, Basil Scott, a senior DS&T official, addressed both subjects. He enumerated a number of factors that made it harder to monitor foreign communications—including the spread of fiber-optic systems, the explosion of cellular phones, and encryption. At the same time, he suggested how information technology could be used to help analysts identify biological and chemical weapon activities, although information indicating such activities may be buried in a mass of data. Scott discussed an assortment of data-mining and data-retrieval techniques that could be employed, including clustering techniques that enable analysts to mine the most useful data sets first, link analysis to establish relationships, time-series analysis to identify time trends, and visualization—which lets analysts see "non-traditional presentations of data" that "can help [them] deal with large and complex data sets."[31]

Exploiting information technology will undoubtedly be a key activity for the directorate, but that should not be its only reason for being. Indeed, if the only significant directorate activities were to be information technology and support to clandestine human intelligence operations, there would be little reason for it to exist as a separate directorate—for the offices involved could be placed comfortably in the intelligence and operations directorates.

But outside those activities there remain many potential challenges. Although analysts have a flood of information to deal with, there can also be a paucity of information concerning topics of crucial importance—including foreign weapons of mass destruction programs and terrorism.

As long as the Office of Technical Collection and the Office of Development and Engineering remain part of the directorate, it retains the potential to make a significant contribution to the technical collection of intelligence. With nations adopting increasingly sophisticated denial and deception strategies to foil collection of information by U.S. imagery and signals intelligence satellites, OTC development of emplaced sensor systems to detect nuclear, chemical, and biological weapons activity and OTC participation in the Special Collection Service may prove to be among the directorate's most productive activities.

As previously noted, the Office of Development and Engineering, particularly as a result of the NRO restructuring, serves as a funnel for CIA personnel into the NRO rather than as a separate program element of the reconnaissance office. But the OD&E can ensure that some of the advantages that resulted from the directorate's dual identity as the NRO's Program B not be lost. The office recruited people from the Directorate of Intelligence, particularly the Office of Scientific and Weapons Research; this influx of personnel helped ensure that those developing reconnaissance satellites did not lose touch with the requirements of the analysts. In 1999, former OD&E director Robert Kohler said that the office felt like an "outcast," with the connection to the rest of the agency being a tenuous one. If the CIA were to back away from the OD&E and the NRO, it would be a "huge loss" to the reconnaissance effort, according to Kohler.[32] Likewise, Gordon Oehler, former director of the Non-Proliferation

Center, has complained that "the centralization of the . . . NRO . . . , where the only major pot of development money remains, removed many of the CIA's best technologists from day-to-day contact with operators and analysts in the rest of the CIA."[33] To reverse or limit such disengagement will require leadership from the top of the directorate.

Another factor in determining the extent to which the directorate prospers in the next decade is whether it continues to identify areas where the activities of other CIA and intelligence community components are deficient and moves to fill those gaps. As already noted, the directorate did not rise to empire status by attempting to duplicate what other agencies or CIA components did well.

Of course, people are another vital element in any future directorate successes. Over the almost forty years since it was created, the directorate has employed exceptional managers and scientists—as demonstrated by the directorate personnel named as CIA trailblazers in 1997, including the first four chiefs of the DS&T (Wheelon, Duckett, Dirks, and Hineman) as well as analysts, scientists, and technical service personnel. Recruiting and retaining such people today—when the technological frontier is often found in Silicon Valley and when corporate salaries far exceed government compensation—are far more difficult tasks than in the past.

It will be up to the leadership of the agency and directorate to ensure that the DS&T's mission involves more than helping analysts sort through data, as well as to make talented individuals realize that there are challenges to be met in the directorate that cannot be matched elsewhere. Robert Kohler does see some hope for the directorate. In early 2001, he noted that Joanne Isham was "trying very hard" and boosting morale, and George Tenet seemed to be listening to her. Kohler was "moderately encouraged."[34] It is hoped that in the succeeding years, the reasons to be encouraged will increase, and the next set of wizards will be up to the challenges that will face them.

APPENDIX 1
DS&T Components, 1963–2001

(Items in bold type indicate offices established the previous year)

January 1, 1963	**Office of Special Activities** **Office of Research and Development** **Office of ELINT**
January 1, 1964	Office of Special Activities Office of Research and Development Office of ELINT **Office of Computer Services** **Office of Scientific Intelligence** **Foreign Missile and Space Analysis Center**
January 1, 1966	Office of Special Activities Office of Research and Development Office of ELINT Office of Computer Services Office of Scientific Intelligence **Office of Special Projects** Foreign Missile and Space Analysis Center
January 1, 1974	Office of Special Activities Office of Research and Development Office of ELINT Office of Scientific Intelligence **Office of Development and Engineering** **Office of Technical Service** **Office of Weapons Intelligence** **National Photographic Interpretation Center**
January 1, 1975	Office of Research and Development Office of ELINT Office of Scientific Intelligence Office of Development and Engineering Office of Technical Service Office of Weapons Intelligence National Photographic Interpretation Center
January 1, 1977	Office of Research and Development Office of ELINT Office of Development and Engineering Office of Technical Service **Foreign Broadcast Information Service** National Photographic Interpretation Center

January 1, 1978	Office of Research and Development **Office of SIGINT Operations** Office of Development and Engineering Office of Technical Service Foreign Broadcast Information Service National Photographic Interpretation Center
January 1, 1989	Office of Research and Development Office of SIGINT Operations Office of Development and Engineering Office of Technical Service **Office of Special Projects** Foreign Broadcast Information Service National Photographic Interpretation Center
January 1, 1994	Office of Research and Development **Office of Technical Collection** Office of Development and Engineering Office of Technical Service Foreign Broadcast Information Service National Photographic Interpretation Center
January 1, 1996	Office of Research and Development Office of Technical Collection Office of Development and Engineering Office of Technical Service **Office of Advanced Projects** **Office of Advanced Analytical Tools** **Clandestine Information Technology Office** Foreign Broadcast Information Service National Photographic Interpretation Center
January 1, 1997	Office of Research and Development Office of Technical Collection Office of Development and Engineering Office of Technical Service Office of Advanced Projects Office of Advanced Analytical Tools Clandestine Information Technology Office Foreign Broadcast Information Service
January 1, 1999	Office of Technical Collection Office of Development and Engineering Office of Technical Service Office of Advanced Analytical Tools Clandestine Information Technology Office Foreign Broadcast Information Service **Investment Program Office**
February 1, 2001	Office of Technical Collection Office of Development and Engineering Office of Technical Service Foreign Broadcast Information Service **Office of Advanced Information Technology** **Office of Advanced Technologies and Programs**

APPENDIX 2
DS&T Leadership

Deputy Director for Research

Herbert J. Scoville	April 15, 1962–June 17, 1963

Deputy Director for Science and Technology

Albert D. (Bud) Wheelon	August 5, 1963–September 26, 1966
Carl E. Duckett (Acting)	September 26, 1966–April 20, 1967
Carl E. Duckett	April 20, 1967–June 1, 1976
Leslie C. Dirks	June 1, 1976–July 3, 1982
Richard Evans Hineman	July 3, 1982–September 5, 1989
James V. Hirsch	September 5, 1989–September 5, 1995
Ruth David	September 15, 1995–September 4, 1998
Joanne O. Isham (Acting)	September 5, 1998–April 1, 1999
Gary L. Smith	April 1, 1999–January 10, 2000
Joanne O. Isham	Jan 10, 2000–

Assistant Deputy Director for Research

Col. Edward B. Giller	June 25, 1962–August 5, 1963

Assistant/Associate Deputy Director for Science and Technology

(Title change from Assistant Deputy Director to Associate Deputy Director was effective May 8, 1973)

Col. Edward B. Giller	August 5, 1963–May 4, 1964
Carl Duckett	May 16, 1966–September 26, 1966
Lloyd Lauderdale	June 5, 1967–March 21, 1969
Donald Steininger	November 1, 1969–June 14, 1974
Sayre Stevens	June 14, 1974–May 17, 1976
Ernest J. Zellmer	June 1, 1976–September 24, 1979
James H. Taylor	September 24, 1979–September 27, 1982
James V. Hirsch	May 2, 1983–September 5, 1989
Gary W. Goodrich	October 16, 1989–December 31, 1995
Peter M. Daniher	January 1, 1996–November 12, 1997
Joanne Isham	November 12, 1997–January 10, 2000
James Runyan	January 10, 2000–

Director, Office of Special Activities (OSA)

James A. Cunningham (Acting)	August 1, 1962–September 4, 1962
Brig. Gen. Jack C. Ledford	September 4, 1962–August 1, 1966
Col. Paul N. Bacalis	August 1, 1966–July 12, 1968
Brig. Gen. Donald H. Ross	July 12, 1968–June 1, 1970
Brig. Gen. Harold F. Knowles	June 1, 1970–July 6, 1971
Brig. Gen. Wendell L. Bevan Jr.	July 6, 1971–August 31, 1974
James Cherbonneaux	Nov. 1, 1974–January 1, 1975

Director, Office of Research and Development (ORD)

Col. Edward B. Giller	November 29, 1962–May 4, 1964
Robert M. Chapman (Acting)	May 4, 1964–March 11, 1965
Robert M. Chapman	March 11, 1965–July 1, 1972
Sayre Stevens	July 1, 1972–June 14, 1974
James V. Hirsch	June 14, 1974–September 22, 1975
Donald L. Haas	September 22, 1975–May 23, 1976
Donald L. Reiser (Acting)	May 23, 1976–October 18, 1976
Frank Briglia (Acting)	October 18, 1976–February 27, 1977
Philip K. Eckman	February 27, 1977–April 1, 1989
Robert A. Herd III	April 1, 1989–July 18, 1996
Russell E. Dressell	July 18, 1996–October 1998

Office of Research and Development abolished effective October 1998.

Director, Office of ELINT (OEL)

George C. Miller	July 30, 1962–June 14, 1971
John N. McMahon	June 14, 1971–May 21, 1973
James V. Hirsch (Acting)	May 21, 1973–June 14, 1974
Robert D. Singel	June 14, 1974–September 22, 1975
James V. Hirsch	September 22, 1975–February 14, 1977

Office of ELINT and Division D merged to form Office of Special Operations effective February 14, 1977.

Director, Office of SIGINT Operations (OSO)

Edward Ryan	February 14, 1977–May 30, 1978
D. Barry Kelly	May 30, 1978–September 28, 1981
A. Roy Burks	September 28, 1981–July 15, 1984
M. Corley Wonus	July 15, 1984–March 21, 1989
Joseph B. Castillo	March 21, 1989–August 23, 1993

Office of SIGINT Operations and the Office of Special Projects (1988) were merged to form the Office of Technical Collection effective August 23, 1993.

Director, Office of Computer Services (OCS)

Joseph Becker	September 16, 1963–June 1, 1966
Charles A. Briggs	June 1, 1966–August 18, 1969
W. Douglas Climenson (Acting)	August 18, 1969–September 1, 1970
John D. Iams	September 1, 1970–April 1, 1973

Office of Computer Services transferred to Directorate of Management and Services and renamed Office of Joint Computer Support, effective April 1, 1973.

Director, Office of Scientific Intelligence (OSI)

Donald Chamberlain	August 22, 1963–June 24, 1973
Karl H. Weber	September 20, 1973–November 22, 1976

OSI transferred to the Directorate of Intelligence, effective November 22, 1976.

Director, Foreign Missile and Space Analysis Center (FMSAC)

Carl E. Duckett	November 7, 1963–May 16, 1966
David S. Brandwein	May 16, 1966–September 4, 1973

Foreign Missile and Space Analysis Center merged with component of OSI to form Office of Weapons Intelligence, effective September 4, 1973.

Director, Special Projects Staff (SPS)

Jackson D. Maxey	July 1964–September 1965

Special Projects Staff became Office of Special Projects on September 15, 1965.

Director, Office of Special Projects (OSP)

John J. Crowley	September 15, 1965–November 16, 1970
Harold L. Brownman	November 16, 1970–March 17, 1973

Office of Special Projects abolished and mission assumed by Office of Development and Engineering effective April 23, 1973.

Director, Office of Development and Engineering (OD&E)

Leslie C. Dirks	April 23, 1973–May 23, 1976
Donald L. Haas	May 23, 1976–August 28, 1978
Bert C. Aschenbrenner (Acting)	August 28, 1978–November 20, 1978
Stephens Crosby (Acting)	November 20, 1978–January 22, 1979
Bernard Lubarsky	January 22, 1979–March 8, 1982
Robert J. Kohler	March 8, 1982–August 17, 1985
Julian Caballero Jr.	August 17, 1985–October 3, 1993
Edmund Nowinski	October 3, 1993–October 16, 1995
Dennis Fitzgerald	October 16, 1995–

Director, Office of Weapons Intelligence (OWI)

David S. Brandwein	September 4, 1973–July 29, 1974
R. Evans Hineman	July 29, 1974–January 6, 1975
Ernest J. Zellmer	January 6, 1975–June 7, 1976
R. Evans Hineman	June 7, 1976–October 22, 1979
E. Wayne Boring	October 22, 1979–February 25, 1980

Office of Weapons Intelligence transferred to Directorate of Intelligence, November 22, 1976.

Director, National Photographic Interpretation Center (NPIC)

Arthur Lundahl	May 4, 1973–July 21, 1973
John J. Hicks	July 21, 1973–May 1, 1978
Col. Lorenzo W. Burroughs (Act.)	May 1, 1978–June 29, 1978
Rutledge P. "Hap" Hazard	June 30, 1978–February 20, 1984
R. M. "Rae" Huffstutler	February 20, 1984–January 25, 1988
Frank J. Ruocco	February 15, 1988–January 2, 1991
Leo A. Hazelwood	February 18, 1991–August 30, 1993
Nancy E. Bone	September 7, 1993–October 1, 1996

Director, Office of Technical Service (OTS)

Sidney Gottlieb	May 4, 1973–May 21, 1973
John N. McMahon	May 21, 1973–July 29, 1974
David S. Brandwein	July 29, 1974–June 2, 1980
M. Corley Wonus	June 2, 1980–July 15, 1984
Peter A. Marino	July 15, 1984–December 1, 1986
Joseph R. DeTrani	December 1, 1986–April 17, 1989
Frank R. Anderson	April 17, 1989–May 20, 1991
Robert G. Ruhle	May 20, 1991–February 20, 1994
Robert W. Manners	February 20, 1994–November 14, 1996
James L. Morris	November 14, 1996–April 4, 1997
Patrick L. Meehan	May 2, 1997–

Director, Foreign Broadcast Information Service (FBIS), transferred from DI to DS&T effective November 22, 1976; HN 1–127, November 16 1976.

Don H. Peterson	November 22, 1976–January 7, 1980
John F. Pereira	January 7, 1980–January 25, 1983
John D. Chandlee	January 25, 1983–January 3, 1986
Harrison S. Markham	January 3, 1986–September 28, 1986
Robert W. Manners	September 28, 1986–March 4, 1991
Wayne R. Schreiner	March 19, 1991–January 11, 1996
J. Niles Riddel	January 11, 1996–

Director, Special Projects Staff (SPS)

Gary W. Goodrich	January 18, 1987–October 12, 1987

Director, Office of Special Projects (OSP)

Gary W. Goodrich	October 12,1987–October 16, 1989
Peter M. Daniher	December 4, 1989–August 26, 1993

Director, Office of Technical Collection (OTC), established August 26, 1993, from merger of OSO and OSP (1987).

Peter M. Daniher	August 26, 1993–January 1, 1996
Patrick L. Meehan (Acting)	January 1, 1996–July 18, 1996
Patrick L. Meehan	July 18, 1996–May 1, 1997
James L. Runyan (Acting)	May 5, 1997–September 2, 1997
James L. Runyan	September 3, 1997–January 10, 2000

Director, Office of Advanced Analytical Tools (AAT)

Susan Gordon	July 18, 1996–October 2000

Director, Office of Advanced Projects (OAP)

Richard D. Platte	July 18, 1996–October 1998

Director, Clandestine Information Technology Office (CITO)

James R. Gosler	May 29, 1996–October 2000

CITO was formed from components of the Office of Technical Service (OTS) and the Office of Technical Collection (OTC). Part of CITO was transferred back to OTC in January 2001, and the rest was absorbed by the Directorate of Operations Information Operations Center.

Director, Office of Advanced Information Technology (AIT)

Larry Fairchild	October 2000–

Director, Office of Advanced Technologies and Programs (ATP)

Unknown	October 2000–

ACRONYMS AND ABBREVIATIONS

AAT	Office of Advanced Analytic Tools
ABM	Antiballistic Missile
ACDA	Arms Control and Disarmament Agency
ADSI	Assistant Director for Scientific Intelligence
AEC	Atomic Energy Commission
AFSC	Air Force Systems Command
AIR	American Institutes for Research
AIT	Office of Advanced Information Technology
APL	Applied Physics Laboratory (Johns Hopkins University)
ARDE	Democratic Revolutionary Alliance
ARS	Advanced Reconnaissance System
ATP	Office of Advanced Technologies and Programs
BND	Bundesnachrichtendienst (West German Foreign Intelligence Service)
CCD	Charge-Coupled Device
CIA	Central Intelligence Agency
CIG	Central Intelligence Group
CIO	Central Imagery Office
CITO	Clandestine Information Technology Office
COMINT	Communications Intelligence
COMIREX	Committee on Imagery Requirements and Exploitation
COMOR	Committee on Overhead Reconnaissance
DCI	Director of Central Intelligence
DCID	Director of Central Intelligence Directive
DDI	Deputy Director for Intelligence
DDP	Deputy Directorate for Plans Deputy Director for Plans
DDR	Deputy Director for Research
DEFSMAC	Defense Special Missile and Astronautics Center
DIA	Defense Intelligence Agency
DMA	Defense Mapping Agency
DNRO	Director National Reconnaissance Office
DOD	Department of Defense
DPD	Development Projects Division
DPS	Development Projects Staff
DS&T	Directorate of Science and Technology
EARL	Edgewood Arsenal Research Laboratories
ELINT	Electronic Intelligence
ERTS	Earth Resources Technology Satellite
ESO	ELINT Staff Officer
FBIS	Foreign Broadcast Information Service
FMSAC	Foreign Missile and Space Analysis Center

FROG	Film-Readout GAMBIT
FSTC	Foreign Science and Technology Center
FTD	Foreign Technology Division
HALSOL	High-Altitude Solar Energy
HN	Headquarters Notice
ICBM	Intercontinental Ballistic Missile
IDF	Israeli Defense Forces
IEG	Imagery Exploitation Group
INR	Bureau of Intelligence and Research
IPO	Investment Program Office
IRBM	Intermediate-Range Ballistic Missile
JCS	Joint Chiefs of Staff
JPRS	Joint Publications Research Service
JRDB	Joint Research and Development Board
LOROP	Long-Range Oblique Photography
MASINT	Measurement and Signature Intelligence
MIRV	Multiple Independent Reentry Vehicles
MPS	Ministry of Public Security (PRC)
MRBM	Medium-Range Ballistic Missile
MRV	Multiple Reentry Vehicles
MSX	Midcourse Space Experiment
NACA	National Advisory Council on Aeronautics
NARA	National Archives and Records Administration
NASA	National Aeronautics and Space Administration
NEL	National Exploitation Laboratory
NIA	National Imagery Agency
NIA	National Intelligence Authority
NIDL	National Information Display Laboratory
NIMA	National Imagery and Mapping Agency
NIE	National Intelligence Estimate
NORAD	North American Aerospace Defense Command
NPIC	National Photographic Interpretation Center
NRO	National Reconnaissance Office
NRP	National Reconnaissance Program
NRPEC	National Reconnaissance Program Executive Committee
NSA	National Security Agency
NSC	National Security Council
NSCID	National Security Council Intelligence Directive
NURO	National Underwater Reconnaissance Office
NVA	North Vietnamese Army
OAP	Office of Advanced Projects
OCS	Office of Computer Services
OD&E	Office of Development and Engineering
OEL	Office of ELINT
OIA	Office of Imagery Analysis
ORD	Office of Research and Development
ORE	Office of Reports and Estimates
OSA	Office of Special Activities
OSI	Office of Scientific Intelligence
OSO	Office of Special Operations

OSO	Office of SIGINT Operations
OSP	Office of Special Projects
OSR	Office of Strategic Research
OSS	Office of Strategic Services
OTC	Office of Technical Collection
OTH	Over-the-Horizon
OTS	Office of Technical Service
OWI	Office of Weapons Intelligence
PBCFIA	President's Board of Consultants on Foreign Intelligence Activities
PDB	President's Daily Brief
PFIAB	President's Foreign Intelligence Advisory Board
PEG	Priority Exploitation Group, NPIC
PIBS	Presidential Intelligence Briefing System
PIC	Photographic Interpretation Center
PID	Photographic Intelligence Division
PPMS	Power and Pattern Measurement System
PRC	People's Republic of China
PSAC	President's Scientific Advisory Committee
RDD	Radiation Detection Device
RPV	Remotely Piloted Vehicle
SAC	Strategic Air Command
SALT	Strategic Arms Limitation Treaty
SAM	Surface-to-Air Missile
SAVA	Special Assistant for Vietnamese Affairs
SCS	Special Collection Service
SCMC	Shuangchengzi Missile Test Complex
SDS	Satellite Data System
SEATO	Southeast Asia Treaty Organization
SEI	Scientific Engineering Institute
SIC	Scientific Intelligence Committee
SIGINT	Signals Intelligence
SLBM	Submarine-Launched Ballistic Missile
SNA	Somali National Alliance
SNIE	Special National Intelligence Estimate
SOD	Special Operations Division
SOSUS	Sound Surveillance System
SRI	Stanford Research Institute
TCP	Technological Capabilities Panel
TIO	Technology Investment Office
TRW	Thompson-Ramo-Woolridge
TSD	Technical Services Division
TSS	Technical Services Staff
UAV	Unmanned Aerial Vehicle
UCLAs	Unilaterally Controlled Latino Assets
USAF	United States Air Force
USIB	United States Intelligence Board
VC	Vietcong

NOTES

Chapter 1: Unexpected Missions

1. Thomas F. Troy, *Donovan and the CIA: A History of the Establishment of the Central Intelligence Agency* (Frederick, Md.: University Publications of America, 1981), pp. 406–407, 471–472.

2. Ibid., pp. 349, 464–465; Christopher Andrew, *For the President's Eyes Only: Secret Intelligence and the American Presidency from Washington to Bush* (New York: HarperCollins, 1995), pp. 168–169.

3. John Ranelagh, *The Agency: The Rise and Decline of the CIA, from Wild Bill Donovan to William Casey* (New York: Simon & Schuster, 1986), p. 112.

4. Ronald Kessler, *Inside the CIA: Revealing the Secrets of the World's Most Powerful Spy Agency* (New York: Pocket Books, 1992), p. 140; Richard M. Bissell with Jonathan E. Lewis and Francis T. Pudlo, *Reflections of a Cold Warrior: From Yalta to the Bay of Pigs* (New Haven: Yale University Press, 1996), p. 98.

5. Center for the Study of Intelligence, *Declassified National Intelligence Estimates of the Soviet Union and International Communism* (Washington, D.C.: Central Intelligence Agency, 1996), pp. 4, 6.

6. Brig. Gen. E. K. Wright, Deputy Director of Central Intelligence, "Establishment and Functions of the Nuclear Energy Group, Scientific Branch, Office of Reports and Estimates," in C. Thomas Thorne Jr. and David S. Patterson (eds.), *Emergence of the Intelligence Establishment* (Washington, D.C.: U.S. Government Printing Office, 1996), pp. 503–505; Charles A. Zeigler and David Jacobson, *Spying Without Spies: Origins of America's Secret Nuclear Surveillance System* (Westport, Conn.: Praeger, 1995), pp. 60–63; George S. Jackson and Martin P. Clausen, *Organizational History of the Central Intelligence Agency, 1950–1953* (Washington, D.C.: Central Intelligence Agency, 1957), p. 3; interview with Henry S. Lowenhaupt, Springfield, Virginia, April 15, 1999.

7. Lowenhaupt interview; CIA Public Affairs Staff, "'Trailblazers' and Years of CIA Service," www.odci.gov/cia, March 13, 1999.

8. David Z. Beckler, Chief of the Intelligence Section, JRDB, "The Critical Situation in Regard to Atomic Energy Intelligence," December 2, 1947, in Thorne and Patterson (eds.), *Emergence of the Intelligence Establishment*, pp. 820–821.

9. Brig. Gen. E. K. Wright, Deputy Director of Central Intelligence, "Operations-Intelligence Relationship of CIG with JRDB," March 13, 1947, in Thorne and Patterson (eds.), *Emergence of the Intelligence Establishment*, pp. 502–503.

10. Ronald E. Doel and Allan A. Needell, "Science, Scientists, and the CIA: Balancing International Ideals, National Needs, and Professional Opportunities," *Intelligence and National Security* 12, 1 (January 1997): 59–81 at p. 62.

11. Ralph L. Clark, Director of Programs Division, to Dr. Vannevar Bush, Chairman, RDB, "CIA Situation," December 3, 1947, in Thorne and Patterson (eds.), *Emergence of the Intelligence Establishment*, pp. 818–819.

12. Doel and Needell, "Science, Scientists, and the CIA," p. 63.

13. Ibid., pp. 63–65; Jackson and Clausen, *Organizational History of the Central Intelligence Agency*, p. VI-14; Brig. Gen. E. K. Wright, DDCI, Memorandum for Assistant Director for Special Operations et al., Subject: Additional Functions of the Office of Special Operations, March 5, 1948, 2000 CIA Release, National Archives and Records Administration (NARA).

14. Doel and Needell, "Science, Scientists, and the CIA," p. 65.

15. Jackson and Clausen, *Organizational History of the Central Intelligence Agency*, p. 1.

16. Allen W. Dulles, William H. Jackson, and Mathias F. Correa, *The Central Intelligence Agency and National Organization for Intelligence* (Washington, D.C.: National Security Council, January 1, 1949), p. 56.

17. Jackson and Clausen, *Organizational History of the Central Intelligence Agency*, pp. VI-3, VI-16, VI-16 n. 2; Ludwell Lee Montague, *General Walter Bedell Smith as Director of Central Intelligence, October 1950–February 1953* (University Park: Pennsylvania State University Press, 1992), p. 174; Robert Blum to Mathias F. Corea, December 18, 1948, in Thorne and Patterson (eds.), *Emergence of the Intelligence Establishment*, p. 902.

18. Doel and Needell, "Science, Scientists, and the CIA," p. 66.

19. Ibid., p. 67.

20. Willard Machle, Assistant Director for Scientific Intelligence, to Rear Admiral Roscoe Hillenkoetter, Director of Central Intelligence, "Inability of OSI to Accomplish Its Mission," September 29, 1949, in Thorne and Patterson (eds.), *Emergence of the Intelligence Establishment*, pp. 1012–1016; Jackson and Clausen, *Organizational History of the Central Intelligence Agency*, p. VI-19; interview with Karl Weber, Oakton, Virginia, May 5, 1999.

21. Machle, "Inability of OSI to Accomplish Its Mission"; Memorandum for the Record, Subject: Responsibilities of the Office of Scientific Intelligence (Summary of discussion between [deleted], OSI and Mr. Piel [deleted] of Management), November 29, 1951, NARA, RG 263, 1998 CIA, Box 209, Folder 3.

22. Director of Central Intelligence Directive 3/3, "Scientific Intelligence," October 28, 1949; Weber interview.

23. Montague, *General Walter Bedell Smith as Director of Central Intelligence, October 1950–February 1953*, pp. 174–175.

24. Ibid., p. 175; Weber interview.

25. Montague, *General Walter Bedell Smith as Director of Central Intelligence, October 1950–February 1953*, p. 176.

26. Ibid., pp. 177–178; Jackson and Clausen, *Organizational History of the Central Intelligence Agency*, pp. VI-59 to VI-60.

27. Montague, *General Walter Bedell Smith as Director of Central Intelligence, October 1950–February 1953*, pp. 177–178; Ranelagh, *The Agency*, pp. 196–197; Jackson and Clausen, *Organizational History of the Central Intelligence Agency*, p. VI-66.

28. Montague, *General Walter Bedell Smith as Director of Central Intelligence, October 1950–February 1953*, p. 179; Director of Central Intelligence 3/4, "Production of Scientific and Technical Intelligence," August 14, 1952; Jackson and Clausen, *Organizational History of the Central Intelligence Agency*, p. VI-74.

29. Montague, *General Walter Bedell Smith as Director of Central Intelligence, October 1950-February 1953*, p. 180.

30. Ranelagh, *The Agency*, pp. 197, 729–730.

31. Central Intelligence Agency Notice No. 20-191-71, "Announcement of Key Positions," June 28, 1955; Central Intelligence Agency, Memo for Awards Committee, National Civil Service League, November 28, 1958.

32. Director of Central Intelligence Directive No. 3/5, "Production of Scientific and Technical Intelligence," February 3, 1959.

33. Doel and Needell, "Science, Scientists, and the CIA," pp. 70–71.

34. Michael Warner, CIA History Staff, Memorandum for the Record, Subject: The Central Intelligence Agency and Human Radiation Experiments: An Analysis of the Findings, February 14, 1995, p. 11.

35. Jackson and Clausen, *Organizational History of the Central Intelligence Agency*, p. 67 n.49.

36. Intelligence Advisory Committee, NIE 11-3A-54, *Summary: The Soviet Atomic Energy Program to Mid-1957*, February 16, 1954, pp. 1–4.

37. *Allen Welsh Dulles as Director of Central Intelligence, 26 February 1953–29 November 1961, Volume II, Coordination of Intelligence* (Washington, D.C.: CIA, 1973), pp. 42–43; Director of Central Intelligence, NIE 11-6-54, *Soviet Capabilities and Probable Programs in the Guided Missile Field*, October 1954, pp. ii-iii, 1.

38. *Allen Welsh Dulles as Director of Central Intelligence*, pp. 46–47, 51n., 58; Annex D to Director of Central Intelligence Directive 3/4, "Terms of Reference for the Guided Missile Intelligence Committee," January 31, 1956; "Summary Statement of IAC Actions Leading to Consideration of a Guided Missile Intelligence Committee," n.d., NARA, RG 263, 1998 CIA Release, Box 188, Folder 6; interview with Henry Plaster, Vienna, Virginia, September 30, 1999.

39. Avner Cohen, *Israel and the Bomb* (New York: Columbia University Press, 1998), p. 84; Office of Scientific Intelligence, CIA, NIE 38–58, *The Netherlands Nuclear Energy Program*, November 10, 1958; Office of Scientific Intelligence, CIA, *The French Nuclear Weapons Program*, November 13, 1959.

40. Henry S. Lowenhaupt, "The Decryption of a Picture," *Studies in Intelligence* 1, 3 (Summer 1957): 41–53.

41. John Marks, *The Search for the "Manchurian Candidate": The CIA and Mind Control* (New York: Norton, 1991), pp. 59, 79, 80, 83; U.S. Congress, Senate Select Committee to Study Governmental Operations with Respect to Intelligence Activities (hereinafter Senate Select Committee), *Final Report, Book I: Foreign and Military Intelligence* (Washington, D.C.: U.S. Government Printing Office, 1976), pp. 390, 395–397.

42. Tim Weiner, "Sidney Gottlieb, 80, Dies; Took LSD to C.I.A.," *New York Times*, March 10, 1999, p. C22; Marks, *The Search for the "Manchurian Candidate,"* pp. 59–60; Evan Thomas, *The Very Best Men, Four Who Dared: The Early Years of the CIA* (New York: Simon & Schuster, 1995), p. 211.

43. Marks, *The Search for the "Manchurian Candidate,"* pp. 24–25, 27; U.S. Congress, Senate Select Committee, *Final Report, Book I*, p. 387.

44. Marks, *The Search for the "Manchurian Candidate,"* pp. 31–32, 44, p. 59.

45. Ibid., pp. 60–61; U.S. Congress, Senate Select Committee, *Final Report, Book I*, p. 390.

46. Marks, *The Search for the "Manchurian Candidate,"* p. 62.

47. Ibid., pp. 61–62; U.S. Congress, Senate Select Committee, *Final Report, Book I*, p. 389.

48. Marks, *The Search for the "Manchurian Candidate,"* pp. 90, 108; Ranelagh, *The Agency*, p. 207.

49. James R. Killian Jr., *Sputnik, Scientists, and Eisenhower: A Memoir of the First Special Assistant to the President for Science and Technology* (Cambridge: MIT Press, 1982), pp. 67–68.

50. Gregory W. Pedlow and Donald E. Welzenbach, *The Central Intelligence Agency and Overhead Reconnaissance: The U-2 and OXCART Programs, 1954–1974* (Washington, D.C.: CIA, 1992), Preface.

51. Donald E. Welzenbach, "Science and Technology: Origins of a Directorate," *Studies in Intelligence* 30, 2 (Summer 1986): 13–26 at 13–15; Victor K. McElheny, *Insisting on the Impossible: The Life of Edwin Land, Inventor of Instant Photography* (Reading, Mass.: Perseus Books, 1998), p. 294.

52. Killian, *Sputniks, Scientists, and Eisenhower*, p. 79; McElheny, *Insisting on the Impossible*, p. 301.

53. Donald Welzenbach, "Din Land: Patriot from Polaroid," *Optics and Photonics News* 5, 10 (October 1996): 22ff; Attachment 1, Memorandum for: Director of Central Intelligence, Subject: A Unique Opportunity for Comprehensive Intelligence, November 5, 1954.

54. Ranelagh, *The Agency*, p. 314.

55. "A Unique Opportunity for Comprehensive Intelligence—A Summary," attachment, Edwin Land to Allen W. Dulles, November 5, 1954.

56. Pedlow and Welzenbach, *The Central Intelligence Agency and Overhead Reconnaissance*, p. 4; R. Cargill Hall, "Post-War Strategic Reconnaissance and the Genesis of Corona," in Dwayne A. Day, John Logsdon, and Brian Latell (eds.), *Eye in the Sky: The Story of the CORONA Spy Satellites* (Washington, D.C.: Smithsonian, 1998), pp. 86–118 at pp. 87–92.

57. Edwin Land to Allen Dulles, November 5, 1954.

58. Pedlow and Welzenbach, *The Central Intelligence Agency and Overhead Reconnaissance*, pp. 32–35, 40; A. J. Goodpaster, "Memorandum of Conference with the President, 0810, 24 November 1954," November 24, 1954, Ann C. Whitman Diary, November 1954, Box 3, Ann C. Whitman File, DDE Papers as President, Dwight David Eisenhower Library (DDEL); Peter Grose, *Gentleman Spy: The Life of Allen Dulles* (Boston: Houghton Mifflin, 1994), p. 405; Chris Pocock, *Dragon Lady: The History of the U-2 Spyplane* (Shrewsbury, England: Airlife, 1989), p. 26; Oral History Interview with Richard Bissell Jr., Columbia University, 1973, p. 42.

59. Bissell with Lewis and Pudlo, *Reflections of a Cold Warrior*, p. 78; Pedlow and Welzenbach, *The Central Intelligence Agency and Overhead Reconnaissance*, pp. 15–16, 30.

60. Peter Wyden, *The Bay of Pigs: The Untold Story* (New York: Simon & Schuster, 1979), p. 13.

61. Ibid., pp. 12–13.

62. Bissell with Lewis and Pudlo, *Reflections of a Cold Warrior*, pp. 98, 105.

63. Ben R. Rich and Leo Janos, *Skunk Works: A Personal Memoir of My Years at Lockheed* (Boston: Little, Brown, 1994), p. 130.

64. Pedlow and Welzenbach, *The Central Intelligence Agency and Overhead Reconnaissance*, p. 66.

65. Ibid., p. 60; Jonathan E. Lewis, "Tension and Triumph: Civilian and Military Relations and the Birth of the U-2 Program," in Robert A. McDonald (ed.), *CORONA: Between the Sun and the Earth: The First NRO Reconnaissance Eye in Space* (Bethesda, Md.: American Society for Photogrammetry and Remote Sensing, 1997), pp. 13–23 at p. 13. Eisenhower was certainly aware that the Air Force had, for a number of years, been conducting electronic and photographic reconnaissance flights that entered Soviet airspace. But it was expected that the U-2s would fly far deeper into the Soviet Union than the military planes—to reach key missile and nuclear targets that the military flights could not be expected to reach.

66. Pedlow and Welzenbach, *The Central Intelligence Agency and Overhead Reconnaissance*, pp. 94–95, 100; Pocock, *Dragon Lady*, p. 25; William E. Burrows, "That New Black Magic," *Air and Space*, December 1998/January 1999, pp. 29–35.

67. Pedlow and Welzenbach, *The Central Intelligence Agency and Overhead Reconnaissance*, pp. 101, 104.

68. Pocock, *Dragon Lady*, p. 27; Pedlow and Welzenbach, *The Central Intelligence Agency and Overhead Reconnaissance*, pp. 104–105.

69. Pedlow and Welzenbach, *The Central Intelligence Agency and Overhead Reconnaissance*, p. 105; Pocock, *Dragon Lady*, p. 27.

70. Pocock, *Dragon Lady*, p. 28.

71. "Soviet Note No. 23," July 10, 1956, White House Corr., Gen. 1956(3), Box 3, John Foster Dulles Papers, White House Memoranda, DDEL; Pedlow and Welzenbach, *The Central Intelligence Agency and Overhead Reconnaissance*, p. 109.

72. Herbert I. Miller, Memorandum for: Project Director, Subject: Suggestions re Intelligence Value of AQUATONE, July 17, 1956, 2000 CIA Release, NARA.

73. Pedlow and Welzenbach, *The Central Intelligence Agency and Overhead Reconnaissance*, pp. 111, 124.

74. Jay Miller, *Lockheed U-2* (Austin, Tex.: Aerofax, 1983), pp. 27, 30; Pedlow and Welzenbach, *The Central Intelligence Agency and Overhead Reconnaissance*, pp. 135, 139.

75. Pedlow and Welzenbach, *The Central Intelligence Agency and Overhead Reconnaissance*, pp. 135, 139, 143; Henry S. Lowenhaupt, "Mission to Birch Woods," *Studies in Intelligence* 12, 4 (Fall 1968): 1–12 at 3.

76. Pedlow and Welzenbach, *The Central Intelligence Agency and Overhead Reconnaissance*, p. 143.

77. Ibid., p. 165.

78. Ibid., p. 168; CIA, "Situation Estimate for Project CHALICE, Fiscal Years 1961 and 1962," March 14, 1960, 2000 CIA Release, NARA.

79. Pedlow and Welzenbach, *The Central Intelligence Agency and Overhead Reconnaissance,* p. 168.

80. Ibid., pp. 174–176; Chris Pocock, *The U-2 Spyplane: Toward the Unknown* (Atglen, Pa.: Schiffer Books, 2000), p. 165; interview with a former CIA official.

81. Evan Thomas, *The Very Best Men* (New York: Simon & Schuster, 1995), p. 218; Pedlow and Welzenbach, *The Central Intelligence Agency and Overhead Reconnaissance*, p. 176; Transcript, "Debriefing of Francis Gary Powers, Tape #2," February 13, 1962, NARA, RG 263, 1998 CIA Release, Box 230, Folder 3.

82. "Testimony of Allen Dulles," *Executive Sessions of the Senate Foreign Relations Committee (Historical Series), Vol. XII, Eighty-sixth Congress–Second Session, 1960* (Washington, D.C.: U.S. Government Printing Office, 1982), p. 285.

83. Ibid.

84. Seymour M. Hersh, *The Samson Option: Israel's Nuclear Arsenal and American Foreign Policy* (New York: Random House, 1991), p. 52.

85. Pedlow and Welzenbach, *The Central Intelligence Agency and Overhead Reconnaissance*, p. 215; Memorandum for: Director of Central Intelligence, Subject: Identification of Special Projects, August 13, 1958, NARA, RG 263, 1998 CIA Release, Box 42, Folder 5.

86. Central Intelligence Agency, "Future of the Agency's U-2 Capability," July 7, 1960, pp. 4, 10; Miller, *Lockheed U-2*, p. 31; Richard M. Bissell Jr., Deputy Director (Plans), Memorandum for: All Members U.S. Government IDEALIST Community, January 4, 1961, 2000 CIA Release, NARA.

87. Wayne Mutza, *Lockheed P2V Neptune: An Illustrated History* (Atglen, Pa.: Schiffer Military/Aviation History, 1996), pp. 109–110; "Lockheed RB-69A 'Neptune,'" www.wpafb.af.mil/museum/research/bombers/b5/b5-62.htm, July 28, 1999.

88. Mutza, *Lockheed P2V Neptune*, pp. 110, 112–113.

89. Ibid., p. 113; Jay Miller, *Skunk Works: The Official History* (North Branch, Minn.: Specialty Press, 1996), p. 58.

90. Frederic C.E. Oder, James C. Fitzpatrick, and Paul E. Worthman, *The CORONA Story* (Washington, D.C.: National Reconnaissance Office, 1997), p. 123; interview with Albert D. Wheelon, Montecito, California, November 11–12, 1998; interview with John McMahon, Los Altos, California, November 17, 1998; Mutza, *Lockheed P2V Neptune*, pp. 113–114; Miller, *Skunk Works*, p. 58.

91. Pedlow and Welzenbach, *The CIA and Overhead Reconnaissance*, p. 260; Thomas P. McIninch, "The OXCART Story," *Studies in Intelligence* 15, 1 (Winter 1971): 1–34 at 2.

92. McIninch, "The OXCART Story," p. 3.

93. Pedlow and Welzenbach, *The Central Intelligence Agency and Overhead Reconnaissance*, pp. 262–263; John L. Sloop, *Liquid Hydrogen as a Propulsion Fuel* (Washington, D.C.: NASA, 1978), pp. 141–167.

94. Pedlow and Welzenbach, *The Central Intelligence Agency and Overhead Reconnaissance*, p. 263; McIninch, "The OXCART Story," p. 3.

95. McIninch, "The OXCART Story," p. 3; Pedlow and Welzenbach, *The Central Intelligence Agency and Overhead Reconnaissance*, pp. 263, 267.

96. Pedlow and Welzenbach, *The Central Intelligence Agency and Overhead Reconnaissance*, pp. 268–269.

97. Ibid., pp. 270–271, 273; McIninch, "The OXCART Story," p. 3.

98. Pedlow and Welzenbach, *The Central Intelligence Agency and Overhead Reconnaissance*, p. 273; Rich and Janos, *Skunk Works*, p. 200.

99. Pedlow and Welzenbach, *The Central Intelligence Agency and Overhead Reconnaissance*, p. 274.

100. Ibid., pp. 274, 278.

101. Brig. Gen. A. J. Goodpaster, Memorandum for the Record, June 2, 1960, Dwight D. Eisenhower Papers, White House Office: Office of Staff Secretary, Subject Series, alpha sub, b.15, F: "Intel Matters (15)," DDEL.

102. Oder, Fitzpatrick, and Worthman, *The CORONA Story*, p. 18.

103. Jeffrey T. Richelson, *America's Secret Eyes in Space: The U.S. KEYHOLE Spy Satellite Program* (New York: Harper & Row, 1990), p. 27; Bissell with Lewis and Pudlo, *Reflections of a Cold Warrior*, p. 135.

104. Oder, Fitzpatrick, and Worthman, *The CORONA Story*, pp. 10, 15.

105. Kenneth E. Greer, "Corona," *Studies in Intelligence*, Supplement, 17 (Spring 1973), reprinted in Kevin C. Ruffner (ed.), *CORONA: America's First Satellite Program* (Washington, D.C.: Central Intelligence Agency, 1995), pp. 3–39 at p. 5; Hall, "Postwar Strategic Reconnaissance and the Genesis of Corona," p. 113.

106. Central Intelligence Agency/National Reconnaissance Office, "CORONA Pioneers," May 25, 1995; interview with Frank Buzard, Rancho Palos Verdes, California, June 11, 1999; Dwayne A. Day, "Development and Improvement of the Corona Satellite," in Day, Logsdon, and Latell (eds.), *Eye in the Sky*, pp. 48–85 at p. 49; Robert A. McDonald, "Corona's Pioneers," in McDonald (ed.)., *CORONA*, pp. 141–152 at p. 145.

107. Robert A. McDonald, "CORONA: A Success for Space Reconnaissance, a Look into the Cold War, and a Revolution for Intelligence," *Photogrammetric Engineering and Remote Sensing* 51, 6 (June 1995): 689–720 at 693; Central Intelligence Agency/National Reconnaissance Office, "CORONA Pioneers."

108. Dwayne A. Day, "The Development and Improvement of the Corona Satellite," in Day, Logsdon, and Latell (eds.), *Eye in the Sky*, pp. 48–85, at p. 50.

109. Buzard interview.

110. Albert D. Wheelon, "CORONA: A Triumph of American Technology," in Day, Logsdon, and Latell (eds.), *Eye in the Sky*, pp. 29–47 at pp. 34–35; Greer, "Corona," pp. 7–8; Bissell with Lewis and Pudlo, *Reflections of a Cold Warrior*, p. 136.

111. Jonathan McDowell, "Launch Listings," in Day, Logsdon, and Latell (eds.), *Eye in the Sky*, pp. 235–246 at p. 236; Day, "The Development and Improvement of the Corona Satellite," p. 49.

112. Day, "The Development and Improvement of the CORONA Satellite," p. 55.

113. Greer, "Corona," at pp. 16–21; McDowell, "Launch Listings," p. 236; Leonard Mosley, *Dulles: A Biography of Eleanor, Allen, and John Foster and Their Family Network* (New York: Dial Press, 1978), p. 432.

114. "The Origin and Evolution of the Corona System," in Day, Logsdon, and Latell (eds.), *Eye in the Sky*, pp. 181–199 at p. 199.

115. Buzard interview.

116. Richelson, *America's Secret Eyes in Space*, p. 40; Greer, "Corona," pp. 3, 22, 24; Dwayne A. Day, John Logsdon, and Brian Latell, "Introduction," in Day, Logsdon, and Latell (eds.), *Eye in the Sky*, pp. 1–18 at p. 10.

117. Interview with a former CIA official.

118. Ibid.

119. J. Michael Selander, "Image Coverage Models for Declassified Corona, Argon, and Lanyard Satellite Photography: A Technical Explanation," in McDonald (ed.), *CORONA*, pp. 177–188, at p. 177; Greer, "Corona," p. 24; Photographic Interpretation Center, Central Intelligence Agency, *Joint*

Mission Coverage Index, Mission 9009, 18 August 1960, September 1960, pp. 115–125 in Ruffner (ed.), *CORONA*, p. 120.

120. Greer, "Corona," p. 24; McDonald (ed.), *CORONA*, p. 718.

121. McDonald (ed.), *CORONA*, pp. 698–700, 715, 718.

122. Director of Central Intelligence, NIE 11-4-57, "Main Trends in Soviet Capabilities and Policies, 1957–1962," November 12, 1957, pp. 26–27; Lawrence C. McQuade, Memorandum for Mr. Nitze, Subject: But Where Did the Missile Gap Go? (Washington, D.C.: Assistant Secretary of Defense, International Security Affairs, May 31, 1963), pp. 7–8.

123. Director of Central Intelligence, NIE 11-4-59, *Main Trends in Soviet Capabilities and Policies, 1959–1964*, February 9, 1960, pp. 51–52.

124. Desmond Ball, *Politics and Force Levels: The Strategic Missile Program of the Kennedy Administration* (Berkeley: University of California Press, 1980), pp. 10, 15–25, 96.

125. Director of Central Intelligence, NIE 11-4-60, "Main Trends in Soviet Capabilities and Policies, 1960–1965," December 1, 1960, p. 52.

126. Director of Central Intelligence, NIE 11-8-61, *Soviet Capabilities for Long-Range Attack*, June 7, 1961, in Donald P. Steury, *Intentions and Capabilities: Estimates on Soviet Strategic Forces, 1950–1983* (Washington, D.C.: Central Intelligence Agency, 1996), pp. 115–119 at pp. 116–117.

127. Jerrold L. Schechter and Peter S. Deriabin, *The Spy Who Saved the World: How a Soviet Colonel Changed the Course of the Cold War* (New York: Scribner's, 1992), pp. 273–274; Director of Central Intelligence, NIE 11-8/1-61, *Soviet Capabilities for Long-Range Attack*, September 21, 1961, p. 4.

128. Director of Central Intelligence, NIE 11-8/1-61, *Soviet Capabilities for Long-Range Attack*, pp. 2, 10–11, 13.

129. National Security Council, NSCID No. 8, "Photographic Interpretation," January 18, 1961.

130. *The Reminiscences of Arthur C. Lundahl*, Oral History Research Office, Columbia University, 1982, pp. 11, 38, 42.

131. Ibid., pp. 51, 56, 57.

132. Ibid., pp. 182, 187, 197; Jack Anderson, "Getting the Big Picture for the CIA," *Washington Post,* November 28, 1982, p. C7; Dino A. Brugioni and Frederick J. Doyle, "Arthur C. Lundahl: Founder of the Image Exploitation Discipline," pp. 159–168 in McDonald (ed.), *CORONA*, at pp. 160–161.

133. *The Reminiscences of Arthur Lundahl*, p. 221; interview with a former CIA official; Office of the Deputy Director (Intelligence), Notice No. 1-130-5, "Photographic Interpretation Center," August 19, 1958.

134. *The Reminiscences of Arthur C. Lundahl*, pp. 197, 201; John Prados, *The Soviet Estimate: U.S. Intelligence and Russian Military Strength* (New York: Dial, 1982), p. 110; Office of the Deputy Director (Intelligence), Notice No. 1-130-5, "Photographic Interpretation Center."

135. *The Reminiscences of Arthur C. Lundahl*, pp. 197–201, 229.

136. Prados, *The Soviet Estimate*, pp. 122–123.

137. Joint Study Group, *Report on Foreign Intelligence Activities of the United States Government*, December 15, 1960, pp. 1, 2.

138. *The Reminiscences of Arthur Lundahl*, pp. 53, 61.

139. Ibid., pp. 299–300; Marion W. Boggs, Memorandum, Subject: Discussion at the 474th Meeting of the National Security Council, Thursday, January 12, 1961, January 13, 1961, Dwight D. Eisenhower Library, Papers 1953–61, Ann Whitman File, pp. 4–9.

140. Boggs, Memorandum, Subject: Discussion at the 474th Meeting of the National Security Council, Thursday, January 12, 1961, pp. 6–7.

141. Ibid., pp. 7–8.

142. Ibid., pp. 8, 9.

143. Ibid., p. 9; *The Reminiscences of Arthur Lundahl*, pp. 301–302.

144. *Allen Welsh Dulles as Director of Central Intelligence, 26 February 1953–29 November 1961: Volume II, Coordination of Intelligence* (Washington, D.C.: Central Intelligence Agency, July 1973), p. 82.

145. Ibid., p. 81.

146. Ibid., pp. 81–82.

147. Charles A. Kroeger Jr., "ELINT: A Scientific Intelligence System," *Studies in Intelligence* 2, 1 (Winter 1958): 71–83; *Allen Welsh Dulles as Director of Central Intelligence*, p. 94; Richard M. Bissell Jr., Deputy Director (Plans), Memorandum for: Major General J. M. Williams, Assistant Chief of Staff for Intelligence USA, et al., Subject: ELINT Requirements Requiring Sensitive Collection, September 9, 1959, 2000 CIA Release, NARA.

148. Olav Riste, *The Norwegian Intelligence Service, 1945–1970* (London: Frank Cass, 1999), pp. 90, 92, 149–150.

149. Robert P. Berman and John C. Baker, *Soviet Strategic Forces: Requirements and Responses* (Washington, D.C.: Brookings Institution, 1982), pp. 106–107; Riste, *The Norwegian Intelligence Service*, p. 105; interview with a former CIA official.

150. Riste, *The Norwegian Intelligence Service*, pp. 147–148.

151. Ibid., p. 149; Central Intelligence Agency, *Cost Reduction Program: FY 1966-FY 1967*, September 1, 1965, p. 9, NARA, RG 263, Entry 36, HRP 89-2/00443, Box 7, File 713; Rolf Tamnes, *The Cold War in the High North* (Oslo: Ad Notam, 1991), pp. 121–122, 212.

152. Interview with Robert Phillips, Rosslyn, Virginia, June 4, 1999.

153. William H. Nance, "Quality ELINT," *Studies in Intelligence* 12, 2 (Spring 1968): 7–19 at 8.

154. Ibid.

155. William E. Burrows, *Exploring Space: Voyages in the Solar System and Beyond* (New York: Random House, 1990), p. 99.

156. Henry G. Plaster, "Snooping on Space Pictures," *Studies in Intelligence* 8, 4 (Fall 1964): 31–39 at 31.

157. Ibid., pp. 31–32.

158. Ibid., p. 32. NSA went on to design and produce special equipment that would show oscilloscope pictures as a signal was being received, with the first two sent to ELINT sites in Hawaii and Alaska. Video transmissions from *Sputnik 9* and *Sputnik 10,* both launched in March 1961, gave verification that the flights carried canine passengers. More important was the ability of NSA to report, 58 minutes into Yuri Gagarin's 108-minute flight on April 12, 1961, that the Soviets had indeed placed a man into orbit and he was alive. See Plaster, "Snooping on Space Pictures," p. 34.

159. James Burke, "Seven Years to Luna 9," *Studies in Intelligence* 10, 3 (Summer 1966): 1–24 at 4–5, 7; Burrows, *Exploring Space*, p. 420.

160. Burrows, *Exploring Space*, p. 420; Burke, "Seven Years to Luna 9," pp. 7–8.

161. Burke, "Seven Years to Luna 9," pp. 8–9; Burrows, *Exploring Space*, pp. 130–131.

162. David C. Martin, *Wilderness of Mirrors* (New York: Harper & Row, 1980), p. 121; Philip Agee, *Inside the Company: CIA Diary* (San Francisco: Stonehill, 1975), Appendix 3; "CIA Historical Program," January 1971, NARA, RG 263, 1998 CIA Release, Box 4, Folder 3.

163. Agee, *Inside the Company*, p. 351.

164. James Bamford, *The Puzzle Palace: A Report on NSA, America's Most Secret Agency* (Boston: Houghton Mifflin, 1982), p. 142.

165. Memorandum for General Maude, Subject: Proposed U.S./U.K. Cooperation within Area 5 of Technical Cooperation Program, May 4, 1951, NARA, RG 341, Entry 214; Pocock, *Dragon Lady*, p. 47–48.

166. Nicholas R. Garofalo, "Present and Future Capabilities of OTH Radars," *Studies in Intelligence* 13, 2 (Spring 1969): 53–61 at 53–54; [deleted], Assistant Chief, DPD-DD/P, Memorandum for: Acting Deputy Director (Plans), Status of CIA Personnel Staff, Project [deleted], July 22, 1960, 2000 CIA Release, NARA.

167. Ibid., pp. 54–55, 60.

168. Thomas Powers, *The Man Who Kept the Secrets: Richard Helms and the CIA* (London: Weidenfeld and Nicolson, 1979), p. 146; Ranelagh, *The Agency*, p. 211; Kevin Whitelaw, "A Killing in the Congo," *U.S. News and World Report,* July 24–31, 2000, p. 63.

169. Ranelagh, *The Agency*, p. 211.

170. U.S. Congress, Senate Select Committee to Study Governmental Operations with Respect to Intelligence Activities, *Alleged Assassination Plots Involving Foreign Leaders* (Washington, D.C.: U.S. Government Printing Office, 1975), pp. 71, 89.

171. J. S. Earman, Inspector General, CIA, *Report on Plots to Assassinate Fidel Castro* (Washington, D.C.: CIA, 1967), pp. 23–24.

172. Ibid., p. 24; Powers, *The Man Who Kept the Secrets*, p. 148.

173. Powers, *The Man Who Kept the Secrets*, p. 150.

Chapter 2: False Start

1. Allen W. Dulles, Memorandum for: Deputy Secretary of Defense, Special Assistant to the President for Science and Technology, Subject: Proposed Curtailment of Project CORONA, December 4, 1958, in NRO Collection of CORONA, ARGON, LANYARD Records (subsequently CAL Records).

2. John Ranelagh, *The Agency: The Rise and Decline of the CIA, from Wild Bill Donovan to William Casey* (New York: Simon & Schuster, 1986), pp. 410, 730.

3. Donald E. Welzenbach, "Science and Technology: Origins of a Directorate," *Studies in Intelligence* 30, 2 (Summer 1986): 13–26 at 22; CIA, N-120-2, Organization and Functions: Office of the Deputy Director (Plans), Establishment of the Development Projects Division, February 18, 1959, NARA, RG 263, 1998 CIA Release, Box 44, Folder 14.

4. Welzenbach, "Science and Technology," p. 22; Albert D. Wheelon, "Genesis of a Unique National Capability," address at CIA, December 19, 1984, p. 9.

5. U.S. Congress, Senate Select Committee to Study Governmental Operations with Respect to Intelligence Activities, *Final Report, Book IV: Supplementary Detailed Staff Reports on Foreign and Military Intelligence* (Washington, D.C.: U.S. Government Printing Office, 1976), p. 77.

6. Welzenbach, "Science and Technology," p. 22.

7. Ibid.

8. Richard M. Bissell Jr., with Jonathan E. Lewis and Francis T. Pudlo, *Reflections of a Cold Warrior: From Yalta to the Bay of Pigs* (New Haven: Yale University Press, 1996), p. 203.

9. Evan Thomas, *The Very Best Men: Four Who Dared—The Early Years of the CIA* (New York: Simon & Schuster, 1995), p. 272.

10. Letter, Richard M. Bissell to John McCone, February 7, 1962.

11. Ibid.

12. Ibid.

13. Ibid.

14. Ibid.; CIA, HN 1-18, February 14, 1962, NARA, CIA Historical Review Program 89-2 RG 263, NN3-263-94-010, Box 1, HS/HC 706, Folder 7.

15. Welzenbach, "Science and Technology," p. 23.

16. John A. McCone, HN 1-8, February 14, 1962; John A. McCone, HN 1-9, February 16, 1962; information provided by CIA Public Affairs Staff.

17. Lt. Gen. Marshall Carter, DDCI, HN 1-15, "Transfer of Special Projects Branch," April 16, 1962, NARA, CIA HRP 89-2, NN3-263-94-010, Box 5, HS/HC 706, Box 7.

18. "Reconsideration of the Missions and Functions of the Deputy Director (Research)," July 3, 1962, 2000 CIA Release.

19. Lt. Gen. Marshall Carter, Deputy Director, HN 1-23, "Deputy Director (Research)," July 30, 1962.

20. Ibid.; Col. Stanley W. Beerli, Assistant Director for Special Activities, Office of Special Activities, OSA HQS Notice No. 1-16, June 20, 1962.

21. Interview with Albert Wheelon, Montecito, California, November 11–12, 1998.

22. Ray S. Cline, *Secrets, Spies, and Scholars: The Essential CIA* (Washington, D.C.: Acropolis, 1976), pp. 4, 54–55, 105, 120, 123, 133, 149, 172, 194; Welzenbach, "Science and Technology," p. 23.

23. Welzenbach, "Science and Technology," pp. 22–23; Cline, *Secrets, Spies, and Scholars*, p. 200.

24. "Reconsideration of the Missions and Functions of the Deputy Director (Research)." Helms did not object to the DDR's conducting "agent-oriented" research that would be useful to the Plans directorate. (John A. Bross, Memorandum for: Deputy Director of Central Intelligence, Subject: [Deleted], December 21, 1962, NARA, RG 263, 1998 CIA Release, Box 47, Folder 15.)

25. Telephone interview with Edward Giller, June 29, 1999; Wheelon interview.

26. "ORD Milestones," September 1966, NARA, TRB, RG 263, 1998 CIA Release, Box 66, Folder 5; "Missions and Responsibilities of the Office of Research and Development," September 26, 1962, NARA, RG 263, 1998 CIA Release, Box 66, Folder 4.

27. "Missions and Responsibilities of the Office of Research and Development."

28. John Marks, *The Search for the "Manchurian Candidate": The CIA and Mind Control* (New York: Norton, 1991), pp. 210, 224; telephone conversation with Bud Wheelon, January 28, 2000.

29. Marks, *The Search for the "Manchurian Candidate,"* pp. 224–225.

30. Ibid., p. 225.

31. Ibid., pp. 225–226.

32. Henry G. Plaster, "Snooping on Space Pictures," *Studies in Intelligence* 8, 4 (Fall 1964): 31–39 at 34; Peter A. Gorin, "ZENIT: The Response to CORONA," in Dwayne A. Day, John M. Logsdon, and Brian Latell (eds.), *Eye in the Sky: The Story of the CORONA Spy Satellites* (Washington, D.C.: Smithsonian, 1998), pp. 157–170 at p. 162.

33. Donald C. Brown, "On the Trail of Hen House and Hen Roost," *Studies in Intelligence* 13, 2 (Spring 1969): 11–19 at 11; Chris Pocock, *The U-2 Spyplane: Toward the Unknown* (Atglen, Pa.: Schiffer Books, 2000), pp. 172–174.

34. Brown, "On the Trail of Hen House and Hen Roost," p. 12.

35. Ibid., pp. 12–13.

36. Gene Poteat, "Stealth, Countermeasures, and ELINT, 1960–1975," *Studies in Intelligence* 42, 1 (1998): 51–59 at 53.

37. Ibid.

38. Ibid.

39. Ibid., p. 55.

40. Ibid.

41. Ibid.

42. Ibid.

43. Ibid.

44. Ibid., pp. 55–56.

45. Ibid., p. 56.

46. Ibid.

47. Robert A. McDonald, "CORONA: Success for Space Reconnaissance, a Look into the Cold War, and a Revolution in Intelligence," *Photogrammetric Engineering and Remote Sensing* 60, 6 (June 1995): 689–720 at 715–716.

48. Gregory W. Pedlow and Donald E. Welzenbach, *The Central Intelligence Agency and Overhead Reconnaissance: The U-2 and OXCART Programs, 1954–1974* (Washington, D.C.: CIA, 1992), p. 200.

49. Ibid., pp. 200–201.

50. Dino Brugioni, *Eyeball to Eyeball: The Inside Story of the Cuban Missile Crisis* (New York: Random House, 1991), p. 105.

51. Pedlow and Welzenbach, *The Central Intelligence Agency and Overhead Reconnaissance*, p. 205.

52. Ibid., p. 206.

53. Ibid., pp. 206–207.

54. Interview with Jack C. Ledford, Arlington, Virginia, October 7, 1999.

55. Ibid.; United States Air Force, Biography: Brigadier General Jack C. Ledford, n.d.

56. Pedlow and Welzenbach, *The Central Intelligence Agency and Overhead Reconnaissance*, p. 207.

57. Ibid.; *Office of Special Projects, 1965–1970, Volume One, Chapters I-II* (Washington, D.C.: CIA, 1973), p. 100; Ledford interview.

58. Pedlow and Welzenbach, *The Central Intelligence Agency and Overhead Reconnaissance*, pp. 207–208.

59. Capt. Sanders A. Laubenthal, *The Missiles in Cuba, 1962: The Role of SAC Intelligence* (Offutt AFB, Nebr.: Strategic Air Command, 1984), pp. 22–26.

60. Pedlow and Welzenbach, *The Central Intelligence Agency and Overhead Reconnaissance*, pp. 208–209.

61. McDonald, "CORONA," p. 700; Director of Central Intelligence, SNIE 13-2-63, "Communist China's Advanced Weapons Program," July 24, 1963, pp. 4, 5–6; National Photographic Interpretation Center, CIA, "Search for Uranium Mining in the Vicinity of A-Ko-Su, China," August 1963, in Kevin Ruffner (ed.), *CORONA: America's First Satellite* (Washington, D.C.: CIA, 1995), pp. 175–183 at p. 176.

62. National Photographic Interpretation Center, CIA, "Chronological Developments of the Kapustin Yar/Vladimirovka and Tyuratam Missile Test Centers, USSR, 1957 Through 1963," November 1963, in Ruffner (ed.), *CORONA*, pp. 191–196 at pp. 192–193; National Photographic Interpretation Center, CIA, "Suspect CW Agent Production Plants—Dzerzhinsk USSR, Changes Since 1962," August 1963, in Ruffner (ed.), *CORONA*, pp. 185–189; National Photographic Interpretation Center, CIA, "Probable Solid Propellants Testing Facilities and Associated Explosives Plants in the USSR," December 1963, in Ruffner (ed.), *CORONA*, pp. 197–214 at pp. 199, 213.

63. Pedlow and Welzenbach, *The Central Intelligence Agency and Overhead Reconnaissance*, p. 289.

64. Thomas P. McIninch, "The OXCART Story," *Studies in Intelligence* 15, 1 (Winter 1971): 1–34 at 11–12.

65. Ibid., pp. 12–13.

66. Ibid., p. 13.

67. Ibid., pp. 13–14; telephone conversation with Albert Wheelon, January 28, 2000.

68. Dwayne A. Day, "The Development and Improvement of the CORONA Satellite," in Dwayne A. Day, John M. Logsdon, and Brian Latell (eds.), *Eye in the Sky: The Story of the CORONA Spy Satellites* (1998), pp. 48–85 at pp. 75–77; McDonald, "CORONA," p. 695.

69. Interview with a former CIA official; Welzenbach, "Science and Technology," p. 24.

70. Dwayne A. Day, "A Failed Phoenix: The KH-6 LANYARD Reconnaissance Satellite," *Spaceflight* 39, 5 (May 1997): 170–174; McDonald, "CORONA," p. 694.

71. Day, "A Failed Phoenix."

72. Frederic C.E. Oder, James C. Fitzpatrick, and Paul E. Worthman, *The CORONA Story* (Washington, D.C.: NRO, 1987), p. 92; Welzenbach, "Science and Technology," p. 26; Herbert Scoville Jr., letter to John A. McCone, April 25, 1963.

73. Herbert Scoville Jr., letter to John A. McCone, April 25, 1963.

74. Roswell Gilpatric, Deputy Secretary of Defense, to Allen W. Dulles, Director of Central Intelligence, September 6, 1961.

75. Robert Perry, *A History of Satellite Reconnaissance, Volume 5: Management of the National Reconnaissance Program, 1960–1965* (Washington, D.C.: NRO, 1969), pp. 42, 47, 51.

76. Ibid., p. 49.

77. Ibid., pp. 49–50; interview with Joseph V. Charyk, June 1, 1999; Herbert R. Scoville Jr., Deputy Director (Research), Memorandum for Dr. Charyk, Subject: SecDef-DCI Agreement on NRO, April 20, 1962.

78. "Agreement Between Secretary of Defense and the Director of Central Intelligence on Responsibilities of the National Reconnaissance Office," May 2, 1962; *Office of Special Projects, 1965–1970, Volume Four: Appendixes B, C, & D & Annex I* (Washington, D.C.: CIA, 1973), p. 6 in CAL Records 2/A/0077; Perry, *A History of Satellite Reconnaissance, Volume 5*, pp. 51–52.

79. Joseph V. Charyk, Memorandum for: NRO Program Directors, NRO Staff, Subject: (S) Organization and Functions of the NRO, July 23, 1962; Gerald K. Haines, *The National Reconnaissance Office: Its Origins, Creation, and Early Years* (Washington, D.C.: NRO, 1997), p. 22; Martin interview; Secretary of the Air Force/Public Affairs, "Biography: Major General John L. Martin, Jr."; telephone interview with Albert Wheelon, May 19, 1997; interview with a former CIA official; Jeffrey T. Richelson, "The Wizards of Langley: The CIA's Directorate of Science and Technology, 1962–1996," *Intelligence and National Security* 12, 1 (January 1997): 82–103; Organization Chart, Office of Special Activities, July 1962; *GRAB: Galactic RAdiation and Background* (Washington, D.C.: NRL, 1997); Dwayne A. Day, "Listening from Above: The First Signals Intelligence Satellite," *Spaceflight* 41, 8 (August 1999): 339–346.

80. Col. John L. Martin Jr., Memorandum for the Record, Subject: 22–23 May Conference on NRO, May 24, 1962; Perry, *A History of Satellite Reconnaissance, Volume 5*, p. 53.

81. Perry, *A History of Satellite Reconnaissance, Volume 5*, p. 61.

82. Ibid., pp. 61, 63–64.

83. Herbert Scoville Jr., Memorandum for: Director, National Reconnaissance Office, Subject: Comments on Organization and Functions of NRO, August 29, 1962.

84. Wheelon interview; interview with John McMahon, Los Altos, California, November 17, 1998.

85. Wheelon interview; McMahon interview.

86. Interview with Edward Giller, June 29, 1999; Wheelon, "Genesis of a Unique National Capability."

87. Scoville, Comments on Organization and Functions of NRO.

88. Perry, *A History of Satellite Reconnaissance, Volume 5*, p. 67.

89. Ibid., pp. 67, 73.

90. Ibid., pp. 71–73.

91. Ibid., p. 73–74.

92. Ibid., p. 74; Wheelon, "Genesis of a Unique National Capability."

93. Perry, *A History of Satellite Reconnaissance, Volume 5*, p. 75.

94. Ibid.

95. National Security Council Intelligence Directive No. 5, "U.S. Espionage and Counterintelligence Activities Abroad," January 18, 1961.

96. Oder, Kirkpatrick, and Worthman, *The CORONA Story*, pp. 90–91; telephone interview with Brockway McMillan, September 15, 1999; Buzard interview.

97. Perry, *A History of Satellite Reconnaissance, Volume 5*, p. 78.

98. Ibid., p. 91; Joseph Charyk, "A Summary Review of the National Reconnaissance Office," February 25, 1963.

99. Perry, *A History of Satellite Reconnaissance*, pp. 93, 96–97.

100. l. Edward Giller, Assistant Deputy Director, Research, Memorandum for the Record, Subject: Meeting Between Mr. McCone and Dr. McMillan–21 March 1963, March 22, 1963, NRO CAL Records, 1/E/0011. Perhaps McCone believed the agreement was more workable because he did not see it as significantly limiting his authority over the DNRO. Thus, in the same meeting, he also voiced his displeasure to Charyk's successor about the state of the satellite reconnaissance program. He also wanted to know if certain instructions he had given to the DNRO had been carried out, obtained a promise from the DNRO to produce a new launch schedule for presentation to the USIB, and instructed him to involve the NRO in the aerial portion of the NRP.

101. John A. McCone, Director of Central Intelligence, and Roswell Gilpatric, "Agreement between the Secretary of Defense and the Director of Central Intelligence on Management of the National Reconnaissance Program," March 13, 1963, p. 1.

102. Ibid., pp. 1–2.

103. Ibid., pp. 3–4.

104. Perry, *A History of Satellite Reconnaissance, Volume 5*, pp. 93–96.

105. Oder, Fitzpatrick, and Worthman, *The CORONA Story*, p. 92; Buzard interview.

106. Oder, Fitzpatrick, and Worthman, *The CORONA Story*, p. 92.

107. Ibid.

108. Ibid.

109. Interview with Herbert Scoville, McLean, Virginia, 1983.

110. Giller interview.

Chapter 3: A New Beginning

1. Donald E. Welzenbach, "Science and Technology: Origins of a Directorate," *Studies in Intelligence* 30, 2 (Summer 1986): 13–26 at 24; interview with John McMahon, Los Altos, California, November 17, 1998.

2. Welzenbach, "Science and Technology," p. 24.

3. Ibid., pp. 24–25.

4. Ibid., pp. 25–26.

5. Ibid., p. 26; Albert D. Wheelon, "Genesis of a Unique National Capability," December 19, 1984, address at CIA, p. 12; CIA, HN 20-49, "Announcement of Assignment to Key Position Deputy Director (Intelligence)," June 4, 1962.

6. Central Intelligence Agency, *R. V. Jones Intelligence Award Ceremony Honoring Dr. Albert Wheelon*, December 13, 1994; Central Intelligence Agency, "Biographic Profile, Albert Dewell Wheelon," May 10, 1966; interview with Albert Wheelon, Montecito, California, November 11–12, 1998; Robert P. Crease and Charles C. Mann, *The Second Creation: Makers of the Revolution in 20th-Century Physics* (New York: Macmillan, 1986), p. 175.

7. Vita, Albert D. Wheelon, April 10, 1999.

8. Wheelon interview; Wheelon, "Genesis of a Unique National Capability," pp. 7–8.

9. Wheelon interview; Wheelon, "Genesis of a Unique National Capability," pp. 8–9; telephone conversation with Bud Wheelon, January 28, 2000.

10. Wheelon interview; telephone conversation with Albert Wheelon, September 16, 1999; Wheelon telephone conversation, January 28, 2000.

11. MSC [Marshall S. Carter], Memorandum for the Director, February 22, 1963.

12. Welzenbach, "Science and Technology," p. 26; Wheelon, "Genesis of a Unique National Capability," p. 12; Wheelon interview; interview with Albert Wheelon, Montecito, California, June 14, 1999.

13. Wheelon interview, June 14, 1999.

14. Ibid.

15. Ibid.

16. Ibid.

17. Ibid.

18. Wheelon, "Genesis of a Unique National Capability," pp. 12–13; Wheelon interview, June 14, 1999; Welzenbach, "Science and Technology," p. 26.

19. Lt. Gen. Marshall S. Carter, Acting DCI, HN 1-36, August 5, 1963, NARA, CIA HRP 89-2, RG 263, NN3-263-94-010, Box 5, HS/HC 706, Folder 7; Diary Notes for Colonel White, August 6, 1963, 2000 CIA Release.

20. Interview with Brig. Gen. Jack C. Ledford, Arlington, Virginia, October 7, 1999.

21. Lt. Gen. Marshall S. Carter, Acting DCI, HN 1-36, August 5, 1963.

22. Wheelon interview, May 11–12, 1998.

23. Telephone interview with Albert Wheelon, April 2, 1997; Wheelon interview, June 14, 1999; interview with Karl Weber, Oakton, Virginia, May 5, 1999.

24. John Ranelagh, *The Agency: The Rise and Decline of the CIA, from Wild Bill Donovan to William Casey* (New York: Simon & Schuster, 1986), p. 491; interview with Albert Wheelon, Montecito, California, March 21, 2000.

25. Ray S. Cline, *Secrets, Spies, and Scholars: Blueprint of the Essential CIA* (Washington, D.C.: Acropolis Books, 1976), pp. 199–200. The battle over OSI was the most important but not the only dispute between Cline and Wheelon. They also clashed over the role of Cline's Collection Guidance Staff and the related issues of the location of the Special Intelligence Staff and the intelligence directorate's access to information about DS&T reconnaissance activities. Wheelon described the conflict over the Collection Guidance Staff as one of Cline's "petty bureaucratic gambits." Of more concern to Wheelon was Cline's drafting of an OSI analyst to help produce an assessment in October 1963 of the significance of Soviet leader Nikita Khrushchev's remarks on abandoning the race to the moon. In a memo to OSI chief Donald Chamberlain, Wheelon noted that Cline had not consulted him (Wheelon) or his deputy (Carl Duckett), nor had he shown Wheelon a copy of the assessment before it was distributed. In his memo, Wheelon noted that "I raised this with Cline yesterday and told him this would have to stop." He instructed Chamberlain to inform everyone in OSI not to take any assignments from Cline unless "you . . . or your designated officer, are in the loop."One battle that was not joined was an attempt to transfer NPIC from Cline's directorate to the DS&T. A December 1963 memo to Wheelon asked him if he had "given thought to . . . Indian wrestling Ray Cline for control of NPIC." The justification offered was NPIC's inactivity in the research and development area. However, Wheelon felt that he already "had enough trouble with Cline," and fighting for NPIC would not be worth a "bruising fight." The best thing the DS&T could do for NPIC, Wheelon believed, was to "give them really good pictures." (Ray S. Cline, Memorandum for: Deputy Director of Central Intelligence, Subject: Rationale for a Central Collection Guidance Function, February 28, 1964; Ray S. Cline [DDI], Memorandum for: Director of Central Intelligence, Subject: Differences of Opinion Regarding Collection Guidance Staff [CGS], March 13, 1964; interview with Albert Wheelon, Montecito, California, November 11–12, 1998; Albert D. Wheelon, Deputy Director for Science and Technology, Memorandum for: Assistant Director/Scientific Intelligence, Subject: Coordination with DD/I, October 31, 1963, 2000 CIA Release; [Deleted], Acting Assistant Director, Special Activities, Memorandum for: Deputy Director (Science and Technology), Subject: National Photographic Interpretation Center, December 31, 1963, 2000 CIA Release; telephone conversation with Albert Wheelon, March 5, 2001.)

26. Systems Analysis Staff, Directorate of Science and Technology, CIA, *A Report on DS&T Intelligence Collection Requirements*, July 12, 1966, p. 7; China Task Force, Central Intelligence Agency, "The Production Effort," July 1965–June 1967, p. 20, NARA, RG 263, CIA HRP 89-2, NN3-263-94-010, Box 9, File HS/HC 735, Folder 2.

27. Wheelon telephone conversations, September 16, 1999, and June 16, 2000.

28. Office of Scientific Intelligence, CIA, *Japanese Nuclear Energy Program*, OSI-SR/65-55, November 1964; Office of Scientific Intelligence, CIA, *Indian Nuclear Energy Program,* November 6, 1964; Office of Scientific Intelligence, Central Intelligence Agency, *Soviet Nuclear Research Reactors*, OSI-SR/64-41, September 22, 1964.

29. Director of Central Intelligence, NIE 11-2-64, *The Soviet Atomic Energy Program*, July 16, 1964, p. 3; Director of Central Intelligence, NIE 11-2A-65, *The Soviet Atomic Energy Program*, May 19, 1965.

30. Donald F. Chamberlain, Director of Scientific Intelligence, Memorandum for: Mr. Charles E. Johnson, Staff Member, National Security Council, Subject: The Nuclear Weapons Capability, October 18, 1965.

31. Weber interview.

32. George McGhee to Secretary of State Dean Rusk, "Anticipatory Action Pending Chinese Demonstration of a Nuclear Capability," September 13, 1961, NARA, RG 59, Records of Policy Planning Staff, 1957–1961; "Telegram from State Department to Embassy in Soviet Union," July 15, 1963, in David M. Mabon and David S. Patterson (eds.), *Foreign Relations of the United States [FRUS], 1961–1963, Volume VII: Arms Control and Disarmament* (Washington, D.C.: Government Printing Office, 1996), p. 801; "Telegram from Embassy in Soviet Union to State Department," July 27, 1963, in Mabon and Patterson (eds.), *FRUS, 1961–1963, Volume VII*, p. 860. Rusk's rejection of the McGhee proposal is noted in handwritten comments that appear on the document.

33. Director of Central Intelligence, SNIE 13-2-63, *Communist China's Advanced Weapons Program*, July 24, 1963, p. 1.

34. John Wilson Lewis and Xue Litai, *China Builds the Bomb* (Stanford, Calif.: Stanford University Press, 1988), p. 114; Joel Ullom, "Enriched Uranium Versus Plutonium: Proliferant Preferences in the Choice of Fissile Material," *Nonproliferation Review* 2, 1 (Fall 1994): 1–15 at 1, 5.

35. Director of Central Intelligence, SNIE 13-2-63, *Communist China's Advanced Weapons Program*, p. 1.

36. Ibid., pp. 2, 4; Lewis and Xue, *China Builds the Bomb*, pp. 134–135.

37. SNIE 13-2-63, *Communist China's Advanced Weapons Program*, p. 2.

38. Gen. Maxwell Taylor, Memorandum for General LeMay et al., "Chinese Nuclear Development," November 18, 1963, NARA, RG 218, Taylor Papers, Box 1.

39. Johnson's study remains classified but is concisely summarized in George W. Rathjens, "Destruction of Chinese Nuclear Weapons Capabilities," December 14, 1964. The paper was produced by Rathjens while he was a staff member of the Arms Control and Disarmament Agency.

40. Robert S. Norris, Andrew S. Burrows, and Richard W. Fieldhouse, *Nuclear Weapons Databook Volume V: British, French, and Chinese Nuclear Weapons* (Boulder, Colo.: Westview, 1994), p. 333.

41. Director of Central Intelligence, SNIE 13-4-64, *The Chances of an Imminent Communist Chinese Nuclear Explosion*, August 26, 1964, p. 1.

42. Ibid., p. 2.

43. Interview with Albert Wheelon, Washington, D.C., April 9, 1997.

44. Interview by William Burr with Allen S. Whiting, Crystal City, Virginia, December 13, 1996; interview with former CIA official, April 7, 1997.

45. "Transcript of Daily Press Briefing, Tuesday, September 29, 1964," RG 59, Records of Special Assistant to Undersecretary for Political Affairs, 1963–1965, Box 2, Psychological Preparations of Chinese Test, October 16, 1964.

46. Donald Chamberlain, AD/SI to DDCI, Subject: Estimated Imminence of a Chinese Nuclear Test, October 15, 1964, in Harriet Dashiell Schwar (ed.), *Foreign Relations of the United States 1964–1968, Volume XXX, China*, (Washington, D.C.: U.S. Government Printing Office, 1998), pp. 107–108.

47. Ibid.

48. Glenn T. Seaborg with Benjamin S. Loeb, *Stemming the Tide: Arms Control in the Johnson Years* (Lexington, Mass.: Lexington Books, 1986), p. 116; V. Gupta and D. Rich, "Locating the Detonation of China's First Nuclear Explosive Test on 16 October 1964," *International Journal of Remote Sensing* 17, 10 (October 1996): 1969–1974.

49. Norris, Burrows, and Fieldhouse, *Nuclear Weapons Databook, Volume V*, p. 345; Willis Armstrong, William Leonhart, William J. McCaffrey, and Herbert C. Rothenberg, "The Hazards of Single-Outcome Forecasting," *Studies in Intelligence* 28, 3 (Fall 1984): 57–70, reprinted in H. Bradford Westerfield (ed.), *Inside the CIA's Private World: Declassified Articles from the Agency's Internal Journal 1955–1992* (New Haven: Yale University Press, 1995), pp. 238–254 at p. 246; Wheelon interview, April 9, 1997.

50. Letter, B. A. Schriever, Commander, Air Force Systems Command, to General Curtis E. LeMay, December 26, 1963.

51. Office of Computer Services, Directorate of Science and Technology, CIA, *OCS Computer System Planning Report*, June 1, 1965. FMSAC's work was aided by help from outside specialists—from contractors as well as the national labs that analyzed the radar signatures and telemetry of satellites and missiles. Telemetry of Soviet reconnaissance satellites was analyzed in an attempt to determine their targets. Another group, at Lawrence Livermore National Laboratory, analyzed Soviet and Chinese nuclear weapons programs. (Albert D. Wheelon, Memorandum for: Director, BPAM, Subject: Replies for Questions by Bureau of the Budget Examiners, November 19, 1964; interview with Albert Wheelon, Montecito, California, November 11–12, 1998.)

52. Albert D. Wheelon and Sidney N. Graybeal, "Intelligence for the Space Race," *Studies in Intelligence* 7, 4 (Fall 1963): 1–13 at 1.

53. Ibid., p. 3.

54. Telephone interview with Edward Proctor, March 16, 1999; Wheelon interview, June 14, 1999; Wheelon interview, November 11–12, 1998.

55. Interview with R. Evans Hineman, Chantilly, Virginia, February 17, 1999; Wheelon interview, April 9, 1997.

56. David S. Brandwein, "The SS-8 Controversy," *Studies in Intelligence* 13, 3 (Summer 1969): 27–35.

57. Ibid.; Director of Central Intelligence, NIE 11-8-63, *Soviet Capabilities for Strategic Attack*, October 18, 1963, p. 12.

58. Wheelon interview, November 11–12, 1998.

59. Interview with former CIA official.

60. Ibid.; Wheelon telephone conversation, September 16, 1999.

61. Wheelon interview, April 9, 1997; telephone conversation with Albert Wheelon, November 29, 1998.

62. Hineman interview.

63. Ibid.

64. Letter, Schriever to LeMay.

65. Ibid.

66. Ibid.

67. Jack E. Thomas, Assistant Chief of Staff, Intelligence, Subject: CIA Foreign Missile and Space Analysis Center, January 2, 1964.

68. Draft of Letter, Gen. Curtis E. LeMay to Gen. B. A. Schriever, AFSC, January 7, 1964.

69. Department of Defense Directive S-5100.43, "Defense Special Missile and Astronautics Center (Defense/SMAC)," April 27, 1964; Richard L. Bernard, "The Defense Special Missile and Astronautics Center," *Cryptologic Spectrum*, Fall 1981, pp. 30–33; Mark Clesh, "Dedication of New Operations Center for DEFSMAC," *Communiqué*, March/April 1998, pp. 42–43.

70. Clesh, "Dedication of New Operations Center for DEFSMAC"; National Security Agency, *A Historical Perspective of DefSMAC with Charles Tevis and Max Mitchell*, 1980 (video); Hineman interview.

71. Nicholas L. Johnson, *Soviet Military Strategy in Space* (London: Jane's, 1987), p. 51; James Harford, *Korolev: How One Man Masterminded the Soviet Drive to Beat America to the Moon* (New York: John Wiley, 1997), pp. 190–200; Director of Central Intelligence, NIE 11-1-65, *The Soviet Space Program*, n.d., pp. 23–24, 28; Director of Central Intelligence, NIE 11-1-67, *The Soviet Space Program*, March 2, 1967, pp. 6–7.

72. Director of Central Intelligence, NIE 11-1-65, *The Soviet Space Program*, p. 27; Director of Central Intelligence, NIE 11-1-67, *The Soviet Space Program*, p. 5.

73. Director of Central Intelligence, NIE 11-1-67, *The Soviet Space Program*, pp. 5–6, 34–35; Harford, *Korolev*, pp. 155–156; William E. Burrows, *Exploring Space: Voyages in the Solar System and Beyond* (New York: Random House, 1990), p. 162.

74. Director of Central Intelligence, NIE 11-1-67, *The Soviet Space Program*, pp. 6, 34–35; Harford, *Korolev*, p. 154; Burrows, *Exploring Space*, p. 134.

75. Hineman interview.

76. Wheelon and Graybeal, "Intelligence for the Space Race," p. 5.

77. Ibid., pp. 4–5.

78. Harford, *Korolev*, p. 152.

79. Frank A. Whitmire and Edward G. Correll, "The Failure of Cosmos 57," *Studies in Intelligence* 10, 3 (Summer 1966): 25–29.

80. Ibid.

81. Ibid.; Director of Central Intelligence, NIE 11-1-67, *The Soviet Space Program*, p. 33.

82. James Burke, "Seven Years to Luna 9," *Studies in Intelligence* 10, 2 (Summer 1966): 1–24 at 20.

83. Ibid.; Burrows, *Exploring Space*, pp. 162–163.

84. Robert C. Berman and John P. Baker, *Soviet Strategic Forces: Requirements and Responses* (Washington, D.C.: Brookings Institution, 1982), p. 104; "Soviets Step Up Testing of First-Line ICBM Systems," *EUCOM Intelligence Report*, April 13, 1966, p. 1.

85. Jerold H. Klaimon, "Reentry Vehicle Analysis," *Studies in Intelligence* 12, 3 (Summer 1968): 23–33.

86. Ibid., p. 24.

87. David S. Brandwein, "Telemetry Analysis," *Studies in Intelligence* 8, 4 (Fall 1964): 21–29 at 23–24.

88. Ibid., p. 24.

89. Ibid., pp. 26–27; Klaimon, "Reentry Vehicle Analysis," p. 28.

90. Director of Central Intelligence, NIE 11-8-64, *Soviet Capabilities for Strategic Attack*, October 8, 1964, p. 41.

91. Central Intelligence Agency, *Cost Reduction Program FY 1966-FY 1967*, September 1, 1965, p. 9, NARA, RG 263, HRP 89-2, Box 7, File HS/HC 713.

92. Olav Riste, *The Norwegian Intelligence Service, 1945–1970* (London: Frank Cass, 1999), pp. 149, 158; Rolf Tamnes, *The United States and the Cold War in the High North* (Oslo: Ad Notam, 1991), pp. 211–212.

93. McMahon interview.

94. Hedrick Smith, "U.S. Aides Say Loss of Post in Iran Impairs Missile-Monitoring Ability," *New York Times*, March 2, 1979, pp. A1, A8; Wheelon interview, April 9, 1997.

95. Interview with William H. Nance, Bethesda, Maryland, May 4, 1999.

96. Smith, "U.S. Aides Say Loss of Post in Iran Impairs Missile-Monitoring Ability."

97. Interview with Robert Phillips, Rosslyn, Virginia, June 4, 1999; Nance interview.

98. Nance interview; U.S. Congress, Senate Foreign Relations Committee, *Fiscal Year 1980 International Security Assistance Authorization* (Washington, D.C.: U.S. Government Printing Office, 1979), p. 366; Wheelon interview, April 9, 1997; Phillips interview.

99. Director of Central Intelligence, NIE 11-8-67, *Soviet Capabilities for Strategic Attack*, October 26, 1967, p. 10; Berman and Baker, *Soviet Strategic Forces*, p. 104; Director of Central Intelligence, NIE 11-8-64, *Soviet Capabilities for Strategic Attack*, October 8, 1964, p. 13.

100. "Soviets Step Up Testing of First-Line ICBM Systems," *EUCOM Intelligence Report*, April 13, 1966; "Soviets Maintaining High Launch Rate for Major ICBM's; SS-11 Crew Training May Be Under Way," *EUCOM Intelligence Report*, August 18, 1966; "Series of SS-11 ICBM Tests to Pacific Impact Area Concluded," *EUCOM Intelligence Report*, September 7, 1966.

101. Frank Eliot, "Moon Bounce Elint," *Studies in Intelligence* 11, 2 (Spring 1967): 59–65 at 64.

102. Ibid., p. 60.

103. N. C. Gerson, "SIGINT in Space," *Studies in Intelligence* 28, 2 (Summer 1984): 41–48 at 47; Directorate of Collection, Office, ACS/Intelligence, U.S. Air Force, *History: Directorate of Collection, Office, ACS/Intelligence 1 July 31–December 1962*, n.d., p. 3; Eliot, "Moon Bounce Elint," pp. 60–61.

104. Eliot, "Moon Bounce Elint," pp. 63–64; Donald C. Brown, "On the Trail of Hen House and Hen Roost," *Studies in Intelligence* 13, 2 (Spring 1969): 11–19 at 13.

105. Brown, "On the Trail of Hen House and Hen Roost," pp. 13–14, 19.

106. Eliot, "Moon Bounce Elint," pp. 61, 64.

107. Ibid., pp. 64–65.

108. William H. Nance, "Quality ELINT," *Studies in Intelligence* 12, 2 (Spring 1968): 7–19 at 7–8; Gene Poteat, "Stealth, Countermeasures, and ELINT, 1960–1975," *Studies in Intelligence* 42, 1 (Spring 1998): 51–59 at 54–55. The specific technical characteristics that fall in the power and coverage categories are maximum beam power, total radiated power, antenna gain, and variation in gain (side and back lobe distribution) (Nance, "Quality ELINT," pp. 7–19 at 10.)

109. Nance, "Quality ELINT," p. 15.

110. Ibid., pp. 16–17.

111. Nicholas R. Garofalo, "Present and Future Capabilities of OTH Radars," *Studies in Intelligence* 13, 2 (Spring 1969): 53–61 at 55.

112. Ibid.; "Telegram from the Department of State to the Embassy in Iran," August 25, 1965, in Nina D. Howland (ed.), *Foreign Relations of the United States, 1964–1968, Volume XXII: Iran* (Washington, D.C.: U.S. Government Printing Office, 1999), pp. 166–167.

113. "The Indian Connection," *India Today*, December 31, 1983, p. 10; Wheelon interview, November 11–12, 1998. "The Indian Connection" and other sources have reported this device to be aimed at monitoring Chinese nuclear tests. Wheelon and McMahon recalled that the Himalaya project was to monitor telemetry.

114. Interview with a former CIA official; Wheelon interview, November 11–12, 1998.

115. Interview with a former CIA official; Ben R. Rich and Leo Janos, *Skunk Works: A Personal Memoir of My Years at Lockheed* (Boston: Little, Brown, 1994), p. 182.

116. Interview with Richard Bissell, Farmington, Connecticut, March 16, 1984.

117. Chris Pocock, *Dragon Lady: The History of the U-2 Spyplane* (Shrewsbury, England: Airlife, 1989), p. 98.

118. Ibid.

119. Ibid., p. 100; Gregory W. Pedlow and Donald E. Welzenbach, *The Central Intelligence Agency and Overhead Reconnaissance: The U-2 and OXCART Programs, 1954–1974* (Washington, D.C.: CIA, 1992), p. 282.

120. Pedlow and Welzenbach, *The Central Intelligence Agency and Overhead Reconnaissance*, p. 282; Pocock, *Dragon Lady*, p. 100.

121. Pocock, *Dragon Lady*, p. 100.

122. Ibid., pp. 100–101; R. E. Lawrence and Harry W. Woo, "Infrared Imagery in Overhead Reconnaissance," *Studies in Intelligence* 11, 3 (Summer 1967): 17–40 at 23.

123. Pocock, *Dragon Lady*, p. 111.

124. Ibid., pp. 102–103, 111; Wheelon interview, November 11–12, 1998.

125. Ledford interview. An undated, but clearly pre-1963, "Inspector General's Survey of Air Activities: Summary of Recommendations" (NARA, RG 263, 1998 CIA Release, Box 45, Folder 5), contained the recommendation that the CIA explore "with the U.S. Navy the feasibility and arrangements necessary for staging of missions from aircraft carriers whenever the target lies beyond the range of U.S.-based U-2s."

126. Ledford interview; Pedlow and Welzenbach, *The Central Intelligence Agency and Overhead Reconnaissance*, pp. 247–248.

127. Pocock, *Dragon Lady*, pp. 107–109; Norris, Burrows, and Fieldhouse, *Nuclear Weapons Databook, Volume V*, p. 407; interview with a former CIA official.

128. Wheelon interview, November 11–12, 1998.

129. David Reade, *The Age of Orion: Lockheed P-3, an Illustrated History* (Atglen, Pa.: Schiffer Military/Aviation History, 1998), p. 104; interview with Robert Singel, Great Falls, Virginia, February 25, 1999.

130. Singel interview; Reade, *The Age of Orion*, p. 105; Wheelon interview, June 14, 1999.

131. Reade, *The Age of Orion*, p. 105.

132. Ibid., p. 106.

133. McMahon interview; Wayne Mutza, *Lockheed P2V Neptune: An Illustrated History* (Atglen, Pa.: Schiffer Military/Aviation History, 1996), p. 115; Wheelon interview, November 11–12, 1998; telephone conversation with Albert Wheelon, January 28, 2000.

134. Singel interview; Wheelon interview, June 14, 1999.

135. Reade, *The Age of Orion*, p. 106. By November 1965, the CIA was involved in another program to modify P-2V7 aircraft for intelligence purposes. That month, representatives from ORD and OSA visited E-Systems at Greenville, Texas, to explore the possibility of using the planes as multi-sensor platforms. A memo noted that the CIA would likely be able to use such an aircraft for reconnaissance of undefended areas where conventional photography was limited because of dense foliage. A March 1966 memo noted that ORD had been directed to run the program and that "the continuation of any OSA program to achieve a low-altitude multi-sensor capability depends directly on the success or failure of this [effort]."The reference to dense foliage and the fact that the NRO was not providing funds for the program suggest that its primary focus was reconnaissance of Southeast Asian territory in support of CIA covert operations. ("Memorandum for the Record, Subject: Visit to [deleted], Project [deleted], November 22, 1965; Memorandum for: see Distribution, Subject: [deleted] Meetings, March 23, 1966, NARA, RG 263, 1998 CIA Release RG 263, Box 45, Folder 5 [both memos]).

136. Wheelon interview, November 11–12, 1998; Wheelon interview, March 21, 2000.

137. Wheelon interview, November 11–12, 1998.

138. Thomas P. McIninch, "The OXCART Story," *Studies in Intelligence* 15 (Winter 1971): 1–34 at 17.

139. Ibid.

140. Ibid., p. 19.

141. Ibid., p. 20; Pedlow and Welzenbach, *The Central Intelligence Agency and Overhead Reconnaissance*, pp. 300–301.

142. McIninch, *The OXCART Story*, p. 20.

143. Ibid., p. 21.

144. Ibid.

145. Ibid., p. 23.

146. Ibid.; Pedlow and Welzenbach, *The Central Intelligence Agency and Overhead Reconnaissance*, pp. 301–302.

147. Pedlow and Welzenbach, *The Central Intelligence Agency and Overhead Reconnaissance*, p. 302.

148. Ibid., p. 307.

149. Ibid.

150. Wheelon interview, November 11–12, 1998.

151. Interview with a former CIA official.

Chapter 4: Space Reconnaissance Wars

1. Interview with a former CIA official.

2. Interview with Albert Wheelon, Washington, D.C., April 9, 1997.

3. Interview with Albert Wheelon, Montecito, California, November 11–12, 1998; Robert Perry, *A History of Satellite Reconnaissance, Volume 5: Management of the National Reconnaissance Program, 1960–1965* (Washington, D.C.: NRO, 1969), pp. 123–124n. in NRO CAL Records, 2/A/0066.

4. Lt. Gen. Marshall S. Carter, DDCI, Memorandum for the Record, Subject: Meeting with Dr. Brockway McMillan, July 23, 1963.

5. Perry, *A History of Satellite Reconnaissance, Volume 5*, p. 120.

6. Office of Public Affairs, Secretary of the Air Force, "General Lew Allen Jr.," September 1981; interview with Gen. Lew Allen Jr., Pasadena, California, June 10, 1999.

7. General Lew Allen Jr. interview.

8. Roswell Gilpatric, Memorandum for the Record, Subject: Mr. McCone's Concerns Regarding NRO, August 22, 1963.

9. *Office of Special Projects, 1965–1970, Volume One, Chapters I-II* (Washington, D.C.: CIA, 1973), pp. 105–106.

10. Letter, Albert D. Wheelon, June 17, 1999.

11. Jonathan McDowell, "Launch Listings," in Dwayne A. Day, John M. Logsdon, and Brian Latell (eds.), *Eye in the Sky: The Story of the CORONA Spy Satellites* (Washington, D.C.: Smithsonian Institution Press, 1998), pp. 235–246 at p. 238.

12. Robert S. McNamara, Secretary of Defense, Memorandum for the Director, National Reconnaissance Office, Subject: Policy Guidance on Management Control over Reconnaissance Programs, October 22, 1963, NRO CAL Records, 1/A/0043.

13. Brockway McMillan, Memorandum for the Director of Central Intelligence, Subject: Management of the CORONA Project, October 28, 1963, NRO CAL Records, 1/A/0044.

14. Wheelon letter.

15. John A. McCone, Memorandum for: General Carter, Dr. Wheelon, September 20, 1963.

16. Brockway McMillan, Director, National Reconnaissance Office, Memorandum for Director of Central Intelligence, Subject: Management of CORONA Project, December 10, 1963, NRO CAL Records, 1/C/0062; Brockway McMillan, Director, National Reconnaissance Office, Memorandum for Director, NRO Program A, Director, NRO Program B, Subject: Responsibility for Operating Management of the CORONA Project, December 10, 1963, NRO CAL Archives, 1/A/0045.

17. Perry, *A History of Satellite Reconnaissance, Volume 5*, p. 134.

18. John A. McCone, Director, to Dr. Brockway McMillan, Director, National Reconnaissance Office, December 13, 1963, NRO CAL Records, 1/A/0047.

19. Albert D. Wheelon, Deputy Director (Science and Technology), Memorandum for: Director of Central Intelligence, Subject: Recommendation re Fubini's proposal, February 3, 1964, NRO CAL Records, 1/C/0067.

20. Brockway McMillan, Director, National Reconnaissance Office, to John McCone, February 4, 1964.

21. Albert D. Wheelon, Deputy Director (Science and Technology), Memorandum for: DCI, DDCI, Subject: Dissolution of CORONA Project Office, March 13, 1964, NRO CAL Records 1/C/0070.

22. Cyrus Vance, Deputy Secretary of Defense, to Lt. Gen. Marshall S. Carter, DDCI, August 28, 1964, NRO CAL Records 1/A/0063.

23. Cyrus R. Vance to John McCone, October 15, 1964, NRO CAL Records; [Deleted] to Albert Wheelon, October 22, 1964, NRO CAL Records, 1/C/0064.

24. Brig. Gen. Jack Ledford, USAF Assistant Director, Special Activities, Memorandum for the Record, Subject: Unsolved Management and Relationship, November 9, 1964, NRO CAL Records, 1/C/0087.

25. John A. McCone, Memorandum for: Honorable Cyrus R. Vance, Deputy Secretary of Defense, Subject: CIA Program B Participation in CORONA, November 17, 1964, NRO CAL Records, 1/A/0079.

26. Lt. Gen. Marshall S. Carter, Deputy Director, to Dr. Brockway McMillan, Director, National Reconnaissance Office, November 17, 1964, NRO CAL Records, 1/A/0080.

27. Directorate of Science and Technology, CIA, *CORONA Program History, Volume II: Governmental Activities*, May 19, 1976, pp. 1–19, in NRO CAL Records, 2/A/0089.

28. Brockway McMillan to [Deleted], June 14, 1965, NRO CAL Records, 1/A/0010.

29. "Examples of the Air Force Impacts on the CORONA Program," March 31, 1965, NRO CAL Records, 1/C/0010.

30. Marshall S. Carter, Lt. Gen. USA, Deputy Director, Memorandum for the Record, Subject: Meeting with Mr. Vance and Dr. McMillan, on Thursday, 25 March, March 26, 1965, NRO CAL Records, 1/A/0096.

31. Ibid.; Jackson D. Maxey, Chief, Special Projects Staff, Memorandum for the Record, Subject: Fact Sheet Regarding the Allegation That Since August 1964 CIA Has Been Withholding Payload Data from the Air Force in the CORONA Program, March 25, 1965, in NRO CAL Records, 1/C/0099.

32. Carter, Memorandum for the Record, Subject: Meeting Mr. Vance and Dr. McMillan.

33. Ibid.

34. "Robert Harry Mathams—Hands-on Intelligence Analyst," n.d.

35. Wheelon interview, November 11–12, 1998.

36. Ibid.

37. Interview with Roy Burks, North Potomac, Maryland, May 10, 1999; Sayre Stevens, "The Soviet BMD Program," in Ashton B. Carter and David N. Schwartz (eds.), *Ballistic Missile Defense* (Washington, D.C.: Brookings Institution, 1984), pp. 182–220 at 192.

38. *United States of America, Plaintiff v. William Peter Kampiles, Defendant,* United States District Court, Northern District of Indiana, Hammond Division, Testimony of Leslie Dirks, November 13, 1978, p. 4.

39. Burks interview; Wheelon interview, November 11–12, 1998.

40. Public Affairs Staff, "Biographical Information on William J. Perry," April 15, 1999; Wheelon interview, November 11–12, 1998; CIA Public Affairs Staff, "DCI Tenet Presents Dr. William J. Perry with Prestigious R. V. Jones Intelligence Award," April 15, 1999. In presenting him with the award, DCI George Tenet noted Perry's "leadership in promoting, modifying, and upgrading our national SIGINT capabilities are legendary." (CIA Public Affairs Staff, "DCI Tenet Presents Dr. William J. Perry with Prestigious R. V. Jones Intelligence Award," April 15, 1999.)

41. Wheelon interview, November 11–12, 1998; Desmond Ball, *Pine Gap: Australia and the U.S. Geostationary SIGINT Satellite Program* (Sydney: Allen & Unwin, 1988), p. 13; Desmond Ball, *A Suitable Piece of Real Estate: American Installations in Australia* (Sydney: Hale & Iremonger, 1980), p. 73; Philip Klass, "U.S. Monitoring Capability Impaired," *Aviation Week and Space Technology*, May 14, 1979, p. 18; telephone conversation with Albert Wheelon, February 8, 2000. Wheelon later recalled how some subordinates told him they were going to establish a committee to pick a code name for the project. Wheelon told them that by the time the name was chosen, the system would be built. Wheelon later noted that he was "impatient, intolerant" with regard to such "traditional time wasters." (Albert Wheelon, Washington, D.C., April 9, 1997.)

42. Wheelon interview, June 14, 1999.

43. McMillan interview; Wheelon interview, November 11–12, 1998, Christopher Anson Pike, "CANYON, RHYOLITE, and AQUACADE: U.S. Signals Intelligence Satellites in the 1970s," *Spaceflight* 37, 11 (November 1995): 381–383; Wheelon telephone interview, April 2, 1997; interview with John McMahon, Los Altos, California, November 17, 1998; Brockway McMillan, Memorandum for the Secretary of Defense, Subject: Comments on NRO and NRP, September 30, 1965, pp. 8–9. Both CANYON and RHYOLITE satellites were to orbit the earth once every twenty-four hours—which is what made them geosynchronous. RHYOLITE, but not CANYON, was geostationary because with virtually a zero-degree inclination, it essentially hovered over a single point at an altitude of 22,300 miles, whereas CANYONs traced a figure eight—drifting from about ten degrees below the equator to ten degrees above. In addition, the perigee and apogee of the orbit were approximately 19,000 and 24,000 miles.

44. Buzard interview.

45. Desmond Ball, *Pine Gap*, p. 55; interview with a former CIA official.

46. Desmond Ball, *Pine Gap*, p. 56.

47. Wheelon interview, April 9, 1997; telephone conversation with Albert Wheelon, October 12, 1999.

48. President's Foreign Intelligence Advisory Board, Memorandum for the President, Subject: National Reconnaissance Program, May 2, 1964, p.2, NRO CAL Records, 6/B/0044.

49. Ibid., p. 2.

50. Ibid., p. 3.

51. Cyrus Vance, Memorandum for McGeorge Bundy, Subject: Memorandum for the President, by the President's Foreign Intelligence Advisory Board, re National Reconnaissance Program, June 2, 1964, LBJ Library, National Security File, Intelligence File, NRO, Box 9.

52. J. Patrick Coyne, Memorandum for Mr. Bundy, Subject: National Reconnaissance Program, June 15, 1964, LBJ Library, National Security File, Intelligence File, "NRO," Box 9.

53. Spurgeon M. Keeny Jr., Memorandum for Mr. Bundy, July 2, 1964, LBJ Library, National Security File, Intelligence File, "NRO," Box 9; telephone interview with Spurgeon Keeny, July 10, 2000; Peter Jessup, "Some Borborygmous Rumblings from the Innards of the NRO," n.d., LBJ Library, National Security File, Intelligence File, "NRO," Box 9. Jessup also noted that the CIA-appointed NRO deputy director, Eugene Kiefer, "is even excluded from the NRO communications routing. When the Air Force has wind that McCone will issue a blast at a USIB meeting, McMillan absents himself and sends Kiefer. The tragicomedy then ensues of McCone blasting his own man."

54. McGeorge Bundy, Memorandum for the Secretary of Defense, the Director of Central Intelligence, Subject: National Reconnaissance Program, n. d., LBJ Library, Intelligence File, NRO, Box 9.

55. John A. McCone, Memorandum for the Record, Subject: Discussion at the NRO Executive Meeting, Attended by McCone, Vance, Fubini, and McMillan, August 12, 1964, NRO CAL Records, 1/A/0062.

56. Directorate of Science and Technology, *CORONA Program History, Volume II: Governmental Activities*, p. 1–18; NRO, *Program Directors of the NRO: ABC&D* (Chantilly, Va.: NRO, 1999), n.p.; Wheelon interview, April 2, 1997. Wheelon recalled that he established the SPS in fall 1963, shortly after he became Deputy Director for Science and Technology. A CIA listing of DS&T staff and office heads gives July 1964 as the official beginning of the staff. The *CORONA Program History* cites September 1 as when the existence of SPS became official.

57. Albert D. Wheelon, Deputy Director for Science and Technology, Memorandum for: Deputy Director of Central Intelligence, Subject: Establishment of a Satellite Office Within the Science and Technology Directorate, February 26, 1965, NRO CAL Records, 2/A/0078.

58. Ibid.

59. Ibid.

60. *Office of Special Projects, 1965–1970, Volume One, Chapters I-II* (Washington, D.C.: CIA, 1973), p. 116.

61. Ibid., p. 118.

62. Perry, *A History of Satellite Reconnaissance, Volume 5*, pp. 186–187.

63. Ibid., p. 187.

64. Ibid., p. 188.

65. Ibid.

66. Ibid., p. 189.

67. Ibid., pp. 174–175, 189.

68. Wheelon letter.

69. John Ranelagh, *The Agency: The Rise and Decline of the CIA, from Wild Bill Donovan to William Casey* (New York: Simon & Schuster, 1986), pp. 413n, 730–731; *Office of Special Projects, 1965–1970, Volume One, Chapters I-II*, p. 120.

70. *Office of Special Projects, 1965–1970, Volume One, Chapters I-II*, p. 6.

71. Albert D. Wheelon, "A Summary of the National Reconnaissance Problem," May 13, 1965, p. 5, NRO CAL Records, 1/D/0008.

72. Ibid., pp. 5–6.

73. Ibid., p. 6.

74. Ibid., pp. 7–10.
75. Ibid., pp. 19–21.
76. Ibid., p. 21.
77. Ibid., pp. 21–22.
78. Ibid., pp. 22–23.
79. Perry, *A History of Satellite Reconnaissance, Volume 5*, p. 195; W. F. Raborn, Director, to Honorable Cyrus R. Vance, Deputy Secretary of Defense, August 13, 1965, NRO CAL Records, 2/A/0078.
80. Cyrus Vance, Deputy Secretary of Defense, and William F. Raborn, Director of Central Intelligence (signatories), "Agreement for Reorganization of the National Reconnaissance Program," August 13, 1965.
81. Ibid.
82. Ibid.; W. F. Raborn, Director of Central Intelligence, to Honorable Cyrus R. Vance, Deputy Secretary of Defense, August 13, 1965, NRO CAL Records, 2/A/0078.
83. Raborn to Vance, August 13, 1965.
84. Ibid.
85. Ibid.; *Office of Special Projects, 1965–1970, Volume One, Chapters I-II*, p. 122.
86. McMillan interview; telephone interview with Albert Wheelon, May 19, 1997; letter from Frank Buzard to author, January 16, 1997; Brockway McMillan, Memorandum for the Secretary of Defense, Subject: Comments on NRO and NRP, pp. 4–5.
87. Directorate of Science and Technology, *CORONA Program History, Volume II, Governmental Activities*, p. 1–20; Frederic C.E. Oder, James C. Fitzpatrick, and Paul E. Worthman, *The CORONA Story* (Washington, D.C.: NRO, November 1987), p. 108; Burks interview.
88. Oder, Fitzpatrick, and Worthman, *The CORONA Story*, pp. 103, 105; Ludwell Lee Montague, *General Walter Bedell Smith as Director of Central Intelligence, October 1950-February 1953* (University Park: Pennsylvania State University Press, 1992), pp. 168–169; Wheelon interview, November 11–12, 1998. Sheldon died in 1987 as part of a suicide pact with his wife Alice, a prominent science fiction writer who used the pseudonym James Triptree Jr. He was bedridden and blind at the time. (Patricia Davis, "Bullets End 2 'Fragile' Lives," *Washington Post*, May 20, 1987, pp. A1, A14.)
89. McDowell, "Launch Listings," p. 238; "Appendix A," in Day, Logsdon, and Latell (eds.), *Eye in the Sky*, pp. 231–233 at p. 233.
90. Oder, Fitzpatrick, and Worthman, *The CORONA Story*, p. 109; "Appendix A," in Day, Logsdon, and Latell (eds.), *Eye in the Sky*, p. 233.
91. Buzard letter to author.
92. Perry, *A History of Satellite Reconnaissance, Volume 5*, p. 106; "Actions Under Way Responsive to Purcell Panel Report Recommendations," attachment to Brockway McMillan, Memorandum for the Director, CIA, Subject: Implementation of the Purcell Panel Recommendations, September 11, 1963; Brockway McMillan, Memorandum for the Director, CIA, Subject: Implementation of the Purcell Panel Recommendations, September 11, 1963.
93. John N. McMahon, Memorandum for [Deleted], Subject: References to the Purcell Panel, December 14, 1964; Perry, *A History of Satellite Reconnaissance, Volume 5*, p. 106; "Actions Under Way Responsive to Purcell Panel Report Recommendations," attachment to Brockway McMillan, Memorandum for the Director, CIA, Subject: Implementation of the Purcell Panel Recommendations, September 11, 1963.
94. Purcell Panel Report, p. 3.
95. Interview with a former CIA official; *Office of Special Projects, 1965–1970, Volume One, Chapters I-II*, p. 2.
96. Wheelon interview, April 9, 1997; Wheelon interview, November 11–12, 1998.
97. Perry, *A History of Satellite Reconnaissance, Volume 5*, pp. 130–131; Albert D. Wheelon, Deputy Director (Science and Technology), to Dr. Brockway McMillan, Director, National Recon-

naissance Office, November 5, 1963; telephone conversation with Albert Wheelon, December 26, 1999.

98. Wheelon to McMillan, November 5, 1963; Brockway McMillan, Director, National Reconnaissance Office, to Dr. Albert D. Wheelon, Deputy Director (Science and Technology), November 18, 1963. The picture of this episode as described in an NRO history is significantly different from that indicated by the memos described here. The history claims that by late November, McMillan had become aware of and annoyed about the Drell group's activities, and his reaction was a barbed comment that he would appreciate receiving more advance notice of such activities affecting NRO's mission. Further, he objected to several of Wheelon's concepts as well as the scope of the group's task and therefore would provide no funds for the project. (Perry, *A History of Satellite Reconnaissance, Volume 5*, pp. 131, 206 n.77.)

99. Wheelon interview, November 11–12, 1998; Wheelon interview, April 9, 1997.

100. Ibid.; Wheelon interview, November 11–12, 1998.

101. Wheelon letter.

102. Ibid.; *Office of Special Projects, 1965–1970, Volume I, Chapters I-II*, pp. 2–3; interview with John McMahon, Los Altos, California, November 17, 1998.

103. *Office of Special Projects, 1965–1970, Volume One, Chapters I-II*, pp. 2–3; McMahon interview.

104. Perry, *A History of Satellite Reconnaissance, Volume 5*, pp. 156, 159.

105. Ibid., pp. 159–160.

106. Ibid., p. 160.

107. Ibid., p. 161.

108. Ibid.

109. Ibid., pp. 162, 176; Wheelon letter.

110. John N. McMahon, Memorandum for: [Deleted], Subject: References to the Purcell Panel, December 14, 1964. Not everyone in the CIA involved in CORONA believed it was necessary to build a new search system. Roy Burks, the field technical director for CORONA at the time, questioned whether it would be possible to replace both the CORONA and GAMBIT systems with a single high-resolution search system. Technical intelligence analysts would not be satisfied, and the difference in going from a resolution of four feet to three feet was hundreds of millions of dollars. If the intelligence community was going to retain the high-resolution system in any event, he believed it made sense to keep down the cost of the search system by extending the focal length of CORONA and staying with the Thor booster. He feared that two very expensive systems would not be affordable. (Interview with Roy Burks, North Potomac, Maryland, May 10, 1999.)

111. Telephone interview with Walter Levison, September 17, 1999; McMillan interview; Perry, *A History of Satellite Reconnaissance, Volume 5*, p. 177. McMillan later recalled that MATCHBOX was proposed by someone from IBM. The promise of attaining high resolution with a smaller optical system would permit smaller and less expensive boosters—which greatly appealed to the Pentagon's Office of Systems Analysis. However, according to McMillan, the physics was "crazy." (Interview with Brockway McMillan, September 15, 1999.)

112. Perry, *A History of Satellite Reconnaissance, Volume 5*, pp. 176, 180; Wheelon interview, November 11–12, 1998.

113. Levison interview.

114. Interview with a former CIA official; Levison interview; telephone interview with Frank Madden, November 3, 2000.

115. Col. Paul Worthman, Memorandum for the Record, Subject: Telephone Conversation with Representatives of the Itek Corporation, February 24, 1965.

116. Col. Paul E. Worthman, Memorandum for the Record, Subject: Itek Discussions with Dr. McMillan and Mr. Land, February 25, 1965.

117. McMahon interview; Burks interview; Wheelon interview, November 11–12, 1998; Perry, *A History of Satellite Reconnaissance, Volume 5*, p. 179; McMillan interview, Levison interview; interview with a former CIA official; Brockway McMillan, Memorandum for Mr. Vance, February 25, 1965.

118. McMahon interview.

119. Telephone conversation with Albert Wheelon, April 13, 2000.

120. Wheelon interview, November 11–12, 1998; telephone conversation with Albert Wheelon, February 8, 2000; McMillan interview; Wheelon telephone conversation, April 13, 2000.

121. Perry, *A History of Satellite Reconnaissance, Volume 5*, p. 195.

122. Ibid., pp. 196–197.

123. Ibid., p. 198.

124. Ibid., p. 194.

125. McMahon interview; John N. McMahon, Memorandum for the Record, Subject: Meeting with Mr. Reber [Deleted] re NRO Problems and Issues, Subject: Participation by [Deleted] and [Deleted], 13 September 1965, 1/E/0045.

126. Burks interview.

127. Perry, *A History of Satellite Reconnaissance, Volume 1: CORONA* (Washington, D.C.: NRO, 1969), p. 162. A former CIA official believes AQUILINE was the initial code name, but it was replaced when officials discovered it had been assigned to another project.

128. Albert Wheelon to Richard Helms, August 2, 1966, CIA 2000 Release.

129. Interview with a former CIA official.

Chapter 5: Change of Command

1. Central Intelligence Agency, The R. V. Jones Intelligence Award Ceremony honoring Dr. Albert D. Wheelon, December 13, 1994.

2. Information provided by CIA Public Affairs Staff.

3. Telephone interview with Albert Wheelon, October 12, 1999.

4. Ibid.

5. Telephone interview with Dino Brugioni, May 21, 1996.

6. Telephone interview with Robert Kohler, July 6, 1999.

7. Interview with Robert Singel, Great Falls, Virginia, February 25, 1999.

8. Interview with a former CIA official.

9. Sherry Sontag and Christopher Drew with Annette Lawrence Drew, *Blind Man's Bluff: The Untold Story of American Submarine Espionage* (New York: Public Affairs, 1998), p. 77; Robert P. Berman and John C. Baker, *Soviet Strategic Forces: Requirements and Responses* (Washington, D.C.: Brookings Institution, 1982), pp. 106–108; William J. Broad, *The Universe Below: Discovering the Secrets of the Deep Sea* (New York: Simon & Schuster, 1997), p. 72; Roy Varner and Wayne Collier, *A Matter of Risk: The Incredible Inside Story of the CIA's Hughes* Glomar Explorer *Mission to Raise a Russian Submarine* (New York: Random House, 1978), pp. 11, 15–16; William J. Broad, "Russia Says U.S. Got Sub's Atom Arms," *New York Times*, June 20, 1993, p. 4; Clyde W. Burleson, *The Jennifer Project* (College Station: Texas A&M, 1997), pp. 19–22.

10. Broad, *The Universe Below*, pp. 72–73; Sontag and Drew, *Blind Man's Bluff*, p. 75.

11. Sontag and Drew, *Blind Man's Bluff*, pp. 76–77, 79; Broad, *The Universe Below*, p. 73; "The Great Submarine Snatch," *Time*, March 31, 1975, pp. 20–27; Burleson, *Jennifer Project*, p. 18.

12. Sontag and Drew, *Blind Man's Bluff*, p. 77.

13. Ibid., pp. 52–53; Broad, *The Universe Below*, p. 63.

14. Broad, *The Universe Below*, p. 74; Sontag and Drew, *Blind Man's Bluff*, pp. 80–81.

15. Sontag and Drew, *Blind Man's Bluff*, p. 81; Broad, *The Universe Below*, p. 74.

16. Burleson, *Jennifer Project*, p. 33; "The Great Submarine Snatch."

17. Burleson, *Jennifer Project*, p. 33; "The Great Submarine Snatch."

18. Sontag and Drew, *Blind Man's Bluff*, p. 82.

19. Ibid., p. 84; John Ranelagh, *The Agency: The Rise and Decline of the CIA* (New York: Simon and Schuster, 1986), p. 601.

20. "The Great Submarine Snatch"; Seymour Hersh, "Human Error Is Cited in '74 Glomar Failure," *New York Times*, December 9, 1976, pp. 1, 55.

21. Sontag and Drew, *Blind Man's Bluff*, p. 83.

22. United States Air Force, "Biography: Brigadier General Jack C. Ledford," n.d.; United States Air Force, "Biography: Major General Paul N. Bacalis," n.d.

23. Telephone interview with Gen. Paul N. Bacalis, December 1, 1999.

24. Gregory W. Pedlow and Donald E. Welzenbach, *The Central Intelligence Agency and Overhead Reconnaissance: The U-2 and OXCART Programs, 1954–1974* (Washington, D.C.: CIA, 1992), pp. 251–253; Chris Pocock, *Dragon Lady: The History of the U-2 Spyplane* (Shrewsbury, England: Airlife Publishing, 1989), p. 115.

25. Memorandum for Record, Subject: Resume of C216C, December 12, 1966, 2000 CIA Release.

26. Pocock, *Dragon Lady*, pp. 112–113.

27. Translation of portion of Colonel Li-Liang, *Piercing the Bamboo Curtain from the Sky*, provided by Joe Donoghue.

28. Pocock, *Dragon Lady*, p. 115; Pedlow and Welzenbach, *The Central Intelligence Agency and Overhead Reconnaissance*, p. 253.

29. Pocock, *Dragon Lady*, p. 115.

30. Interview with John McLucas, Washington, D.C., May 25, 1995.

31. Letter, David Packard to Richard M. Helms, December 9, 1969; David Packard, Memorandum for: Dr. McLucas, Subject: Consolidation of CIA and SAC U-2 Fleet (TS), December 8, 1969.

32. Donald H. Ross to [deleted], December 25, 1969, 2000 CIA Release; Col. Charles P. Wilson, *Strategic and Tactical Aerial Reconnaissance in the Near East* (Washington, D.C.: Washington Institute for Near East Policy, 1999), p. 58.

33. Pedlow and Welzenbach, *The Central Intelligence Agency and Overhead Reconnaissance*, p. 256.

34. Pedlow and Welzenbach, *The Central Intelligence Agency and Overhead Reconnaissance*, p. 256; Wilson, *Strategic and Tactical Reconnaissance in the Near East*, p. 58.

35. Pedlow and Welzenbach, *The Central Intelligence Agency and Overhead Reconnaissance*, p. 256; Wilson, *Strategic and Tactical Reconnaissance in the Near East*, p. 58.

36. Pedlow and Welzenbach, *The Central Intelligence Agency and Overhead Reconnaissance*, p. 310; Thomas P. McIninch, "The OXCART Story," *Studies in Intelligence* 15, 1 (Winter 1971): 1–34 at 30; Brig. Gen. Jack C. Ledford, Director (Special Activities), Briefing Note for the Director of Central Intelligence, Subject: Bureau of the Budget Recommendations for the OXCART Program, November 16, 1965.

37. Pedlow and Welzenbach, *The Central Intelligence Agency and Overhead Reconnaissance*, p. 310; McIninch, "The OXCART Story," p. 30; [Deleted] Assistant for Programs, Research and Development, Special Activities, Memorandum for: Director of Special Activities, Subject: Comments to W. R. Thomas III Memorandum to the Director, BOB, July 27, 1966, Draft, 2000 CIA Release.

38. McIninch, "The OXCART Story," p. 23.

39. Pedlow and Welzenbach, *The Central Intelligence Agency and Overhead Reconnaissance*, p. 310; McIninch, "The OXCART Story," p. 31.

40. McIninch, "The OXCART Story," p. 31; Pedlow and Welzenbach, *The Central Intelligence Agency and Overhead Reconnaissance*, p. 309.

41. Pedlow and Welzenbach, *The Central Intelligence Agency and Overhead Reconnaissance*, p. 309.

42. Walter Rostow, Memorandum for the President, December 27, 1966; "OXCART/SR-71 Background Papers," Attachment to Col. Abbot C. Greenleaf, Memorandum for Dr. Foster, Dr. Enthoven, Dr. Flax, Gen. Carroll, Gen. Steakley, January 1968; Pedlow and Welzenbach, *The Central Intelligence Agency and Overhead Reconnaissance*, p. 310; McIninch, "The OXCART Story," p. 31.

43. Pedlow and Welzenbach, *The Central Intelligence Agency and Overhead Reconnaissance*, pp. 302–303, 310.

44. Ibid., pp. 302–303.

45. Director of Central Intelligence, NIE 11-3-67, *Soviet Strategic Air and Missile Defenses*, November 9, 1967, pp. 1, 9, 20–21.

46. Pedlow and Welzenbach, *The Central Intelligence Agency and Overhead Reconnaissance*, p. 303.

47. Ibid.

48. Ibid.

49. Ibid., pp. 303–304.

50. Ibid., pp. 304–305; McIninch, "The OXCART Story," p. 25.

51. Pedlow and Welzenbach, *The Central Intelligence Agency and Overhead Reconnaissance*, p. 305; McIninch, "The OXCART Story," p. 27.

52. Bacalis interview.

53. Paul F. Crickmore, *Lockheed SR-71: The Secret Missions Exposed* (London: Osprey, 1993), pp. 26–28; Pedlow and Welzenbach, *The Central Intelligence Agency and Overhead Reconnaissance*, p. 305; McIninch, "The OXCART Story," p. 27; NPIC, *Black Shield Mission X-001, 31 May 1967,* June 1967, 2000 CIA Release.

54. Pedlow and Welzenbach, *The Central Intelligence Agency and Overhead Reconnaissance*, p. 306; McIninch, "The OXCART Story," pp. 27–28; NPIC, *Black Shield Mission BX-6705, 20 June 1967,* June 1967, 2000 CIA Release; NPIC, *Black Shield Mission BX-6706, 30 June 1967,* July 1967, 2000 CIA Release.

55. Pedlow and Welzenbach, *The Central Intelligence Agency and Overhead Reconnaissance*, p. 307; Crickmore, *Lockheed SR-71,* pp. 30–31.

56. NPIC, *Black Shield Mission BX-6723, 17 September 1967,* November 1967, p. 1, 2000 CIA Release; NPIC, *Black Shield Mission BX-6725, 4 October 1967,* December 1967, pp. 1–2, 2000 CIA Release; NPIC, *Black Shield Mission BX-6732, 28 October 1967,* December 1967, p. 1, 2000 CIA Release.

57. Pedlow and Welzenbach, *The Central Intelligence Agency and Overhead Reconnaissance*, pp. 310–311.

58. 9th SRW, *History of the 9th Strategic Reconnaissance Wing, 1 October–31 December 1967*, n.d., pp. 43–44; Pedlow and Welzenbach, *The Central Intelligence Agency and Overhead Reconnaissance*, p. 310.

59. Pedlow and Welzenbach, *The Central Intelligence Agency and Overhead Reconnaissance*, pp. 310–311.

60. Ibid., p. 311.

61. Paul H. Nitze, Deputy Secretary of Defense, Memorandum for Director, National Reconnaissance Office, Chairman, Joint Chiefs of Staff, Subject: OXCART and SR-71 Operations, December 29, 1967.

62. Pedlow and Welzenbach, *The Central Intelligence Agency and Overhead Reconnaissance*, p. 307; McIninch, "The OXCART Story," p. 28.

63. Crickmore, *Lockheed SR-71*, pp. 32–33.

64. Pedlow and Welzenbach, *The Central Intelligence Agency and Overhead Reconnaissance*, pp. 307, 309; Lt. Gen. Joseph F. Carroll, Director, DIA, Memorandum for the Chairman, Joint Chiefs of Staff, Subject: Requirement for a Second BLACK SHIELD Mission over North Korea, January 29, 1968, LBJ Library, National Security File, Intelligence File, "NRO," Box 9.

65. McIninch, "The OXCART Story," p. 32.

66. Ibid.

67. Ibid., pp. 32–33; Pedlow and Welzenbach, *The Central Intelligence Agency and Overhead Reconnaissance*, p. 313.

68. L. K. White, Deputy Director for Support, "Announcement of Assignment to Key Position, Office of the Deputy Director for Science and Technology," HN 20-115, September 13, 1963; "ORD Milestones," n.d.; Albert D. Wheelon, Deputy Director for Science and Technology, General Notice No. 12, May 5, 1964; L. K. White, Deputy Director for Support, "Announcement of Assignment to Key Position, Office of the Deputy Director for Science and Technology, Office of Research and Development," HN 20-197, March 19, 1965. All NARA, RG 263, 1998 CIA Release, Box 66, Folder 5.

69. John Marks, *The Search for the "Manchurian Candidate": The CIA and Mind Control* (New York: Norton, 1991), p. 227.

70. Michael Warner, CIA History Staff, Memorandum for the Record, Subject: The Central Intelligence Agency and Human Radiation Experiments: An Analysis of the Findings, February 14, 1995, pp. 7–8; Memorandum for: Director of Research and Development, Subject: Transfer of Funds to EARL for Follow-Up Study of Medical Volunteers, February 17, 1971. CIA, congressional, and DOD investigators subsequently could not determine whether such tests ever took place.

71. Interview with Victor Marchetti, October 12, 1999.

72. Ibid.; John Ranelagh, *The Agency*, p. 208.

73. Ranelagh, *The Agency*, p. 208.

74. Memorandum for: [Deleted], [Deleted] Views on Trained Cats [Deleted] for [Deleted] Use, n.d.

75. Interview with a former CIA official.

76. Ibid.

77. Ibid.

78. Ibid.

79. Ibid.; Marchetti interview.

80. Interview with a former CIA official.

81. Kirsten Lundberg, "The SS-9 Controversy: Intelligence as Political Football," Kennedy School of Government, C16-89-884.0, Case Program, 1989, p. 1; William Beecher, "Soviet Missile Deployment Puzzles Top U.S. Analysts," *New York Times*, April 14, 1969, pp. 1, 39.

82. Lundberg, "The SS-9 Controversy," p. 2; John Prados, *The Soviet Estimate: U.S. Intelligence Analysis and Russian Military Strength* (New York: Dial Press, 1982), p. 210; John Newhouse, *War and Peace in the Nuclear Age* (New York: Knopf, 1989), p. 215.

83. Lundberg, "The SS-9 Controversy," p. 2; Prados, *The Soviet Estimate*, pp. 209–210.

84. Lundberg, "The SS-9 Controversy," p. 3; Anne Hessing Cahn, *Killing Détente: The Right Attacks the CIA* (University Park: Pennsylvania State University Press, 1998), p. 93; Prados, *The Soviet Estimate*, p. 208.

85. Director of Central Intelligence, NIE 11-8-68, *Soviet Strategic Attack Forces*, in Donald P. Steury (ed.), *Intentions and Capabilities: Estimates on Soviet Strategic Forces, 1950–1953* (Washington, D.C.: CIA, 1996), pp. 239–251 at pp. 249–250.

86. Lundberg, "The SS-9 Controversy," p. 5.

87. Prados, *The Soviet Estimate*, p. 208.

88. Extracts from David S. Brandwein's Personal Notebook, provided to author.

89. Ibid.

90. Lundberg, "The SS-9 Controversy," pp. 5–6.

91. Ibid., p. 7.

92. Ibid., pp. 7, 11.

93. Ibid., p. 13; Cahn, *Killing Détente*, pp. 93–96.

94. Extract from Brandwein diary, June 6, 1969.

95. Peter Grose, "U.S. Intelligence Doubts First-Strike Goal," *New York Times*, June 19, 1969, pp. 1, 10.

96. Extract from Brandwein diary.

97. Cahn, *Killing Détente*, p. 97; U.S. Congress, Senate Select Committee to Study Governmental Operations with Respect to Intelligence Activities, *Final Report, Book I: Foreign and Military Intelligence* (Washington, D.C.: U.S. Government Printing Office, 1976), p. 78; extract from Brandwein diary. Helms, however, dropped a paragraph from the memo that reemphasized the view that the Soviet Union was not seeking a first-strike capability. An assistant to Laird objected to the paragraph, noting that it was a direct contradiction of Laird's position and he was about to make a speech claiming that an ABM system was essential. Helms complied by dropping the paragraph from the main text, only to have it restored as a footnote by the director of the State Department's Bureau of Intelligence and Research. (Russell Jack Smith, *The Unknown CIA: My Three Decades with the Agency* [New York: Berkley, 1992], p. 243; U.S. Congress, Senate Select Committee to Study Governmental Operations with Respect to Intelligence Activities, *Final Report, Book I: Foreign and Military Intelligence*, p. 78.)

98. Lundberg, "The SS-9 Controversy," p. 13.

99. Ibid., p. 14.

100. "Statement by the Director, Senate Foreign Relations Committee," June 23, 1969, NARA, RG 263, 1998 CIA Release, Box 182, Folder 8.

101. U.S. Congress, Senate Committee on Foreign Relations, *Intelligence and the ABM* (Washington, D.C.: U.S. Government Printing Office, 1969), pp. 3, 13; Lundberg, "The SS-9 Controversy," pp. 16–17.

102. Extract from Brandwein diary.

103. Lundberg, "The SS-9 Controversy," pp. 17–18.

104. Ibid. p. 18; Cahn, *Killing Détente*, p. 98.

105. Nicholas R. Garafalo, "Present and Future Capabilities of OTH Radars," *Studies in Intelligence* 13, 1 (Spring 1969): 53–61 at 55.

106. Ibid., p. 56.

107. Ibid.; Robert S. Norris, Andrew S. Burrows, and Richard W. Fieldhouse, *Nuclear Weapons Databook, Volume V: British, French, and Chinese Nuclear Weapons* (Boulder, Colo.: Westview, 1994), p. 362.

108. Desmond Ball, *Pine Gap: Australia and the U.S. Geostationary Signals Intelligence Satellite Program* (Sydney: Allen & Unwin, 1988), p. 57.

109. Interview with Roy Burks, North Potomac, Maryland, May 10, 1999; interview with John McMahon, Los Altos, California, November 17, 1998.

110. Ball, *Pine Gap*, pp. 57–58, 61.

111. John Noble Wilford, "A Secret Payload Is Orbited by U.S.," *New York Times*, August 7, 1968, p. 7; Air Force Eastern Test Range, *Eastern Test Range Index of Missile Launchings, July 1968–June 1969* (Patrick AFB, Fla.: AFETR, 1969), p. 3; Christopher Anson Pike, "CANYON, RHYOLITE, and AQUACADE," *Spaceflight* 37, 11 (November 1995): 381–383.

112. Pike, "CANYON, RHYOLITE, and AQUACADE"; interview with a former CIA official; Ball, *Pine Gap*, p. 18; Philip J. Klass, "U.S. Monitoring Capability Impaired," *Aviation Week and Space Technology*, May 14, 1979, p. 18.

113. Ball, *Pine Gap*, p. 16.

114. Interview with a former CIA official.

115. Ibid.

116. Interview with Henry Plaster, Vienna, Virginia, September 30, 1999.

117. Interview with a former CIA official.

118. Ibid. A third camera was carried on five HEXAGON missions. The film of this twelve-inch mapping camera was fed into the final film capsule and returned at the end of the mission. A secondary experimental system was used on some early missions to transmit pictures by radio signals—essentially

the same system that had failed when it operated on SAMOS. The results were no better this time, and the system was eventually jettisoned.

119. Ibid.; "Space Reconnaissance Dwindles," *Aviation Week and Space Technology*, October 6, 1980, pp. 18–20.

120. Interview with a former CIA official.

121. Curtis Peebles, "The Guardians," *Spaceflight*, November 1978, pp. 381ff.

122. William Burrows, *Deep Black: Space Espionage and National Security* (New York: Random House, 1986), p. 239.

123. Warren F. Carey and Myles Maxfield, "Intelligence Implications of Disease," *Studies in Intelligence* 16, 1 (Spring 1972): 71–78 at 71.

124. Ibid., pp. 71–72.

125. Ibid., pp. 74, 76.

126. Ibid., p. 76.

127. Ibid., pp. 76–77.

128. Ibid., p. 77.

129. Ibid.

Chapter 6: Empire

1. "Introduction: Producing National Intelligence Estimates," in Donald P. Steury (ed.), *Intentions and Capabilities: Estimates on Soviet Strategic Forces, 1950–1983* (Washington, D.C.: Central Intelligence Agency, 1996), p. xvi.

2. Telephone conversation with Sayre Stevens, November 11, 1998; undated, untitled, CIA summary of functions of selected offices, circa 1975.

3. *The Reminiscences of Arthur C. Lundahl*, Columbia University, Oral History Research Office, 1982, p. 302.

4. Ibid.. p. 303.

5. Ibid., p. 305.

6. Telephone interview with Dino Brugioni, May 21, 1996.

7. Ibid.

8. Interview with R. M. Huffstutler, Falls Church, Virginia, March 23, 1999; Brugioni interview; telephone interview with Edward Proctor, March 16, 1999. According to R. M. "Rae" Huffstutler, there was some opposition to the transfer of NPIC. Dino Brugioni recalled that this opposition included Edward Proctor, the Deputy Director for Intelligence. Proctor recalled that he recommended the transfer.

9. John Ranelagh, *The Agency: The Rise and Decline of the CIA, from Wild Bill Donovan to William Casey* (New York: Simon & Schuster, 1986), pp. 545–546, 732; William Colby and Peter Forbath, *Honorable Men: My Life in the CIA* (New York: Simon & Schuster, 1978), p. 332.

10. Colby and Forbath, *Honorable Men*, pp. 333, 335–336.

11. Interview with John McMahon, Los Altos, California, November 17, 1998; U.S. Congress, Senate Select Committee on Intelligence, *Nomination of John N. McMahon* (Washington, D.C.: U.S. Government Printing Office, 1982), p. 18.

12. McMahon interview.

13. Ibid.

14. Fred Emery, *Watergate: The Corruption of American Politics and the Fall of Richard Nixon* (New York: Times Books, 1994), pp. 52–53; Thomas Powers, *The Man Who Kept the Secrets: Richard Helms and the CIA* (London: Weidenfeld and Nicolson, 1979), p. 253.

15. McMahon interview; Ranelagh, *The Agency*, pp. 552–553.

16. McMahon interview.

17. H. Keith Melton, *CIA Special Weapons and Equipment: Spy Devices of the Cold War* (New York: Sterling Publishing, 1994), pp. 16, 21, 28, 30, 48.

18. Ibid., pp. 64, 66, 68, 70, 72–77, 78–79, 87, 92–93, 96–97.

19. Ibid., pp. 107–109, 110–111. Not all CIA officers were enthralled by every creation of the technical services unit. John Stockwell recalled being handed a slender notebook that included a pad of soluble rice paper, which he could supposedly gobble down if captured. He wrote that "like many OTS gimmicks this was a classroom toy which had little use in the field," explaining that a case officer would not want to make irreplaceable notes on a pad that would dissolve "at the slightest touch of rain or sweat." (John Stockwell, *In Search of Enemies: A CIA Story* [New York: Norton, 1978], p. 98.)

20. U.S. Congress, House Select Committee on Intelligence, *U.S. Intelligence Agencies and Activities: Intelligence Costs and Fiscal Procedures, Part 1* (Washington, D.C.: U.S. Government Printing Office, 1975), p. 543; Memorandum for: Deputy Director for Science and Technology, Subject: Functional Relationships Between the Office of Research and Development and the Office of Development and Engineering, July 18, 1973, NARA, RG 263, 1998 CIA Release, Box 66, Folder 4.

21. *United States of America v. Christopher John Boyce,* Reporter's Transcript, Volume 5, District Court, Central District of California, Hon. Robert J. Kelleher, CR-77-131-RJK, April 20, 1977, pp. 971–972; U.S. Congress, Senate Select Committee on Intelligence, *Nomination of John N. McMahon*, p. 18.

22. Jonathan McDowell, "US Reconnaissance Satellite Programs, Part I: Photoreconnaissance," *Quest* 4, 2 (Summer 1995): 22–31 at 31.

23. Director of Central Intelligence, NIE 11-8-71, *Soviet Forces for Intercontinental Attack*, October 21, 1971, p. 10; Director of Central Intelligence, NIE 11-8-70, *Soviet Forces for Intercontinental Attack*, November 24, 1970, pp. 4–5; Director of Central Intelligence, NIE 11-8-72, *Soviet Forces for Intercontinental Attack*, October 26, 1972, p. 22; Robert P. Berman and John C. Baker, *Soviet Strategic Forces: Requirements and Responses* (Washington, D.C.: Brookings Institution, 1982), pp. 106–107.

24. Philip J. Klass, "U.S. Monitoring Capability Impaired," *Aviation Week and Space Technology*, May 14, 1979, p. 18.

25. Ibid.

26. [James Cunnningham], DD/OSA, Memorandum for: Deputy for Technology/OSA, Subject: A Covert Reconnaissance Satellite, April 17, 1963.

27. Ibid.

28. Interview with a former CIA official.

29. Merton E. Davies and William R. Harris, *RAND's Role in the Evolution of Balloon and Satellite Observation Systems and Related U.S. Space Technology* (Santa Monica, Calif.: RAND, 1988), p. 75.

30. Interview with Albert Wheelon, Montecito, California, March 21, 2000.

31. Interview with a former CIA official; telephone conversation with Albert Wheelon, February 12, 2000.

32. Joint Chiefs of Staff, "Point Paper for Luncheon with President's Foreign Intelligence Advisory Board," June 5, 1970.

33. Donald Neff, *Warriors for Jerusalem: The Six Days That Changed the Middle East* (New York: Simon & Schuster, 1984), pp. 201–202; Ze'ev Schiff, *A History of the Israeli Army: 1874 to the Present* (New York: Macmillan, 1985), pp. 127, 130.

34. Schiff, *A History of the Israeli Army*, pp.133, 134.

35. Neff, *Warriors for Jerusalem*, pp. 203–204; Schiff, *A History of the Israeli Army*, p. 140.

36. Interview with a former CIA official; interview with Robert McNamara, January 20, 1989, Washington, D.C.

37. [Leslie Dirks], Chief, Design and Analysis Division, Office of Special Projects, Subject: Briefing to General Maxwell Taylor on Photographic Satellite Support to Middle East Crisis, 31 August 1967, September 8, 1967.

38. [Leslie Dirks], Chief, Design and Analysis Division, Office of Special Projects, Memorandum for: Director, NRO Staff, Subject: General Maxwell Taylor's Inquiries Concerning the Application of Photographic Satellites in Crisis Situations," September 5, 1967.

39. John N. McMahon, Acting Director of Special Projects, Memorandum for: Director for Science and Technology, Subject: Assessment of KH Information in Light of the Soviet Invasion of Czechoslovakia, August 30, 1968.

40. Interview with a former CIA official; Cynthia Grabo, "The Watch Committee and the National Indications Center: The Evolution of U.S. Strategic Warning," *International Journal of Intelligence and Counterintelligence* 3, 3 (Fall 1989): 363–386.

41. Interview with a former CIA official.

42. Roland S. Inlow, "How the Cold War and Its Intelligence Problems Influenced CORONA Operations," in Robert A. McDonald (ed.), *CORONA: Between the Sun and the Earth, the First NRO Reconnaissance Eye in Space* (Bethesda, Md.: American Society for Photogrammetry and Remote Sensing, 1997), pp. 221–229 at p. 228; remarks of W. Y. Smith at Conference on "Piercing the Curtain: CORONA and the Revolution in Intelligence," May 23–24, 1995, George Washington University, Washington, D.C.

43. Interview with a former CIA official. A dissenting view came from the Office of Strategic Research of the Directorate of Intelligence. OSR was asked to assess what its analysts would have predicted if they had access to the photography throughout the period leading up to the invasion. According to OSR, even access to photography on a daily basis from July 1 to August 19 would not have enabled them to say "with any reasonable certainty that the Soviets were going to invade." (John N. McMahon, Acting Director of Special Projects, Memorandum for: Director for Science and Technology, Subject: Assessment of KH Information in Light of the Soviet Invasion of Czechoslovakia, August 30, 1968.)

44. Ibid.

45. Ibid.

46. Ibid.

47. Bruce C. Clarke Jr., Special Assistant to the DDI for Special Projects, Memorandum for: Mr. Borel et al., Subject: DDI Requirements in Connection with New Reconnaissance System, August 11, 1966; interview with Albert Wheelon, Montecito, California, June 14, 1999.

48. Interview with a former CIA official.

49. Ibid.

50. Ibid.

51. Ibid.; Memorandum for President's File, Subject: President's Foreign Intelligence Advisory Board, Meeting with the President, June 4, 1971.

52. Interview with a former CIA official.

53. Gregory W. Pedlow and Donald E. Welzenbach, *The Central Intelligence Agency and Overhead Reconnaissance: The U-2 and OXCART Programs, 1954–1974* (Washington, D.C.: CIA, 1992), p. 257.

54. U.S. Air Force, "Biography, Brigadier General Wendell L. Bevan Jr.," July 15, 1970, with updates.

55. Secretary of Defense, Memorandum for Director of Central Intelligence, Subject: Management of the U-2R Fleet, n.d.; Pedlow and Welzenbach, *The Central Intelligence Agency and Overhead Reconnaissance*, p. 257.

56. Pedlow and Welzenbach, *The Central Intelligence Agency and Overhead Reconnaissance*, p. 256; Chris Pocock, *Dragon Lady: The History of the U-2 Spyplane* (Shrewsbury, England: Airlife, 1989), p. 119.

57. Pedlow and Welzenbach, *The Central Intelligence Agency and Overhead Reconnaissance*, p. 257; Pocock, *Dragon Lady*, p. 120.

58. Pedlow and Welzenbach, *The Central Intelligence Agency and Overhead Reconnaissance*, p. 257; Pocock, *Dragon Lady*, p. 120; Memo B/Gen Wendell L. Bevan to [deleted], June 26, 1974.

59. CIA Inspector General, *Inspector General's Survey of the Office of Research and Development*, October 1972, pp. 5–6, 74, NARA, RG 263, 1998 CIA Release, Box 66, Folder 2; Sayre Stevens remarks, "DS&T 35th Anniversary: Celebrating 50 Years of CIA History," July 24, 1997, videotape.

60. CIA Inspector General, *Inspector General's Survey of the Office of Research and Development*, pp. 16, 42.

61. Interview with Sayre Stevens, Springfield, Virginia, March 18, 1999; interview with James Hirsch, Fairfax, Virginia, February 12, 1999; Sayre Stevens remarks, "DS&T 35th Anniversary." Not everyone saw the approach of Stevens's predecessor as sterile. Gene Poteat noted that research is always controversial, especially if it is not directed—that is, not targeted on fulfilling a requirement specified by a consumer. But in his view, ORD's search for technological breakthroughs before identifying specific customers led to important discoveries, such as large-scale integrated circuits. (Interview with Gene Poteat, McLean, Virginia, April 25, 2000.)

62. Hirsch interview; Stevens interview; National Foreign Assessment Center, CIA, *The Soviet Earth Resources Satellite Program*, June 1980, p. 8; "Project UPSTREET," CIA Public Affairs Fact Sheet, n.d.

63. Hirsch interview.

64. Stevens interview; Bob Preston, *Plowshares and Power: The Military Use of Civil Space* (Washington, D.C.: National Defense University Press, 1994), pp. 55–56; James B. Campbell, *Introduction to Remote Sensing* (New York: Guilford, 1987), pp. 118–122.

65. Campbell, *Introduction to Remote Sensing*, p. 135.

66. Stevens interview; "Project UPSTREET"; "History Biological Sciences Division—1963 Through 1968," NARA, RG 263, 1998 CIA Release, Box 66, Folder 5.

67. National Foreign Assessment Center, CIA, *The Soviet Earth Resources Satellite Program*, p. 8; "Project UPSTREET."

68. Hirsch interview.

69. Ibid.

70. Stevens interview; CIA Inspector General, *Inspector General's Survey of the Office of Research and Development*, p. 80.

71. Stevens interview, March 18, 1999.

72. Jim Schnabel, *Remote Viewers: The Secret History of America's Psychic Spies* (New York: Dell, 1997), pp. 86, 120; "Harold E. Puthoff," www.firedocs.com/remoteviewing/oooh/people/puthoff.html; "Russell Targ," www.firedocs.com/remoteviewing/oooh/people/targ.html; Martin Gardner, "Distant Healing and Elizabeth Targ," *Skeptical Inquirer*, March/April 2001, pp. 12–14.

73. Schnabel, *Remote Viewers*, p. 87.

74. Martin Gardner, "Zero-Point Energy and Harold Puthoff," *Skeptical Inquirer*, May/June 1998, pp. 13–15, 60; Harold Puthoff, "To Whom It May Concern," May 31, 1970.

75. Kenneth A. Kress, "Parapsychology In Intelligence: A Personal Review and Conclusions," *Studies in Intelligence* 21, 4 (Winter 1977): 7–17 at 8.

76. Ibid.; H. E. Puthoff, "CIA-Initiated Remote Viewing at Stanford Research Institute," *Journal of Scientific Exploration* 10, 1 (1996): 63–76 at 64–65.

77. Schnabel, *Remote Viewers*, p. 97.

78. John D. La Mothe, *Controlled Offensive Behavior—USSR (U)*, (Washington, D.C.: DIA, July 1972). The paper was actually authored by a member of the Medical Intelligence Office, Office of the Surgeon General, Department of the Army, and approved and issued by DIA. La Mothe clearly believed in paranormal phenomena, considered the *National Enquirer* a legitimate research resource and felt it worth quoting the opinion of astrologer Sybil Leek that "there is great danger that within the next ten years the Soviets will be able to steal our top secrets by using out-of-body spies." (p. 30.; also see P. T. Van Dyke and M. L. Juncosa, *Paranormal Phenomena: Briefing on a Net Assessment Study* [Santa Monica, Calif.: RAND, January 1973]).

79. Puthoff, "CIA-Initiated Remote Viewing," pp. 65–66; Kress, "Parapsychology in Intelligence," pp. 8–9; Schnabel, *Remote Viewers*, p. 108.

80. Kress, "Parapsychology in Intelligence," p. 9.

81. Puthoff, "CIA-Initiated Remote Viewing," p. 68.

82. Interview with John McMahon, Los Altos, California, November 17, 1998.

83. Schnabel, *Remote Viewers*, pp. 106, 111.

84. Ibid., pp. 107–108; Harold E. Puthoff and Russell Targ, *Perceptual Augmentation Techniques: Final Report (Covering the Period January 1974 through February 1975,) Part Two—Research Project* (Menlo Park, Calif.: Stanford Research Institute, December 1, 1975), p. 4.

85. Puthoff and Targ, *Perceptual Augmentation Techniques: Final Report*, pp. 6–7.

86. Ibid., p. 7.

87. Kress, "Parapsychology in Intelligence," p. 10; Schnabel, *Remote Viewers*, p. 111.

88. Kress, "Parapsychology in Intelligence," p. 10; Schnabel, *Remote Viewers*, p. 112; James Bamford, *The Puzzle Palace: A Report on NSA, America's Most Secret Agency* (Boston: Houghton Mifflin, 1982), p. 169.

89. Harold E. Puthoff and Russell Targ, *Perceptual Augmentation Techniques, Part One—Technical Proposal,* SRI No. ISH 73–146, October 1, 1973; Memorandum for the Record, Subject: Verification of Remote Viewing Experiments at Stanford Research Institute, November 9, 1973, pp. 2–3.

90. Memorandum for the Record, Subject: Verification of Remote Viewing Experiments at Stanford Research Institute, p. 4.

91. Schnabel, *Remote Viewers*, pp. 112–113.

92. Memorandum for the Record, Subject: Verification of Remote Viewing Experiments at Stanford Research Institute, p. 5.

93. Schnabel, *Remote Viewers*, p. 120.

94. Memorandum for the Record, Subject: Verification of Remote Viewing Experiments at Stanford Research Institute, pp. 6–7.

95. Ibid., p. 8.

96. Ibid., p. 9.

97. Bamford, *The Puzzle Palace*, p. 408; Schnabel, *Remote Viewers*, p. 97.

98. Kress, "Parapsychology in Intelligence," p. 10; telephone conversation with Sayre Stevens, November 11, 1999; interview with Sayre Stevens, Springfield, Virginia, March 18, 1999.

99. Kress, "Parapsychology in Intelligence," p. 10.

100. Russell Targ and Harold Puthoff, "Information Transmission Under Conditions of Sensory Shielding," *Nature*, October 18, 1974, pp. 602–607; "Investigating the Paranormal," *Nature*, October 18, 1974, pp. 559–560. A subsequent note challenged the validity of Puthoff and Targ's research. See David Marks and Richard Kammann, "Information Transmission in Remote Viewing Experiments," *Nature*, August 17, 1978, pp. 680–681. Also see David Marks and Richard Kammann, *The Psychology of the Psychic* (Buffalo, N.Y.: Prometheus Books, 1980).

101. Kress, "Parapsychology in Intelligence," p. 11; U.S. Congress, Senate Select Committee on Intelligence, *Nomination of John N. McMahon*, p. 19; McMahon interview; information provided by the CIA Public Affairs Staff; interview with James V. Hirsch, Fairfax, Virginia, February 12, 1999.

102. D. Stillman, "An Analysis of a Remote-Viewing Experiment of URDF-3," Los Alamos Scientific Laboratory, December 4, 1975, p. 4; Schnabel, *Remote Viewers*, p. 120.

103. Schnabel, *Remote Viewers*, p. 120; Michael Dobbs, "Deconstructing the Death Ray," *Washington Post*, October 17, 1999, pp. F1, F4.

104. Stillman, "An Analysis of Remote-Viewing Experiment of URDF-3," p. 5.

105. Ibid., p. 11.

106. Ibid., p. 12.

107. Ibid., pp. 13–14, 17, 18.

108. Ibid., p. 18.

109. Ibid., p. 25.
110. Ibid., p.27.
111. Ibid., p. 28.
112. Dobbs, "Reconstructing the Death Ray."
113. Puthoff and Targ, *Perceptual Augmentation Techniques: Final Report*, p. 9; Kress, "Parapsychology in Intelligence," p. 14.
114. Kress, "Parapsychology in Intelligence"; Schnabel, *Remote Viewers*, pp. 177–178.
115. Kress, "Parapsychology in Intelligence," p. 14.
116. Ibid.; Hirsch interview.
117. Kress, "Parapsychology in Intelligence," p. 15.
118. Ibid.
119. Ibid., pp. 15–16; Schnabel, *Remote Viewers*, passim; Jeremiah O'Leary, "Turner Says U.S. Didn't Bug Park," *Washington Times*, August 9, 1977, pp. A1, A6. The *Post* article was John L. Wilhelm, "Psychic Spying?" *Washington Post*, August 7, 1977, pp. B1, B5; interview with Gene Poteat, McLean, Virginia, April 25, 2000.
120. Joseph E. Perisco, *Piercing the Reich: The Penetration of Nazi Germany by American Secret Agents During World War II* (New York: Ballantine Books, 1979), pp. 201–203.
121. Interview with a former CIA official.
122. McMahon interview.
123. Jeffrey M. Lenorovitz, "CIA Satellite Data Link Study Revealed," *Aviation Week and Space Technology*, May 2, 1977, pp. 25–26.
124. Testimony of Leslie Dirks, *United States of America v. Christopher John Boyce (CR-77-131-RJK)*, Reporter's Transcript, *Volume 5*, District Court, Central District of California, April 20, 1977, pp. 976, 983; Robert Lindsey, *The Falcon and the Snowman: A True Story of Friendship and Espionage* (New York: Simon & Schuster, 1979), p. 215.
125. Testimony of Leslie Dirks, pp. 984–986.
126. Lindsey, *The Falcon and the Snowman*, p. 214.
127. Testimony of Leslie Dirks, pp. 1001–1002; Lindsey, *The Falcon and the Snowman*, p. 218.
128. Lenorovitz, "CIA Satellite Data Link Study Revealed."
129. Lindsey, *The Falcon and the Snowman*, p. 218; testimony of Leslie Dirks, p. 994.
130. "The Great Submarine Snatch," *Time*, March 31, 1975, pp. 20–27; Roy Varner and Wayne Collier, *A Matter of Risk: The Incredible Inside Story of the CIA's Hughes* Glomar Explorer *Mission to Raise a Russian Submarine* (New York: Random House, 1978), p. 134; William Broad, *The Universe Below: Discovering the Secrets of the Deep Sea*, (New York: Simon & Schuster, 1997), pp. 255–256.
131. William Colby and Peter Forbath, *Honorable Men: My Life in the CIA* (New York: Simon & Schuster, 1978), pp. 389, 413.
132. "The Great Submarine Snatch"; Varner and Collier, *A Matter of Risk*, p. 144.
133. Seymour Hersh, "Human Error Is Cited in '74 Glomar Failure," *New York Times*, December 9, 1976, pp. 1, 55; Clyde W. Burleson, *The Jennifer Project* (College Station: Texas A&M, 1997), pp. 112, 133; Sherry Sontag and Christopher Drew with Annette Lawrence Drew, *Blind Man's Bluff: The Untold Story of American Submarine Espionage* (New York: Public Affairs, 1998), pp. 191, 196; Broad, *The Universe Below*, p. 79. A June 1993 report issued by a panel of experts under the office of Russian president Boris Yeltsin claimed that the United States had recovered two warheads. The amount of radiation the panel suggested was removed from the sub would be consistent with that contained by two nuclear torpedoes. The panel's claim was said to be made on the basis of Russian information, not Western press accounts—perhaps indicating that the Soviet navy had used minisubs to investigate the wreckage subsequent to U.S. press reports of the recovery operation. (William J. Broad, "Russia Says U.S. Got Sub's Atom Arms," *New York Times*, June 20, 1993, p. 4; "CIA Raising USSR Sub Raises Questions," *FBIS-SOV-92-145*, July 28, 1992, pp. 15–16.)
134. Hersh, "Human Error Cited in '74 Glomar Failure."

135. "CIA Raising USSR Sub Raises Questions," *FBIS-SOV-92-145*, July 28, 1992, pp. 15–16; CIA, "Burial at Sea," videotape, September 4, 1974.

136. Colby and Forbath, *Honorable Men*, pp. 414–417. According to one account, the sunken sub would not have had anything worth recovering. In late 1974, the USS *Seawolf* was sent back to the site. Its reconnaissance showed, according to a high-ranking naval official, that "It dissolved just like that, like an Alka-Seltzer in water. . . . It spread all over acres on the ocean floor. According to another official, "there was no possibility to recover anything more." (Sontag and Drew, *Blind Man's Bluff*, p. 197.)

137. Ranelagh, *The Agency*, pp. 624–625; Colby, *Honorable Men*, pp. 7–10.

138. Stevens interview, March 18, 1999.

139. Interview with a former CIA official.

140. Seymour M. Hersh, *The Samson Option: Israel's Nuclear Arsenal and American Foreign Policy* (New York: Random House, 1991), p. 240.

141. Ibid., p. 239.

142. Ibid.; Arthur Kranish, "CIA: Israel Has 10–20 Weapons," *Washington Post*, March 15, 1976, p. A2.

143. Kranish, "CIA: Israel Has 10–20 Weapons."

144. Andrew and Leslie Cockburn, *Dangerous Liaison: The Inside Story of the U.S.-Israeli Covert Relationship* (New York: HarperCollins, 1991), p. 94.

Chapter 7: Cracks in the Empire

1. Information provided by CIA Public Affairs Staff.

2. Robert Lindsey, *The Falcon and the Snowman: A True Story of Friendship and Espionage* (New York: Simon & Schuster, 1979), p. 287.

3. Interview with Robert Phillips, Rosslyn, Virginia, June 4, 1999.

4. Interview with Philip Eckman, Alexandria, Virginia, May 16, 2000.

5. Telephone interview with Sayre Stevens, May 29, 1996; interview with Sayre Stevens, Springfield, Virginia, March 18, 1999.

6. Stevens telephone interview; Stevens interview.

7. Interview with R. Evans Hineman, Chantilly, Virginia, February 17, 1999.

8. Interview with R. M. (Rae) Huffstutler, Falls Church, Virginia, March 23, 1999; Stevens telephone interview.

9. Interview with a former CIA official; Stevens interview; Huffstutler interview.

10. Interview with Henry Plaster, Vienna, Virginia, September 30, 1999; Eckman interview.

11. Interview with Philip Eckman, Alexandria, Virginia, May 16, 2000.

12. Ibid.; Philip Eckman, "Some Random Thoughts and Musings on ORD," n.d.

13. Eckman, "Some Random Thoughts and Musings on ORD."

14. Ibid.

15. Anthony Kenden, "U.S. Reconnaissance Satellite Programs," *Spaceflight*, July 1978, pp. 243ff.

16. William E. Burrows, *Deep Black: Space Espionage and National Security* (New York: Random House, 1986), p. 227.

17. Interview with a former CIA official; Jeffrey T. Richelson, *America's Secret Eyes in Space* (New York: Harper & Row, 1990), p. 362.

18. John Noble Wilford, "Spy Satellite Reportedly Aided in Shuttle Flight," *New York Times*, October 20, 1981, p. C4.

19. James Janesick and Morley Blouke, "Sky on a Chip: The Fabulous CCD," *Sky and Telescope*, September 1987, pp. 238–242; Burrows, *Deep Black*, p. 244.

20. James R. Janesick and Morley M. Blouke, "Introduction to Charged Couple Device Imaging Sensors," in Kosta Tsipis (ed.), *Arms Control Verification: The Technologies That Make It Possible* (New

York: Pergamon-Brassey's, 1985), p. 104; Curtis Peebles, *Guardians: Strategic Reconnaissance Satellites* (Novato, Calif.: Presidio Press, 1987), pp. 118–119.

21. Burrows, *Deep Black*, p. 244.

22. Ibid., p.247; interview with a former CIA official.

23. Interview with a former CIA official.

24. Jeffrey Richelson, "The Satellite Data System," *Journal of the British Interplanetary Society* 37, 5 (1984): 226–228.

25. Ibid.; telephone conversation with Albert Wheelon, February 15, 2000.

26. John Pike, "Reagan Prepares for War in Outer Space," *CounterSpy* 7, 1 (September-November 1982): 17–22; James Bamford, "America's Supersecret Eyes in Space," *New York Times Magazine*, January 13, 1985, pp. 39ff.

27. Richelson, *America's Secret Eyes in Space*, p. 362.

28. Interview with a former CIA official.

29. Ibid.

30. E. H. Knoche, Deputy Director of Central Intelligence, Memorandum for the Record, Subject: Meeting with National Security Adviser Brzezinski, December 30, 1976.

31. Burrows, *Deep Black*, p. 226.

32. Ibid.

33. Ibid.

34. Ibid., pp. 228–229; interview with a former CIA official.

35. Interview with a former CIA official.

36. Lindsey, *The Falcon and the Snowman*, pp. 49, 54.

37. Ibid., pp. 54–63; James Bamford, *The Puzzle Palace: A Report on NSA, America's Most Secret Agency* (Boston: Houghton Mifflin, 1982), pp. 512–514.

38. Harry Rostizke, *KGB: The Eyes of Russia* (New York: Doubleday, 1981), p. 203; Bamford, *The Puzzle Palace*, p. 514; Lindsey, *The Falcon and the Snowman*, pp. 164–168.

39. Rositze, *KGB*, pp. 203–204; Bamford, *The Puzzle Palace*, pp. 520–521.

40. Rositze, *KGB*, p. 204; Bamford, *The Puzzle Palace*, p. 521.

41. *United States of America v. Christopher John Boyce, CR-77-131-RJK,* United States District Court, Central District of California, Volume 5, Reporter's Transcript of Proceedings, April 20, 1977, pp. 957–1008.

42. Lindsey, *The Falcon and the Snowman*, p. 287.

43. *United States of America v. Christopher John Boyce, CR-77-131-RJK,* pp. 1008–1009, 1012.

44. Ibid., p. 1013; Lindsey, *The Falcon and the Snowman*, p. 287.

45. Bamford, *The Puzzle Palace*, pp. 521–522; Philip J. Klass, "U.S. Monitoring Capability Impaired," *Aviation Week and Space Technology*, May 14, 1979, p. 18; Burrows, *Deep Black*, p. 192; interview with Bernard Lubarsky, May 9, 2000.

46. Andrew Tully, *Inside the FBI* (New York: Dell, 1987), p. 45; George Lardner Jr., "Spy Rings of One," *Washington Post Magazine*, December 4, 1983, pp. 60–65.

47. Henry Hurt, "CIA in Crisis: The Kampiles Case," *Reader's Digest*, June 1979, pp. 65–72.

48. Tully, *Inside the FBI*, p. 45; Lardner, "Spy Rings of One"; Stansfield Turner, *Secrecy and Democracy: The CIA in Transition* (Boston: Houghton Mifflin, 1985), p. 65; interview with a former CIA official; Arthur S. Hulnick, *Fixing the Spy Machine: Preparing American Intelligence for the Twenty-first Century* (Westport, Conn.: Praeger, 1999), p. 104 n.14.

49. Turner, *Secrecy and Democracy*, p. 69.

50. Lardner, "Spy Rings of One"; Peebles, *Guardians*, p. 120; *United States of America v. William Peter Kampiles*, United States District Court, Northern District of Indiana, November 6, 1978, Direct Testimony of Donald E. Stukey, pp. 804–808.

51. *United States of America v. William Peter Kampiles*, Direct Testimony of Donald E. Stukey, p. 809; *United States of America v. William Peter Kampiles*, Direct Testimony of Vivian Psachos, p. 259;

Lardner, "Spy Rings of One"; Tully, *Inside the FBI*, p. 42–43; Griffin Bell, *Taking Care of the Law* (New York: William Morrow, 1982), p. 119.

52. Tully, *Inside the FBI*, pp. 43–44; Hurt, "CIA in Crisis"; Thomas O'Toole and Charles Babcock, "CIA 'Big Bird' Satellite Manual Was Allegedly Sold to the Soviets," *Washington Post*, August 23, 1978, pp. A1, A16; Michael Ledeen, "A Mole in Our Midst," *New York*, October 2, 1978, pp. 55–57; James Ott, "Espionage Trial Highlights CIA Problems," *Aviation Week and Space Technology*, November 27, 1978, pp. 21–23; David Wise, "The Spy Who Wouldn't Die," *GQ*, July 1998, pp. 148ff.

53. Tully, *Inside the FBI*, p. 52; *United States of America v. William Kampiles,* Direct Testimony of James Murphy, p. 352.

54. Bell, *Taking Care of the Law*, p. 121.

55. Ott, "Espionage Trial Highlights CIA Problems."

56. *United States of America v. William Peter Kampiles,* Direct Testimony of Leslie Dirks, pp. 6, 8.

57. Ibid., pp. 10, 12.

58. Ibid., p. 13.

59. Ott, "Espionage Trial Highlights CIA Problems."

60. Ibid.

61. Tully, *Inside the FBI*, pp. 48, 55.

62. Ibid., p. 56.

63. Interview with Roy Burks, North Potomac, Maryland, May 10, 1999.

64. Interview with Robert Singel, Great Falls, Virginia, February 25, 1999; Burks interview.

65. Michael E. Ruane, "Ex-CIA Employee Has Saluted Tiny Paper Soldiers Since '20s," *Dallas Morning News*, February 28, 1999, p. 9F; "Appointment of Eight Special Assistants to the President for National Security Affairs," White House, February 11, 1987; private information.

66. Phillips interview.

67. Ibid.; Burks interview.

68. Bob Woodward, *VEIL: The Secret Wars of the CIA, 1981–1987* (New York: Simon & Schuster, 1987), p. 313.

69. Burks interview.

70. Laurence Stern, "U.S. Tapped Top Russians' Car Phones," *Washington Post*, December 5, 1973, pp. A1, A16; Ernest Volkman, "U.S. Spies Lend an Ear to Soviets," *Newsday*, July 12, 1977, p. 7; Michael Frost and Michel Gratton, *Spyworld: Inside the Canadian and American Intelligence Establishments* (Toronto: Doubleday Canada, 1994), p. 60.

71. Stern, "U.S. Tapped Top Russians' Car Phones"; Volkman, "U.S. Spies Lend an Ear to Soviets"; Bill Gertz, "CIA Upset Because Perle Detailed Eavesdropping," *Washington Times*, April 15, 1987, p. 2A.

72. Jack Anderson, "CIA Eavesdrops on Kremlin Chiefs," *Washington Post*, September 16, 1971, p. F7.

73. Patrick Tyler, *A Great Wall: Six Presidents and China—An Investigative History* (New York: Public Affairs, 1999), pp. 83–84, 157.

74. Burks interview; Phillips interview.

75. Burks interview.

76. Ibid.

77. Woodward, *VEIL*, p. 314.

78. NRO, *Deputy Directors of the NRO*, 1997, n.p.; "Office of Development and Engineering," no date, portion of CIA document obtained under the Freedom of Information Act (FOIA); "Office of Research and Development," no date, portion of CIA document obtained under the FOIA.

79. Lubarsky interview.

80. Ibid.; "Office of Development and Engineering."

81. Biography, Jeffrey K. Harris; private information.

82. NRO, "Biography: Dennis Fitzgerald," 1997.

83. NRO, "David A. Kier, National Reconnaissance, Technical Director," April 1997; private information.

84. Interview with former CIA officials.

85. Lubarsky interview; private information.

86. Dial Torgeson, "U.S. Spy Devices Still Running at Iran Post," *International Herald Tribune*, March 7, 1979, pp. A1, A8.

87. Hedrick Smith, "U.S. Aides Say Loss of Post in Iran Impairs Missile-Monitoring Ability," *New York Times*, March 2, 1979, pp. A1, A8.

88. William Sullivan, *Mission to Iran* (New York: W. W. Norton, 1981), pp. 21–22.

89. U.S. Congress, House Permanent Select Committee on Intelligence, *Iran: Evaluation of U.S. Intelligence Performance Prior to November 1978* (Washington, D.C.: U.S. Government Printing Office, 1979), pp. 6, 7; Central Intelligence Agency, *Iran in the 1980s* (Washington, D.C.: CIA, August 1977), p. iii.

90. Interview with a former CIA official.

91. Torgeson, "U.S. Spy Devices Still Running at Iran Post."

92. Desmond Ball, *Pine Gap: Australia and the U.S. Geostationary Signals Intelligence Program* (Sydney: Allen & Unwin, 1988), pp. 58–59.

93. Torgeson, "U.S. Spy Devices Still Running at Iran Post."

94. Ibid.; Cyrus Vance, *Hard Choices: Critical Years in America's Foreign Policy* (New York: Simon & Schuster, 1983), p. 342; William Branigan, "Iran's Airmen Keep U.S. Listening Posts Intact and Whirring," *Washington Post*, May 20, 1979, p. A20.

95. Smith, "U.S. Aides Say Loss of Post in Iran Impairs Missile-Monitoring Ability."

96. Vance, *Hard Choices*, pp. 354–355.

97. Burks interview. On Teal Amber, see L. E. Dean, C. R. Johnson, and H. J. Strasler, "Teal Amber I," *Journal of Defense Research*, Special Issue 78-3, 1978, pp. 151–170.

98. Interview with William H. Nance, Bethesda, Maryland, May 4, 1999.

99. Ibid.

100. John Newhouse, *War and Peace in the Nuclear Age* (New York: Knopf, 1989), p. 224; Robert S. Ross, *Negotiating Cooperation: The United States and China, 1969–1989* (Stanford, Calif.: Stanford University Press, 1995), p. 45; William Burr (ed.), *The Kissinger Transcripts: The Top-Secret Talks with Beijing and Moscow* (New York: New Press, 1999), pp. 50–51, 170–171, 204; Tyler, *A Great Wall,* p. 98.

101. Nance interview.

102. Ibid.

103. Tyler, *A Great Wall*, pp. 205–207.

104. Ibid., pp. 277–278.

105. Philip Taubman, "U.S. and Peking Jointly Monitor Russian Missiles," *New York Times*, June 18, 1981, pp. A1, A14; Murrey Marder, "Monitoring: Not-So-Secret-Secret," *Washington Post*, June 19, 1981, p. 10.

106. Tyler, *A Great Wall*, p. 284.

107. Nance interview.

108. Robert Gates, *From the Shadows: The Ultimate Insider's Account of Five Presidents and How They Won the Cold War* (New York: Simon & Schuster, 1996), p. 123.

109. David Bonavia, "Radar Post Leak May Be Warning to Soviet Union," *The Times* (London), June 20, 1981, p. 5; Tyler, *A Great Wall*, p. 284.

110. Tyler, *A Great Wall*, pp. 278, 285; "Spying on Russia, with China's Help," *U.S. News & World Report*, June 29, 1981, p. 10; Taubman, "U.S. and Peking Joint Monitor Russian Missiles"; Robert C. Toth, "U.S., China Jointly Track Firings of Soviet Missiles," *Los Angeles Times*, June 19, 1981, pp. 1, 9; Walter Pincus, "U.S. Seeks A-Test Monitoring Facility," *Washington Post*, March 19, 1986, p. A8.

111. Communication from former CIA officer.

112. Antonio J. Mendez with Malcolm McConnell, *The Master of Disguise: My Secret Life in the CIA* (New York: Morrow, 1999), p. 269.

113. Ibid.; Jean Pelletier and Claude Adams, *The Canadian Caper* (New York: William Morrow, 1981), pp. 59–60, 79, 196.

114. Mendez with McConnell, *The Master of Disguise*, p. 267; CIA Public Affairs Staff, "'Trailblazers' and Years of CIA Service," 1997.

115. Mendez with McConnell, *The Master of Disguise,* pp. 270, 272–273.

116. Ibid., pp. 275–276.

117. Antonio J. Mendez, "A Classic Case of Deception," *Studies in Intelligence*, Winter 1999–2000, pp. 1–16 at pp. 2–3.

118. Ibid., p. 3.

119. Ibid., p. 3; Mendez with McConnell, *The Master of Disguise*, pp. 128, 277–278.

120. Mendez with McConnell, *The Master of Disguise*, p. 278.

121. Ibid., pp. 280–282; Mendez, "A Classic Case of Deception," p. 4; Michael E. Ruane, "Seeing Is Deceiving," *Washington Post*, February 15, 2000, pp. C1, C8.

122. Mendez with McConnell, *The Master of Disguise*, pp. 284–286; Ruane, "Seeing Is Deceiving."

123. Mendez, "A Classic Case of Deception."

124. Mendez with McConnell, *The Master of Disguise*, pp. 296, 298; Mendez, "A Classic Case of Deception," p. 6.

125. Mendez with McConnell, *The Master of Disguise*, pp. 298, 301–305; Ruane, "Seeing Is Deceiving"; Mendez, "A Classic Case of Deception," p. 7.

126. Mendez with McConnell, *The Master of Disguise*, pp. 339–340; Ruane, "Seeing Is Deceiving."

Chapter 8: Breaking Down Barriers

1. Interview with R. Evans Hineman, Chantilly, Virginia, February 17, 1999; *United States of America, Plaintiff v. Samuel L. Morison, Defendant, Case No. Y-84-00455*, United States District Court, District of Maryland, Baltimore, October 15, 1985, Transcript of Trial Before the Honorable Joseph H. Young, pp. 443–444; "DS&T Leadership History," n.d., provided by CIA Public Affairs Staff.

2. Interview with James V. Hirsch, Fairfax, Virginia, February 12, 1999; telephone interview with Robert Kohler, July 6, 1999; "DS&T Leadership History."

3. *DS&T 35th Anniversary: Celebrating 50 Years of CIA History*, July 24, 1997, video.

4. Ibid.; Hineman interview.

5. "DS&T Leadership History"; Hineman interview.

6. "DS&T 35th Anniversary"; Hineman interview.

7. A phone interview with Thomas Twetten, March 12, 2001.

8. Warren E. Leary, "The Dream of Eternal Flight Begins to Take Wing," *New York Times*, January 12, 1999, pp. D1, D6; Stuart F. Brown, "The Eternal Airplane," *Popular Science*, April 1994, pp. 70, 100; interview with Philip Eckman, Alexandria, Virginia, May 16, 2000; interview with a former CIA official.

9. Brown, "The Eternal Airplane"; David A. Fulghum, "Solar-Powered UAV to Fly at Edwards," *Aviation Week and Space Technology*, October 4, 1993, p. 27; "Environmental Research Aircraft and Sensor Technology: Pathfinder, Past Flight Information," www.dfrc.nasa.gov/Projects/erast/Projects/Pathfinder/pastinfo.html, November 1, 1998.

10. Leary, "The Dream of Eternal Flight"; "Environmental Research Aircraft and Sensor Technology: Pathfinder," www.dfrc.nasa.gov/Projects/erast/Projects/Pathfinder/pastfltinfo.html, November 1, 1998. In November 1998, a successor to PATHFINDER, with a 206-foot wingspan and the designation CENTURION, made its debut, flying at just over 80,000 feet and able to stay aloft for

fourteen to fifteen hours during daylight. It is expected to be capable of flying at over 100,000 feet. Scientists hope the vehicle will provide data to help in the development of another advanced UAV, HELIOS, which is expected to be able to remain over a target for months using an energy storage system to power the aircraft at night. Projected possible uses for the aircraft include monitoring the upper atmosphere, long-term monitoring of ocean storms, and forest and crop monitoring.

11. John Boatman, "USA Planned Stealthy UAV to Replace SR-71," *Jane's Defence Weekly*, December 17, 1994, pp. 1, 3; David A. Fulghum and Peter A. Wall, "Long-Hidden Research Spawns Black UAV," *Aviation and Space Technology*, September 25, 2000, pp. 28–29; private information.

12. Fulghum and Wall, "Long-Hidden Research Spawns Black UAV"; Boatman, "USA Planned Stealthy UAV to Replace SR–71."

13. Fulghum and Wall, "Long-Hidden Research Spawns Black UAV"; Boatman, "USA Planned Stealthy UAV to Replace SR–71"; private information.

14. Fulghum and Wall, "Long-Hidden Research Spawns Black UAV"; Boatman, "USA Planned Stealthy UAV to Replace SR–71"; U.S. Congress, Senate Committee on Armed Services, *Department of Defense Authorization for Appropriations for Fiscal Year 1994 and the Future Years Defense Program* (Washington, D.C.: U.S. Government Printing Office, 1993), p. 477.

15. Peter Kornbluh, *Nicaragua: The Price of Intervention, Reagan's War Against the Sandinistas* (Washington, D.C.: Institute for Policy Studies, 1987), pp. 18–20.

16. James Le Moyne, "The Secret War Boils Over," *Newsweek*, April 11, 1983, pp. 46–50; Joanne Omang, "Historical Background to the CIA's Nicaraguan Manual," in *Psychological Operations in Guerrilla Warfare* (New York: Vintage, 1985), pp. 15, 22; "A Secret War for Nicaragua," *Newsweek*, November 8, 1982, pp. 42–53; Kornbluh, *Nicaragua*, pp. 22–23; Robert C. Toth, "CIA Covert Action Punishes Nicaragua for Salvador Aid," *New York Times*, April 18, 1984, pp. A1, A12.

17. Ronald Reagan, National Security Decision Directive 17, "National Security Directive on Cuba and Central America," January 4, 1982. Top Secret.

18. LeMoyne, "Secret War Boils Over"; Kornbluh, *Nicaragua*, pp. 23–24, 40.

19. "The CIA Blows an Asset," *Newsweek*, September 3, 1984, pp. 48–49.

20. Kornbluh, *Nicaragua*, p. 48; Philip Taubman, "U.S. Officials Say C.I.A. Helped Nicaraguan Rebels Plan Attacks," *New York Times*, October 16, 1984, pp. 1, 22; "Oct. 10 Assault on Nicaraguans Is Laid to C.I.A.," *New York Times*, April 18, 1994, pp. A1, A12.

21. Kornbluh, *Nicaragua*, p. 48; Taubman, "U.S. Officials Say C.I.A. Helped Nicaraguan Rebels Plan Attacks"; "Oct. 10 Assault on Nicaraguans Is Laid to C.I.A."; John Prados, *President's Secret Wars: CIA and Pentagon Covert Operations from World War II Through the Persian Gulf* (Chicago: Ivan R. Dee, 1996), p. 415; Capt. James M. Martin, "Sea Mines in Nicaragua," *Proceedings of the U.S. Naval Institute* 116, 9 (September 1990): 111–116.

22. Kornbluh, *Nicaragua*, pp. 48–50; Hedrick Smith, "Britain Criticizes Mining of Harbors Around Nicaragua," *New York Times*, April 7, 1984, pp. 1, 4; Fred Hiatt and Joanne Omang, "CIA Helped to Mine Ports in Nicaragua," *Washington Post*, April 7, 1984, p. 1; Philip Taubman, "Americans on Ship Said to Supervise Nicaragua Mining," *New York Times*, April 8, 1984, pp. 1, 12; Martin, "Sea Mines in Nicaragua."

23. Prados, *President's Secret Wars*, p. 413; Memorandum for Robert C. MacFarlane, From: Oliver L. North, Constantine Menges, Subject: Special Activities in Nicaragua, March 2, 1984, in National Security Archive, *Nicaragua: The Making of U.S. Policy, 1978–1990* (Alexandria, Va.: Chadwyck-Healey, 1991), Document No. 01994.

24. Kornbluh, *Nicaragua*, pp. 48–50; Smith, "Britain Criticizes Mining of Harbors Around Nicaragua"; Hiatt and Omang, "CIA Helped to Mine Ports in Nicaragua"; Taubman, "Americans on Ship Said to Supervise Nicaragua Mining"; American Embassy Managua to Secretary of State, Washington, D.C., Subject: Soviet Ship Damaged by Mine at Puerto Sandino, 211755 March 1984 in National Security Archive, *Nicaragua: The Making of U.S. Policy*, Document No. 02017.

25. Duane R. Claridge, *A Spy for All Seasons: My Life in the CIA* (New York: Scribner's, 1996), p. 205; Leslie H. Gelb, "Officials Say CIA Made Mines with Navy Help," *New York Times*, June 1, 1984, p. A4; Claridge, *A Spy for All Seasons*, p. 386.

26. *United States of America, Plaintiff v. Samuel L. Morison*, pp. 1022–1024.

27. Interview with Robert M. Huffstutler, Falls Church, Virginia, March 23, 1999; Résumé, Robert M. Huffstutler, n.d.

28. Hineman interview; Huffstutler interview; John J. Hicks, Director, National Photographic Interpretation Center, Memorandum for: Deputy Director for Science and Technology, Subject: Use of Photointerpreter and Supporting Resources, July 25, 1975. The problem persists to this day. In fall 1999, Congress threatened to cut the funding for the next generation of imagery satellites unless the administration came up with sufficient funds to pay for a processing and exploitation capability to match the new generation's collection capability. (Vernon Loeb and Walter Pincus, "New Spy Satellites at Risk Because Funding Is Uncertain, Pentagon Told," *Washington Post*, November 12, 1999, p. A7.)

29. Hineman interview.

30. Huffstutler interview.

31. Ibid.

32. Ibid.

33. Ibid.

34. Hineman interview; Huffstutler interview.

35. Huffstutler interview.

36. Ibid.

37. Ibid.

38. Ibid.

39. Nigel Hawkes, Geoffrey Lean, David Leigh, Robin McKie, Peter Pringle, and Andrew Wilson, *Chernobyl: The End of the Nuclear Dream* (New York: Vintage, 1986), pp. 99–103.

40. Stephen Engelberg, "U.S. Says Intelligence Units Did Not Detect the Accident," *New York Times*, May 2, 1986, p. A9.

41. Hawkes, Lean, Leigh McKie, Pringle, and Wilson, *Chernobyl*, p. 122; Huffstutler interview.

42. "Meltdown," *Newsweek*, May 12, 1986, pp. 20–35; Boyce Rensberg, "Explosion: Graphite Fire Suspected," *Washington Post*, April 30,1986, pp.A1, A17; Carl M. Cannon and Mark Thompson, "Threat to Soviets Grows, U.S. Spy Photos Indicate," *Miami Herald*, April 30, 1986, pp.1A, 14A.

43. "Meltdown."

44. Robert C. Toth, "Satellites Keep Eye on Reactor," *Los Angeles Times*, May 2, 1986, p. 22.

45. "Meltdown"; Bernard Gwertzman, "Fire in Reactor May Be Out, New U.S. Pictures Indicate; Soviet Says Fallout Is Cut," *New York Times*, May 2, 1986, pp.A1, A8.

46. Philip M. Boffey, "U.S. Panel Calls the Disaster in the Ukraine the Worst Ever," *New York Times*, May 4, 1986, pp. 1, 20.

47. Serge Schemann, "Soviet Mobilizes a Vast Operation to Overcome the Disaster," *New York Times*, May 19, 1986, p. A8.

48. Walter Pincus and Mary Thornton, "U.S. to Orbit 'Sigint' Craft from Shuttle," *Washington Post*, December 19, 1984, pp.A1, A8-A9.

49. Edward H. Kolcum, "Night Launch of Discovery Boosts Secret Military Satellite into Orbit," *Aviation Week and Space Technology*, November 27, 1989, p. 29; private information.

50. James Gerstenzang, "Shuttle Lifts Off with Spy Cargo," *Los Angeles Times*, January 25, 1985, pp. 1, 11; "Final Launch Preparations Under Way for Signal Intelligence Satellite Mission," *Aviation Week and Space Technology*, November 6, 1989, p. 24; interview with Bernard Lubarsky, Alexandria, Virginia, May 9, 2000; interview with a former CIA official.

51. Kohler interview.

52. Lubarsky interview; telephone conversation with Albert Wheelon, November 15, 1999; Kohler interview, July 6, 1999.

53. Kohler interview.

54. Ibid.

55. Ibid.

56. Ibid.

57. Ibid.

58. Ibid.

59. Ibid.; Wheelon telephone conversation; telephone conversation with Albert Wheelon, February 15, 2000.

60. Wheelon telephone conversation, November 15, 1999; Wheelon telephone conversation, February 15, 2000.

61. Kohler interview.

62. List of Directors, Office of Development and Engineering, n.d.

63. Interview with a former CIA official.

64. Lubarsky interview; Jeffrey T. Richelson, *America's Space Sentinels: DSP Satellites and National Security* (Lawrence: University Press of Kansas, 1999), pp. 131–136.

65. Richelson, *America's Space Sentinels,* pp. 131–136.

66. Ruth Marcus and Joe Pichirallo, "Chin Believed Planted in U.S. as Spy," *Washington Post*, December 6, 1985, pp. A1, A22; Philip Shenon, "Former C.I.A. Analyst Is Arrested and Accused of Spying for China," *New York Times*, November 24, 1985, pp. 1, 31; Joe Pichirallo, "Ex-CIA Analyst Gave Secrets to China for 30 Years, FBI Says," *Washington Post*, November 24, 1985, pp. A1, A24.

67. Pichirallo, "Ex-CIA Analyst"; Stephen Engelberg, "30 Years of Spying for China Is Charged," *New York Times*, November 27, 1985, p. B8.

68. Pichirallo, "Ex-CIA Analyst"; "A Chinese Agent in the CIA?" *Newsweek*, December 2, 1985, p. 49.

69. Marcus and Pichirallo, "Chin Believed Planted in U.S. as Spy"; Philip Shenon, "U.S. Says Spy Suspect Had Access to Highly Classified Data," *New York Times*, January 3, 1986, p. A12; Michael Wines, "Bigger Role Laid to Suspected Spy," *Los Angeles Times*, November 28, 1985, pp. 1, 10; *United States of America v. Larry Wu Tai Chin aka Chin Wu-Tai*, United States District Court for the Eastern District of Virginia, Alexandria Division, Criminal No. 85-00263-A, January 2, 1986, pp. 2–3, 14.

70. Joe Pichirallo, "Retiree Kept Close CIA Ties," *Washington Post*, November 27, 1985, pp. A1, A10; Robin Toner, "Bail Denied Ex-CIA Worker in China Spy Case," *New York Times*, November 28, 1985, p. B8; Joe Pichirallo, "Ex-CIA Analyst Gave Secrets to China," *Washington Post*, November 24, 1985, pp. A1, A24.

71. "'Ministry of State Security' Set Up on Mainland China," *Issues and Studies*, July 1983, pp. 5–8; Nicholas Eftimiades, "China's Ministry of State Security: Coming of Age in the International Arena," *Intelligence and National Security* 8, 1 (January 1993): 23–43; "Chinese Official Said Exposer of CIA Turncoat," *Washington Post*, September 5, 1986, p. A18; Michael Wines, "Spy Reportedly Unmasked by China Defector," *Los Angeles Times*, September 5, 1986, pp. 1, 12; Daniel Southerland, "China Silent on Reported Defection of Intelligence Official," *Washington Post*, September 4, 1986, p. A30.

72. "Chinese Official Said to Be Exposer of CIA Turncoat"; Wines, "Spy Reportedly Unmasked by China Defector"; Thomas Allen and Norman Polmar, *Merchants of Treason: America's Secrets for Sale from the* Pueblo *to the Present* (New York: Delacorte, 1988), p. 302.

73. Ronald Kessler, *Spy vs. Spy: Stalking Soviet Spies in America* (New York: Scribner's, 1988), pp. 202–203.

74. Remarks by William O. Studeman, Deputy Director of Central Intelligence, at the Symposium on "National Security and National Competitiveness: Open Source Solutions," December 1, 1992, McLean, Va., p. 4; Robert Pear, "Radio Broadcasts Report Protests Erupting All over China," *New York Times*, May 23, 1989, p. A14.

75. Bob Woodward, *VEIL: The Secret Wars of the CIA, 1981–1987* (New York: Simon & Schuster, 1987), p. 32; NBC, *Inside the KGB: Narration and Shooting Script*, May 1993, p. 39.

76. Peter Earley, *Confessions of a Spy: The Real Story of Aldrich Ames* (New York: Putnam, 1997), p. 117.

77. Ibid., p. 118.

78. Ibid.

79. Ibid., pp. 118–119, 197.

80. Interview; "Seismic Sensors," *Intelligence Newsletter*, January 17, 1990, p. 2.

81. Hineman interview.

82. John O. Koehler, *STASI: The Untold Story of the East German Secret Police* (Boulder, Colo.: Westview Press, 1998), p. 295.

83. Hineman interview.

84. Ibid.

85. Ibid.; CIA document fragment, "Office of Special Projects," July 22, 1988.

86. Interview with Robert Phillips, Rosslyn, Virginia, June 4, 1999.

87. Ibid.

Chapter 9: A New World

1. Benjamin B. Fischer (ed.), *At Cold War's End: U.S. Intelligence on the Soviet Union and Eastern Europe 1989–1991* (Washington, D.C.: Central Intelligence Agency, 1999), p. xi.

2. Ibid.

3. Interview with James V. Hirsch, Fairfax, Virginia, February 12, 1999; remarks of James V. Hirsch, "DS&T 35th Anniversary: Celebrating 50 Years of CIA History," July 24, 1997, videotape.

4. Remarks of James V. Hirsch, "DS&T 35th Anniversary,."

5. Ibid.

6. Hirsch interview.

7. Ibid.

8. Bob Woodward, *The Commanders* (New York: Simon & Schuster, 1991), p. 206.

9. Ibid.

10. Ibid., p. 207; Michael R. Gordon and Bernard Trainor, *The General's War: The Inside Story of The Conflict in the Gulf* (Boston: Little, Brown, 1994), pp. 9–10.

11. U.S. News & World Report, *Triumph Without Victory: The Unreported History of the Persian Gulf War* (New York: Times Books, 1992), pp. 21–22.

12. Ibid., p. 32.

13. Gordon and Trainor, *The General's War*, p. 25.

14. Ibid., pp. 24–25; Woodward, *The Commanders*, pp. 208, 216, 218–219.

15. U.S. News & World Report, *Triumph Without Victory*, pp. 7–9; George Bush, National Security Directive 45, "U.S. Policy in Response to the Iraqi Invasion of Kuwait," August 20, 1990, p. 2.

16. Richard Hallion, *Storm over Iraq: Air Power and the Gulf War* (Washington, D.C.: Smithsonian Institution, 1992), p. 159; George Bush, National Security Directive 54, "Responding to Iraqi Aggression in the Gulf," January 15, 1991.

17. Doug Waller, *The Commandos: The Inside Story of America's Secret Soldiers* (New York: Simon & Schuster, 1994), p. 243; U.S. News & World Report, *Triumph Without Victory*, p. 212.

18. Bill Gertz, "New Spy Satellite, Needed to Monitor Treaty, Sits on Ground," *Washington Times*, October 20, 1987, p. A5; Bob Woodward, *Veil: The Secret Wars of the CIA 1981–1987* (New York: Simon & Schuster, 1987), p. 221; private information.

19. Douglas Isbell and Vincent Kiernan, "Long-Delayed Atlantis Flight Orbits Military Spy Satellite," *Space News*, March 5–11, 1990, p. 12; Edward H. Kolcum, "Atlantis Lofts AFP-731 Recon-

naissance Satellite," *Aviation Week and Space Technology*, March 5, 1990, p. 22; Warren E. Leary, "Problems Are Reported with New Spy Satellite," *New York Times*, March 18, 1990, p. 20; Patrick E. Tyler, "Satellite Fails," *Washington Post*, March 17, 1990, pp. A1, A11.

20. Warren E. Leary, "Debris from Secret U.S. Satellite Is Burning Up in Fall from Space," *New York Times*, March 22, 1990, p. A24; "Soviets Claim Reconnaissance Satellite Launched by Atlantis Has Failed," *Aviation Week and Space Technology*, March 26, 1990, p. 23; "Shuttle Spy Satellite Has Not Reentered," *Spaceflight*, January 1991, p. 4; private information.

21. Private information.

22. Ibid.

23. Ibid.

24. Ibid.

25. Ibid.

26. Douglas G. Armstrong, "The Gulf War's Patched-Together Air Intelligence," *Naval Institute Proceedings*, November 1992, pp. 109–111; Desmond Ball, *Intelligence in the Gulf War* (Canberra, Australia: SDSC, Australian National University, 1991), pp. 32, 34.

27. Craig Covault, "Space Recon of Iraq Taxes CIA Operations," *Aviation Week and Space Technology*, September 3, 1990, pp. 30–31.

28. Interview with Patrick Eddington, Centerville, Virginia, April 12, 1999.

29. Ibid.

30. Covault, "Space Recon of Iraq Taxes CIA Operations; U.S. News & World Report, *Triumph Without Victory*, p. 277; Thomas Christie et al., *Desert Storm SCUD Campaign* (Arlington, Va.: Institute for Defense Analyses, 1992), p. IV-6.

31. Department of Defense, *Conduct of the Persian Gulf War, Final Report to Congress* (Washington, D.C: DOD, April 1992), C-14 to C-15; Rick Atkinson, *Crusade: The Untold Story of the Persian Gulf War* (Boston: Houghton Mifflin, 1993), p. 265.

32. E. C. Aldridge Jr., Director, NRO, to David L. Boren, Chairman, Senate Select Committee on Intelligence, November 21, 1988.

33. Ibid.

34. Ibid.; Rear Adm. Robert K. Geiger and D. Barry Kelly, *NRO Restructure Study, Final Report, Volume II* (Washington, D.C.: NRO, 1989).

35. Kelly and Geiger, *NRO Restructure Study, Final Report, Volume II*, p. 16.

36. Letter, Secretary of Defense Richard Cheney and Director of Central Intelligence William Webster to Senator David Boren, Chairman, Senate Select Committee on Intelligence.

37. Ibid.

38. U.S. Congress, Senate Select Committee on Intelligence, *NRO Headquarters Project* (Washington, D.C.: U.S. Government Printing Office, 1995), p. 37; U.S. Congress, House Permanent Select Committee on Intelligence, *NRO Headquarters Facility* (Washington, D.C.: U.S. Government Printing Office, 1995), p. 2.

39. U.S. Congress, House Permanent Select Committee on Intelligence, *NRO Headquarters Facility*, p. 19; U.S. Congress, Senate Select Committee on Intelligence, *NRO Headquarters Project*, p. 52; Letter from Mary Jo Kingsley, Chief Information Access and Release Center, NRO, to author, August 9, 1996.

40. Martin C. Faga, Memorandum for the Secretary of Defense, Subject: DCI Task Force on the NRO-INFORMATION MEMORANDUM," May 19, 1992; George Bush, National Security Directive 67, "Intelligence Capabilities, 1992–2005," March 30, 1992.

41. DCI Task Force on the National Reconnaissance Office, *Report to the Director of Central Intelligence, DCI Task Force on the National Reconnaissance Office, Final Report*, April 1992, p. 2.

42. Ibid., p. 6.

43. U.S. Congress, Senate Select Committee on Intelligence and House Permanent Select Committee on Intelligence, *S. 2198 and S. 421 to Reorganize the United States Intelligence Community* (Washington, D.C.: U.S. Government Printing Office, 1993), p. 18.

44. Ralph Vartabedian, "Air Force Spy Satellite Unit Leaving California," *Los Angeles Times* (Washington ed.), October 16, 1992, pp. A1, A5; Ralph Vartabedian, "Air Force Spy Satellite Unit Leaving Southland," *Los Angeles Times*, October 16, 1992, pp. A1, A12; Vincent Kiernan, "NRO Streamlines to Cut Intelligence Bureaucracy," *Space News*, December 7–13, 1992, pp. 1, 29.

45. Ronald Kessler, *Inside the CIA: Revealing the Secrets of the World's Most Powerful Spy Agency* (New York: Pocket Books, 1992), pp. 77–78; CIA document fragment, July 22, 1988.

46. Interview with a former CIA official.

47. Interview with Robert Phillips, Rosslyn, Virginia, June 4, 1999.

48. Hirsch interview.

49. Vernon Loeb, "After-Action Report," *Washington Post Magazine*, February 27, 2000, pp. 7ff.

50. Ibid.

51. Ibid.

52. Ibid.

53. R. Jeffrey Smith, "Tracking Aideed Hampered by Intelligence Failures," *Washington Post*, October 8, 1993, p. A19.

54. Loeb, "After-Action Report."

55. Ibid.

56. Ibid.

57. Ibid.

58. CIA, "DCI Speech on New Frontiers in Breast Cancer Screening," October 11, 1994.

59. Sam Grant and Peter C. Oleson, "Breast Cancer Detection Research," *Studies in Intelligence*, Semiannual Unclassified Edition, No. 1, 1997, pp. 27–34 at pp. 27–28.

60. Grant and Oleson, "Breast Cancer Detection Research."

61. Ibid.

62. Tom Bowman and Scott Shane, "Espionage from the Front Lines," *Baltimore Sun*, December 8, 1995, pp. 1A, 20A–21A.

63. Ibid.; Howard Kurtz, "Pollard: Top Israelis Backed Spy Ring," *Washington Post*, February 28, 1987, p. A8.

64. Seymour Hersh, "The Wild East," *Atlantic Monthly*, June 1994, pp. 61–86.

65. Bowman and Shane, "Espionage from the Front Lines."

66. Ibid.

67. Ibid.

68. Ibid.

69. Ibid.; Seymour Hersh, *"The Target Is Destroyed": What Really Happened to Flight 007 and What America Knew About It* (New York: Random House, 1986), p. 4.

70. Bowman and Shane, "Espionage from the Front Lines."

71. Ibid.

72. Ibid.

73. Ibid. By mid-1994, individuals from the military services were being seconded to work for the SCS, after cover problems had been overcome. Four Air Intelligence Agency (AIA) candidates were selected to participate in the program, designated SENSOR SILVER. (Joyce M. Hons, Juan R. Jimenez, Gabriell G. Marshall, and Johnny D. Ford, *History of the Air Intelligence Agency, 1 January–31 December 1994, Volume I* [San Antonio, Tex.: AIA, December 1995], p. 39.)

74. R. Jeffrey Smith, "Pentagon Has Spent Millions on Tips from Trio of Psychics," *Washington Post*, November 29, 1995, pp. A1, A18; "U.S. Agencies Used Psychics for Years for 'Remote Viewing,'" *Washington Times*, November 30, 1995, p. A12; Steven Emerson, *Secret Warriors: Inside the Covert Military Operations of the Reagan Era* (New York: Putnam, 1988), pp. 65–66.

75. Smith, "Pentagon Has Spent Millions on Tips from Trio of Psychics"; R. Jeffrey Smith and Curt Suplee, "'Psychic Arms Race' Had Several Funding Channels," *Washington Post*, November 30, 1995, pp. A1, A13; "U.S. Agencies Used Psychics for Years for 'Remote Viewing.'"

76. Smith and Suplee, "'Psychic Arms Race' Had Several Funding Channels."

77. Douglas Waller, "The Vision Thing," *Time*, December 11, 1995, p. 48; Martin Gardner, "Claiborne Pell: The Senator from Outer Space," *Skeptical Inquirer,* March/April 1996, pp. 12–15.

78. Hirsch interview; Office of Public Affairs, "CIA Statement on 'Remote Viewing,'" September 6, 1995.

79. Information about AIR is accessible from its web site: www.air-dc.org.

80. Michael D. Mumford, Andrew M. Rose, and David M. Goslin, *An Evaluation of Remote Viewing: Research and Applications* (Washington, D.C.: American Institutes for Research, September 29, 1995), pp. 1–3 to 1–4.

81. Ibid., pp. 1–4 to 1–5.

82. Ibid., p. E-1; Ray Hyman, "Evaluation of the Military's Twenty-Year Program on Psychic Spying," *Skeptical Inquirer*, March/April 1996, pp. 24–26; Ray Hyman, "Parapsychological Research: A Tutorial Review and Critical Appraisal," *Proceedings of the IEEE* 74, 6 (June 1986): 823–849; Smith, "Pentagon Has Spent Millions on Tips from Trio of Psychics"; Mumford, Rose, and Goslin, *An Evaluation of Remote Viewing*, p. E-2.

83. Mumford, Rose, and Goslin, *An Evaluation of Remote Viewing*, p. E-3.

84. Ibid., p. E-4.

85. Ibid. For a critique of the AIR report's conclusions as well as claims of bias in its preparation, see Edwin C. May, "The American Institutes for Research Review of the Department of Defense's STAR GATE Program: A Commentary," *Journal of Scientific Exploration* 10, 1 (1996): 89–107.

86. Hirsch interview.

Chapter 10: Agile Intelligence

1. Telephone interview with James Hirsch, April 11, 2000.

2. Ibid.; interview with Steven Koonin, Pasadena, California, March 22, 2000.

3. Vita, Steven E. Koonin, n.d.; Koonin interview.

4. Hirsch telephone interview.

5. Interview with Ruth David, Arlington, Virginia, February 22, 1999; CIA, Public Affairs, "Ruth A. David, Deputy Director of Science and Technology, Central Intelligence Agency," n.d.

6. CIA, Public Affairs, "Ruth A. David, Deputy Director of Science and Technology, Central Intelligence Agency"; "Meet the CEO," www.anser.org/aboutanser/meetceo.html; David interview.

7. CIA, Public Affairs, "Ruth A. David, Deputy Director for Science and Technology, Central Intelligence Agency."

8. Ibid.; CIA Public Affairs, "DS&T Leadership History," n.d.; interview with Robert Phillips, Rosslyn, Virginia, June 4, 1999.

9. David interview.

10. Ibid.; Ruth David, "Prologue," to Frederick Thomas Martin, *Top Secret Intranet: How U.S. Intelligence Built INTELINK-The World's Largest, Most Secure Network* (Upper Saddle River, N.J.: Prentice-Hall PTR, 1998), p. xix.

11. David interview.

12. David, "Prologue," to Martin, *Top Secret Intranet*, p. xx; Ruth David, speech to Armed Forces Communications Electronics Association, January 1998, p. 7.

13. David, speech to Armed Forces Communications Electronics Association, p. 8.

14. Ibid., pp. 14–15.

15. Ibid., pp. 10, 14.

16. CIA Office of Public Affairs, "Restructuring in the DS&T," 1996.

17. "Computer Scientists,(AAT)," www.cia.gov/cia/employment/jobpostings/comsciad.htm.

18. Clarence A. Robinson, "Intelligence Agency Adjusts as Mission Possible Unfolds," *Signal*, October 1998.

19. Ibid.

20. Ibid.

21. David interview; CIA Public Affairs, "Restructuring in the DS&T."

22. Jeffrey T. Richelson, "CIA's Science and Technology Gurus Get New Look, Roles," *Defense Week*, August 19, 1996, p. 6.

23. CIA Public Affairs, "Restructuring in the DS&T"; private information.

24. Phillips interview.

25. Phillips interview; interview with Philip Eckman, Alexandria, Virginia, May 16, 2000; "Public Support Swells for CIA's FBIS Program," *Secrecy and Government Bulletin*, July 1996; "Costly Cuts?" *Newsweek*, November 25, 1996, p. 6. As of February 1995, FBIS had fourteen foreign bureaus located in Abidjan, Ivory Coast; Amman, Jordan; Asunción, Paraguay; Bangkok, Thailand; Chiva Chiva, Panama; Hong Kong; Islamabad, Pakistan; London, UK; Mbabane, Swaziland; Nicosia, Cyprus; Okinawa, Japan; Seoul, Republic of Korea; Tel Aviv, Israel; and Vienna, Austria. Domestically, in addition to its Reston, Virginia, headquarters, FBIS operated a bureau in Key West.

26. FBIS, "Overview for CNC Conference," n.d.

27. Phillips interview.

28. Ibid.

29. "Public Support Swells for CIA's FBIS Program."

30. U.S. Congress, House of Representatives, House Permanent Select Committee on Intelligence, *Intelligence Authorization Act for Fiscal Year 1998, Report 105-135, Part 1* (Washington, D.C.: U.S. Government Printing Office, 1997), pp. 23–24.

31. Stephen Barr, "Monitoring Service Spared in Latest Crisis," *Washington Post*, February 6, 1997, p. A21. In 1997, FBIS did complete a transition, started in 1995, from the production of hard-copy reports—including the FBIS Daily Report and the Joint Publications Research Service translations—as a step toward purely electronic transmission. (FBIS, "Overview for CNC Conference, n.d., Slide 5.)

32. U.S. Congress, House of Representatives, House Permanent Select Committee on Intelligence, *Intelligence Authorization Act for Fiscal Year 1998*, p. 24.

33. Ibid.

34. Peter Maass, "From His Bed, CIA's Best Makes His Breakthroughs," *Washington Post*, April 21, 1996, pp. A1, A20; CIA, "'Trailblazers' and Years of CIA Service," 1997.

35. Maass, "From His Bed, CIA's Best Makes His Breakthroughs."

36. Ibid.

37. Ibid.

38. Ibid.

39. Ibid.

40. Robert M. Gates, Director of Central Intelligence, *Statement on Change in CIA and the Intelligence Community*, April 1, 1992, p. 28.

41. H.R. 4165, "National Security Act of 1992," 1992; S. 2198, "Intelligence Reorganization Act of 1992," 1992.

42. Robert M. Gates, Director of Central Intelligence, *Statement on Change in CIA and the Intelligence Community*, April 1, 1992, p. 28; telephone conversation with R. Evans Hineman, February 24, 2000.

43. Central Imagery Office, *Briefing Slides*, 1992.

44. Department of Defense Directive 5105.26, "Central Imagery Office," May 6, 1992; Central Imagery Office, *Briefing Slides*, pp. 2–3; Director of Central Intelligence Directive 2/9, "Management of National Imagery Intelligence," June 1, 1992.

45. Central Imagery Office, *Briefing Slides*, p. 2.

46. Statement of John Deutch before Senate Select Committee on Intelligence, April 26, 1995, pp. 8–9.

47. "DCI Plans a National Imagery Agency," *Communiqué*, August 1995, pp. 1, 8; DCI, "Terms of Reference for National Imagery Agency," circa May 1995.

48. Central Intelligence Agency, "National Imagery and Mapping Agency Proposed to Congress," November 28, 1995.

49. Ibid.

50. Interview with John N. McMahon, Los Altos, California, November 17, 1998.

51. Interview with James V. Hirsch, Fairfax, Virginia, February 12, 1999; CIA, Office of Public Affairs, "Unclassified Imagery Analysis Presentation," n.d.

52. Hirsch interview.

53. Ibid. Until 1994, OIA and NPIC were two distinct organizations. In 1994, NPIC assumed responsibility for staffing and managing OIA. At the same time, a number of OIA managers moved into positions at NPIC. The change, according to Patrick Eddington, was not one that he or others at NPIC felt was beneficial. He noted that NPIC, in the Navy Yard, lived a separate life from the CIA and that there were different cultures. In his view, NPIC was more independent and felt no obligation to support the intelligence directorate's conclusions, had a more exacting standard in its analysis of imagery, offered more extensive training to its analysts, and had a broader customer base—which included State, Defense, the Federal Emergency Management Agency, and Commerce. Whereas OIA never maintained an extensive database, the NPIC's National Data System was available to the entire intelligence community. The reorganization, according to Eddington, threw NPIC into "a state of turmoil" and made it "a less exciting and rewarding place to work." (Interview with Patrick Eddington, Centreville, Virginia, April 12, 1999. Also see Patrick Eddington, *Gassed in the Gulf: The Inside Story of the Pentagon-CIA Cover-Up of Gulf War Syndrome* ([Washington, D.C.: Insignia, 1997], p. 25.)

54. Interview with R. Evans Hineman, Chantilly, Virginia, February 17, 1999.

55. Interview with Patrick Eddington, Centreville, Virginia, April 12, 1999.

56. Eddington, *Gassed in the Gulf*, p. 151.

57. U.S. Congress, Senate Select Committee on Intelligence, *Special Report of the Senate Select Committee on Intelligence, United States Senate, January 4, 1995 to October 3, 1996* (Washington, D.C.: U.S. Government Printing Office, 1997), pp. 7–8. There was also some concern about the proposed merger from Defense Mapping Agency officials, who feared that their formal inclusion in the intelligence community might have a negative impact on the relationship with foreign nations who provide mapping information.

58. NIMA, "National Imagery and Mapping Agency Established," October 1, 1996.

59. First "Announced NRO Payload," *Spaceflight* 39, 3 (March 1997): 77. In 1995, the NRO and CIA had acknowledged the launch dates associated with the CORONA, ARGON, and LANYARD programs, the last of which was in May 1972.

60. Vincent Kiernan, "Titan 4 Launches Spy Satellite from Vandenberg AFB," *Space News*, December 7–13, 1992, p. 26; Craig Covault, "Advanced KH-11 Broadens U.S. Recon Capability," *Aviation Week and Space Technology*, January 6, 1997, pp. 24–25; Craig Covault, "New Intelligence Ops Debut in Iraqi Strikes," *Aviation Week and Space Technology*, December 21–28, 1998, pp. 124–125; William Harwood, "Titan Boosts Military Payload for Ninth Consecutive Success," *Space News*, December 11–17, 1995, p. 26; private information.

61. Interview with Bernard Lubarsky, Alexandria, Virginia, May 16, 2000; private information.

62. Barbara Crosette, "U.S. Seeks to Prove Mass Killings," *New York Times*, August 11, 1995, p. A3; Bill Gertz, "New Chinese Missiles Target All of East Asia," *Washington Times*, July 10, 1997, pp. A1, A16; Tim Weiner, "U.S. Suspects India Prepares for Nuclear Test," *New York Times*, December 15, 1995, p. A6; Elaine Sciolino, "U.S. Says It's Won Votes to Maintain Sanctions on Iraq," *New York Times*, March 5, 1995, pp. 1, 9; Bill Gertz, "Libyans Stop Work on Chemical Plant," *Washington Times*, June 24, 1996, p. A4; Joseph S. Bermudez Jr., "North Korea Set for More Ballistic Missile Tests," *Jane's Defence Weekly*, October 23, 1996, p. 5.

63. CIA Office of Public Affairs, "Hypertext Systems," n.d.

64. CIA, Office of Public Affairs, "Information Retrieval," n.d.

65. CIA, Office of Public Affairs, "Image Perspective Transformation Modeling and Visualization," n.d. circa 1996.

66. CIA Public Affairs, "Dual-Use Technology Projects: Law Enforcement and the Environment," 1996.

67. Ibid.; "Once-Secret Technology Assists Cancer Detection," *Signal*, June 1995, pp. 66–67; CIA, Public Affairs, "Facial Recognition Program," n.d.

68. Interview with Gene Poteat, McLean, Virginia, April 25, 2000; Philip Eckman, "Some Random Thoughts and Musings on ORD," n.d. Previously, according to former ORD director Philip Eckman, OD&E competed with ORD for funds and also was the agency's executive authority for decisions on funding reconnaissance projects, making it both "judge and jury." According to Eckman, that had been a sore point for many years, "since it was generally acknowledged that ORD had the lion's share of innovative proposals each year, yet never received more than about 20% of the funds." (Philip Eckman, "Some Random Thoughts and Musings on ORD," n.d.)

69. David interview.

70. McMahon interview; Poteat interview.

71. Hineman interview.

72. Hirsch interview.

73. David interview.

Chapter 11: Uncertain Future

1. CIA, "CIA's Deputy Director for Science and Technology to Become CEO of Public Service Research Institute," June 22, 1998; "History," www.anser.org/aboutanser/history.html.

2. CIA, "CIA's Deputy Director for Science and Technology to Become CEO of Public Service Research Institute."

3. Interview with Robert Singel, Great Falls, Virginia, February 25, 1999.

4. Interview with Philip Eckman, Alexandria, Virginia, May 16, 2000.

5. "Joanne Isham," www.odci.gov/cia, 1998; CIA Public Affairs, "DCI Tenet Announces Appointment of Deputy Directors for Science and Technology," January 12, 2000; CIA Public Affairs, "Joanne O. Isham, Deputy Director for Science and Technology," January 13, 2000.

6. Vernon Loeb, "Inside Information," www.washingtonpost.com, January 10, 2000; interview with R. Evans Hineman, Chantilly, Virginia, February 17, 1999.

7. CIA, "Director of Central Intelligence Appoints Dr. Gary L. Smith, Deputy Director for Science and Technology," March 24, 1999.

8. "Profile of APL," www.jhuapl.edu/profile/profile.htm; "MSX Satellite Passes Rocket Tracking Test," *Space News*, April 24–30, 1997, p. 10.

9. CIA, "Director of Central Intelligence Appoints Dr. Gary L. Smith, Deputy Director for Science and Technology."

10. Ibid.

11. CIA Public Affairs, "DCI Tenet Announces Appointment of Deputy Director for Science and Technology," January 12, 2000.

12. Vernon Loeb, "CIA Science Chief Quits; Deputy Named," *Washington Post*, January 14, 2000, p. A25; private information.

13. CIA Public Affairs, "DCI Tenet Announces Appointment of Deputy Director for Science and Technology."

14. Telephone conversation with CIA spokesman, January 21, 2000.

15. Loeb, "CIA Science Chief Quits; Deputy Named"; telephone interview with Gordon Oehler, October 5, 2000.

16. CIA Public Affairs, "James L. Runyan, Associate Deputy Director for Science and Technology," January 2000.

17. Private information.

18. Letter, Joanne O. Isham to Albert Wheelon, October 13, 2000.

19. CIA, "DS&T Realignment Overview," n.d.

20. Ibid.; CIA, "DS&T Response to Author's Questions," February 9, 2001.

21. Tabassum Zakaria, "CIA Using 'Data Mining' Technology to Find Nuggets," Reuters, March 2, 2001.

22. Ibid.

23. Gary H. Anthes, "Cloak & Dagger IT," www.computerworld.com, accessed February 6, 2001; Rick E. Yannuzzi, "In-Q-Tel: A New Partnership Between the CIA and the Private Sector," *Defense Intelligence Journal* 9, 1 (Winter 2000).

24. Anthes, "Cloak & Dagger IT."

25. Ibid.

26. Neil King Jr., "Small Start-Up Helps the CIA to Mask Its Moves on the Web," *Wall Street Journal,* February 12, 2001, pp. B1, Bb.

27. Ibid.

28. CIA, "DS&T Response to Author's Questions"; private information.

29. CIA, "DS&T Realignment Overview."

30. Ibid.

31. Basil H. Scott, "A 21st Century CIA—Meeting Challenges, Realizing Opportunities," April 4, 1999, www.odci.gov/dst.

32. Telephone interview with Robert Kohler, July 6, 1999.

33. Gordon Oehler, "Warning and Detection," in Sidney D. Drell, Abraham D. Sofaer, and George D. Wilson, *The New Terror: Facing the Threat of Biological and Chemical Weapons* (Stanford, Calif.: Hoover Institution Press, 1999), pp. 138–151 at p. 143.

34. Telephone interview with Robert Kohler, February 1, 2001.

SOURCES

Interviews (Dates without locations indicate a telephone interview)

Lew Allen: Pasadena, California, June 10, 1999.
Paul Bacalis: December 1, 1999.
Richard Bissell: Farmington, Connecticut, January 6, 1984; Farmington, Connecticut, March 16, 1984.
Dino Brugioni: May 21, 1996.
Roy Burks: North Potomac, Maryland, May 10, 1999.
Frank Buzard: Rancho Palos Verdes, California, June 11, 1999.
Joseph Charyk: June 1, 1999.
Ruth David: Arlington, Virginia, February 22, 1999.
Philip Eckman: Alexandria, Virginia, May 16, 2000.
Patrick Eddington: Centreville, Virginia, April 12, 1999.
Edward Giller: June 29, 1999.
R. Evans Hineman: Chantilly, Virginia, February 17, 1999.
James V. Hirsch: Fairfax, Virginia, February 12, 1999.
R. M. Huffstutler: Falls Church, Virginia, March 23, 1999.
Robert Kohler: July 6, 1999; February 1, 2001.
Steven Koonin: Pasadena, California, March 22, 2000.
Jack C. Ledford: Arlington, Virginia, October 7, 1999.
Walter Levison: September 17, 1999.
Henry S. Lowenhaupt: Springfield, Virginia, April 15, 1999.
Bernard Lubarsky: Alexandria, Virginia, May 9, 2000.
Arthur Lundahl: October 19, 1988; July 27, 1989.
Frank Madden: November 3, 2000.
Victor Marchetti: October 12, 1999.
John Martin: September 7, 1996.
John McMahon: Los Altos, California, November 17, 1998.
Brockway McMillan: September 15, 1999.
William H. Nance: Bethesda, Maryland, May 4, 1999.
Gordon Oehler: October 5, 2000.
Robert Phillips: Rosslyn, Virginia, June 4, 1999.
Henry Plaster: Vienna, Virginia, September 30, 1999.
Gene Poteat: McLean, Virginia, April 25, 2000.
Edward Proctor: March 10, 1999.
Robert Singel: Great Falls, Virginia, February 25, 1999.
Sayre Stevens: May 29, 1996; Springfield, Virginia, March 18, 1999.

Thomas Twetten: March 12, 2001.
Karl Weber: Oakton, Virginia, May 5, 1999.
Albert Wheelon: April 2, 1997; Washington, D.C., April 9, 1997; May 19, 1997; Montecito, California, May 11–12, 1998; November 29, 1998; Montecito, June 14, 1999; Montecito, March 21, 2000.

Government/Contractor Documents, Publications, and Videos (excluding memos, letters, and press releases)

"Agreement Between Secretary of Defense and the Director of Central Intelligence on Responsibilities of the National Reconnaissance Office." May 2, 1962.
Air Force Eastern Test Range, *Eastern Test Range Index of Missile Launchings, July 1968–June 1969.* Patrick AFB, Fla.: AFETR, 1969.
Allen Welsh Dulles as Director of Central Intelligence, 26 February 1953–29 November 1961, Volume II, Coordination of Central Intelligence. Washington, D.C.: Central Intelligence Agency, 1973.
Armstrong, Willis, William Leonhart, William J. McCaffrey, and Herbert C. Rothenberg. "The Hazards of Single-Outcome Forecasting." *Studies in Intelligence* 28, 3 (Fall 1984): 57–70.
Bernard, Richard L. "The Defense Special Missile and Astronautics Center." *Cryptologic Spectrum*, Fall 1983, pp. 30–33.
Brandwein, David S. "Telemetry Analysis." *Studies in Intelligence* 8, 4 (Fall 1964): 21–29.
______. "The SS-8 Controversy." *Studies in Intelligence* 13, 3 (Summer 1969): 27–35.
Brown, Donald C. "On the Trail of Hen House and Hen Roost." *Studies in Intelligence* 13, 2 (Spring 1969): 11–19.
Burke, James. "Seven Years to Luna 9." *Studies in Intelligence* 10, 3 (Summer 1966): 1–24.
Bush, George. National Security Directive 45. "U.S. Policy in Response to the Iraqi Invasion of Kuwait," August 20, 1990.
______. National Security Directive 54. "Responding to Iraqi Aggression in the Gulf," January 15, 1991.
Carey, Warren F., and Myles Maxfield. "Intelligence Implications of Disease." *Studies in Intelligence* 16, 1 (Spring 1972): 71–78.
Center for the Study of Intelligence. *Declassified National Intelligence Estimates of the Soviet Union and International Communism.* Washington, D.C.: Central Intelligence Agency, 1996.
Central Imagery Office. *Briefing Slides,* 1992.
Central Intelligence Agency. *The French Nuclear Energy Weapons Program*, November 13, 1959.
______. "Future of the Agency's U-2 Capability," July 7, 1960.
______. *Cost Reduction Program FY 1966–FY 1967*, September 1, 1965, NARA/CP, TRB, RG 263, Entry 36, HRP 89-2/00443, Box 7, File 713.
______. "Biographic Profile, Albert Dewell Wheelon," May 10, 1966, NARA, MRB, RG 263.
______. *Burial at Sea*, September 4, 1974. Videotape.
______. *Iran in the 1980s*, August 1977.
______. *R. V. Jones Intelligence Award Ceremony Honoring Dr. Albert Wheelon*, December 13, 1994.
______. *DS&T 35th Anniversary: Celebrating 50 Years of CIA History*, July 24, 1997. Videotape.
Central Intelligence Agency and National Reconnaissance Office. "CORONA Pioneers," May 25, 1995.
Central Intelligence Agency, Photographic Interpretation Center. *Joint Mission Coverage Index, Mission 9009, 18 August 1960*, September 1960. In Kevin C. Ruffner (ed.), *CORONA: America's First Satellite Program.* Washington, D.C.: Central Intelligence Agency, 1995.
Charyk, Joseph. "A Summary Review of the National Reconnaissance Office," February 25, 1963.

China Task Force, Central Intelligence Agency. "The Production Effort," July 1965–June 1967, NARA, RG 263, CIA HRP 89-2, NN3-263-94-010, Box 9, File HS/HC 735, Folder 2.
"CIA Raising USSR Sub Raises Questions." *FBIS-SOV-92-145*, July 28, 1992, pp. 15–16.
Clesh, Mark. "Dedication of New Operations Center for DEFSMAC," *Communiqué*, March/April 1998, pp. 42–43.
David, Ruth. Speech to Armed Forces Communications Electronics Association, January 1998.
Davies, Merton, and William R. Harris. *RAND's Role in the Evolution of Balloon and Satellite Observation Systems and Related U.S. Space Technology.* Santa Monica, Calif.: RAND, 1988.
"DCI Plans a National Imagery Agency." *Communiqué*, August 1995, pp. 1, 8.
DCI Task Force on the National Reconnaissance Office. *Report to the Director of Central Intelligence, DCI Task Force on the National Reconnaissance Office, Final Report*, April 1992.
Dean, L. E., C. R. Johnson, and H. J. Strasler. "Teal Amber I." *Journal of Defense Research*, Special Issue 78-3, 1978, pp. 151–170.
"Debriefing of Francis Gary Powers, Tape #2." February 13, 1962, NARA, RG 263, 1998 CIA release, Box 230, Folder 3.
Department of Defense. DOD Directive S-5100.43, "Defense Special Missile and Astronautics Center (Defense/SMAC)," April 27, 1964.
______. *Conduct of the Persian Gulf War, Final Report to Congress.* Washington, D.C.: Department of Defense, April 1992.
______. DOD Directive 5105.26, "Central Imagery Office," May 6, 1992.
Department of State. "Transcript of Daily Press Briefing, Tuesday, September 29, 1964."
Deutch, John. Statement before Senate Select Committee on Intelligence, April 26, 1995.
Director of Central Intelligence. NIE 11-6-54, *Soviet Capabilities and Probable Programs in the Guided Missile Field*, October 1954.
______. NIE 11-4-57, *Main Trends in Soviet Capabilities and Policies, 1957–1962*, November 12, 1957.
______. NIE 11-4-59, *Main Trends in Soviet Capabilities and Policies, 1959–1964*, February 9, 1960.
______. NIE 11-4-60, *Main Trends in Soviet Capabilities and Policies, 1956–1965*, December 1, 1960.
______. NIE 11-8-61, *Soviet Capabilities for Long Range Attack*, June 7, 1961.
______. NIE 11-8/1-61, *Soviet Capabilities for Long Range Attack*, September 21, 1961.
______. SNIE 13-2-63, *Communist China's Advanced Weapons Program*, July 24, 1963.
______. NIE 11-8-63, *Soviet Capabilities for Strategic Attack*, October 18, 1963.
______. NIE 11-2-64, *The Soviet Atomic Energy Program*, July 16, 1964.
______. SNIE 13-4-64. *The Chances of an Imminent Communist Chinese Nuclear Explosion*, August 26, 1964.
______. NIE 11-8-64, *Soviet Capabilities for Strategic Attack*, October 8, 1964.
______. NIE 11-1-65. *The Soviet Space Program*, 1965.
______. NIE 11-2A-65, *The Soviet Atomic Energy Program*, May 19, 1965.
______. NIE 11-1-67, *The Soviet Space Program*, March 2, 1967.
______. NIE 11-8-67, *Soviet Capabilities for Strategic Attack*, October 26, 1967.
______. NIE 11-3-67, *Soviet Strategic Air and Missile Defenses*, November 9, 1967.
______. NIE 11-8-70, *Soviet Forces for Intercontinental Attack*, November 24, 1970.
______. NIE 11-8-71, *Soviet Forces for Intercontinental Attack*, October 21, 1971.
______. NIE 11-8-72, *Soviet Forces for Intercontinental Attack*, October 26, 1972.
______. DCID 3/3, "Scientific Intelligence," October 28, 1949.
______. DCID 3/4, "Production of Scientific and Technical Intelligence," August 14, 1952.
______. DCID 3/5, "Production of Scientific and Technical Intelligence," February 3, 1959.
______. DCID 2/9, "Management of National Imagery Intelligence," June 1, 1992.

Directorate of Collection, Office, ACS/Intelligence, Air Force. *History: Directorate of Collection, Office, ACS/Intelligence 1 July–31 December 1962*, n.d.

Directorate of Science and Technology, CIA. *CORONA Program History, Volume II: Governmental Activities*, May 1976.

Dulles, Allen W., William H. Jackson, and Mathias F. Correa. *The Central Intelligence Agency and National Organization for Intelligence.* Washington, D.C.: National Security Council, 1949.

Earman, J. S., Inspector General, CIA. *Report on Plots to Assassinate Fidel Castro.* Washington, D.C.: CIA, 1967.

Eliot, Frank. "Moon Bounce Elint." *Studies in Intelligence* 11, 2 (Spring 1967): 59–65.

Fischer, Benjamin B. (ed.) *At Cold War's End: U.S. Intelligence on the Soviet Union and Eastern Europe 1989–1991.* Washington, D.C.: Central Intelligence Agency, 1999.

Foreign Broadcast Information Service. "Overview for CNC Conference," n.d.

Garofalo, Nicholas R. "Present and Future Capabilities of OTH Radars." *Studies in Intelligence* 13, 2 (Spring 1969): 53–61.

Gates, Robert M. *Statement on Change in CIA and the Intelligence Community*, April 1, 1992.

Geiger, Rear Adm. Robert, and D. Barry Kelly. *NRO Restructure Study, Final Report, Volume II.* Washington, D.C.: NRO, 1989.

Gerson, N. C. "SIGINT in Space." *Studies in Intelligence* 28, 2 (Summer 1984): 41–48.

GRAB: Galactic Radiation and Background. Washington, D.C.: Naval Research Laboratory, 1997.

Grant, Sam, and Peter C. Oleson. "Breast Cancer Detection Research." *Studies in Intelligence*, Semiannual Unclassified Edition No. 1, 1997, pp. 27–34.

Greer, Kenneth E. "Corona." *Studies in Intelligence*, Supplement, 17 (Spring 1973).

Haines, Gerald K. *The National Reconnaissance Office: Its Origins, Creation, and Early Years.* Washington, D.C.: NRO, 1997.

Hons, Joyce M., Juan R. Jimenez, Gabriell G. Marshall, and Johnny D. Ford. *History of the Air Intelligence Agency, 1 January–31 December 1994, Volume I.* San Antonio, Tex.: AIA, 1995.

Howland, Nina D. (ed.). *Foreign Relations of the United States, 1964–1968, Volume XXII: Iran.* Washington, D.C.: U.S. Government Printing Office, 1999.

Inspector General, CIA. *Inspector General's Survey of the Office of Research and Development*, October 1972.

"Inspector General's Survey of Air Activities: Summary of Recommendations," circa 1962.

Intelligence Advisory Committee. NIE 11-3A-54, *Summary: The Soviet Atomic Energy Program to Mid-1957*, February 16, 1954.

Jackson, George S., and Martin F. Clausen. *Organizational History of the Central Intelligence Agency, 1950–1953.* Washington, D.C.: Central Intelligence Agency, 1957.

Joint Study Group. *Report on Foreign Intelligence Activities of the United States Government*, December 15, 1960.

Klaimon, Jerold H. "Reentry Vehicle Analysis." *Studies in Intelligence* 12, 3 (Summer 1968): 23–33.

Kress, Kenneth A. "Parapsychology in Intelligence: A Personal Review and Conclusions." *Studies in Intelligence* 21, 4 (Winter 1977): 7–17.

Kroeger, Charles A., Jr. "ELINT: A Scientific Intelligence System." *Studies in Intelligence* 2, 1 (Winter 1958): 71–83.

LaMothe, John D. *Controlled Offensive Behavior–USSR (U).* Washington, D.C.: DIA, 1972.

Laubenthal, Capt. Sanders A. *The Missiles in Cuba, 1962: The Role of SAC Intelligence.* Offutt AFB, Nebr.: Strategic Air Command, 1984.

Lawrence, R. E., and Harry W. Woo. "Infrared Imagery in Overhead Reconnaissance." *Studies in Intelligence* 11, 3 (Summer 1967): 17–40.

Lowenhaupt, Henry S. "The Decryption of a Picture." *Studies in Intelligence* 1, 3 (Summer 1957).

______. "Mission to Birch Woods." *Studies in Intelligence* 12, 4 (Fall 1968): 1–12.

Mabon, David M., and David S. Patterson (eds.). *Foreign Relations of the United States, 1961–1963, Volume VII: Arms Control and Disarmament.* Washington, D.C.: U.S. Government Printing Office, 1996.

McCone, John A., Director of Central Intelligence, and Roswell Gilpatric, Deputy Secretary of Defense. "Agreement Between the Secretary of Defense and the Director of Central Intelligence on Management of the National Reconnaissance Program," March 13, 1963.

McIninch, Thomas P. "The OXCART Story." *Studies in Intelligence* 15, 1 (Winter 1971): 1–34.

Mendez, Antonio. "A Classic Case of Deception." *Studies in Intelligence*, Unclassified Edition, Winter 1999–2000, pp. 1–16.

Montague, Ludwell Lee. *General Walter Bedell Smith as Director of Central Intelligence, October 1950–February 1953.* University Park: Pennsylvania State University Press, 1992.

Mumford, Michael D., Andrew D. Rose, and David M. Goslin. *An Evaluation of Remote Viewing: Research and Applications.* Washington, D.C.: American Institutes for Research, September 29, 1995.

Nance, William H. "Quality ELINT." *Studies in Intelligence* 12, 2 (Spring 1968): 7–19.

National Foreign Assessment Center, CIA. *The Soviet Earth Resources Satellite Program*, June 1980.

National Photographic Interpretation Center, CIA. "Search for Uranium Mining in the Vicinity of A-Ko-Su, China," August 1963. In Kevin C. Ruffner (ed.), *CORONA: America's First Satellite Program.* Washington, D.C.: Central Intelligence Agency, 1995, pp. 175–183.

______."Suspect CW Agent Production Plants—Dzerzhinsk USSR, Changes Since 1962," August 1963. In Kevin C. Ruffner (ed.), *CORONA: America's First Satellite Program.* Washington, D.C.: Central Intelligence Agency, 1995, pp. 185–189.

______. "Chronological Developments of the Kapustin Yar/Vladimirovka and Tyuratam Missile Test Centers, USSR, 1957 Through 1963," November 1963. In Kevin C. Ruffner (ed.), *CORONA: America's First Satellite Program.* Washington, D.C.: Central Intelligence Agency, 1995, pp. 191–196.

______. "Probable Solid Propellants Testing Facilities and Associated Explosives Plants in the USSR," December 1963. In Kevin C. Ruffner (ed.), *CORONA: America's First Satellite Program.* Washington, D.C.: Central Intelligence Agency, 1995, pp. 197–214.

______*Black Shield Mission X–001, 31 May 1967,* June 1967.

______*Black Shield Mission BX–6705, 20 June 1967,* June 1967.

______*Black Shield Mission BX–6706, 30 June 1967,* July 1967.

______*Black Shield Mission BX–6723, 17 September 1967,* November 1967.

______*Black Shield Mission BX–6725, 4 October 1967,* December 1967.

______*Black Shield Mission BX–6732, 28 October 1967,* December 1967.

National Reconnaissance Office. *Deputy Directors of the NRO.* Chantilly, Va.: NRO, 1997.

______. "Biography: Dennis Fitzgerald." Chantilly, Va.: NRO, 1997.

______. *Program Directors of the NRO: ABC&D.* Chantilly, Va.: NRO, 1999.

National Security Agency. *A Historical Perspective of DefSMAC with Charles Tevis and Max Mitchell*, 1980. Video.

National Security Council. NSCID No. 5, "U.S. Espionage and Counterintelligence Activities Abroad," January 18, 1961.

______. NSCID No. 8, "Photographic Interpretation," January 18, 1961.

9th Strategic Reconnaissance Wing. *History of the 9th Strategic Reconnaissance Wing, 1 October–31 December 1967*, n.d.

Oder, Frederic C.E., James C. Fitzpatrick, and Paul E. Worthman. *The CORONA Story.* Washington, D.C.: National Reconnaissance Office, 1997.

Office of Computer Services, Directorate of Science and Technology, CIA. *OCS Computer System Planning Report*, June 1, 1965.

Office of Scientific Intelligence, Central Intelligence Agency. *Indian Nuclear Energy Program,* November 6, 1964.

______. *Japanese Nuclear Energy Program,* OSI-SR/65-55, November 1964.

______. *Soviet Nuclear Research Reactors*, OSI-SR/64-41, September 22, 1964.

Office of Special Projects, 1965–1970, Volume One, Chapters I-II. Washington, D.C.: CIA, 1973.

Office of Special Projects, 1965–1970, Volume Four: Appendixes B, C, and D. Washington, D.C.: CIA, 1973.

"ORD Milestones," September 1966, NARA, TRB, RG 263, 1998 CIA Release, Box 66, Folder 5.

Pedlow, Gregory W., and Donald E. Welzenbach. *The Central Intelligence Agency and Overhead Reconnaissance: The U-2 and OXCART Programs, 1954–1974.* Washington, D.C.: CIA, 1992.

Pekel, Kent. "Integrity, Ethics, and the CIA," *Studies in Intelligence*, Unclassified Edition, Spring 1998, pp. 85–94.

Perry, Robert. *A History of Satellite Reconnaissance, Volume 5: Management of the National Reconnaissance Program, 1960–1965.* Washington, D.C.: NRO, 1969.

Plaster, Henry G. "Snooping on Space Pictures." *Studies in Intelligence* 8, 4 (Fall 1964): 31–39.

Poteat, Gene. "Stealth, Countermeasures, and ELINT, 1960–1975." *Studies in Intelligence* 42, 1 (1998): 51–59.

Psychological Operations in Guerrilla Warfare. New York: Vintage, 1985.

Puthoff, Harold E., and Russell Targ. *Perceptual Augmentation Techniques, Part One—Technical Proposal.* SRI No. ISH 73–146, October 1, 1973.

______. *Perceptual Augmentation Techniques: Final Report (Covering the Period January 1974 through February 1975, Part Two—Research Project).* Menlo Park, Calif.: Stanford Research Institute, December 1, 1975.

Rathjens, George W. "Destruction of Chinese Nuclear Weapons Capabilities." ACDA, December 14, 1964.

Reagan, Ronald. National Security Decision Directive 17, "National Security Directive on Cuba and Central America," January 4, 1982.

Ruffner, Kevin C. (ed.). *CORONA: America's First Satellite Program.* Washington, D.C.: CIA, 1995.

Schwar, Harriet Dashiell (ed.). *Foreign Relations of the United States, 1964–1968, Volume 30: China.* Washington, D.C.: U.S. Government Printing Office, 1998.

Scott, Basil H. "A 21st Century CIA—Meeting Challenges, Realizing Opportunities," April 4, 1999. www. odci.gov/dst.

Secretary of the Air Force/Public Affairs. "Biography: Major General John L. Martin Jr.," n.d.

______. "Biography: General Lew Allen Jr.," September 1981.

"Series of SS-11 ICBM Tests to Pacific Impact Area Concluded." *EUCOM Intelligence Report*, September 7, 1966.

Sloop, John L. *Liquid Hydrogen as a Propulsion Fuel.* Washington, D.C.: NASA, 1978.

"Soviets Maintaining High Launch Rate for Major ICBMs: SS-11 Crew Training May Be Under Way." *EUCOM Intelligence Report*, August 18, 1966.

"Soviets Step Up Testing of First-Line ICBM Systems." *EUCOM Intelligence Report*, April 13, 1966.

"Statement by the Director, Senate Foreign Relations Committee," June 23, 1969.

Steury, Donald P. (ed.). *Intentions and Capabilities: Estimates on Soviet Strategic Forces, 1950–1983.* Washington, D.C.: CIA, 1996.

Stillman, D., "An Analysis of a Remote-Viewing Experiment of URDF-3." Los Alamos, Los Alamos Scientific Laboratory, December 4, 1975, p. 4.

Studeman, William O., Deputy Director of Central Intelligence. Remarks at Symposium on "National Security and National Competitiveness: Open Source Solutions," December 1, 1992, McLean, Va.

Systems Analysis Staff, Directorate of Science and Technology, CIA. *A Report on DS&T Intelligence Collection Requirements*, July 12, 1966.

"Testimony of Allen Dulles." *Executive Sessions of the Senate Foreign Relations Committee (Historical Series), Vol. XII, Eighty-sixth Congress–Second Session, 1960.* Washington, D.C.: U.S. Government Printing Office, 1982.

Thorne, C. Thomas, Jr., and David S. Patterson (eds.). *Emergence of the Intelligence Establishment.* Washington, D.C.: U.S. Government Printing Office, 1996.

United States Air Force, "Biography: Major General Paul N. Bacalis," n.d.

______. "Biography: Brigadier General Jack C. Ledford, n.d.

______. "Biography: Brigadier General Wendell L. Bevan Jr., July 15, 1970, with updates.

United States of America v. Christopher John Boyce. Reporter's Transcript, District Court, Central District of California, Hon. Robert J. Kelleher, CR-77-131-RJK, April 20, 1977.

United States of America v. Larry Wu Tai Chin aka Chin Wu-Tai. United States District Court, Eastern District of Virginia, Alexandria Division, Criminal No. 85-00263-A, January 2, 1986.

United States of America v. William Kampiles. United States District Court, Northern District of Indiana, November 6, 1978.

U.S. Congress, House Permanent Select Committee on Intelligence. *Iran: Evaluation of U.S. Intelligence Performance Prior to November 1978.* Washington, D.C.: U.S. Government Printing Office, 1979.

______. *NRO Headquarters Facility.* Washington, D.C.: U.S. Government Printing Office, 1995.

______. *Intelligence Authorization Act for Fiscal Year 1998, Report 105–135, Part 1.* Washington, D.C.: U.S. Government Printing Office, 1997.

U.S. Congress, House Select Committee on Intelligence. *U.S. Intelligence Agencies and Activities: Intelligence Costs and Fiscal Procedures, Part 1.* Washington, D.C.: U.S. Government Printing Office, 1975.

U.S. Congress, Senate Committee on Armed Services. *Department of Defense Authorization for Appropriations for Fiscal Year 1994 and the Future Years Defense Program.* Washington, D.C.: U.S. Government Printing Office, 1993.

U.S. Congress, Senate Foreign Relations Committee. *Intelligence and the ABM.* Washington, D.C.: U.S. Government Printing Office, 1969.

______. *Fiscal Year 1980 International Security Assistance Authorization.* Washington, D.C.: U.S. Government Printing Office, 1979.

U.S. Congress, Senate Select Committee on Intelligence. *Nomination of John McMahon.* Washington, D.C.: U.S. Government Printing Office, 1982.

______. *S. 2198 and S. 421 to Reorganize the United States Intelligence Community.* Washington, D.C.: U.S. Government Printing Office, 1993.

______. *NRO Headquarters Project.* Washington, D.C.: U.S. Government Printing Office, 1995.

______. *Special Report of the Senate Select Committee on Intelligence, United States Senate, January 4, 1995 to October 3, 1996.* Washington, D.C.: U.S. Government Printing Office, 1997.

U.S. Congress, Senate Select Committee to Study Governmental Operations with Respect to Intelligence Activities. *Alleged Assassination Plots Involving Foreign Leaders.* Washington, D.C.: U.S. Government Printing Office, 1975.

______. *Final Report, Book I: Foreign and Military Intelligence.* Washington, D.C.: U.S. Government Printing Office, 1976.

______. *Final Report, Book IV: Supplementary Detailed Staff Reports on Foreign and Military Intelligence.* Washington, D.C.: U.S. Government Printing Office, 1976.

Welzenbach, Donald E. "Science and Technology: Origins of a Directorate." *Studies in Intelligence* 30, 2 (Summer 1986): 13–26.

Wheelon, Albert D,. and Sidney Graybeal. "Intelligence for the Space Race." *Studies in Intelligence* 7, 4 (Fall 1963): 1–13.

Whitmire, Frank A., and Edward G. Correll. "The Failure of Cosmos 57." *Studies in Intelligence* 10, 3 (Summer 1966): 25–29.

Books and Monographs

Agee, Philip. *Inside the Company: CIA Diary.* San Francisco: Stonehill, 1975.

Allen, Thomas, and Norman Polmar. *Merchants of Treason: America's Secrets for Sale from the* Pueblo *to the Present.* New York: Delacorte, 1988.

Andrew, Christopher. *For the President's Eyes Only: Secret Intelligence and the American Presidency from Washington to Bush.* New York: HarperCollins, 1995.

Atkinson, Rick. *Crusade: The Untold Story of the Persian Gulf War.* Boston: Houghton Mifflin, 1993.

Ball, Desmond. *Politics and Force Levels: The Strategic Missile Program of the Kennedy Administration.* Berkeley: University of California Press, 1980.

______. *A Suitable Piece of Real Estate: American Installations in Australia.* Sydney: Hale & Iremonger, 1980.

______. *Pine Gap: Australia and the U.S. Geostationary SIGINT Satellite Program.* Sydney: Allen & Unwin, 1988.

______. *Intelligence in the Gulf War.* Canberra, Australia: SDSC, Australian National University, 1991.

Bamford, James. *The Puzzle Palace: A Report on NSA, America's Most Secret Agency.* Boston: Houghton Mifflin, 1982.

Beck, Melvin C. *Secret Contenders: The Myth of Cold War Counterintelligence.* New York: Sheridan Square, 1984.

Bell, Griffin. *Taking Care of the Law.* New York: William Morrow, 1982.

Berman, Robert P., and John C. Baker. *Soviet Strategic Forces: Requirements and Responses.* Washington, D.C.: Brookings Institution, 1982.

Bissell, Richard M., with Jonathan E. Lewis and Francis T. Pudlo. *Reflections of a Cold Warrior.* New Haven: Yale University Press, 1996.

Broad, William. *The Universe Below: Discovering the Secrets of the Deep Sea.* New York: Simon & Schuster, 1997.

Brugioni, Dino. *Eyeball to Eyeball: The Inside Story of the Cuban Missile Crisis.* New York: Random House, 1991.

Burleson, Clyde W. *The Jennifer Project.* College Station, Tex.: Texas A&M, 1997.

Burr, William (ed.). *The Kissinger Transcripts: The Top-Secret Talks with Beijing and Moscow.* New York: New Press, 1998.

Burrows, William E. *Deep Black: Space Espionage and National Security.* New York: Random House, 1986.

______. *Exploring Space: Voyages in the Solar System and Beyond.* New York: Random House, 1990.

Cahn, Anne Hessing. *Killing Détente: The Right Attacks the CIA.* University Park: Pennsylvania State University Press, 1998.

Campbell, James B. *Introduction to Remote Sensing.* New York: Guilford, 1987.

Claridge, Duane R. *A Spy for All Seasons: My Life in the CIA.* New York: Scribner's, 1996.

Cline, Ray S. *Secrets, Spies, and Scholars: Blueprint of the Essential CIA.* Washington, D.C.: Acropolis, 1976.

Cockburn, Andrew, and Leslie Cockburn. *Dangerous Liaison: The Inside Story of the U.S.-Israeli Covert Relationship.* New York: HarperCollins, 1991.

Cohen, Avner. *Israel and the Bomb.* New York: Columbia University Press, 1998.

Colby, William, with Peter Forbath. *Honorable Men: My Life in the CIA.* New York: Simon & Schuster, 1978.

Crease, Robert P. and Charles C. Mann. *The Second Creation: Makers of the Revolution in 20th-Century Physics.* New York: Macmillan, 1986.

Crickmore, Paul F. *Lockheed SR-71: The Secret Missions Exposed.* London: Osprey, 1993.

Day, Dwayne A., John Logsdon, and Brian Latell (eds.). *Eye in the Sky: The Story of the CORONA Spy Satellites*. Washington, D.C.: Smithsonian, 1998.
Drell, Sidney, Abraham D. Sofaer, and George D. Wilson (eds.). *The New Terror: Facing the Threat of Biological and Chemical Weapons*. Stanford, Calif.: Hoover Institution Press, 1999.
Earley, Peter. *Confessions of a Spy: The Real Story of Aldrich Ames*. New York: Putnam, 1997.
Eddington, Patrick G. *Gassed in the Gulf: The Inside Story of the Pentagon-CIA Cover-Up of Gulf War Syndrome*. Washington, D.C.: Insignia, 1997.
Emerson, Steven. *Secret Warriors: Inside the Covert Military Operations of the Reagan Era*. New York: Putnam, 1988.
Emery, Fred. *Watergate: The Corruption of American Politics and the Fall of Richard Nixon*. New York: Times Books, 1994.
Frost, Michael, and Michel Gratton. *Spyworld: Inside the Canadian and American Intelligence Establishments*. Toronto: Doubleday Canada, 1994.
Gates, Robert. *From the Shadows: The Ultimate Insider's Account of Five Presidents and How They Won the Cold War*. New York: Simon & Schuster, 1996.
Gordon, Michael, and Bernard Trainor. *The General's War: The Inside Story of the Conflict in the Gulf*. Boston: Little, Brown, 1994.
Grose, Peter. *Gentleman Spy: The Life of Allen Dulles*. Boston: Houghton Mifflin, 1994.
Hallion, Richard. *Storm over Iraq: Air Power and the Gulf War*. Washington, D.C.: Smithsonian Institution, 1992.
Harford, James. *Korolev: How One Man Masterminded the Soviet Drive to Beat America to the Moon*. New York: John Wiley, 1997.
Hawkes, Nigel, Geoffrey Lean, David Leigh, Robin McKie, Peter Pringle, and Andrew Wilson. *Chernobyl: The End of the Nuclear Dream*. New York: Vintage, 1986.
Hersh, Seymour H. *"The Target is Destroyed": What Really Happened to Flight 007 and What America Knew About It*. New York: Random House, 1986.
______. *The Samson Option: Israel's Nuclear Arsenal and American Foreign Policy*. New York: Random House, 1991.
Hulnick, Arthur S. *Fixing the Spy Machine: Preparing American Intelligence for the Twenty-first Century*. Westport, Conn.: Praeger, 1999.
Johnson, Nicholas L. *Soviet Military Strategy in Space*. London: Jane's, 1987.
Kessler, Ronald. *Spy vs. Spy: Stalking Soviet Spies in America*. New York: Scribner's, 1988.
______. *Inside the CIA: Revealing the Secrets of the World's Most Powerful Spy Agency*. New York: Pocket Books, 1992.
Killian, James R., Jr. *Sputnik, Scientists, and Eisenhower: A Memoir of the First Special Assistant to the President for Science and Technology*. Cambridge: MIT Press, 1982.
Koehler, John O. *STASI: The Untold Story of the East German Secret Police*. Boulder, Colo.: Westview Press, 1998.
Kornbluh, Peter. *Nicaragua: The Price of Intervention, Reagan's War Against the Sandinistas*. Washington, D.C.: Institute for Policy Studies, 1987.
Lewis, John Wilson, and Xue Litai. *China Builds the Bomb*. Stanford, Calif.: Stanford University Press, 1988.
Lindsay, Robert. *The Falcon and the Snowman: A True Story of Friendship and Espionage*. New York: Simon & Schuster, 1979.
Marks, David, and Richard Kammann. *The Psychology of the Psychic*. Buffalo, N.Y.: Prometheus Books, 1980.
Marks, John. *The Search for the "Manchurian Candidate": The CIA and Mind Control*. New York: Norton, 1991.
Martin, David C. *Wilderness of Mirrors*. New York: Harper & Row, 1980.

Martin, Frederick Thomas Martin. *Top-Secret Intranet: How U.S. Intelligence Built INTELINK–The World's Largest, Most Secure Network*. Upper Saddle River, N.J.: Prentice-Hall PTR, 1998.

McDonald, Robert A. (ed.). *CORONA: Between the Sun and the Earth, the First NRO Reconnaissance Eye in Space*. Bethesda, Md.: American Society for Photogrammetry and Remote Sensing, 1997.

McElheny, Victor K. *Insisting on the Impossible: The Life of Edwin Land, Inventor of Instant Photography*. Reading, Mass.: Perseus Books, 1998.

Melton, Keith. *CIA Special Weapons and Equipment: Spy Devices of the Cold War*. New York: Sterling Publishing, 1994.

Mendez, Antonio, with Malcolm McConnell. *The Master of Disguise: My Secret Life in the CIA*. New York: Morrow, 1999.

Miller, Jay. *Lockheed U-2*. Austin, Tex.: Aerofax, 1983.

______. *Skunk Works: The Official History*. North Branch, Minn.: Specialty Press, 1996.

Mosley, Leonard. *Dulles: A Biography of Eleanor, Allen, and John Foster and Their Family Network*. New York: Dial Press, 1978.

Mutza, Wayne. *Lockheed P2V Neptune: An Illustrated History*. Atglen, Pa.: Schiffer Military/Aviation History, 1996.

Neff, Donald. *Warriors for Jerusalem: The Six Days That Changed the Middle East*. New York: Simon & Schuster, 1984.

Newhouse, John. *War and Peace in the Nuclear Age*. New York: Knopf, 1989.

Norris, Robert S., Andrew S. Burrows, and Richard W. Fieldhouse. *Nuclear Weapons Databook Volume V: British, French, and Chinese Nuclear Weapons*. Boulder, Colo.: Westview, 1994.

Peebles, Curtis. *Guardians: Strategic Reconnaissance Satellites*. Novato, Calif.: Presidio Press, 1987.

Pelletier, Jean, and Claude Adams. *The Canadian Caper*. New York: William Morrow, 1981.

Perisco, Joseph E. *Piercing the Reich: The Penetration of Nazi Germany by American Secret Agents During World War II*. New York: Ballantine Books, 1979.

Pocock, Chris. *Dragon Lady: The History of the U-2 Spyplane*. Shrewsbury, England: Airlife, 1989.

______. *The U-2 Spyplane: Toward the Unknown*. Atglen, Pa.: Schiffer Books, 2000.

Powers, Thomas. *The Man Who Kept the Secrets: Richard Helms and the CIA*. London: Weidenfeld and Nicolson, 1979.

Prados, John. *The Soviet Estimate: U.S. Intelligence and Russian Military Strength*. New York: Dial, 1982.

______. *Presidents' Secret Wars: CIA and Pentagon Covert Operations from World War II Through the Persian Gulf*. Chicago: Elephant Paperbacks, 1996.

Preston, Bob. *Plowshares and Power: The Military Use of Civil Space*. Washington, D.C.: National Defense University Press, 1994.

Ranelagh, John. *The Agency: The Rise and Decline of the CIA, from Wild Bill Donovan to William Casey*. New York: Simon & Schuster, 1986.

Reade, David. *The Age of Orion: Lockheed P-3, an Illustrated History*. Atglen, Pa.: Schiffer Military/Aviation History, 1998.

Rich, Ben R., and Leo Janos. *Skunk Works: A Personal Memoir of My Years at Lockheed*. Boston: Little, Brown, 1994.

Richelson, Jeffrey T. *America's Secret Eyes in Space: The U.S. KEYHOLE Spy Satellite Program*. New York: Harper & Row, 1990.

______. *America's Space Sentinels: DSP Satellites and National Security*. Lawrence: University Press of Kansas, 1999.

Riste, Olav. *The Norwegian Intelligence Service, 1945–1970*. London: Frank Cass, 1999.

Ross, Robert S. *Negotiating Cooperation: The United States and China, 1969–1989*. Stanford, Calif.: Stanford University Press, 1995.

Rostizke, Harry. *KGB: The Eyes of Russia*. New York: Doubleday, 1981.
Schechter, Jerrold L., and Peter S. Deriabin. *The Spy Who Saved the World: How a Soviet Colonel Changed the Course of the Cold War.* New York: Scribner's 1992.
Schiff, Ze'ev. *A History of the Israeli Army: 1874 to the Present*. New York: Macmillan, 1985.
Schnabel, Jim. *Remote Viewers: The Secret History of America's Psychic Spies*. New York: Dell, 1997.
Seaborg, Glenn T., with Benjamin S. Loeb. *Stemming the Tide: Arms Control in the Johnson Years*. Lexington, Mass.: Lexington Books, 1986.
Smith, Russell Jack. *The Unknown CIA: My Three Decades with the Agency*. New York: Berkley, 1992.
Sontag, Sherry, and Christopher Drew, with Annette Lawrence Drew. *Blind Man's Bluff: The Untold Story of American Submarine Espionage*. New York: Public Affairs, 1998.
Stockwell, John. *In Search of Enemies: A CIA Story*. New York: Norton, 1978.
Sullivan, William. *Mission to Iran*. New York: W. W. Norton, 1981.
Tamnes, Rolf. *The Cold War in the High North*. Oslo: Ad Notam, 1991.
Thomas, Evan. *The Very Best Men: Four Who Dared: The Early Years of the CIA*. New York: Simon & Schuster, 1995.
Troy, Thomas F. *Donovan and the CIA: A History of the Establishment of the Central Intelligence Agency*. Frederick, Md.: University Publications of America, 1981.
Tsipis, Kosta (ed.). *Arms Control Verification: The Technologies That Make It Possible*. New York: Pergamon-Brassey's, 1985.
Tully, Andrew. *Inside the FBI*. New York: Dell, 1987.
Turner, Stansfield. *Secrecy and Democracy: The CIA in Transition*. Boston: Houghton Mifflin, 1985.
Tyler, Patrick. *A Great Wall: Six Presidents and China—An Investigative History*. New York: Public Affairs, 1999.
U.S. News and World Report. *Triumph Without Victory: The Unreported History of the Persian Gulf War*. New York: Times Books, 1992.
Vance, Cyrus. *Hard Choices: Critical Years in America's Foreign Policy*. New York: Simon & Schuster, 1983.
Varner, Roy, and Wayne Collier. *A Matter of Risk: The Incredible Inside Story of the CIA's Glomar Explorer Mission to Raise a Russian Submarine*. New York: Random House, 1978.
Waller, Doug. *The Commandos: The Inside Story of America's Secret Soldiers*. New York: Simon & Schuster, 1994.
Westerfield, H. Bradford (ed.). *Inside the CIA's Private World: Declassified Articles from the Agency's Internal Journal, 1955–1992*. New Haven: Yale University Press, 1995.
Wilson, Col. Charles P. *Strategic and Tactical Aerial Reconnaissance in the Near East*. Washington, D.C.: Washington Institute for Near East Policy, 1999.
Woodward, Bob. *VEIL: The Secret Wars of the CIA, 1981–1987*. New York: Simon & Schuster, 1987.
______. *The Commanders*. New York: Simon & Schuster, 1991.
Wyden, Peter. *The Bay of Pigs: The Untold Story*. New York: Simon & Schuster, 1979.
Ziegler, Charles A., and David Jacobson. *Spying Without Spies: Origins of America's Secret Nuclear Surveillance System*. Westport, Conn.: Praeger, 1995.

Articles and Book Chapters

Anderson, Jack. "CIA Eavesdrops on Kremlin Chiefs." *Washington Post*, September 16, 1971, p. F7.
______. "Getting the Big Picture for the CIA." *Washington Post*, November 28, 1982.
Armstrong, Douglas G. "The Gulf War's Patched-Together Air Intelligence." *Naval Institute Proceedings*, November 1992, pp. 109–111.

Bamford, James. "America's Supersecret Eyes in Space." *New York Times Magazine*, January 13, 1985, pp. 39ff.

Barr, Stephen. "Monitoring Service Spared in Latest Crisis." *Washington Post*, February 6, 1997, p. A21.

Beecher, William. "Soviet Missile Deployment Puzzles Top U.S. Analysts." *New York Times*, April 14, 1969.

Bermudez, Joseph S., Jr. "North Korea Set for More Ballistic Missile Tests." *Jane's Defence Weekly*, October 23, 1996, p. 5.

Boatman, John. "USA Planned Stealth UAV to Replace SR-71." *Jane's Defence Weekly*, December 17, 1994, pp. 1, 3.

Boffey, Philip M. "U.S. Panel Calls the Disaster in the Ukraine the Worst Ever." *New York Times*, May 4, 1986, pp. 1, 20.

Bonavia, David. "Radar Post Leak May Be Warning to Soviet Union." *The Times* (London), June 20, 1981, p. 5.

Bowman, Tom, and Scott Shane. "Espionage from the Front Lines." *Baltimore Sun*, December 8, 1995, pp. 1A, 20A–21A.

Branigan, William. "Iran's Airmen Keep U.S. Listening Posts Intact and Whirring." *Washington Post*, May 20, 1979, p. A20.

Broad, William J. "Russia Says U.S. Got Sub's Atom Arms." *New York Times*, June 20, 1993, p. 4.

Brown, Stuart F. "The Eternal Airplane." *Popular Science*, April 1994, pp. 70, 100.

Brugioni, Dino, and Frederick J. Doyle. "Arthur C. Lundahl: Founder of the Image Exploitation Discipline." In Robert A. McDonald (ed.), *CORONA: Between the Sun and the Earth: The First NRO Reconnaissance Eye in Space*. Bethesda, Md.: American Society for Photogrammetry and Remote Sensing, 1997, pp. 159–168.

Burrows, William E. "That New Black Magic." *Air and Space*, December 1998/January 1999, pp. 29–35.

Cannon, Carl M., and Mark Thompson. "Threat to Soviets Grows, U.S. Spy Photos Indicate." *Miami Herald*, April 30, 1986, pp. 1A, 14A.

"A Chinese Agent in the CIA?" *Newsweek*, December 2, 1985, p. 49.

"Chinese Official Said Exposer of CIA Turncoat." *Washington Post*, September 5, 1986, p. A18.

"The CIA Blows an Asset." *Newsweek*, September 3, 1984, pp. 48–49.

"Costly Cuts?" *Newsweek*, November 25, 1996, p. 6.

Covault, Craig. "Space Recon of Iraq Taxes CIA Operations." *Aviation Week and Space Technology*, September 3, 1990, pp. 30–31.

______. "Advanced KH-11 Broadens U.S. Recon Capability." *Aviation Week and Space Technology*, January 6, 1997, pp. 24–25.

______. "New Intelligence Ops Debut in Iraqi Strikes." *Aviation Week and Space Technology*, December 21–28, 1998, pp. 124–125.

Crosette, Barbara. "U.S. Seeks to Prove Mass Killings." *New York Times*, August 11, 1995, p. A3.

Day, Dwayne A. "A Failed Phoenix: The KH-6 LANYARD Reconnaissance Satellite." *Spaceflight* 39, 5 (May 1997): 170–174.

______. "The Development and Improvement of the Corona Satellite." In Dwayne A. Day, John Logsdon, and Brian Latell (eds.), *Eye in the Sky: The Story of the CORONA Spy Satellites*. Washington, D.C.: Smithsonian, 1998, pp. 48–85.

______. "Listening from Above: The First Signals Intelligence Satellite." *Spaceflight*, 41, 8 (August 1999): 339–346.

Dobbs, Michael. "Deconstructing the Death Ray." *Washington Post*, October 17, 1999, pp. F1, F4.

Doel, Ronald E., and Allan A. Needell. "Science, Scientists, and the CIA: Balancing International Ideals, National Needs, and Professional Opportunities." *Intelligence and National Security* 12, 1 (January 1997): 59–81.

Eftimiades, Nicholas. "China's Ministry of State Security: Coming of Age in the International Arena." *Intelligence and National Security* 8, 1 (January 1993): 23–43.

Engelberg, Stephen. "30 Years of Spying for China Is Charged." *New York Times*, November 27, 1985, p. B8.

______. "U.S. Says Intelligence Units Did Not Detect the Accident." *New York Times*, May 2, 1986, p. A9.

"Final Launch Preparations Under Way for Signal Intelligence Satellite Mission." *Aviation Week and Space Technology*, November 6, 1989, p. 24.

Fulghum, David A. "Solar-Powered UAV to Fly at Edwards." *Aviation Week and Space Technology*, October 4, 1993, p. 27.

Fulghum, David A., and Robert A. Wall. "Long-Hidden Research Spawns Black UCAV." *Aviation Week and Space Technology*, September 25, 2000, pp. 28–29.

Gardner, Martin. "Claiborne Pell: The Senator from Outer Space." *Skeptical Inquirer* 20, 2 (March/April 1996), pp. 12–15.

______. "Zero-Point Energy and Harold Puthoff." *Skeptical Inquirer*, May/June 1998, pp. 13–15.

______. "Distant Healing and Elizabeth Targ." *Skeptical Inquirer*, March/April 2001, pp. 12–14.

Gelb, Leslie H. "Officials Say CIA Made Mines with Navy Help." *New York Times*, June 1, 1984, p. A4.

Gerstenzang, James. "Shuttle Lifts Off with Spy Cargo." *Los Angeles Times*, January 25, 1985, pp. 1, 11.

Gertz, Bill. "CIA Upset Because Perle Detailed Eavesdropping." *Washington Times*, April 15, 1987, p. 2A.

______. "New Spy Satellite, Needed to Monitor Treaty, Sits on Ground." *Washington Times*, October 20, 1987, p. A5.

______. "Libyans Stop Work on Chemical Plant." *Washington Times*, June 24, 1996, p. A4.

______. "New Chinese Missiles Target All of East Asia." *Washington Times*, July 10, 1997, pp. A1, A16.

Gorin, Peter A. "ZENIT: The Response to CORONA." In Dwayne A. Day, John Logsdon, and Brian Latell (eds.), *Eye in the Sky: The Story of the CORONA Spy Satellites*. Washington, D.C.: Smithsonian, 1998, pp. 157–170.

Grabo, Cynthia. "The Evolution of U.S. Strategic Warning." *International Journal of Intelligence and Counterintelligence* 3, 3 (Fall 1989): 363–386.

"The Great Submarine Snatch." *Time*, March 31, 1975, pp. 20–27.

Grose, Peter. "U.S. Intelligence Doubts First-Strike Goal." *New York Times*, June 19, 1969.

Gupta, V., and D. Rich. "Locating the Detonation of China's First Nuclear Explosive Test on 16 October 1964." *International Journal of Remote Sensing* 17, 10 (October 1996): 1969–1974.

Gwertzman, Bernard. "Fire in Reactor May Be Out, New U.S. Pictures Indicate; Soviet Says Fallout Is Cut." *New York Times*, May 2, 1986, pp. A1, A8.

Hall, Cargill. "Post-War Strategic Reconnaissance and the Genesis of Corona." In Dwayne A. Day, John Logsdon, and Brian Latell (eds.), *Eye in the Sky: The Story of the CORONA Spy Satellites*. Washington, D.C.: Smithsonian, 1998, pp. 86–118.

Harwood, William. "Titan Boosts Military Payload for Ninth Consecutive Success." *Space News*, December 11–17, 1995, p. 26.

Hersh, Seymour. "Human Error Is Cited in '74 Glomar Failure." *New York Times*, December 9, 1976, pp. 1, 55.

______. "The Wild East." *Atlantic Monthly*, June 1994, pp. 61–86.

Hiatt, Fred, and Joanne Omang. "CIA Helped to Mine Ports in Nicaragua." *Washington Post*, April 7, 1984, p. 1.

Hurt, Henry. "CIA in Crisis: The Kampiles Case." *Reader's Digest*, June 1979, pp. 65–72.

Hyman, Ray. "Parapsychological Research: A Tutorial Review and Critical Appraisal." *Proceedings of the IEEE* 74, 6 (June 1986): 823–849.

______. "Evaluation of the Military's Twenty-Year Program on Psychic Spying." *Skeptical Inquirer*, March/April 1996, pp. 24–26.

"The Indian Connection." *India Today*, December 31, 1983, p. 10.

Inlow, Roland. "How the Cold War and Its Intelligence Problems Influenced CORONA Operations." In Robert A. McDonald (ed.), *CORONA: Between the Sun and the Earth: The First NRO Reconnaissance Eye in Space*. Bethesda, Md.: American Society for Photogrammetry and Remote Sensing, 1997, pp. 221–229.

"Investigating the Paranormal." *Nature*, October 18, 1974, pp. 559–560.

Isbell, Doug, and Vincent Kiernan. "Long-Delayed Atlantis Flight Orbits Military Spy Satellite." *Space News*, March 5–11, 1990, p. 12.

Janesick, James, and Morley Blouke. "Introduction to Charge-Coupled Devices Imaging Sensors." In Kosta Tsipis (ed.), *Arms Control Verification: The Technologies That Make It Possible*. New York: Pergamon-Brassey's, 1985.

______. "Sky on a Chip: The Fabulous CCD." *Sky and Telescope*, September 1987, pp. 238–242.

Kenden, Anthony. "U.S. Reconnaissance Satellite Programmes." *Spaceflight*, July 1978, pp. 243ff.

Kiernan, Vincent. "NRO Streamlines to Cut Intelligence Bureaucracy." *Space News*, December 7–13, 1992, pp. 1, 29.

______. "Titan 4 Launches Spy Satellite from Vandenberg AFB." *Space News*, December 7–13, 1992, p. 26.

King, Neil, Jr. "Small Start-Up Helps the CIA to Mask Its Moves on the Web." *Wall Street Journal*, February 12, 2001.

Klass, Philip. "U.S. Monitoring Capability Impaired." *Aviation Week and Space Technology*, May 14, 1979.

Kolcum, Edward H. "Night Launch of Discovery Boosts Secret Military Satellite into Orbit." *Aviation Week and Space Technology*, November 27, 1989, p. 29.

______. "Atlantis Lofts AFP-731 Reconnaissance Satellite." *Aviation Week and Space Technology*, March 5, 1990, p. 22.

Kranish, Arthur. "CIA: Israel Has 10–20 Weapons." *Washington Post*, March 15, 1976, p. A2.

Kurtz, Howard. "Pollard: Top Israelis Backed Spy Ring." *Washington Post*, February 28, 1987, p. A8.

Lardner, George. "Spy Rings of One." *Washington Post Magazine*, December 4, 1983, pp. 60–65.

Leary, Warren E. "Problems Are Reported with New Spy Satellite." *New York Times*, March 18, 1990, p. 20.

______. "Debris from Secret U.S. Satellite Is Burning Up in Fall from Space." *New York Times*, March 22, 1990, p. A24.

______. "The Dream of Eternal Flight Begins to Take Wing." *New York Times*, January 12, 1999, pp. D1, D6.

Ledeen, Michael. "A Mole in Our Midst." *New York*, October 2, 1978, pp. 55–57.

Le Moyne, James. "The Secret War Boils Over." *Newsweek*, April 11, 1983, pp. 46–50.

Lenorovitz, Jeffrey M. "CIA Satellite Data Link Study Revealed." *Aviation Week and Space Technology*, May 2, 1977, pp. 25–26.

Lewis, Jonathan E. "Tension and Triumph: Civilian and Military Relations and the Birth of the U-2 Program. In Robert A. McDonald (ed.), *CORONA: Between the Sun and the Earth, the First NRO Reconnaissance Eye in Space*. Bethesda, Md.: American Society for Photogrammetry and Remote Sensing, 1997.

Loeb, Vernon. "New Spy Satellites at Risk Because Funding Is Uncertain, Pentagon Told." *Washington Post*, November 12, 1999, p. A7.

______. "CIA Science Chief Quits, Deputy Named." *Washington Post*, January 14, 2000, p. A25.

______. "After-Action Report." *Washington Post Magazine*, February 27, 2000, pp. 7ff.

Lundberg, Kirsten. "The SS-9 Controversy: Intelligence as Political Football." Kennedy School of Government, C16-89-884.0, Case Program, 1989.

Maass, Peter. "From His Bed, CIA's Best Makes His Breakthroughs." *Washington Post*, April 21, 1996, pp. A1, A20.

Marcus, Ruth, and Joe Pichirallo. "Chin Believed Planted in U.S. as Spy." *Washington Post*, December 6, 1985, pp. A1, A22.

Marder, Murrey. "Monitoring: Not-So-Secret-Secret." *Washington Post*, June 19, 1981, p. 10.

Marks, David, and Richard Kammann. "Information Transmission in Remote Viewing Experiments." *Nature*, August 17, 1978, pp. 680–681.

Martin, Capt. James M. "Sea Mines in Nicaragua." *Proceedings of the U.S. Naval Institute* 116, 9 (September 1990): 111–116.

May, Edwin C. "The American Institutes for Research Review of the Department of Defense's STAR GATE Program: A Commentary." *Journal of Scientific Exploration* 10, 1 (1996): 89–107.

McDonald, Robert A. "CORONA: A Success for Space Reconnaissance, a Look into the Cold War, and a Revolution for Intelligence." *Photogrammetric Engineering and Remote Sensing* 61, 6 (June 1995): 689–720.

McDowell, Jonathan. "U.S. Reconnaissance Satellite Programs, Part I: Photoreconnaissance." *Quest* 4, 2 (Summer 1995): 22–31.

______. "Launch Listings." In Dwayne A. Day, John Logsdon, and Brian Latell (eds.), *Eye in the Sky: The Story of the CORONA Spy Satellites*. Washington, D.C.: Smithsonian, 1998.

"Meltdown." *Newsweek*, May 12, 1986, pp. 20–35.

"'Ministry of State Security' Set Up on Mainland China." *Issues and Studies*, July 1983, pp. 5–8.

"MSX Satellite Passes Rocket Tracking Test." *Space News*, April 24–30, 1997, p. 10.

"Oct. 10 Assault on Nicaraguans Is Laid to C.I.A.." *New York Times*, April 18, 1994, pp. A1, A12.

Oehler, Gordon. "Warning and Detection." In Sidney Drell, Abraham D. Sofaer, and George D. Wilson (eds.), *The New Terror: Facing the Threat of Biological and Chemical Weapons*. Stanford, Calif.: Hoover Institution Press, 1999.

O'Leary, Jeremiah. "Turner Says U.S. Didn't Bug Park." *Washington Times*, August 9, 1977, pp. A1, A6.

Omang, Joanne. "Historical Background to the CIA's Nicaraguan Manual." In *Psychological Operations in Guerrilla Warfare*. New York: Vintage, 1985.

"Once-Secret Technology Assists Cancer Detection." *Signal*, June 1995, pp. 66–67.

O'Toole, Thomas, and Charles Babcock. "CIA 'Big Bird' Satellite Manual Was Allegedly Sold to the Soviets." *Washington Post*, August 23, 1978, pp. A1, A16.

Ott, James. "Espionage Trial Highlights CIA Problems." *Aviation Week and Space Technology*, November 27, 1978, pp. 21–23.

Pear, Robert. "Radio Broadcasts Report Protests Erupting All over China." *New York Times*, May 23, 1989, p. A14.

Peebles, Curtis. "The Guardians." *Spaceflight*, November 1978, pp. 381 ff.

Pichirallo, Joe. "Ex-CIA Analyst Gave Secrets to China for 30 Years, FBI Says." *Washington Post*, November 24, 1985, pp. A1, A24.

______. "Retiree Kept Close CIA Ties." *Washington Post*, November 27, 1985, pp. A1, A10.

Pike, Christopher Anson. "CANYON, RHYOLITE, and AQUACADE: U.S. Signals Intelligence Satellites in the 1970s." *Spaceflight* 37, 11 (November 1995): 381–383.

Pike, John. "Reagan Prepares for War in Outer Space." *CounterSpy* 7, 1 (September–November 1982), pp. 17–22.

Pincus, Walter. "U.S. Seeks A-Test Monitoring Facility." *Washington Post*, March 19, 1986, p. A8.

Pincus, Walter, and Mary Thornton. "U.S. to Orbit 'Sigint' Craft from Shuttle." *Washington Post*, December 19, 1984, pp. A1, A8–A9.

"Public Support Swells for CIA's FBIS Program." *Secrecy and Government Bulletin*, July 1996.

Puthoff, Harold E. "CIA-Initiated Remote Viewing at Stanford Research Institute." *Journal of Scientific Exploration* 10, 1 (Spring, 1996): 63–76.

Rensberg, Boyce. "Explosion: Graphite Fire Suspected." *Washington Post*, April 30, 1986, pp. A1, A17.

Richelson, Jeffrey. "The Satellite Data System." *Journal of the British Interplanetary Society* 37, 5 (1984): 226–228.

______. "CIA's Science and Technology Gurus Get New Look, Roles." *Defense Week*, August 19, 1996, p. 6.

______. "The Wizards of Langley: The CIA's Directorate of Science and Technology, 1962–1996." *Intelligence and National Security* 12, 1 (January 1997): 82–103.

Robinson, Clarence A. "Intelligence Agency Adjusts as Mission Possible Unfolds." *Signal*, October 1998.

Ruane, Michael E. "Ex-CIA Employee Has Saluted Tiny Paper Soldiers Since '20s." *Dallas Morning News*, February 28, 1999, p. 9F.

______. "Seeing Is Deceiving." *Washington Post*, February 15, 2000, pp. C1, C8.

Schemann, Serge. "Soviet Mobilizes a Vast Operation to Overcome the Disaster." *New York Times*, May 19, 1986, p. A8.

"A Secret War for Nicaragua." *Newsweek*, November 8, 1992, pp. 42–53.

"Seismic Sensors." *Intelligence Newsletter*, January 17, 1990, p. 2.

Selander, J. Michael. "Image Coverage Models for Declassified Corona, Argon, and Lanyard Satellite Photography–a Technical Explanation." In Robert A. McDonald (ed.), *CORONA: Between the Sun and the Earth, the First NRO Reconnaissance Eye in Space*. Bethesda, Md.: American Society for Photogrammetry and Remote Sensing, 1997.

Shenon, Philip. "Former C.I.A. Analyst Is Arrested and Accused of Spying for China." *New York Times*, November 24, 1985, pp. 1, 31.

______. "U.S. Says Spy Suspect Had Access to Highly Classified Data." *New York Times*, January 3, 1986, p. A12.

"Shuttle Spy Satellite Has Not Reentered." *Spaceflight*, January 1991, p. 4.

Smith, Hedrick. "U.S. Aides Say Loss of Post in Iran Impairs Missile-Monitoring Ability." *New York Times*, March 2, 1979, pp. A1, A8.

______. "Britain Criticizes Mining of Harbors Around Nicaragua." *New York Times*, April 7, 1984, pp. 1, 4.

Smith, R. Jeffrey. "Tracking Aideed Hampered by Intelligence Failures." *Washington Post*, October 8, 1993, p. A19.

______. "Pentagon Has Spent Millions on Tips from Trio of Psychics." *Washington Post*, November 29, 1995, pp. A1, A18.

Smith, R. Jeffrey, and Curt Suplee. "'Psychic Arms Race' Had Several Funding Channels." *Washington Post*, November 30, 1995, pp. A1, A13.

Southerland, Daniel. "China Silent on Reported Defection of Intelligence Official." *Washington Post*, September 4, 1986, p. A30.

"Soviets Claim Reconnaissance Satellite Launched by Atlantis Has Failed." *Aviation Week and Space Technology*, March 26, 1990, p. 23.

"Space Reconnaissance Dwindles." *Aviation Week and Space Technology*, October 6, 1980, pp. 18–20.

"Spying on Russia, with China's Help." *U.S. News and World Report*, June 29, 1981, p. 10.

Stern, Laurence,. "U.S. Taped Top Russians' Car Phones." *Washington Post*, December 5, 1973, pp. A1, A16.

Stevens, Sayre. "The Soviet BMD Program." In Ashton D. Carter and David N. Schwartz (eds.), *Ballistic Missile Defense*. Washington, D.C.: Brookings Institution, 1984, pp. 182–220.

Targ, Russell. "Remote Viewing at Stanford Research Institute in the 1970s: A Memoir." *Journal of Scientific Exploration* 10, 1 (Spring 1996): 77–88.

Targ, Russell, and Harold Puthoff. "Information Transmission Under Conditions of Sensory Shielding." *Nature*, October 18, 1974, pp. 602–607.

Taubman, Philip. "U.S. and Peking Jointly Monitor Russian Missiles." *New York Times*, June 18, 1981, pp. A1, A14.

______. "Americans on Ship Said to Supervise Nicaragua Mining." *New York Times*, April 8, 1984, pp. 1, 12.

______. "U.S. Officials Say C.I.A. Helped Nicaraguan Rebels Plan Attacks." *New York Times*, October 16, 1984, pp. 1, 22.

Toner, Robin. "Bail Denied Ex-CIA Worker in China Spy Case." *New York Times*, November 28, 1985, p. B8.

Torgeson, Dial. "U.S. Spy Devices Still Running at Iran Post." *International Herald Tribune*, March 7, 1979, pp. A1, A8.

Toth, Robert C. "U.S., China Jointly Track Firings of Soviet Missiles." *Los Angeles Times*, June 19, 1981, pp. 1, 9.

______. "CIA Covert Action Punishes Nicaragua for Salvador Aid." *New York Times*, April 18, 1984, pp. A1, A12.

______. "Satellites Keep Eye on Reactor." *Los Angeles Times*, May 2, 1986, p. 22.

Tyler, Patrick. "Satellite Fails." *Washington Post*, March 17, 1990, pp. A1, A11.

Ullom, Joel. "Enriched Uranium Versus Plutonium: Proliferant Preferences in the Choice of Fissile Material." *Nonproliferation Review* 2, 1 (Fall 1994): 1–15.

"U.S. Agencies Used Psychics for Years for 'Remote Viewing.'" *Washington Times*, November 30, 1995, p. A12.

Vartabedian, Ralph. "Air Force Spy Satellite Unit Leaving California." *Los Angeles Times* (Washington ed.), October 16, 1992, pp. A1, A5.

______. "Air Force Spy Satellite Unit Leaving Southland." *Los Angeles Times*, October 16, 1992, pp. A1, A12.

Volkman, Ernest. "U.S. Spies Lend an Ear to Soviets." *Newsday*, July 12, 1977, p. 7.

Waller, Douglas. "The Vision Thing." *Time*, December 11, 1995, p. 48.

Weiner, Tim. "U.S. Suspects India Prepares for Nuclear Test." *New York Times*, March 5, 1995, pp. 1, 9.

______. "Sidney Gottlieb, 80, Dies: Took LSD to C.I.A.." *New York Times*, March 10, 1999.

Welzenbach, Donald. "Din Land: Patriot from Polaroid." *Optics and Photonics News* 5, 10 (October 1996): 22ff.

Wheelon, Albert D. "Genesis of a Unique National Capability." Address at CIA, December 19, 1985.

______. "CORONA: A Triumph of American Technology." In Dwayne A. Day, John Logsdon, and Brian Latell (eds.), *Eye in the Sky: The Story of the CORONA Spy Satellites*. Washington, D.C.: Smithsonian, 1998.

Whitelaw, Kevin. "A Killing in the Congo." *U.S. News and World Report,* July 24–31, 2000, p. 63.

Wilford, John Noble. "A Secret Payload Is Orbited by U.S." *New York Times*, August 7, 1968, p. 7.

______. "Spy Satellite Reportedly Aided in Shuttle Flight." *New York Times*, October 20, 1981, p. C4.

Wilhelm, John L. "Psychic Spying?" *Washington Post*, August 7, 1977, pp. B1, B5.

Wines, Michael. "Bigger Role Laid to Suspected Spy." *Los Angeles Times*, November 28, 1985, pp. 1, 10.

______. "Spy Reportedly Unmasked by China Defector." *Los Angeles Times*, September 5, 1986, pp. 1, 12.

Wise, David. "The Spy Who Wouldn't Die." *GQ*, July 1998, pp. 148ff.

Yannuzzi, Rick E. "In-Q-Tel: A New Partnership Between the CIA and the Private Sector." *Defense Intelligence Journal* 9, 1 (Winter 2000).

Zakaria, Tabassum. "CIA Using 'Data Mining' Technology to Find Nuggets." Reuters, March 2, 2001.

Internet

Anthes, Gary H. "Cloak and Dagger IT." www.computerworld.com, accessed February 6, 20001.
"Environmental Research Aircraft and Sensor Technology: Pathfinder, Past Flight Information." www.dfrc.nasa.gov/Projects/erast/Projects/Pathfinder/pastinfo.html.
"Harold E. Puthoff." www.firedocs.com/remoteviewing/oooh/people/puthoff.html.
"Lockheed RB-69A 'Neptune.'" www.wpafb.af.mil/museum/research/bombers/b5/b5-62.htm.
Loeb, Vernon. "Inside Information." www.washingtonpost.com, accessed January 10, 2000.
"Meet the CEO." www.anser.org/aboutanser/meetceo.html.
"Profile of APL." www.jhuapl.edu/profile/profile.htm.
"Russell Targ." www.firedocs.com/remoteviewing/oooh/people/targ/html.

Other

NBC. *Inside the KGB: Narration and Shooting Script*, May 1993.
Oral History Interview with Richard Bissell Jr., Columbia University, 1973.
The Reminiscences of Arthur C. Lundahl. Oral History Research Office, Columbia University, 1982.

INDEX